JOHN M. CUNNINGHAM JR.

TURFMEN

AND THE

PRODIGAL

A STORY OF OLD MOBILE

Turfmen and the Prodigal
Ashland Park Books
Mobile, Alabama

ISBN: 978-1-7322488-4-7
Cover Design: Teddi Black
Interior Format: Megan McCullough
Contact Information: ashlandparkbooks@gmail.com
Website: www.theauthorscove.com

To all the horsemen and horsewomen,
past and present

In the 1800s a lot of swamps were near Mobile, so yellow fever was a constant threat during late spring and summer. Many who could afford to do so left the town during its fever season and returned in the fall when it again bustled with activity and cotton came down from Alabama's rivers for export.

Spring Hill, west of Mobile, was one such haven from fever epidemics. It remained separate from the town till 1956. This fact gave me the inspiration to create the fictional Spring Hill Jockey Club.

Mobile's historical jockey club was founded in 1823 and in 1837, it built the town's popular Bascombe Race Course. Other race courses followed. Because I wanted everything in this book to be fiction, I did not include the Bascombe Course in my story.

CAST OF CHARACTERS

The Prodigal

Gideon Deshler, cotton factor and planter

Free Servants

Thaddeus Johnson, butler and footman
Katie Johnson, Thaddeus's wife, cook, and maid
Isaac Vincent, gardener

Slaves

Uriah, driver
Liza, Uriah's girlfriend
Amos, carpenter

Deshler's Overseer

John Spears

Henshaw Family

Earl Henshaw, owner of Henshaw's Jewelry Emporium

Luke Henshaw, Earl Henshaw's son

Hannah Louise, Earl Henshaw's daughter

The Turfmen

Quarles Family

Joe Quarles, businessman and planter

Gloria Quarles, Joe's wife

Sam Quarles, Joe's brother, a planter

Horsemen

Finn Rattigan, trainer

Marcus Adams, jockey

Pete Webster, jockey

Dickson Williams, groom

Horses

Johnny Boy (aka JB)
Applecart
Green Legs, former champion, now deceased

Washburn Family

Owen Washburn, planter

Lorelei Washburn, Owen's wife

Bob Glenville, Lorelei's brother

Rufus Frederickson

Horsemen

Pomeroy Wilkins, trainer
Hezekiah Hanks, jockey
Jacob Styler, groom

Horse

Lightning Bolt

Other Characters

Henry Cadwallader, cotton factor and Gideon Deshler's boss
Reverend Jonas Eagleton, Gideon Deshler's former pastor
Stephen Hamilton, Gideon Deshler's next door neighbor and former friend
Mary Hamilton, Stephen's sister
Daniel Lyman, employee of Henshaw's Jewelry Emporium
Charles Rhodes, employee of Henshaw's Jewelry Emporium
Isham Tivington, architect and builder
Cole Tivington, architect and builder
Austin Vanderporte, professional gambler

PART ONE

MAY–AUGUST

1852

PROLOGUE

Gideon Deshler, standing in his boat's stern while spring's heat scorched his neck, pondered his foe's demise. Clattering oarlocks punctuated his thundering thoughts. Their duel wouldn't last long. One pistol ball in Sam Quarles's heart, that's all it would take.

Up ahead, on the Alabama River, a sandy island commanded Gideon's attention. That's where he'd kill Sam. He didn't want to kill him. He must. Sam insulted his late wife, Harriet, thus, Sam had left Gideon no choice. Gideon's friend and dueling second, Owen Washburn, worked an oar alongside their physician Dr. Turnbull, who also rowed. Owen had negotiated the duel with Sam's second, his younger brother Joe, and they'd settled on having it here at Sam's plantation, Locksley.

Gideon scowled at Sam's boat. His legs braced, Sam stood erect. His remorseless pecan-colored eyes flashed. Joe and Sam's doctor rowed fast and hard.

In Mobile some sixty miles south, dueling was illegal. Every participant in this affair, except Sam, lived there. It'd been outlawed in the whole state of Alabama. This spot ensured no one would discover their fight, unless of course a steamboat happened by, in which case they'd likely receive fair warning from her whistle and paddles as she rounded a bend.

No one would be arrested today. Gideon muttered, a habit he'd developed since Harriet's death. Mouth shut again, his musings resumed. Kill Sam. Or would it be murder, if murder is what dueling truly was? Murder, or an affair of honor on the field of honor, on the island of honor.

Gideon's boat glided up on the island. Owen shipped his oars, hopped out and dropped its small anchor onto the hard sand. Dr. Turnbull climbed over the gunwales.

Two crows launched off the island and landed on the opposite riverbank. They strutted and cawed, spectators hurrahing the pending contest. From a live oak's sprawling, low-hanging branch on the same bank, a turkey vulture witnessed the affair. Beneath it, a coiled cottonmouth basked in the late afternoon sun.

Gideon gestured at the black pistol case on the boat's stern seat.

Owen grabbed it. Sam's craft bumped the sand alongside them.

Sam stared stoically at Gideon, stepped toward the middle of the island. He was a tall man, barrel-chested and solid as granite. His close-cropped brown beard hugged his square chin, reminding Gideon of a chin strap. Had this been fisticuffs instead of a duel, Gideon realized he'd not stand a chance. Sam calling Harriet, a … No, he wouldn't think it. Sam insulted her memory, so today, Sam must and would die.

Gideon ground his teeth. Impassive, respectful, the rules duelists were expected to follow when they faced each other in combat, rules he struggled to abide by. He opened his mouth to speak, clamped his jaw, swallowed an angry mutter. Sam and his stoic stare, he was trying to abide by the rules as well, Gideon hoped.

Owen and Joe knelt and opened their pistol cases.

"Care to come watch me load, Quarles?" Owen asked.

Joe waved him off. "I trust you."

Pistols at half-cock, they proceeded to load the weapons.

"Racing your horses again come winter?" Owen measured out his gunpowder.

"I am." Joe poured his powder down his flintlock's barrel. "And perhaps in New Orleans this fall."

Gideon strolled to Owen and received his pistol in his left hand, held it at his side, its muzzle aimed at the ground. Owen kept his own pistol ready to keep the contest fair.

Sam received his pistol from Joe. Joe kept his loaded smoothbore at his side to ensure the same goal of fairness.

The physicians posted themselves beside a large bush.

"Gentlemen." Joe stepped between them. "Remain at your posts unless Washburn and me say otherwise. When Washburn drops his handkerchief, the fight will commence. As Mister Washburn and I agreed, Mister Deshler will have the first shot. If neither man is hit they will maintain their posts, and we will reload your weapons to repeat the fight. Once a man is hit, either dead or wounded, the matter of honor is satisfied."

"Is everything understood?" Owen said.

Gideon and Sam nodded.

Joe stepped back.

"On my signal, gentlemen." Owen raised his handkerchief. It floated to the ground.

Sam and Gideon shifted their pistols to their opposite hands. Gideon fired first.

1

Mobile, Alabama

May 22, 1852

Gideon stumbled behind Owen down the steamboat's gangplank onto one of the Mobile River's quays. Except for several small boats laboring past and a smattering of Irish stevedores off-loading freight by boats' flickering lanterns, Mobile's riverfront was deserted. The city's fish market on Government Street's wharf emitted a stench that mingled with other unpleasantries. The entire riverfront. *Ugh!* It stank.

His life stank even worse. No Harriet to hug him and welcome his arrival, no son to laugh and call him "Daddy." It was as though a concrete wall blocked everything joyful from soothing the pain that afflicted his heart. He dreaded going inside his house.

With winter's arrival, Mobile's modest population would swell, transformed into a cotton city, packed with planters from the state's interior regions. Owen, who resided not far from Three Mile Creek, west of Mobile, lived closer than most planters and was one of Gideon's clients.

As his second, in accordance with dueling's rules, Owen and Dr. Turnbull went to assist Sam, but Joe turned them back before they could reach Gideon's fallen foe.

When Gideon climbed back into his boat, Joe's angry voice rang out. "Murderer!"

With every step he took, Joe's word shrieked in Gideon's ears.

Owen tugged his narrow chin. "I reckon Lorelei's plumb worried about me."

"She knew about the duel?"

"Can't hide much of anything from her. She'll say nothing, long as I'm still alive. She didn't like what Sam called your Harriet either, and the way she and Quarles's wife get along—"

"Like a couple of bobcats fighting over food," Gideon said. "Could you stay with me a little longer tonight?"

"I'm sorry. I do need to get on back."

"Why?'

"Because I need to."

"Oh."

On the way home Gideon listened to Owen's jabbering about horses and horse racing. He bragged on Comet, the Thoroughbred he'd purchased for Lorelei, and his retired champion Sir Walter, winner of several small races and three major stakes races during his two-year career. He mentioned his grooms, his favorite jockey—George Moore—and his trainer, Tyce Mann.

Gideon feigned interest by asking occasional questions, but his blaring thoughts muffled his friend's words. Harriet wouldn't have approved of his duel. Nor would his late parents, who'd also bought into all this religious mumbo jumbo. *Bah.* He didn't care. He had to kill Sam. Sam gave him no choice, on account of his offending Harriet's honor. Real men defended a lady's honor, and he was a first-class gentleman.

Many females died during childbirth. A sad fact of life. It wasn't fair. It just wasn't fair, females dying and their babies dying. Harriet dying and his newborn son dying. It just wasn't fair, wasn't right. Her sweet image played in his thoughts—her ivory heart-shaped face framed by bountiful brown ringlets, her joy at their expected child growing inside her womb, the grand plans they'd had for him or her, the many months he'd prayed for her safety during childbirth and the health of his child … Gideon swore at the next memory, the day the doctor announced the devastating news: "I'm sorry, Mister Deshler. Your wife has died, but your son survived."

Well, the doctor was wrong. Gideon stifled a tear and glared at the starless iron sky. Yes, his dear son survived, for all of two days. He turned off Government Street's flagstone banquette, Owen alongside him.

While his nose fought the city's dust wafting on a mild breeze, Gideon led Owen through his home's gate, up a short oyster-shell path and climbed several steps onto its white-pillared gallery.

Thaddeus, his butler and footman, closed the front door behind him. "Shall I see Mister Washburn's horse saddled, sir?"

Gideon nodded and spotted Thaddeus's wife, Katie, watching them through a window.

"I shall bring the animal around front." Thaddeus, whistling "How Firm a Foundation," headed for the stable behind the house, his long limbs making quick strides.

Gideon flinched. Thaddeus, a talented whistler, almost always whistled some kind of religious song even when he'd ordered him not to do it. Like Katie and Isaac Vincent, his gardener, Thaddeus Johnson was free, all of them manumitted by his parents and allowed to remain in the state with the consent of its senate and legislature.

Gideon's mother, brave enough to take the risk and violate the law, and with his father's approval, gave them a basic education once they'd been freed—reading and writing and arithmetic and spelling. Had she been caught she'd have suffered a huge fine. She, however, believed such education would help them learn the Bible better as well as serve the household in a more efficient manner.

Many of Mobile's free black women, such as Katie, worked in white homes while its free black men did skilled labor. Katie, among other duties, served Gideon as his maid and cook. She once had a kitchen girl who'd helped her but sadly, the girl perished in one of Mobile's fever epidemics a few years ago. Isaac, though he understood that a kitchen was a woman's domain, often helped her these days because, as he once said, he enjoyed "fixing a fine meal." Thaddeus and Isaac were among the city's few free black men working in white households. Many such households used Irish immigrants instead.

Gideon shoved his hands in his trouser pockets and shifted his feet.

"You'll still be paying Lorelei and me a call tomorrow, won't you, my friend?" Owen asked.

"You bet. I'd like to see that new horse of yours, that Comet."

"And that you will. Lorelei and I'll be looking for you. He's going to be faster than Frank Quarles's Green Legs ever was."

"I wouldn't know. I never saw that horse run."

Owen flashed a confident grin. "Trust me. I saw Green Legs run before he was killed. On more than one occasion. That horse was fast, for certain. But Comet would make him eat dust. And despite what Joe thinks," Owen huffed, "my father did not kill that animal."

"I believe you." Gideon had heard a little about Green Legs, who'd died suddenly a few years ago, but he knew very little about that unfortunate event.

Thaddeus led Owen's chestnut Morgan to him. "I pray the good Lord will give you a safe trip, Mister Washburn."

Owen grunted, swung into his saddle and cantered up Government Street.

"Go on home, Thaddeus." Gideon's fist covered his yawn. "I'm off to bed."

"Tomorrow's Sunday, sir."

"And the day after tomorrow is Monday. Be up Spring Hill by two o'clock."

"On a Sunday, sir? On the Lord's Day?"

"Blast it. Have it your way. My parents spoiled you by giving you the Sabbath day off. I have something to do tomorrow anyway."

"I reckon you won't be going to church, Mister Deshler?"

"Leave."

"We're all praying for you, sir. Every Sunday and every day."

"Good for you." Gideon trudged into his house.

Thaddeus, Katie and Isaac were part of a black congregation sponsored by his late parents' Methodist church. Religion made them feel better, he supposed, just like it did his parents. He'd heard them pray for the freedom of all enslaved people. He snickered. Lots of good prayer would do them.

"Go ahead and pray, Thaddeus. Maybe the ceiling will answer you." Gideon stepped down the hall to his pantry, muttering. "That's what I need. A big bottle of white wine before I go to bed." Since Owen deprived him of a longer visit, he'd drink wine and go to sleep. He hoped. In his pantry, he grabbed a bottle from his wine rack and stared at it. He let loose a loud sigh. "Wine, you are a good friend." His leaden feet carried him into his study. He plopped down at a desk, slouched. "Drink up, Gideon. Find peace. Imbibe." He drank it all then laid his head on the desk, wept and fell into slumber.

2

River Rose—
Three Mile Creek, Alabama
May 23, 1852

Longleaf pines rustled in a gentle breeze while Gideon guided his horse up a narrow dirt road several miles north of Three Mile Creek. Another mile remained before he reached the turnoff for River Rose, Owen's magnificent estate. Provided Owen's wife, Lorelei, didn't kick him out of their home for overstaying his welcome, he hoped for quality time with his friend and a good chance to observe Owen's newest Thoroughbred acquisition, Comet.

On his left, a black flash parted thick grass. He gripped the derringer he always carried for protection, despite the fact that carrying a concealed weapon violated state law. He waited for the flash to reveal itself. "Dumb bull snake. I might've killed you." Gideon continued on his way. The serpent slithered across the road.

Gideon scratched his chest. "Well now, today is Sunday, isn't it?" He laughed. "Why Gideon Deshler, my dear sir, you almost forgot." He laughed again. Louder.

At a second turnoff, he guided his mount onto River Rose's dirt lane. A hawk circled low over the treetops. Spotted his prey, no doubt. A rabbit? A squirrel? Lower the hawk circled, swooped down out of sight. Death, life's curse, claimed all creatures. Sam met his end. One day he would too. Had his killing Sam been a crime? No, he'd fought him on the square.

Met his end? The thought surfaced again. What is the end, when a person dies? Where did Sam go after he was killed? Certainly not Hell. That place didn't exist.

Gideon steered his horse around a sharp bend. His late parents believed in Hell, and they also believed in Heaven. Although he did love his parents, loved them greatly, sometimes their morals were too strict and discipline too severe. That day long ago when his teacher caught him cheating on an arithmetic test and told his mother, his mother spanked him so hard he'd never forgotten its stings. "Bah." What his parents had taught him about religion and morals in his childhood and youth … Were those things true? No, none of it was true.

Gideon rode past River Rose's cotton acreage. Ten dogtrot cabins stood on his right. On his left was a larger log house, Tom Zeller's quarters. A most unpleasant individual, Zeller, but a good overseer is what Owen said.

Up ahead rose a mansion, its upper story stucco and painted pale red. Its ground floor was red brick. Huge white columns fronted its rows of French doors. Owen's late father William, shortly upon his arrival from Tennessee, purchased it from a Frenchman who'd fallen on hard times and moved back to Martinique. Mister Washburn had considered having it painted white like many Anglo houses, but for whatever reason, he never did.

A cast iron horse guarded its white picket gate. Sunbeams shimmered off its massive hipped roof's four dormers. Spacious wraparound galleries hugged its upper and lower floors. From its upper gallery to earth, a steep staircase descended.

Owen and Lorelei lived on the second floor. The first floor they used for storage and dining.

Gideon's father had arrived in Mobile a year before Mister Washburn, accompanied by Thaddeus and Katie who were a few years older than he and married. Later, soon after his father purchased his plantation, Selah, on the Alabama River, his father purchased Isaac.

Gideon dismounted and led his horse through the gate. He started to tie his animal's reins to a hitching post when a wiry slave raced to him. "I got it, Mistah Deshler."

Gideon tossed him the reins.

The slave eyed him warily.

Lorelei, a petite blonde, came out the front door. Her deep yellow skirt rustled over numerous petticoats. Two inches taller than Owen, she possessed bright brown doe-eyes set inside a flawless oval face. A small emerald ring adorned her finger, a coral bracelet circled her thin wrist.

Once Gideon and Owen shook hands, Lorelei put on her affected, dimpled smile. Gideon loathed it.

"Your coat's unbuttoned, Mister Deshler." She pointed at it.

He glanced down. *Shrug.*

"If you don't button it, I will."

Gideon swore under his breath. Mrs. Washburn didn't know her place.

"Stop it, Lorelei," Owen snapped. "Our friend's come to see Comet."

"I know he has, Husband, but I do expect your friends to have proper manners."

The barracuda. Gideon buttoned his coat. What was she about to do to him? Make him leave?

Lorelei shoved Owen. "Quit standing there. Show him."

Owen frowned at her before saying, "Well, let's go."

Gideon cleared his throat. Lorelei's bossy attitude left a taste in his mouth as delightful as castor oil. He followed Owen down a pebbled path threading camellia bushes till they arrived at Owen's Thoroughbred stables, a two-story structure with a large cupola on its pine roof.

"My horsemen live on the second floor," Owen said. "I tried getting Tyce manumitted a few years ago. The state legislature didn't approve it."

"Tyce is that trainer you mentioned to me?"

Owen nodded. They strolled past the twenty stalls on its first floor. Every upper stall door, save two, were opened.

"Beautiful horses." Gideon patted the brown nose of one that hung out its head to catch the breeze.

"That they are." Owen stopped at the first stall, a white number "1" painted on its lower door. From inside it, a coal-black horse locked its large brown eyes on him.

George Moore, a small man whom Owen often referred to as his "number one jockey" stepped out of the tack room. Owen gestured him to the black horse and opened the stall's lower door. "Here he is, Gideon," Owen said. "Our next champion, Comet."

Gideon whistled. The animal's head looked near perfect. It was long and narrow like the ivory black knight in his chess set. "He's a handsome beast."

Owen turned to George. "Bridle him up."

George ducked back inside the tack room. Soon he returned, saddle pad and blanket in hand. A groom, who carried the bridle and exercise saddle, came with him. Comet's chiseled head hung low and his ears twitched back and forth. They tacked him up.

Gideon reached out to pet Comet's shoulder.

"Don't do that," Lorelei snapped.

Gideon withdrew his hand and stared at her quizzically.

Again, she pasted on her affected smile. "He doesn't like being petted there." Lorelei approached Comet slowly, whispered in the horse's ear, reached up and stroked his forehead twice. "See here. This is what my gentleman likes."

Comet, his breaths slow, nuzzled her.

"I'll thank you not to try and pet his shoulders again." She narrowed her eyes at him, as though he was a naughty child.

Barracuda. Gideon turned from her and concentrated on Owen. "How'd you come across him?"

"Paid one-thousand fifty dollars for him from a friend of a friend over in Mississippi. Comet's sire had been one of Mississippi's great Thoroughbreds and once belonged to Mister William J. Minor. Comet comes from a pedigree of champions, is what he says. The things I've read about him confirmed it. A fine-looking animal, wouldn't you agree?" He acknowledged Tyce, who'd joined them. "George and Tyce accompanied me. They suggested I purchase him."

Gideon studied Comet's powerful hindquarters.

George pointed at them. "Look at how strong-looking they are."

"His forequarters too," Gideon said.

"You like him, sah?" Tyce asked.

"Indeed." Gideon bobbed his head. His Thorougbreds didn't come close to this animal. Since he didn't race them, he owned a mere two. Perhaps, once he learned more about the sport, he'd give them a try. "What makes you so sure Comet'll be a champion? I remember your father once told me it took years of training before a man could be sure about the quality of a horse's racing ability."

"Comet won several races against other two-year-olds before we bought him, came in second a few times, what his previous owner said. He's racing with three-year-olds this year."

"He'll win because he's my horse." Lorelei's tone implied he'd asked a stupid question. "His owner couldn't turn down our monetary offer. If he knows what's good for him, Comet'll win me, us, lots of money." She shot George a look that warned him her words were meant for him too.

Gideon turned his head and coughed. Why did Owen ever marry Bossy Lorelei?

"Mister Troye will paint his portrait next week." Lorelei lifted her chin high.

"The equine artist who teaches at Spring Hill Academy?" Gideon asked.

"Who else would I want to do it?" Lorelei gave Comet another quick pat. "He painted some of my father's Thoroughbreds last year."

"Lorelei's father owns three outstanding horse farms." A gleam surfaced on Owen's face. "Well sir, her brother Bob'll inherit two of them." Owen's voice quivered with excitement. "And you know what, friend? He's leaving me his beautiful Valley Horse Farm, up in the Tennessee Valley, in his will. Why, two thousand acres of some of the greatest horse country I've ever seen. Just the land I'd asked him for once he passed on."

Gideon nudged him. "You'll be set with that, what with all your land down here as well."

"Sitting pretty as a peacock." Owen rocked back on his heels. "Still won't be enough, though. I'm looking at buying more land. Sir Walter brought my father prominence."

"Where's Sir Walter now?" Gideon asked.

"Out in the pasture with some broodmares," Owen said. "He's been enjoying the good life and making me decent money siring foals. Provided Comet proves to be the winner we expect, I'll be breeding him too. He'll bring me thousands of dollars. My dream, my friend? Stables throughout the South and horses that know how to win, to win my own fame in equine society." Owen patted Comet. "I'll become the greatest turfman in the whole entire South, owner of more horse land and horses than my dear father ever dreamed possible."

Lorelei flicked her wrist at George impatiently. "Put Comet through his paces. Let Mister Deshler see what he can do."

Tyce grasped George's left knee as he bent it, reins in his left hand. A bounce and a jump, and George was in the saddle. He clucked at Comet and guided him toward the track.

Owen rested his hand on Gideon's shoulder. "I reckon I told you this a few months back, but let me say it again. At last—"

"At last, it is good to have our fellowship and fun renewed," Gideon said.

Owen clapped his shoulders. "I concur."

Gideon grinned. Finally, he could enjoy good times with friends who helped him forget his cares. All he needed now, to make his life complete, was a fine lady to wed. Without a wife, without someone to help heal his lonely heart … Sometimes, he wished he'd die.

3

MOBILE, ALABAMA

JULY 24, 1852

Gideon crossed a mausoleum's long summer shadow. Perspiration coursed his cheeks. He turned left at a path's intersection and, dazed, passed Magnolia Cemetery's tombs.

Isaac accompanied him pushing a lawnmower Gideon's parents had purchased many years ago during a vacation in England. The machine was invented there by an engineer named Edwin Budding, or so Gideon had heard. Isaac claimed it made his gardening easier, better and faster than using a scythe, he'd said.

Easier? Gideon scoffed. So far, this summer's weeks had been days of misery. Of course, as a cotton factor, he kept busy helping his clients upriver in the state's fertile Black Belt. He bought supplies and the equipment planters needed to keep their plantations operating and made frequent trips to Selah, the plantation he'd inherited from his father. Outside of this, he devoted most all of his free time playing poker at Shakespeare's Row, a gaming establishment for Mobile's gentlemen, and drinking wine every night at home. He wished his thoughts could rush up the cotton season, for he'd push his brain so hard to do it, it'd burst. Busyness and fine wine occupied his desolation. Surely, upon the season's arrival, he wouldn't imbibe as much.

Harriet's gravesite halted them. High grass and tall weeds smothered hers and their son Billy's plots. Their gravestones, inconspicuous granite markers bearing their names and the year and month they died, "January, 1851," stood side-by-side. His parents' marker thrust skyward, a tall obelisk atop a grass-smothered plinth. On the platform, a scripture was inscribed: "For me to live is Christ, and to die is gain." Beneath it, the reference: "Philippians 1:21."

Gideon looked away. That verse. That verse. Death wasn't gain. It it was oblivion. A bay boat explosion killed his father in 1849, a few months after he and Harriet wed. A heart attack robbed his mother's life months later. A scream welled inside him ... silent ... painful.

Harriet's image flashed through his mind, her face aglow as she stood in her father's parlor clad in her silk wedding gown, her pastor and their friends gathered close to witness their marriage ceremony.

He shut his eyes, opened them again when Isaac's lawnmower, its wheels rattling on its cylinder and its blades scissoring grass, passed him. Isaac paused and removed his floppy straw hat, then mopped his broad furrowed brow. "Mrs. Harriet sure was a nice lady. Mighty good Christian folks, she and your parents were." Isaac glanced at him, his wideset hazel eyes the epitome of compassion.

Compassion for who? For him, 'cause he wasn't like the rest of his family? 'Cause he'd abandoned the faith? He'd wrestled with faith during his years of mourning. Mourning first for his parents, then for Harriet and little Billy. For a while after their passing, he'd attended church sporadically till finally, he quit his faith. Thus ended his struggles regarding religion, but not his struggles with misery.

Isaac resumed mowing Gideon's parents' plots. Back and forth, his strides slow and easy, the gardener moved in front of their headstones.

"Deshler."

Gideon started at Joe Quarles's familiar bass voice. Joe's wife, Gloria, crooked her gloved hand around Joe's elbow. From beneath her poke bonnet, black ringlets framed her oval face.

"Sam's still alive," Joe said.

"Didn't kill him, eh? I should've aimed better."

"You did shoot him in the chest, but let me tell you, your pistol ball hit his ribs and fractured one. At first, we feared you'd killed him.

Fortunately you missed his heart. He required some surgery, but he'll live, Doctor Lytle says. He's on bed rest for now. He'll be in some pain for the rest of his life."

Gideon smiled to himself. Sam, in pain for the rest of his life? *Good.*

"His full recovery will take a few months, Mister Deshler, thanks to you." Gloria huffed in disgust. "I declare, all you men ever want to do is fight each other in those abominable duels. It is against the law. Both of you know that."

Gideon studied her serious face, a woman who prided herself on formalities and etiquette and obedience to the law, Lorelei Washburn's total opposite.

Gloria's fingers laced Joe's fingers.

"We don't fight at the racetrack, dear," Joe said. "My jockey club forbids it."

"I didn't want to fight him." A lie. He'd jumped at the opportunity.

"He had no right to insult her. I agree." Gloria withdrew her hand from Joe's. "I've already spoken to him in that regard. But I do declare, you also had no right to shoot him. You men could've settled matters more peaceably. Both of you were wrong."

"Have you seen Washburn's new acquisition yet?" Joe asked, changing the subject.

Gideon swatted a mosquito on his neck. "Yes, 'cept I don't know much about Thoroughbred racing, so I can't answer any of your questions about him much. I can only tell you Comet owns a powerful set of legs."

Joe steered his wife toward his parents' marker. "It takes more than that to make a champion."

Gloria wiggled her fingers goodbye, cut short their conversation.

Gideon swatted at three mosquitoes.

"Pretty near done, sir." Isaac pushed the mower swiftly, sweat streaked his face.

"Mow it again."

"Again, Mister Gideon?"

"You heard me. Yes!"

4

BELLE GLADE HORSE FARM AND PLANTATION
MOBILE BAY'S EASTERN SHORE
AUGUST 6, 1852

Elvira Sturgis twirled her bullwhip and cackled at her parents'
skinny little servant whom she'd backed against the attic's corner.
"Don't pilfer those eggs again, Becky." Her whip popped and
just missed Becky's face. "Next time, I'll put a bigger hurt on you."

Her lips drawn into a thin line, Becky wiped the blood off her
copper-colored cheeks. "I ain't stole it." Her eyes spit fire.

"Don't you lie to me." Elvira raised her whip to strike again.
Becky dodged it by bolting to a window that overlooked Mobile
Bay's Eastern Shore. Up flew her hands. Elvira's rawhide snapped
the servant's scarred knuckles. "Lower those hands, girl."

"You lower your whip, Devil Woman."

Elvira tossed her whip against the wall, seized Becky's arms and
flung her onto the floor. "Stand up, Imbecile."

Becky's glower assessed her master and mistress's daughter.

"I said stand up, else I'll take you down to the bay and toss you
in it for the crabs to eat."

Becky gained her footing and spat.

"Get your sorry self on downstairs and dust the breakfront like Mother told you. We've got the Washburns coming here soon. Your dusting should've been done by now."

Becky limped to the attic's door.

"Stop," Elvira snapped.

Becky halted, her posture rigid.

"Next time you call me Devil Woman, Becky, I swear I will kill you."Elvira popped her whip. "And I will toss your corpse to the sharks." She popped the whip again. "Leave. Tell Elkins I said put tallow on your cuts."

Limping, Becky descended the steps.

"Dumb girl." Elvira stuck her whip's handle in a crimson sash tied round her waist. She was weary of Becky's foolishness. As tiny as Becky was, she had no fear of her, not like the other slaves. The only way to prevent an uprising was making them more scared of her than she was of them. If she didn't get that girl in line ... Suddenly light-headed, she steadied her weak knees. No, Becky may be a nuisance, but she'd never try to kill her or her family ... yet ... frighten her into obedience? She'd better find a way to do it to that stubborn little imbecile. Soon.

On the floor beneath her, she entered her mother Margaret's bedroom, where she was crocheting. Mrs. Sturgis set aside her work to peer at Elvira above her spectacles, which she seldom wore except when crocheting, knitting or reading. "A pity your father's not here right now."

"I put just as big a hurt on them as he does when they get out of line." Elvira admired the pink lace collar her mother was making. "I rather enjoy doing it."

"If we don't keep control of them no telling what they may do to to us."

Elvira picked up a tortoiseshell comb off her mother 's bureau. "Ours may turn on us like Mamaw's and Papaw's did. They're all beasts."

"That was a horrible uprising my parents were killed in. An event we Virginians will never forget." Mrs. Sturgis took off her spectacles.

"I'm glad you and Father moved here before that happened" Elvira set down the comb. "Y'all might've been killed in it too."

"Your father's sworn to me from the day it happened that no slave would ever kill us." Her mother put her crochet work into a small sewing basket. "Elvira, we really must talk."

"Why?"

"You're twenty years old. You're a beautiful lady. It's time you go back to courting. Quit spurning every man who desires your elegant companionship."

"And quit showing them my pet?" Elvira fingered a button on her white lace bodice.

"For now. You don't want to scare anymore of them off."

"Not every gentleman's scared of them. After what Mister Culpepper did to me—"

"Oh, stop thinking about that scoundrel. You want to end up a spinster?"

Spinster? Care for Cousin Lacie's brood? *Never.* She abhorred children. Her mother was right. The only way she could keep socializing with society's respectable crowd was to get married. Forget all the men in her life who'd betrayed her affections, who'd cheated on her, who'd used her. Above everyone else, forget that low-down, good-for-nothing Mister Adam Culpepper, who'd fled to parts unknown. She never wanted to see that man again. "I want a rich man, Mother, who has no fear of Hell because he knows it's a myth. An atheist like us. Not some fool who believes in religious fabrications." And a man she could use like Mister Culpepper had used her.

"Now that's my sweetheart. Go check on Becky and the other servants for me."

"Yes ma'am."

Elvira stepped down and around the spiral staircase into their home's central hall. As she entered the music room, her doorbell tinkled. She turned and waited for their butler to allow their visitors' entrance. She stepped back into the hallway and smiled a greeting. Finally, the Washburns had arrived.

Owen tossed his calling card atop similar cards in the silver salver the butler extended. "Here, Elkins." Owen gave the butler his top hat.

Elkins hung it on a hat tree in the foyer.

Ugh. Lorelei was wearing her ugly purple skirt. It looked like her dunderhead brother Bob had selected its fabric. Elvira forced aside her distaste for her friend's fashion sense, collected her etiquette to play the polite hostess and approached her. They gave each other quick hugs.

"Lorelei, dear," Elvira said, "I'm so glad you and your husband accepted our dinner invitation. Please, do come in."

Mrs. Sturgis came down the stairs. "Good afternoon, Mister Washburn."

Owen bowed. "Good afternoon, Mrs. Sturgis. Is your husband home?"

"He's gone out to take care of some business. He'll be back soon," Mrs. Sturgis said.

"Before we get down to some serious dining, I have something to ask him."

"A legal question, Mister Washburn?" Elvira said.

"Another matter. Your father's an excellent lawyer, but I don't require his legal advice today."

Mrs. Sturgis led them to the music room where Becky dusted its breakfront's mahogany cabinets.

"That's a good girl, Becky." Mrs. Sturgis gestured the servant out of the room. "Shoo, now. I think we may have some cornbread in the kitchen. You may have some if you like."

Becky curtsied, departed.

"You must want to talk to him about Thoroughbreds." Mrs. Sturgis turned back to Owen. "That would be my next guess."

"Yes ma'am. And our jockey club's ball."

Lorelei gave brief attention to Elvira's whip, tucked in her dress's sash. "Are your servants causing trouble again, Elvira?"

"Nothing I can't handle." Elvira touched the whip.

Mrs. Sturgis gestured at a rosewood armchair. "Please, do sit down." She clapped. "Elkins. Come here."

The butler stepped into the parlor.

"Bring our guests some tea."

"Yes ma'am." Elkins left.

Owen pulled up chairs for the ladies. Once they were seated, he sat on a settee.

"Mrs. Sturgis." Lorelei gestured at Owen. "My husband here—"

"We have a friend," Owen said before Lorelei could finish. "He may be a good match for you, Elvira."

"Really?" Elvira tried to sound perky. Even though she possessed a talent at pretending, she wasn't sure she succeeded this time.

"He was my best friend back when we were children, till his parents' religion interfered."

"Now look here, you two," Elvira said. "Everyone knows I'm not religious."

"Neither is he," Lorelei said quickly. "He used to be. He's not anymore."

"Continue." Mrs. Sturgis's austere gaze followed a servant who entered the room with a tray bearing teacups on sucers.

"A year before he attended the university in Tuscaloosa, he adopted his parents' Methodism." Owen received his cup and saucer.

"He and my husband parted ways after that." Lorelei got her tea off the tray. "He didn't know we were courting, nor did we invite him to our wedding."

"I remember your wedding." Elvira clasped her hands in her lap. "So beautiful it was. That's what I want when I get married. A wedding right here at my home with just a few friends."

"Shush, dear." Mrs. Sturgis sipped her tea. "Let our guests finish." She sipped more tea. "Do continue, Mister Washburn. We're listening."

"Reckon there's not much more to say, ma'am." Owen cradled his teacup before clinking it on its saucer. "He got married too, without our knowledge since we'd ended our friendship. Two years ago, his wife died birthing a baby. Their newborn died a couple days later. He told me he'd prayed long and hard for them, but nothing happened. He struggled a lot during his years of mourning until, six months ago, he finally kicked God out of his life."

Elvira giggled. Kicked God out of his life? When God didn't exist?

"His name's Gideon Deshler, Mrs. Sturgis."

"Mister Deshler?" Mrs. Sturgis's jaw dropped. "He lives in Spring Hill, does he not? A few miles from us, I think. His cottage looks quite nice."

"I've seen him before." Elvira offered a quick smile. "A few times, out in his yard at his big house on Government Street. He does cut a fine figure of a man."

Owen rested his teacup on his knee. "You know him?" He sipped his tea again.

"Only the gossip." Mrs. Sturgis set her tea on a side table. "We never associate with hypocrites who move in religious circles."

"That's why we only know about him, what we've heard, but don't really know him," Elvira said. "I've never been formally introduced."

"Darling, you simply must meet him." Lorelei leaned forward. "You'll like him once you get to know him. Why, you two would make a wonderful couple. Besides, ever since his Harriet and only son died, the poor man's been powerful lonely."

Lost his religion? Good looks? Wealthy? Elvira hung on her friend's subtle message—*lonely.* Ever since that fancy-dressed New Orleans lawyer Mister Culpepper absconded with her substantial dowry the day before their marriage, yes, that's it. By "helping" a lonely man who shared her devout atheism, she may find in him a husband she could use and control, in the same way that scoundrel Culpepper used her. "How'd you think he'd feel about my pet?"

Owen brightened. "He wouldn't be scared of it. We used to hunt them back when we were boys."

"My goodness." Elvira fluttered her hands. "I simply must make his acquaintance." *Much obliged, Mister Adam Culpepper.* Vengeance on men was now her motto.

Owen hastened alongside Elvira's father, Edward Sturgis, to Sturgis's dusty red horse barn and the angry shout inside it. What in blazes …? Owen was curious to find out what happened.

"A hunnerd!" a familiar voice screamed. "You gained ten big'uns this month, Ned."

They ducked through the barn's opened double doors. Two grooms exited stalls, mucking rakes in hand.

"Out. Both of you," Sturgis roared.

The boys dropped their rakes and fled.

Sturgis swaggered to the Fairbanks floor scale standing between twenty stalls, ten on each side. Owen watched and listened.

Sturgis's jockey, Ned Jenkins, though shorter than his angry trainer Robert Alcorn, stood almost eye-level with him. Owen recalled that Robert, likewise a slave, had once been both a jockey and a groom.

Like all jockeys, they were slightly built and wore boy-sized shirts. Robert's beard was a mere tuft hanging off his narrow chin.

"What's this ruckus about?" Sturgis asked Robert. Robert gestured angrily at the platform scale. "He's done gained ten pounds, sah. He's a hunnerd big'uns now."

"Are you becoming a hippopotamus on us, Ned?" Chuckling, though his shrewd black eyes signaled his dearth of amusement, Sturgis snatched a quirt off a nearby wall rack. He raised it to smack Ned.

Ned flinched.

He wiggled his quirt beneath Ned 's broad nose. "We can get our weight down to eighty pounds, can't we?" He chuckled again. "You won't ride Mystified at a hundred pounds, will you?"

"Naw sah," Ned said.

"You may race one of my four-year-olds at that weight, except I do not want that. You will ride Mystified, won't you? Like I want you to do, won't you?"

Ned sucked in a deep breath and nodded.

Sturgis smacked the quirt on a stall door. "You have exactly one month to get your weight down. To eighty pounds."

Ned nodded slowly.

Again, Sturgis chuckled. "You know what will happen if you fail to lose weight, do you not?"

Ned nodded again … slowly.

"You would find it distasteful, wouldn't you, Ned?"

"Yas Massa."

Sturgis pivoted and headed out of the barn. Over his shoulder, he shouted, "Starve him if you have to, Robert."

"I'll see it gets done, sah," Robert said.

"You'd better." Sturgis tossed aside the quirt. Back out in the open air, he clapped Owen on the shoulders. "Ned's a good boy. He's just got to learn to stop stuffing his face."

"Reckon it's the only way our jockeys can learn, being firm with them."

"Quite correct."

At Sturgis's racetrack, riders exercised horses. One horse stood out, his sorrel steed Mystified, a handsome beast. The rider had him moving at a slow trot.

Owen and Sturgis folded their arms atop the white fence's top rail and watched.

"Mystified has a good stride," Owen said. "Smooth and long. Lorelei's brother Bob has some fine Thoroughbreds too. I keep trying to purchase one of them from him."

"Young Glenville won't sell?"

"Reckon not. He's mule-stubborn when it comes to his racehorses. Can't say I blame him."

"Will he be entering any on our track this season?'

Owen shrugged. "Haven't heard. Guess what his and Lorelei's father did, though? A few months ago, old Mister Glenville added me to his will."

"Splendid. And?"

"And he's leaving me Valley Farms." Owen's pulse quickened. He envisioned a map of Alabama with numerous red dots on it, representing all the horse farms he hoped to one day own.

"I've seen Valley Farms. A beautiful place, nestled near the Appalachian Mountains." Sturgis pulled a cigar from his shirt pocket. "Bob will get his other two farms, I presume."

"Yes sir."

"Maybe you two could form a partnership."

Owen wasn't overly fond of his brother-in-law, but perhaps he could tolerate him as a business partner. He'd worry about it if, and when, the time came.

"Young Washburn, I do believe Mystified will do well this race season." Sturgis tapped his cigar on a fence post. "He's a handsome devil. My favorite. He may not be as fast as your Comet, but I expect he'll beat any of Joe's horses. That's all I care about right now. Beating Quarles's Thoroughbreds."

"Beating Joe?" Owen flashed a smile. "It'd suit me just fine. Joe's determined to reclaim his father's status in the turf world, but I'm counting on Comet to prove I'm still the better breeder and judge of horses."

"A tragedy what happened between your father and Frank Quarles."

"My father was innocent." Owen kicked a clod of dirt.

"And as a lawyer who studied all the evidence in that case and the lack thereof, that is likewise my verdict. He'd have been kicked out of the jockey club had he been determined guilty. Even put in jail."

"It's a sad fact Quarles's father never believed in his innocence, not even after we accused Frank's groom."

"Oh, Frank's little groom boy was guilty, all right. A sad fact the incident evolved into bad blood between you and Joe." Sturgis chomped his unlit cigar.

Mystified and his rider slow-trotted past them, two lengths ahead of the other horses and riders.

Sturgis waved his cigar. "Orley, move him at a fast trot once more around the track."

Orley did what he was told. The others fast-trotted behind him. Mystified and the other horses, their hoofs pounding dirt, soon made more trots past them.

"Cool them down after this lap," Sturgis yelled to the riders. To Owen, he genially said, "Now, young Washburn. What did you tell my wife you wanted to discuss?"

"Sir," Owen cleared his throat, "since you're president of our jockey club and all, I was wondering. Would it be permissible for me to invite a friend to our autumn dance?"

"A turfman?"

"Not exactly. A prospect."

"Prospect for whom?"

"For Elvira. His name's Gideon Deshler."

Sturgis's terrier brows arched. "A rich cotton factor, I'm aware of that fact. Isn't he of a religious persuasion?"

"Not anymore, sir. He's forsaken religion. He's more of the atheist persuasion now. Owns lots of acreage up near Montgomery, a nice cottage here in Spring Hill on ten acres of land and a sizable house on Government Street."

Sturgis took his cigar from his mouth and stuck it in his coat pocket. "Not a large house like mine is here."

"Uh, that's true, sir. His parents built theirs about twenty years ago."

"As did mine. I added an extra floor and an attic when I took ownership and decided to reside here year-round. Looks more like a mansion now, don't you think?"

"Yessir."

"Deshler works for that old fanatic, Cadwallader."

"That's true, but Gideon doesn't buy in to Cadwallader's religion. And he might be a good turfman one day. He was my closest friend from way back."

Deep in thought, Sturgis's brow furrowed as he tugged his heavy white beard.

Freddy, one of Sturgis's jockeys, hastened to him. "Sah, the tack room's cleaned up an' organized real good now."

"I'll inspect it in a minute. Go see Robert for your weigh-in."

Freddy lit out for the horse barn.

"Please, sir," Owen said. "Would it be all right for you, or me, to send him an invitation to our dinner and dance? To meet Elvira, sir?"

"We'll arrange a meeting with him at the track."

"A capital idea. I sure would like him to get more interested in our sport, since we're such good friends and all."

"Always room for more of us turfmen, young Washburn. Come. I need to discuss a few things with my overseer. Probably has my hands working the east field today."

Owen matched Sturgis's pace. "I'm delighted your wife is having Lorelei and me over for dinner tonight."

"We look for a delightful evening as well."

"Your invitation gave us an excuse to make this a short vacation. I've rented us a room for the weekend at the hotel in Point Clear."

"I'm surprised it had a vacancy this time of year."

"So were we. Lorelei loves Point Clear ."

"So does my Elvira. Our girls will have a chance to spend more time together." Sturgis draped his arm around Owen's shoulders and winked. "We'll discuss Joe's chances of becoming as good a turfman as his father after supper."

"Not much of a chance, sir."

Their laughter exploded.

5

DUNDEE HORSE FARM AND PLANTATION
TENSAW RIVER, ALABAMA
AUGUST 7, 1852

Joe Quarles strolled toward his whitewashed horse barn on his cotton and Thoroughbred farm, Dundee, Gloria's hand in his. Dundee was a huge spread a few miles north of Mobile, on the Tensaw River. It'd been named for the Scottish town, his grandmother's birthplace. Pleasant odors of hay and horses mingled as they drew close. To Joe, everything about horses was pleasant.

As often as he could, Joe traveled to Dundee to check on his horses, horsemen and field hands. His overseer managed Dundee's farm operations while his stables' trainer, Finn Rattigan, a redheaded Irishman whose temper was as fiery as his hair, managed his Thoroughbreds and horsemen. All of his horsemen, except Rattigan, were slaves.

Both a businessman and a turfman, Joe resided on Mobile's outskirts, on Spring Hill Road. Visits to Dundee, these were his vacations.

Joe's strides were swift, long. "Gloria, my sweet, let me tell you this. One day I'll be as great a turfman as my father. Johnny Boy will prove it on the tracks."

Gloria swung their arms back and forth. "JB? That cantankerous colt? Why I do declare, my darling. You jest."

"Truly I do not, my dear. He's got lots of spirit, and he's quite smart. Rattigan and I noticed it the first time we saw him over in Louisiana last month."

"My dear, sweet husband, you know full well a great champion needs more than that, He also needs a talented jockey, like Mister Adam Bingaman's Abe."

"You sound like my father."

"He knew a lot about horses."

"Well, everything he knew, he taught me." His elbow bumped Gloria's. "We have good jockeys at my stables, dear wife. Not everyone can own a slave with Abe's talents. However, once we channel JB's spirit in the right direction, once we get him trained, he'll win. Washburn's horse doesn't put the scare in me. Don't let it put the scare in you either."

"Me? Scared?" She drew him to a halt. Her tapered, gloved fingers cupped his chin. They kissed.

What a wonderful taste, her lips. And from a wonderful lady. He opened his mouth to speak.

Gloria continued. "Why should I be scared? I declare, why if our JB doesn't win, we still have your company's lumberyard and this farm. You can always go into business with my father if you ever desire."

Joe, smiling, nudged her aside. She had never taken horse racing seriously, not like he did. Nor did she have any love for Lorelei Washburn or her brother Bob, a turfman living near Opelika. "My company's hotel? It's not as nice as the new Battle House." Two other hotels burned down in 1850, leaving his the only one standing until the Battle House's recent opening. His firm already had plans in the works for improvements. "Besides, that's not the point. Status among my fellow turfmen. That's the point." He resumed his stride.

"Regaining your father's status. That's all you care about."

"You know Washburn's father stole this farm's reputation. And why, our Johnny will become the stud every owner will want his mare to breed with." Excited by the thought of Johnny Boy becoming a famous champion, he raised his voice.

"He'll get this farm's reputation back. Turfmen throughout our Southland will send their mares to foal with him. It'll be like it was when Father was alive. He was as well-known as those Kentucky breeders and why, I tell you, I'll become more famous than my father in the equine world. Greater than William Minor and Duncan Kenner too. Dundee's name will once again be heralded throughout the racing world."

"An almost impossible dream, my love."

"You don't believe in me?"

"Mister Quarles! The *capall!*" A short, muscular white man—Finn Rattigan—sprinted to them. "JB, the *capall*, the horse, sir, has escaped his stall. I feared something bad would happen when those crows started strutting around the horse barn. Bad luck, they are."

"Crows had nothing to do with it, you superstitious Irishman," Joe snapped. "Saddle Sadie for me."

"Dickson. James. Tom. Hurry!" Rattigan yelled.

The three grooms he'd called sprinted to them.

"Pete, Marcus," Joe yelled at the jockeys, who quit their daily exercise routine with the other jockeys and exercise riders.

The Morgan Sadie and two Thoroughbreds were tacked up quickly. Rattigan assisted Pete Webster into his saddle. Joe helped Marcus Adams into his before he climbed aboard Sadie.

Johnny Boy, a dark chestnut three-year-old, kept a good distance ahead of Joe and his jockeys. He swerved around live oaks and dogwoods, his mane blowing wildly, his thundering hoofs kicking up grass and dirt.

Sadie worked up a lather and gained on the jockeys, though they still lagged behind Johnny Boy, way ahead.

Johnny Boy leaped over a short garden fence, plowed between two tall camellia bushes and hurdled the opposite fence into a field where horses grazed. He scattered five of them before halting at a big plantation bell on the edge of a cotton field where slaves were working.

When Johnny stopped, Joe and the jockeys overtook him.

Joe scratched his forearm. Was Johnny Boy too tired to keep running? Judging by his tight lower lip and stiff ears, the colt was tense. "Pete, Marcus. Nice and easy now. Don't spook him."

Slowly, the jockeys approached on their mounts.

"He ain't a bad animal, Massa." Pete twirled his lasso.

"Jus' got a li'l mind of his own," Marcus said.

Two rabbits hopped out of some nearby brush. Johnny Boy bolted past the slaves' cabins.

"Get him!" Joe yelled.

Sam Quarles stood in the horse barn's entrance and tapped his sister-in-law's elbow. "This is more entertaining than bears doing somersaults."

"Who needs a circus when we have JB?" Gloria said.

Sam waved at Joe then winced. A pain pricked his chest. He'd mended enough from his wound to be up and about a little. Only with his doctor's reluctant permission had he been able to come downriver to visit Joe and handle some Locksley business in Mobile, though the city's business season wouldn't officially start till November. He'd written Joe two weeks ago about his planned visit, and he'd brought with him his three servants—Sallie, Zacchaeus and Reuben—who always accompanied him on his trips.

Joe acknowledged Sam's greeting before he turned his attention back to the task at hand—the battle to get Johnny Boy into his stall after the long chase.

His ears pinned behind his raised head, Johnny Boy jerked Pete's and Marcus's lassos looped round his neck. He snorted, opened wide his mouth and displayed a fierce set of teeth.

"Look at those ivories," Sam said, amused. "Don't let him bite your head off, Pete. He may get ahold of your big ole beard."

"Easy, boy." Pete let his lasso slacken. "Easy. Ea…sy."

"You be a good horse now." Marcus's lasso also slackened. His voice was as gentle as Pete's.

"If you are looking for this Irishman's opinion, Mister Quarles, I think we should shoot JB." Rattigan spoke from the far end of the stables, his brogue thick despite the ten years he'd lived in the States. "He ought to be broken in by now. The horse is crazy."

Joe ran his hand through his disheveled blond hair. "His previous owners gave up on him, but I'm no quitter. Get him trained the proper way, he'll be a winner. He's got the determination of a champion. I see it."

Johnny Boy's high-pitched scream rattled the barn's rafters. He reared on his hind legs, his forelegs slammed the pine floor inches from Marcus's head.

When Pete tried leading him into his stall, Johnny Boy attacked. Pete backed against a post and dodged the Thoroughbred's teeth by a hair.

Marcus lifted his lasso.

Johnny Boy quit resisting and stared at him.

"Come on now, JB." Marcus's tone was soft. "You're a good boy. Please be a good boy. Please get back in your stall."

Johnny Boy flinched.

Sam nudged Gloria. "JB's going to be trouble."

Gloria nodded.

"Good boy." Slowly, Marcus touched Johnny Boy's chest. "We ain't gonna hurt you none." His fingers moved, ever so cautiously, to pet him.

For reasons known only to Johnny Boy, the colt lowered his head and raised his ears and simmered down long enough for Marcus to stroke his forehead. Several minutes passed. Patiently, talking to him like a father comforting a distressed child, Marcus led Johnny Boy into his stall. Marcus slipped his and Pete's lassos off the horse's neck and stepped back to the center of the barn.

"It appears JB's starting to take a shine to you, Marcus," Joe said.

"Marcus should be the one to work with and ride him, sir. In this Irish trainer's opinion, of course." Rattigan watched Pete and Marcus duck inside the tack room to set their lassos back in place. "JB is a special case, he is."

"Special indeed." Joe stepped to Marcus when he came out of the tack room. "Marcus, JB's your horse. You will have him ready no later than early spring, but by our club's racing season is even better."

"Yas sah. I can do that."

"That's why I'm letting you handle him." Joe strode past Marcus, his hand outstretched for Sam's. "Welcome, brother. I received your letter. We are delighted to have you visit us. You are doing well?"

"As well as can be expected. Not fully mended yet. I need to be careful I don't lift anything too heavy. Might fracture another rib. Anyway, I'm going to Mobile this Monday to take care of some farm business. I'll also play a little poker at Shakespeare's Row."

"You'll probably see Deshler there."

"I hope so." Sam sneered.

"Will you spend the week with us there?"

"You have a mighty good cook at your place. Think I will. Sallie, Zacchaeus and Reuben are with me, of course. They're in your house at the moment."

"They'll share my servants' quarters and help them out with their chores, as usual." Joe led the way to his single-story cottage.

Sam understood why his brother never cared for big fancy mansions, for just like their father, Joe invested most of his money in horses and racing. "Why strut around like a cock of the walk flaunting one's wealth?" Joe once told him. "To impress those who didn't move in his social station? A stupid notion, that."

Oftentimes, he'd told Sam that if he couldn't regain their father's reputation, if he couldn't achieve greatness soon and keep his promise to their father … "Sam, I tell you, if I can't become like our father, I'd rather be dead." Joe's often uttered words worried Sam.

Try hard as he might, Sam couldn't dissuade his brother of this notion. He considered trying it again during his visit, but would it do any good? Probably not.

6

AUGUST 13, 1852

annah Louise Henshaw offered a warm smile while she handed the elderly lady her change. "Why, thank you kindly, Mrs. Ridley. You are one of our emporium's favorite customers."

Mrs. Ridley slipped the gold link bracelet around her fragile wrist and brought her shaky hand up to her face. A small gold heart pendant, a ruby inside the heart, dangled from it. Her gentle face beamed. "It's lovely, Hannah Louise. Simply lovely. Your father owns the best jewelry emporium in the South. He and your brother make the finest jewelry and watches I've ever seen."

Hannah placed Mrs. Ridley's cash in a metal drawer beneath the convex counter. "I'm so glad you like it. I hope your husband will too."

"He will, he will, I know he will."

"Good afternoon, Mrs. Ridley." Earl Henshaw, Hannah's father, stepped onto the sales floor from his back office with Mrs. Ridley's nephew, Paul. "Is my daughter treating you well?"

"Spoiling me as usual." She returned Hannah's smile. "You have a beauty of a daughter, Mister Henshaw, inside and out."

Hannah pulled in her smile. *Me, beautiful?* She'd never seen herself in that light, but Mrs. Ridley always said nice things about people even when what she said wasn't true.

"Would you be courting anyone?" Mrs. Ridley's pale blue eyes twinkled.

Hannah shook her head and blushed.

"Aunt Eunice," Paul Ridley said, exasperated. "What folks are doing and aren't doing is none of our concern."

"Of course, it's not." She patted Hannah's hand. "I know you'll find a good man one day, a special someone just for you."

Hannah, blushing deeper, averted Mrs. Ridley's kind gaze. "Yes ma'am."

"It is not good for man to live alone, Sister." Luke Henshaw moved toward them after seeing another customer out the store's door.

Hannah huffed. "Oh, Luke. Stop it. Look at you. You're older than me, and you still don't have a young lady in your life."

"Haven't found her yet, about the size of it all."

Hannah frowned at her brother. If he'd quit wearing all that Macassar oil on his hair, maybe he would find a wife.

"Well, I know you'll find a wonderful wife and make the perfect husband, Lucas Henshaw." Mrs. Ridley beamed.

"Most certainly." Paul moved out from behind the counter. "Now Aunt Eunice, we really must catch the bay boat back to Point Clear."

"It is the fever season, ma'am," Luke said.

"Why don't y'all move away this time of year, Mister Henshaw?" Mrs. Ridley's countenance turned serious. "I know you can afford it."

"I'm a member of the Can't Get Away Club," Earl said.

Mrs. Ridley brightened. "My, my. I quite forgot. You brave gentlemen do such a fine job helping the sick folk during our fever epidemics."

"Aunt Eunice." Paul tugged Mrs. Ridley's arm. "Come along. Please."

"Well, good day to you all." Mrs. Ridley waved at Hannah and her family as she headed for the door.

Paul and Luke stepped alongside her, Paul on her left and Luke on her right, steadying her by her forearms. They assisted her out of Henshaw's Jewelry Emporium and up a carriage block into a fancy barouche carriage, where their driver awaited them.

Hannah didn't think the sweet lady had many years left on this earth.

"Mrs. Ridley's a fine person." Charles Rhodes, a slightly overweight employee who approached her father's age, spoke from behind a glass ring case he was cleaning.

"A pity she's an Episcopalian," Earl said.

Hands on her hips, Hannah's eyes widened. "Oh, Daddy. Whatever's wrong with being an Episcopalian?"

"Nothing, dear daughter. I just wish she'd join our Methodist church. She's such a pleasant person, with such a positive outlook on things. John Wesley was an Anglican, you remember, and he stayed an Anglican even after God used him to start our Methodist movement."

"The Episcopalians came out of the Anglican church after the Revolution," Luke said as he reentered the store.

"And our denomination sprang out of Brother Wesley's Methodist movement, right here in America," Hannah said, chuckling to herself. *Take that, Luke. You aren't the only one who knows history.* "And Granddaddy Henshaw was friends with the great Francis Asbury."

"Wrong, wrong, wrong." Luke stepped past her. "Grandaddy was close friends with Bishop Coke. Isn't that right, Father?

"That's right," Earl said.

Hannah slapped her hands on her hips. "Well, humph. Bishop Coke and Bishop Asbury worked together." She held her head high on her way to the cameo display. "If he was close friends with Bishop Coke, he'd have been friends with Bishop Asbury too." *Score a point for me.*

The door's bell tinkled. Another customer entered.

Hannah turned from the display. Julia Smith. They'd best keep an eye on that little thief.

His workday ended, Gideon ate a quick sandwich before he headed for Shakespeare's Row, a block of brick buildings in Mobile's business district. Though some men played games of chance near the riverfront, they were society's lowest of the low. Not so, Shakespeare's Row's clientele.

Due to its reputation for integrity, not to mention its location, Shakespeare's game rooms catered to wealthy patrons like himself. The disreputable and undesirable were banned from its premises.

Gideon approached its arched entrance when a familiar voice boomed behind him.

"Deshler. Look at me. I'm alive and stomping like a bull about to charge a matador."

Gideon pivoted.

Sam swaggered to him from an insurance office down the street. "Your blame pistol ball." He winced. "Not the kind of souvenir I like."

"You asked for it," Gideon said, "and you'll get another one if you insult Harriet's memory again."

"I'll be the one doing the killing next time we duel, Deshler." Sam poked his chest. "How old are you now? Twenty-eight, I think?"

Gideon nodded.

"Next time we fight, you won't live to be twenty-nine." Sam headed for the door. "Got your money ready for our poker game tonight?"

"I hope you have your money ready for my wallet, Quarles."

"Hah! It'll be me taking all your money tonight, Deshler, for that souvenir you gave me." Sam's boisterous laughter drew curious stares from passersby.

"Mister Deshler." A girl in a blue-and-white checkered dress called to him from Henshaw's Jewelry Emporium across the street.

Gideon groaned. Why'd Hannah have to show up? He should've expected she'd confront him sooner or later, seeing how her father's store stood directly opposite this place.

On her approach, Hannah dodged four stray cows and two hogs. Stray animals were a common sight in the city. Gideon regretted its aldermen had done little to stop their nuisances.

"Who is that pretty little thing?" Sam asked, grinning. "You know her?"

"Nobody special." Gideon ducked inside Shakespeare's Row before Hannah could stop him. Right on his heels, Sam swaggered through the establishment's door while the young lady kept calling Gideon's name.

In a game room, one of many such rooms in Shakespeare's Row, tobacco fogs swirled over tables beneath gaslit chandeliers. Murmurs punctuated whirring roulette wheels. Along a far wall, men played games of twenty-one and faro. Billiard balls cracking against each other echoed from an adjoining room.

Gideon never played roulette, though he did sometimes play billiards. Occasionally, he engaged in twenty-one and faro. Poker, though, was the pastime he loved. Men who stood beside him at the bar, imbibing their liquors of choice, conversed. The entire place smelled of liquor and tobacco. He purchased his beer before he joined three other players, including Sam, at a poker table.

"Oh ho, Sam." Cole Tivington, one of Joe and Sam's friends, a wealthy architect and builder like his father Isham, shuffled the cards after he coughed. "You are still alive. You mean to tell me that Deshler didn't kill you?"

Sam cracked his knuckles. "I'm invincible."

"So was Green Legs." Isham laid his pipe across a marble ashtray. "On the track."

"Green Legs was the best and fastest four-year-old in the state," Sam said. "He would've probably won a big race in New Orleans if old Frank Washburn hadn't killed him."

Gideon bristled. "Owen's father didn't kill him. No proof was found." His olive face impassive, Cole petted his brown mustache. "The alleged lawyer Sturgis was his friend. Not exactly impartial when he studied the evidence. A wonder Washburn's and Joe's fathers never fought a duel over it."

"Other people agreed with Mister Sturgis, is what I heard." Gideon quaffed his beer. "Ask Owen if you want to know why they didn't fight one, 'cause I sure as blazes don't know."

"At the track, they found what appeared to be a lot of morphine crystals mixed in with Green Legs's feed." Cole stared hard at him beneath hooded eyes.

"Morphine?" Gideon's interest returned.

"What good ears you have, Deshler." Cole chuckled.

Isham cleared his throat. "Are we done prattling and ready to play some serious cards?"

"One more shuffle, please, Father." Cole passed the deck to Isham, then coughed again.

Gideon figured it was the room's tobacco smoke that provoked Cole's coughs, for he'd never seen him cough in places where no one smoked. He straightened a stack of coins and considered the late Green Legs. Whoever did kill that horse might still be out and around. If such was the case, that person might also kill one of Joe's horses before a big race. That is, if that person held a grudge against Joe. He'd wager lots of money on Joe and Owen's feud going beyond words if that happened. Unfortunately, Owen's marksmanship lacked accuracy. Would either of them drug a horse? He received the cards Isham dealt him. He didn't know. He hoped Owen and Joe didn't get into a duel. Not that he cared what happened to Joe. He didn't. However, he didn't want Owen to get killed.

Accompanied by her father and Luke, Hannah walked home. Thankfully, Julia didn't try stealing anything today, probably because they kept watching her.

A dog trotted past. Boys lugging short ladders scurried along the street, leaning them against lamp posts, climbing them and lighting the gas lamps before evening settled in.

While her father and Luke conversed, she pondered Mister Deshler's recent rudeness. He'd once been a fine Christian gentleman. His falling away from his faith troubled her. Her mother Martha passed away, a victim of the fever, in '39, but it didn't embitter her father or Luke. Instead, it made their faith stronger. She was in Heaven, completely healed. They were all confident of it. Could it be Mister Deshler's faith, which he had back when his sweet Harriet was alive, wasn't as strong as she'd once believed? What about when his parents died? Why didn't that embitter him then?

"Why do men fall away from their faith, Daddy?" The question popped out of Hannah's mouth unbidden.

"For many reasons," her father said.

"Some of Paul's friends deserted him," Luke said. "Remember what he told Timothy in his second letter, 'For Demas hath forsaken me.' This grieved Paul. Do you know why Demas forsook him?"

Hannah rolled her eyes. "Go ahead. Say it. I know you want to tell us." Though she admired her brother's sharp mind and the way he memorized scriptures, sometimes he could use a little humility by not showing off his brain.

Luke looked at their father, who nodded for him to continue.

"Because Demas loved the world more than he did God," Luke said. "That's what Paul told Timothy— 'having loved this present world.' The great apostle wrote, 'For Demas hath forsaken me, having loved this present world.'"

Hannah hastened ahead, her skirts rustling. "Mister Deshler sure has let the world get ahold of him."

"The pleasures of sin are for a season," her father said.

"Oh, it will be a short season, Daddy dear. I'll pray for it."

"I fear he's going to have to learn some hard lessons first."

"Hard lessons are what it takes with a lot of people, Sister." Luke strode up alongside her. "God loves His children enough to discipline them back into the straight and narrow, like Father and Mother did to us when we were children."

"I'm not eating tonight." Hannah pulled a small testament from her reticule.

"I'll allow you mean you're going on one of your fasts," Luke said.

"I'll give you tomorrow off, too, if you need it," Earl said.

Hannah stopped in her tracks, which brought her father to a stop. "Thank you, Daddy."

She slipped her testament back inside her reticule. "God's prodigal son will return to Him. I'm quite sure of it."

After she made a quick supper for her family, Hannah closed her bedroom door, took off her bonnet, unbuttoned her white kid gloves and pulled them off her dainty hands. These she set on a dressing table beside its large mirror.

She continued changing out of her day clothes into her more comfortable nightgown while Luke and her father bustled around the house to finish various chores. They owned no slaves, for they opposed that sinful institution. Like her father said many times, it was an abomination. However, they kept this opinion to themselves. A few years ago, some friends had been run out of town because of their abolitionist views.

Their Methodist denomination's founder, John Wesley, disapproved of slavery, yet their denomination had split over the issue a few years ago.

Nor did they have freeborn servants or Irish immigrants in their household's employ, though a few of their friends did. Her family was middle class, and her father owned several houses he rented out for extra income, a few of them on Mobile Bay's Eastern Shore. He was generous almost to a fault and lived a modest lifestyle. Money was nothing more than a means to live and support his family and God's work. Such was his philosophy. Unlike the city's wealthy citizens, who fled Mobile during the fever season, they lived in the city year-round. Because of swamps near the town, yellow fever posed a constant threat except during fall and winter.

Clad now in her nightgown, she knelt beside her bed. Her hands clasped beneath her chin, she gazed out a window. "Dear Lord," she began, gasping and chest heaving from her travail, "I don't understand about Gideon. I mean Mister Deshler. Why has he wandered so far from You?" She choked on a sob. "He used to walk with You, Lord. He used to …" Another moan stuck in her throat for a moment. "Please, Lord Jesus, do whatever it takes. Do whatever it takes to bring him back into Your fold."

She collapsed face down on her carpet, arms outstretched. Her prayers for Gideon soared up, beyond her home, the trees and the heavens.

No moon, no stars, nor the sound of bullfrogs in Gideon's dismal garden. He plodded past his camellia bushes. Inside his home, he lit the hallway's gas jets. Three flickering chandeliers lent light to this bleak space. He tossed his brown deerskin gloves on a blue velvet wing chair.

Sam and Cole *did* take most of his money tonight. Two hands, a meager two hands of poker he'd won. Not that he couldn't afford losing all that money. It was the fact that he'd lost it to Sam and to Cole.

"Cheaters." Gideon's shout echoed. He lit another gas jet in the front parlor. In the midst of it was an ebony table on cabriole legs that stood between a settee and another chair. Atop this table was a blue porcelain vase filled with long-stemmed artificial roses, which she'd placed there one month before she died. He lifted a rose from it. *Sweet Harriet.* He set the rose back in its place.

Gideon shuddered. "This place is a tomb."

He stepped to Harriet's portrait above the Italian marble fireplace. She'd posed for it in her silk indigo gown, her white evening gloves stretching up her arms to her elbows, the year before she passed.

Those beautiful brown ringlets framing her angelic face. He reached toward her cheek. Such soft eyes, such captivating "pearls." He lowered his hand. "I'm sorry, dear wife. My faith has abandoned me."

The memory of the day lingered. They'd met in his former church during an evangelistic meeting when she'd accompanied her father, a small planter, who was visiting the city from a neighboring county at the time.

And on a Saturday afternoon, Gideon mustered his nerve and made his approach during a church social. Harriet gazed up at him from her plate of food, drew him into lively conversation, and … her merriment ….

He turned from her portrait. He'd get Thaddeus to turn it around tomorrow. Coming into this place every night without hearing her vivacious voice … He picked up his father's Bible from off a side table, opened it and read his father's words on its front page:

Gideon Lawrence Deshler, born July 27, 1825. A healthy boy. God is good.

Healthy. He was born healthy. He flung the Bible across the floor. His face flushed. He shook his fists at his chandelier and released what resembled a roar. "My Billy wasn't born healthy. My Billy died."

He turned off the parlor's gas jets and stalked down the hall. Wine was what he needed. A big bottle of wine to help him sleep. He hated this lonely place. He'd go back up to Spring Hill tomorrow.

7

Spring Hill, Alabama

August 14, 1852

Gideon peeked out Owen's carriage window as the vehicle jounced up a low rise. In the distance, cows roamed in and out of thick woods. The Spring Hill Race Track's iron grille gate, after they passed through it, soon receded. At last, they'd arrived. A nine-foot-high brick wall— a barrier to the world—enclosed the track's acreage.

Seated opposite him, Owen plucked his watch from his vest pocket. "One o'clock. Blue skies. No clouds. A perfect afternoon for a little match race."

"Sounds like it's going to be fun." While their carriage bumped along, Gideon shrouded himself in his thoughts. The Spring Hill Race Track. For times too many to count, he'd passed it. He even remembered, during his childhood, watching the trees being felled and the land being cleared for its construction. Today marked his first venture onto its premises. His employer, Mister Henry Cadwallader, often hunted here with his grandsons.

His parents disapproved of horse racing because of the gambling that went with it. A pity, that. They didn't know how to have fun.

Another glance out. Up ahead, a massive grandstand capped by a large cupola dwarfed the wall. Atop the cupola was a staff, its dark blue flag snapping and popping in the breeze. He imagined winter's racing crowds, gentlemen and ladies of various social classes, backgrounds and ages come to watch the Thoroughbreds run. "This November, I'll be among them," he said.

Owen slipped his watch back in his vest pocket. "What was that?"

"Said I'd be among the racing crowds this November."

"That you will, my friend. That you will."

Crowds. Wonderful crowds. Somehow, talking to people lifted his spirits and eased his emptiness.

Owen's driver halted the carriage's team then opened the carriage door for Owen and Gideon to climb out.

"Those are for the spectators' carriages and horses." Owen pointed at a long row of red brick sheds ten columns deep.

"Impressive," Gideon said.

"This November, every one of them will be occupied. Let me show you around before we meet Mister Sturgis. He won't mind waiting." He told his driver to stay put. "George and Tyce should've arrived by now as well."

"Looking forward to seeing more of this place." Gideon followed Owen along an oyster shell path, past several booths.

"Proprietors rent those booths during race season," Owen said. "They minister to our visitors' needs for physical refreshment. It helps our club make additional income."

"Will anyone be selling beer?" Gideon asked.

"A certainty, except our club has a track rule. Only two beers per patron. Any drunks get caught we give them a kick in the britches for the rest of the season. We always post warning signs to that effect. Go get drunk somewhere else, we tell them. We're a respectable track."

"Good rule." *Two beers? Dumb rule.* "How long is your club's season?"

"We race four days. Monday, Tuesday, Friday and Saturday. One week."

"Where are the stables?"

Owen picked up his pace. They turned toward the grandstand and track. Gideon scanned up the stand, past row upon row of seats, one row upon the other. People. Horses. A carefree, worry-free day. He needed it. "How many folks can sit in it?"

"The Citizens' Stand? Some fifteen thousand folks, thereabouts. We let them sit in it for free."

Gideon pointed at another grandstand. "What about the one over yonder?"

"I'll show you." Owen led the way.

At this second grandstand, Owen stepped up through a wide gate onto the front row. "This is the Ladies' Stand, except they don't come up the steps the way I showed you."

"How, then?"

"This way."

Gideon went with him behind the stand, where an arched gateway led to a flight of concrete stairs.

"This gateway lets them park their carriages so they can get in and out easily in bad weather." Owen pointed at the stairs. "Let's go."

Gideon accompanied him up into an airy room.

"Our saloon," Owen said.

Gideon licked his lips. Beer, wine. He could taste the drinks now. He stepped into a sunbeam dancing off dusty tables and chairs. Dust motes swirled around him. At a large window, he viewed the clay oval track below. When racing season began ... he slumped. This saloon was too big. He imagined lively folks swarming past him as though he were a post. Strangers couldn't just ignore him. He couldn't come here by himself. He wanted, needed, a pretty lady on his arm. Elvira Sturgis? Depended on her beauty. Beautiful and a good conversationalist, that's what he needed most. He'd heard rumors about her, but he never gave much credence to gossip and hearsay. Maybe he'd seen her a few times, unaware of who she was.

Gideon turned back toward other, smaller windows positioned high above the bar and its liquor shelves. A rich blue carpet covered every inch of the floor.

"This saloon is for any specially invited guest," Owen said. "You will be one of those specially invited."

"Many thanks, Owen." He just hoped Elvira was a looker.

Next, Gideon toured the Citizens' Stand's basement, where the jockeys weighed and changed into their liveries and race stewards could relax. Platform scales and lockers stood along the walls. Benches and two small tables occupied the center.

He followed Owen out to the track. They traveled along the white rail fence circling it. Owen called his attention to a small stand for the club's officers and timers and their track's manager, Mister Harold Keelson and his wife.

A tall man drew near. Wiry of build with an angular face and a thick white beard, whose hair reminded Gideon of snow piled atop his head, he waved his cigar at them. "Ready for some racing, young Washburn?"

"I'm eager for it, sir." Owen nudged Gideon forward. "Gideon, this is Mister Edward Sturgis, president of our club. Mister Sturgis, permit me to introduce to you Mister Gideon Deshler."

Sturgis stuck out his hand. "Pleased to make your acquaintance, young man."

Gideon gripped it firmly. "It is an honor to meet you as well, sir." He spoke the truth. It was, indeed, an honor to finally meet this man, whose court cases and legal victories were often reported in the city's newspapers. And, yes, he had seen him before, at the cotton warehouses near One Mile Creek. Sturgis and a factor from a different firm had been discussing a matter. Mister Sturgis seemed friendly enough.

Sturgis led them to an area behind the track, what he called the backside. They passed down a path piercing rows of brick stalls and stopped at two horse vans beneath an oak tree.

Gideon tilted his head at a large brick building in the middle of a pasture. Sidelights framed its fancy oak door. Recessed windows glinted.

"We use it for our club's meetings," Sturgis said.

"Also, our annual ball," Owen said. "We used to have our dinners and balls at members' homes, but we haven't since we built that two years ago."

Sturgis and Owen stepped up to the waiting horsemen.

Although he knew George and Tyce from Owen's farm, Gideon had never seen Sturgis's jockey and trainer. George walked Comet backward. The horse's hoofs clattered down a short ramp out of his van. Tyce and the other trainer assisted the jockeys into their saddles.

"Where's Ned?" Owen's eyes raked the area.

"The boy's still getting his weight down," Sturgis said. "Freddy's riding in his place." He aimed his forefinger at his jockey. "Freddy, you and Robert take the animals to their poles. Don't do any racing till we get there."

"George, you and Tyce go with them," Owen said.

The jockeys walked the horses to the track with their trainers afoot.

Sturgis offered Gideon a cigar.

Gideon stared at it.

"Go ahead, young man. Take one." He placed the cigar in Gideon's palm and closed Gideon's fingers around it. "Cuban tobacco. Or perhaps you prefer excellent Carolina tobacco?"

Should he tell this man he didn't smoke? It might insult him, supposing he refused the cigar. He wasn't willing to do that on account of his chance of meeting his daughter. He stuck the cigar into his shirt pocket. "If it's all right, Mister Sturgis, I'll save it for later."

"Of course." Sturgis stepped toward the starting poles. "I hear you work for Cadwallader."

"It's true, sir."

"Do you share Cadwallader's religious fantasies?"

"No sir."

Comet, or else the other horse on the track, snorted.

Sturgis twirled his cigar between his fingers. "At what point in your life did you arrive at the conclusion that God and the Bible were fables?"

"When my wife and son died a little over a year ago." Gideon tried to sound matter-of-fact about his tragedy. "Upon my parents' deaths, my doubts began."

"I'm sorry for their passing."

"Tell him about Selah," Owen said.

Sturgis's brows lifted. "Selah?"

"My plantation near Montgomery," Gideon said.

"That's right. Young Washburn told me you owned a plantation." He cocked his head. "All right, young man. Let's hear about it."

"I inherited it from my father."

"Good. Very good." Sturgis draped his arm around Gideon's shoulders. "How many acres?"

"One thousand two hundred and fifty."

"Slaves?"

"One hundred, sir. All upriver at Selah. My overseer manages it for me. He's worked for my family for years. Very dependable, as far as overseers go."

"Is it your intention to purchase more slaves in the future?"

"Well, I do have the money to buy more. It's just—" Gideon's mind scrambled for an acceptable explanation. "It's just, well, I ... yessir. I will buy more if the opportunity arrives. I'm not as wealthy as Mister Wade Hampton, but I do possess a healthy income."

"I'm no Wade Hampton either. None of us can match his wealth, the South's richest man, him. Tell me about your domestic staff."

"Only three, sir."

"Slaves?"

Gideon hesitated. Who did Mister Sturgis think he was? A witness sitting on the stand during a trial? The man was a lawyer, all right, the way he pelted him with questions. Fortunately, he maintained a friendly tone and demeanor. Such things could be deceptive, though, a lesson he'd learned from hard experience. "No, sir. They're all free. They worked for my parents, so they continued working for me after my folks died."

"I remember now. Young Washburn told me that."

"I did, sir," Owen said.

They halted at the starting poles, where Freddy sat astride Mystified and George, Comet. Tyce stood in the starter's box holding a red flag.

"Are you interested in horse racing, young Deshler?" Sturgis slipped his unlit cigar back in his coat pocket.

"Quite possibly, once I learn more about it."

"Good. Very good. Maybe I'll take up your game one day. Poker, isn't it?"

"Yes sir." Gambler that he was, Gideon reached for his wallet in his trouser pocket. "Mister Sturgis, will you permit me to make a wager?"

"Which horse?"

"Since Owen and I have been friends a long time, I'm wagering one-hundred dollars on Comet's victory today."

"Reckon I'll match that." Owen whipped out his leather. "On my horse, naturally."

Sturgis withdrew his wallet. "I'll wager two hundred on my Mystified so we'll have a four-hundred-dollar purse."

"Provided Comet wins, Gideon and I will split the purse half and half," Owen said.

"My Mystified waxes victorious, I'll collect two hundred from each of you," Sturgis said.

Owen and Gideon nodded their agreement.

"Good. Very good." He stabbed his finger at the jockeys. "Freddy, the inside lane. George, the next lane over."

His flag raised straight and high, Tyce looked at Sturgis. The trainer's brows lifted. "Ready, sah?"

Sturgis and Owen plucked their stopwatches from their vests' pockets.

"Ready," Sturgis said, his and Owen's fingers poised to start their clocks. "Go."

Tyce lowered the flag.

Mystified and Comet took off at swift gallops.

Up to the first turn, they galloped neck and neck. Then Mystified gained ground on the backstretch. George steered Comet closer to Mystified, forced Mystified to lug the inside rail.

"Break away from him, Freddy," Sturgis yelled.

George and Freddy leaned over their horses' necks and popped them with their quirts.

"Faster!" Owen screamed.

Mystified galloped past Comet ... one, two, three ....

"Four lengths ahead." Sturgis clapped. "Attaboy, Mystified."

"There goes my money." Gideon opened his wallet.

"No. No," Sturgis cried. "Look at him."

Gideon glanced up. Mystified dropped back, Comet forged ahead on the second turn. Faster and farther, Comet galloped down the front stretch and finished first.

George and Freddy slowed their lathered mounts to a walk.

"One minute fifty-two seconds," Owen said. "Give him a cool down, George."

George, now dismounted, led Comet back to the track.

Sturgis shot Freddy a frosty smile. "You're lucky this wasn't a serious race, Freddy boy. Cool Mystified down then we'll go home."

Freddy led Mystified close behind George.

"I'll send you the money tomorrow. Is that acceptable?" Sturgis mopped his brow with his handkerchief.

"It is, sir," Owen said.

"Good. Very good. We'll do it again. Mystified needs more work. Ned's a better jockey than Freddy, anyway. Guess I won't be racing him in New Orleans before Christmas. Perhaps in its spring season next year."

"Comet will be racing at the Metairie Track come spring," Owen said.

"You haven't entered him in New Orleans for its fall season?" Sturgis folded his sweaty handkerchief.

"I've not entered any of my horses. Like you, I've decided to wait for New Orleans's spring season. Comet'll get his chance here this November."

"Well, I wish you luck." Sturgis shook Gideon's and Owen's hands. "It was nice meeting you, young Deshler."

"I enjoyed meeting you also," Gideon said.

"I'll drive y'all to your carriage after the cool down."

The horses' cool down finished, Gideon and Owen climbed into Sturgis's carriage, the horse vans following, and Gideon set himself to wondering whether he'd have a chance to meet Elvira. He glanced at Mister Sturgis seated opposite him. He'd dispatch Thaddeus to Mister Sturgis's house with a calling card and hope for a similar response from him. Suppose Mister Sturgis didn't respond with his own card or send a return card in an envelope? He pushed this thought to the back of his mind and participated in Sturgis's and Owen's conversation.

8

Awake on his cot, Ned grumbled and rolled onto his side in his shoebox-shaped room above Sturgis's stable. Though his straw mattress was tolerably comfortable, sleep deserted him. The scent of pine riding a moonlight breeze wafted through his window. Nocturnal nature's sounds, flitting mosquitoes and a coyote from some far off somewhere howled its song.

He didn't understand why it always happened, but every time Old Man Sturgis put him on a special diet to shrink his weight his body, for the first few days, weakened him to the point of collapse and around the fourth day thereabouts, his cravings ended. Also, a measure of strength returned. He thought he'd die during those first few days of eating meager fare. Three weeks had passed since he'd stepped on those scales at one hundred pounds. Next week he'd step on that awful thing again. Eighty pounds, the old man said. He'd better weigh eighty pounds by next weekend, else no telling what sort of cruelty the old devil would inflict.

Although horsemen like himself enjoyed certain privileges denied the slaves working the fields, such as going to another turfman's horse farm alone, slavery was still sinful. Many a day, he'd wanted the old man to send him to Natchez, in Mississippi, to the horse farm where his father worked as a farrier and his mother a seamstress. She made and mended clothes for everyone in their master's family as well as for the horsemen and other slaves. He hadn't seen them in years, not since that awful day when Old Man Sturgis bought him and brought him to this terrible place when he was a stable boy. Since his growing stopped at five feet, the old man had him trained for being a jockey. He hated it.

Every day, he thought about his parents, envisioned the tears watering his mother's eyes when he was taken from her, his father's broad face twisted with deep lines of agony and waving his final farewell. Were they still alive? On some nights he wept, for although it'd been years, he missed them. And they probably missed him. If only he knew … if he knew they were alive … if he could just see them again.

Well, he was a man now, as much as Sturgis was a man. He'd never seen the old fool beat a horse, but he had no problem beating slaves. Devil Woman Elvira's cruelty convinced him witches existed, because she was one. Her cruelty was worse than the overseer's. She'd even branded a few slaves for what she called "pleasure."

The devil woman's pets. Anyone with any sense ought to be scared of them. Rattlesnakes. Why'd she like them dangerous critters? She had no sense at all. If anyone was touched in the head, it was that woman.

A screech owl winging close to his window jerked him out of bed. He leaned out the window to search for the evening predator. He liked birds, his enjoyment of them he'd shared with his mother. Most every day, she'd watch them winging their way into trees while she sat in her room or on her cabin porch, working her needle and thread through fabric. She'd taught him things about certain birds' habits she'd learned through her watching. He wished he knew how to read so he could learn more about them. He wished he had a paper and pencil, so he could draw them. They were free, flying high above peoples' troubles. Many days, he wished he could fly from his bondage. Maybe next time Old Man Sturgis sent him to Tennessee for horses. But that depended on who went with him, if anyone did. Becky, no, he couldn't flee without her.

He gasped. A tiny figure headed for the detached kitchen midway between the servants' quarters and the stables. *Becky*.

"I see her, Ned," Robert snapped. "Stick your head back inside that window." He bounded down the outside stairs.

Freddy and the other jockeys and grooms, their heads poked out their rooms' windows, spotted her too. Ned's heart hammered out of fear for Becky. It looked like she was sticking a key in the kitchen's lock. Stole it from Old Missus?

Elvira hurried with her parents to the kitchen. From her window, while taking down her hair, she'd seen Becky go inside it.

Her father shoved Robert aside and filled the kitchen's doorway. "What's happening here?"

"She was making Ned a sandwich, sah," Robert said. "I was telling her to get back to her room."

"Better listen to the boy, Becky." His cold eyes slid toward Elvira. "Else I'll let you and my daughter have another conversation." An icy chuckle laced Sturgis's warning.

Elvira grinned. Another chance to whip that troublemaker. It'd be a pleasure.

Mrs. Sturgis snatched Becky's right arm, Elvira snatched her left.

"Ouch." Becky's face twisted. "You're hurting me."

With her mother, Elvira dragged Becky back to her quarters.

9

SPRING HILL, ALABAMA

AUGUST 29, 1852

Am I late? Am I late? Gideon fumbled his watch out of his vest pocket, dropped it when he tried to unlatch its lid. Attached to its fob, it dangled. His clammy hands gathered it up and popped it open. One minute till six o'clock.

Whew. He'd arrived at the Sturgises' Spring Hill home a minute earlier than the designated time on their supper invitation. He whipped out his handkerchief and mopped his hands' sweat. He must get ahold of his nerves. Stay calm. Ste-eady. Calm. She's only a female.

All day he'd fought the urge to arrive earlier, to glimpse Elvira before their formal introduction, yet suppose he appeared overeager? He couldn't appear overeager. He might not like her. Suppose he did take a fancy to her. Would she fancy him?

He hitched his mount, cleared his throat, squared his top hat then stepped onto the gallery. He jerked the tiny brass doorbell's short cord.

A butler admitted him inside and received his hat.

"Gideon Deshler has arrived at the invitation of Mister and Mrs. Edward Sturgis." He tossed his card on the butler's salver and kept two more handy, one for Elvira and another for her mother, since this was his first visit. Each card had a corner turned down, an indication he was visiting the entire family, though he'd mainly come to set his eyes upon Miss Sturgis.

"The missus is upstairs still getting dressed, sir. Master is in the pantry. I will inform him of your arrival." The butler departed.

As Gideon's gaze roamed the hall, it screamed *Turfman*. Horse sculptures, horse paintings, shiny race trophies on a glass-enclosed shelf, wallpaper that depicted horses and racing. Everything equine encompassed him, except the tall pewter candlestick on a pedestal table at the parlor's entrance. Along the corridor's right wall, a maroon-carpeted staircase descended.

Because Sturgis divulged no clue at the racetrack regarding whether he'd receive such an invitation, Gideon had fretted these past weeks. Fortunately, Sturgis did respond with his card accompanied by an invitation. A chance to meet a gorgeous lady, provided Elvira possessed the physical attributes Owen claimed.

Only a good wife, a lady as lovely as his Harriet, could remedy the sickness in his heart. His beer and wine, though they helped, were mere bandages on his forsaken existence. A fine, handsome lady. Indeed. *The cure.*

Sturgis ducked out of a room midway down the hall. "You're on time, young Deshler."

"I fear punctuality is one of my faults," Gideon said.

"Nonsense. I like a man who's on time. I regret our supper is a little behind schedule, however." He winked. "You know how ladies are, always taking their own sweet time prettying themselves up for us gents." He indicated the parlor.

Were they always behind schedule? It wasn't proper, really, for a hostess not to be dressed and punctual when their party started. Elvira, supposing she proved to be worth the wait, well, he'd happily overlook this breach of etiquette.

Hopefully, Mister Sturgis wouldn't offer him another cigar and wouldn't ask about the cigar he'd given him at the track because he'd have to lie. In truth, he'd tossed it into One Mile Creek the last time he'd visited his cotton firm's warehouses.

"The paintings on your walls," Gideon said. "Did Mister Troye paint them?"

"A few. I'm trying to hire him to paint Mystified when he has the leisure to do so. Every turfman I know makes demands on his time, but he's assured me he would. Have you seen his painting of Comet yet?"

"Yes sir. Mister Troye's artistic reputation is well-deserved. I wonder whether he's painted Johnny Boy yet."

"Quarles's new acquisition?" Sturgis sat on a settee.

"I've heard part of the story behind his and Owen's feud." Gideon settled into a leather wing chair. "Something about Quarles's father's horse getting killed. Green Legs, they called him?"

The butler entered the parlor.

With a flick of his wrist, Sturgis barked an order like an army sergeant. "Elkins, the wine cellar. Two champagnes." He reached for a walnut cigar box on his side table, flipped it open and offered one to Gideon. "Carolina tobacco."

Gideon took one. "Thank you, sir." He slipped in into his shirt pocket. Waiting for Elvira ... With his handkerchief, he mopped sweat off his palms.

Sturgis produced a penknife from his trousers. He proceeded to snip off one end of his cigar. "Green Legs had lots of wins in his short career." He touched his cigar to a lighter on the table beside him, brought it up and smoked.

Gideon eyed the hallway's staircase. "I understand he was expected to win a big race in New Orleans when he died suddenly."

"Back in '49."

"Owen told me his father's horse, Sir Walter, was Green Legs's biggest rival on the tracks."

"An accurate statement. Green Legs and Sir Walter arrived at the track early on the morning of their race day and ate before their exercise. The race was scheduled for the afternoon."

"And Green Legs's feed had morphine in it?" Gideon glanced back at the staircase. Why was Elvira taking so blame long?

"Way more than forty grains were mixed inside it, Doctor Harrison, our club's veterinary surgeon, said. He collapsed before he could race and died shortly after." Sturgis blew a smoke ring. "Frank's little groom boy who was supposed to be taking care of him was the guilty party."

"How so?"

Sturgis tapped cigar ashes in an ash tray. "You know slaves, how they love to deny things they've done and lie all the time, which is what this groom did. Ole Frank Quarles believed the boy innocent and believed to his dying breath that my good friend William Washburn committed the crime. Not a shred of evidence implicated William. Frank sold the boy to a turfman in north Mississippi for his own good and safety in case someone down here tried hurting him because he killed Green Legs."

As though it hurried Elvira's appearance, Gideon tapped his foot. "Why'd Frank, I mean Mister Quarles, still blame Owen's father after the groom got the blame?"

"Because they were such fierce rivals on the track." Sturgis set his cigar on his ashtray. "And it didn't help Frank's case that he was a braggart and a most insipid fellow."

Elkins brought the champagne. Gideon grasped his beverage off its tray and sipped it as he wandered to a stack of racing magazines on a small table beside a window. "I'm curious. How did Green Legs's death ruin Mister Quarles's reputation as a breeder?"

"Upon Green Legs's death, Sir Walter became *the* horse to beat in Alabama." Sturgis sipped his champagne once Elkins departed the room. "Sir Walter didn't win every race, but did win six out of the seven he'd competed in during his second year of racing. This made William the most prominent Thoroughbred breeder in the state. Not a single one of Frank's other horses came close to defeating Sir Walter. Sir Walter dominated more races before he was retired."

Umm. Gideon sipped his champagne.

Sturgis's eyes flashed. "Horse murderers ought to be hung."

Soft steps and feminine giggles descended the staircase.

Sturgis stood.

Gideon's impatience propelled him into the hall.

A young brunette, decked out in a pink organdy dress and adorned with a sapphire necklace and long sapphire earrings, stepped off the bottommost stair. Her skin resembled white marble and her lips, red as a rosebud. Fragrant perfume cloaked her, her dark lashes fluttered, amusement danced in her violet eyes.

Gideon gulped down his words as his gaze followed her grasping hand, clad in pale pink gloves. Her fingers marched up and down his frock coat's broad lapel. He gaped.

"Well, hello to you Mister Gideon Deshler." Elvira's sultry voice, threaded by a tone sweet as peppermint candy, floated his direction.

He swallowed again. Words. He needed words. "M-Miss Sturgis?"

"Elvira." She cocked her head and gave him a coy look. "I have heard the absolute world about you. It is such a pleasure to at last make your acquaintance."

Gideon's brain whirled, scrambled for words.

"Would you be so kind as to escort me to the dining room, Mister Deshler?"

Gideon stammered and offered his arm. "Of-of course."

Her arm looped around his, they strolled through a pantry where servants busied themselves making final meal preparations, passed a raised door on the floor that he assumed led to a wine cellar and entered the dining room.

Fine china and silverware, goblets and table linens were neatly arranged on a white tablecloth. Above them hung a chandelier that spread light every direction. A punkah also hung from the ceiling and attached to it was a red velvet cord held by a youth waiting to fan them during their meal.

Gideon collected his composure and joined the conversation. He recalled seeing Elvira now, on more than one occasion in the city with her mother. He'd always admired her from afar. She was so ravishing, he could scream. Between glimpses of her and his food, he managed to cut his roast beef into edible portions.

Upon Mister Deshler's departure, Elvira changed out of her cumbersome clothes and jewelry and put on her nightgown. Whenever she could get away with it, in private, she preferred wearing a single petticoat beneath her dress rather than layers of them like other ladies did. It may affect her dress's appearance, but who cared when she wore a mere single one in private. Too many petticoats were too much to manage, as well as too hot, especially in summer.

She lit a lantern and headed for the whitewashed shed behind the garden, where her pet lived. Her limbs moved easier, quicker in her nightgown. Next time she and her family traveled north, she hoped she could buy one of those Bloomer dresses she'd read about, a short skirt with trousers, a sort of Turkish-style dress. She disapproved of Miss Amelia Bloomer's temperance campaign, that was true enough, but she respected her sense of fashion. A lady could move with greater ease in a Bloomer dress. Men might disapprove, but … She swore. She could care less what men thought about things

Men weren't good for anything anymore, except as tools for ladies to manipulate and use. Her father had always given her what she wanted. So did Mister Culpepper, whom she'd fallen for when they first met at the Metairie Track in New Orleans two years ago. At the time, he seemed so generous, calling her pet names and flattering her parents. He was a lawyer same as her father. Their meeting led him to move to Mobile, get hired by her father's firm and then start their courtship … and his deceit.

Inside the shed, she held high her lantern. Its jaundiced glow illuminated a wire cage that contained a mouse. She set the lantern on a short table, reached inside the cage and clutched the unsuspecting rodent from behind.

"No escape now, little fellow." She brought the quivering mouse up to her face. Softheaded girls squealed at the sight of tiny ole mice. Not her. Squealing and carrying on like the sky was falling was silly.

In a terrarium atop a table lived her pet rattlesnake. She slid her fingers toward its pocked lid. Her father's voice sounded in the doorway. "Did you like Mister Deshler, honey?"

"Yes, Father. I did."

The coiled snake buzzed its rattle and lifted its triangular head toward its midnight meal. She dropped the rodent into its terrarium then dropped the lid over it.

"Suitable enough to court?"

Elvira's pet lunged at the mouse.

She stroked the terrarium's glass side while the snake's distended jaws clamped the mouse. "Mister Deshler seemed quite intelligent. I wonder whether he enjoys reading good literature."

"He might."

"A turfman, Father? Can you do it? Can you make a turfman out of him?"

"Have I ever denied you anything, my sweet daughter?"

"Of course not."

"Of course not. I'll do my best to see if I can persuade him to join my jockey club." He kissed her forehead and brushed her arm as he moved up alongside her to watch the snake finish devouring its meal.

She'd spoken the truth to her father. She did like Mister Gideon Deshler. That brown curl in his hair, that swept past his forehead, reminded her of Mister Culpepper in an analytical sense. Could she ever love a man again, even one that possessed the looks of an Adonis? Looks that Mister Deshler possessed?

"Have you decided what you'll name your new pet?" her father asked.

"Gideon."

"Gideon?"

She clutched his nightshirt. "Don't tell Mister Deshler."

"That ought to be the last thing you worry about, Elvira honey."

She welcomed her father's arm circling her when he blew out the lantern's candle. *Gideon. Yes.* It was the perfect name for a snake.

PART TWO

SEPTEMBER-OCTOBER

1852

10

Dundee Horse Farm and Plantation
Tensaw River, Alabama
September 4, 1852

Joe Quarles's rapid strides toward the walking ring left Rattigan puffing behind him. Nearby, on the one-mile track, Dundee's riders exercised Joe's horses, something they usually did in the ring. This day, however, Johnny Boy had to be tested alone.

"Did JB do better this week?" Joe's fast-swinging arms cut the air chest-high.

"Aye." Rattigan's shorter legs struggled to keep up. "Marcus has trained him well to this date, and Johnny Boy has since grown accustomed to his saddle and other tack."

"Let's try to slow trot him." Joe slackened his pace to let the Irishman catch up.

"With Marcus in the saddle, of course." Rattigan moved up alongside. "The exercise lads and grooms are fearful of Johnny Boy. I tell them not to ignore him, that it only makes his behavior worse. We must correct JB's behavior, not ignore it. Marcus and I have worked toward that end. Marcus is our only horseman brave enough to give a go at riding him."

"Sounds like I made a good decision, giving Marcus the main responsibility for training him."

"Aye. But it is this Irishman's opinion that if Marcus cannot ride him, riding him is an impossibility. In which case, it is this Irishman's opinion that we shoot Johnny Boy. A more worthless *capall*, in all my years of racing, including in my old country, I have never set me eyes upon."

"Let me tell you, Rattigan, buying that *capall*, as your Gaelic tongue calls him, was partly your idea."

"An idea I now regret."

Joe warmed. He hoped Rattigan wasn't serious about killing Johnny Boy, because if he did kill him, or any of his horses, he'd fire him quick as lightning and have him locked in jail for the rest of his livelong days.

At the ring's white rail fence, Joe crossed his forearms on its top rail. Inside the fence Johnny Boy, a lead loosely looped around his long neck, was tied to the same top rail.

Pete and a groom clasped the cheek pieces on Johnny Boy's bridle to steady the colt. The groom's fingers quivered.

Marcus adjusted the saddle.

Sweat puddled the groom's forehead and pooled his linen shirt. His lips trembled.

"Don't let JB know you're scared of him," Pete told the groom.

"I-I think he already knows." The groom sounded hoarse. "Hurry, M-Marcus. P-Please."

Johnny Boy's ears twitched. He stamped a hoof, snorted and jerked his head to free himself from the horsemen's grips but despite Johnny Boy's best efforts, they held him tight.

Marcus finished cinching the saddle.

"Go ahead, Marcus. Let's see you slow trot him," Joe said.

"Right directly, Massa Joe."

Rattigan stepped through the paddock gate and assisted Marcus into the saddle. Pete slid the lead's loop off Johnny Boy's neck. Before the horse's front hoofs flew at them, he and the groom barreled beneath the lowest fence rail. Rattigan bolted out the gate. Johnny Boy loosed short, high-pitched neighs.

"JB is angry." Rattigan puffed from his sprint.

"A horse with an attitude." Joe slapped the fence rail. "What an animal!"

With another high-pitched neigh, Johnny bucked and moved quickly around the ring, humping his back.

Marcus kept a tight grip on the reins while he pulled up JB's head. Finally, Marcus slow-trotted him around the ring for two laps then brought him to a stop. Johnny Boy snorted as though disgusted.

Rattigan strode into the paddock and took the reins.

"JB has spirit." Joe punched the fence post. "Love it! You all right, Marcus?"

"Yas sah. Jus' dandy fine." Marcus whacked dust off his trousers.

BELLE GLADE HORSE FARM AND PLANTATION
MOBILE BAY'S EASTERN SHORE
SEPTEMBER 4, 1852

When Ned stepped off the scales, he tensed and dared not look his master in the eye, for that would be like threatening a vicious guard dog.

"Ninety-five pounds." Sturgis removed the counterweight from the balance bar's hook and slapped it in Robert's hand. "You heard what I told you a few weeks ago, Ned. I said you have to be eighty pounds. Mystified's three years old. He can't be carrying a lot of weight in his races."

Ned fastened his attention on the barn's pine floor.

"What am I going do with you, boy? The other jockeys keep their weight down, but you keep feeding your ugly face. I had planned to enter you and Mystified in a race over in New Orleans, except the way you keep eating, I'm not taking you to New Orleans. Not entering you or any jockey in a race there or at any track until you get your weight down."

Robert cleared his throat.

"Robert, send Ned to the manure pile and reduce his diet further. Ned's weight better be down to eighty pounds by the end of this month, else you're going to be in worse trouble than him." Sturgis stalked off, chuckling.

Ned shuffled his feet. "I'm sorry, Robert. Don't yell at me. I tried hard losing weight."

Robert reached up beneath his faded trainer's cap and set it back of his bald head. "I ain't gonna yell at you. We both tried powerful hard, you and me. Old Man Sturgis is getting his just reward one day."

"Hate how I gotta sit in all that horse manure me and Jeremiah piled up."

"I'm powerful sorry, Ned. You're a good man."

"Do you think you could get someone to bring me some water?"

"I will try. Trying's all I can do."

Ned scowled. "Trying is all any of us can do. I hate that old man and that old man's family."

Robert spat. "You ain't alone in that hate."

Ned trudged out of the barn past the race track where his fellow jockeys, in five layers of clothing, walked laps. Twenty-five miles every day, Old Man Sturgis made them do it, even when lightning flashed all around them and thunder rolled. It was meant to keep their weight down. He wished he was doing that instead of having all that foul-smelling manure piled up to his neck. Since all the walking he'd done didn't help him lose enough weight, the horse manure was supposed to steam it off. That's what the old man always said. He'd be piled up in horse manure for a whole week. The closer he drew to its stench, the more his nose rebelled. Dread seized him. "Escape outta this hole. Dear Lord, please. There's gotta be a way."

11

MOBILE, ALABAMA

SEPTEMBER 6, 1852

Gideon ascended his office building's steep stairs to its second floor, paused to catch his wind, then continued down the hall's green carpet. He whipped out a handkerchief and blew his stuffy nose. *Bah.* He wasn't in the mood to hear Cadwallader's Monday morning question, what he always asked his employees soon as they arrived.

At a paneled door, he groaned. Engraved on its brass sign were the words, "Cadwallader and Company, Cotton Factors." He entered, removed his silk top hat and hung it on a hat tree.

Shouts of stevedores in their Irish brogues and the clatter of wagons echoed from the street below, one block from the Mobile River. Foul odors from the riverfront drifted through the office's opened windows. A steamboat's whistle blew. Business, picking up.

Gideon glanced at the mahogany desk commanding the room's farthest end. Behind it, Mister Cadwallader sat in an oak swivel chair reading *Hunt's Merchants' Magazine*. His iron-colored hair, thinned out over his seventy-plus years, uncovered a small mole on his pate. His hunting and fishing and long constitutionals kept him in fine physical shape for a man his age.

Gideon yanked a ledger out of a pine desk's drawer, fumbled through its pages while debits and credits flashed past him. *Hurry up. Get it over with. Ask me your stupid question.*

Silence prevailed.

Had Mister Cadwallader set down his magazine? Gideon peeked at him out the corner of his eye. Not yet.

Another steamboat's whistle shrilled from the river, followed by a blast, the boat's steam exploding through its stacks, he hoped.

Ten minutes ticked on the wall clock.

Mister Cadwallader turned his magazine's pages.

The clock ticked on.

Mister Cadwallader's chair creaked.

Gideon coughed. For attention. His employer was aware of his arrival. The man's hearing was as sensitive as a dog's. Still, he didn't ask the question.

"Mister Cadwallader." Gideon finally spoke after he closed his ledger.

"No returns from the New Orleans Mint for July." Mister Cadwallader brought his magazine up closer to his face. "Gold deposits from California are—"

"Sir."

Mister Cadwallader set aside his magazine. "Yes?"

"Sir, you didn't ask me your Monday morning question."

"Well, did you?"

"No sir. I did not. I did not attend divine services yesterday." He slid the ledger into his desk drawer. There, he was glad that expectation, his employer's question, was over. Church? That word never failed to stir up a bit of guilt for not attending it. He worked his jaw and gritted his teeth. Never would he go again. Not ever.

"Your decision."

"Yes sir. It is." Gideon reached for a lower drawer on the side of his desk.

Mister Cadwallader pulled an inkwell and pen from his desk drawer. "I'll no longer query you regarding your religious disinclinations, Gideon. I admired your father. He was my friend. When I assumed leadership of this company upon my father's passing, he was my best and most dependable employee."

Gideon flinched. "I'm not dependable? Like my father, I mean?" Gideon eyed him, unsure whether he wanted an answer.

Gravely, Mister Cadwallader stared at him. "I am praying for you, Gideon."

"Yes sir." Let Cadwallader go ahead and pray for him if it made him happy. Prayer worked about as good as a wooden mule pulling a wagon.

Boyd Eason closed the door upon entry. A Yankee from New York, he'd been employed here going on five years. His wife, however, was from Mobile.

"Good morning, Boyd," Mister Cadwallader said pleasantly. "Did you attend divine services yesterday?"

"We did, sir, and what a marvelous sermon my wife and I heard." Eason was as animated as a butterfly.

No, Eason, I did not attend church, so don't ask me if I did. Cursing silently, Gideon hoped that self-righteous Yankee would shut up.

Eason hung his top hat next to Gideon's.

"Once everyone arrives," Mister Cadwallader said, "we'll begin our day with prayer."

Prayer. That dumb word again. Gideon slammed his client's records on his desk. He wasn't about to waste his time praying to the ceiling.

The only reason he lived in this city was on account of his parents, their Government Street house and their property he'd inherited up Spring Hill. Also, he did need to take care of his loved ones' graves.

His father had enjoyed living close to the Gulf of Mexico, but this town had started to weary him. Yet how could he leave? He'd just met Elvira, who like Harriet, was neither bashful nor unattractive. Harriet's memory pricked him. He threw himself into the day's business.

12

MOBILE, ALABAMA

SEPTEMBER 7, 1852

Hannah dropped the emporium's receipts in a drawer behind the counter when a large, grinning fellow swaggered through its entrance. She remembered him from last month, but never learned his name.

"Well, well, bust my buttons, pretty lady. This where you work?" The man reached inside his dark green vest's watch pocket. "I'll bet you don't remember seeing me going into Shakespeare's Row with Mister Deshler." He slipped his watch off its fob and set it on the counter. He stepped closer. "Folks call me Sam. I'm quite wealthy. Have a large plantation up the Alabama River."

"How may we be of service, sir?" Hannah cleared her throat. What would it take to stop this annoying man's chatter?

"You are a pretty thing. Has anyone ever told you that?" Sam winked at her.

Earl emerged from his office in the back of the store. "Is there something we can do for you, sir?"

Relieved her father had taken over, Hannah sighed.

"My watch died, and I don't have time to bury it."

Earl opened its back. "The mainspring's broken."

"Aha. The spring has sprung." Sam straightened. "Can you fix it?"

"Perhaps. Luke? Over here a minute, son."

Luke sauntered out of a side room, his workroom beside the cameo display.

Earl set the watch in Luke's palm. "This gentleman's watch needs a new mainspring. How long do you think the repair will take?"

Luke examined it briefly. "Unfortunately, we don't have any mainsprings in the store right now." He brought the watch closer to his squinting eyes. "Hmm. There may be some other things needing fixing as well. I'll allow it may take several weeks."

Sam winked at Hannah again. "I've got the patience of a cat watching a pretty canary in a cage. I'm from out of town, and, like I was telling the lovely lady here, this cat's wallowing in money like pigs wallow in mud."

"Sir, if you please." Luke pulled a sheet of paper in front of him. "Let's finish our business. I need your name and address."

"Samuel K. Quarles." He flashed a grin. "Call me Sam. I fancy the short form of my illustrious name." He winked at Hannah.

Hannah huffed and went to Mister Rhodes, who was helping a customer at the ring case. She pondered the name: *Samuel Quarles.* It sounded familiar. *Could he be?* She'd ask her and find out. Hannah kept her back turned till Samuel K. Quarles left.

Hours later, while Hannah opened a box of bracelets to hang on a display rack, the emporium's doorbell tinkled. She groaned. The Sturgis women—Mrs. Margaret and daughter Elvira—entered. Women they were, for they were hardly ladies in Hannah's opinion, though she kept such notions to herself. Why on earth must she deal with them today?

"Hello there, darling." Elvira swept on her like a hawk. "I want a new brooch."

Hannah forced herself to keep her manners friendly. "I do think we have some in stock, Elvira."

"I am Miss Sturgis to you, you little girl." Elvira tweaked Hannah's cheek.

Hannah bit back her retort. *Miss Sturgeon, as in a fish.* "Come. I'll show you what we have." While she led Elvira to the display she silently asked for God's help. She reached inside a glass case and handed Elvira a diamond brooch while Mrs. Sturgis studied the cameo display.

Elvira turned the brooch over in her hand. "This is shaped like some kind of bird."

"A swan," Hannah said. "A most graceful bird."

Elvira set the brooch atop the counter. "Graceful. Like the grace of your so-called god."

Hannah reached for it to put it back. Elvira slapped down her hand. "Don't you dare put that fowl back unless I tell you to do it." Elvira pinned Hannah's hand to the case and studied other brooches. "I'll try." She pointed at it. "The panthera leo."

"It's a lioness," Hannah said.

"I know it's a lion, you softheaded girl. That's what I just said. You are obviously ignorant of scientific taxonomy. If you'd read as much as I do, you'd be as smart as me."

If I was as smart as you, I'd be a rock. Hannah stifled her sarcasm. "You take your hand off me, I'll get it for you."

Elvira's hand lifted.

Hannah pulled the brooch from its place.

Elvira snatched it and turned it over several times. "Pretty diamond eyes. Love diamonds."

"The lioness's head and fangs are made of eighteen karat yellow gold. Her tongue is a ruby."

"You think I'm blind? I can see that."

"No, Elvira," Hannah said. "I don't think you're blind. I think you're rude."

Elvira stroked the lioness's fangs. "If you expect me to purchase this, little girl, you will refrain from calling me rude." She set the brooch on the counter. "How much?"

"Five hundred dollars."

"I'll pay two hundred for it. On credit."

"Five hundred. Now."

"Two hundred."

"That one's a display. We'll have to have one made for you, naturally. Five hundred." Hannah planted her small fists on the counter. "Your daddy can afford it. He's not exactly poor."

"Like you are?" Elvira pinched Hannah's cheek. "I'm purchasing this one, little girl, with Mother's permission. For two hundred dollars."

"Five hundred." Hannah rose on tiptoes and glared at her. "I'm sure your mother will grant you permission. You're more spoiled than a rotten apple."

"Tut, tut. You shouldn't be judging us good heathen folk."

"Five hundred, Miss Sturgis." Earl, who'd been observing the argument from his office, strode forward. "Five hundred today, you can have the display."

Minutes later, Elvira's mother tossed five hundred dollars at him and stormed out, leaving cameos strewn across their display's counter.

Hannah struggled to contain herself as she helped her father set the cameos back in their respective places. She'd so wanted not to lose her temper, but loving the Sturgis family came mighty hard. She slapped a cameo on a shelf. How dare they expect to pay a lower price when they could afford the full price. She returned the final cameo to its proper spot.

Gideon guzzled his beer then thrust his mug at the game room's bartender. "Fill 'er up, Lloyd."

Lloyd wiped clean a shot glass with a dish towel. "Don't you figure you've had enough? It is your fifth one."

"I'm celebrating."

"Celebrating?" Lloyd set aside the shot glass.

"I got a letter from her father. He's given me permission."

"Permission?"

"To court her. His daughter. She accepted my suit and sent me a letter asking me to call on her."

Lloyd picked up another shot glass and wiped it. "Which girl?"

"The one I told you about the other day. Elvira Sturgis. A first-rate lady she is. The most beautiful creature this side of the Mason-Dixon Line." He raised high his mug and thrust it at Lloyd again. "Now fill 'er up. To the brim."

With his elbows propped on the bar, Gideon scanned the poker tables. Though his drinking had dulled his mental acuity, he nevertheless retained some clarity of thought. Through his blurry vision, he searched the room for Sam and the Tivingtons. No sign of them yet, though he did spot Austin Vanderporte, a frequent visitor this time of year. How could he be missed in that bright red cravat he always wore? And his dark brown suit. A gamester he was, a traveling man whose family roots were a mystery, who made his living playing cards and other games of chance. A steamboat gambler as well. Gideon had no use for dapper professional gamblers like Vanderporte. Not many respectable folks did.

Three strangers at a table engaged in conversation. They looked friendly enough. Before he could join them and strike up a conversation, someone entered the room. He focused. A young man … medium-build, average height, black hair slicked back. *Luke Henshaw*. Why'd he come to this place? Going to stand on a table and preach? He turned back to the bar to receive his beer.

"I can't sell you another one, Mister Deshler," Lloyd said. "I'll get fired if you get drunk on account of me selling you too much."

Gideon raised his mug in a toast. "Number six, Lloyd, my good man. My last one tonight and my celebration, it has officially ended."

"It ends now." Luke's stern voice rang out.

As Luke's firm hands clasped Gideon's shoulders from behind, Gideon stiffened. "Get your dirty paws off me."

"Time to go home."

"I got me a new girl. A real sure-fire looker." Gideon quaffed his beer. He gestured at Lloyd. "Fill 'er up."

Lloyd puffed irritably. "I told you that was the last one. I can't lose my job. We got rules about drunks in this establishment."

Luke tugged Gideon's arm.

"Let go of me," Gideon snarled, "else I'll feed my fist to your teeth."

"Come on." Luke tugged him harder.

Gideon shrugged him off. "All right. No poker tonight. 'Sides, I got to go to work for Cadwallader again tomorrow." He laid money on the table, payment for his drinks.

Back on the street, Luke led him into his family's emporium.

Gideon surveyed the store's darkened room.

"Father and Hannah have gone home," Luke said. "I had to finish work on a watch for a customer, so I elected to stay a few hours longer. Wait a minute. Let me light the gas jets."

When the emporium's chandelier flickered on, numerous glass cases displayed glittering jewelry. Necklaces and earrings adorned sales racks. Clocks of varied sizes and shapes either hung on walls or sat on shelves. The establishment was a treasure trove so enormous it'd spark a pirate's envy.

"Why'd you come get me?" Gideon wobbled up to Luke.

"Because I'm your friend," Luke said. "Or have you forgotten?"

"Not anymore you're not. You don't have the kind of money I have. You're beneath my social class." Gideon didn't expect his words would have much of an effect on Luke. He knew him well enough to know he never took insults personally, nor did social status impress him.

"Well, this low-class poverty-stricken ex- friend of yours promised himself he'd go check on you tonight out of concern."

"Hannah put you up to it?"

"I put myself up to it. We're all concerned about you, as is Reverend Eagleton and everyone in our church."

"You mean you dragged me all the way away from my celebration because you care about me?"

Luke gestured at a cushioned Windsor chair angled next to a pier mirror. "Sit down. We need to talk."

Gideon, though he swayed a little, sat. "Talk about what?"

"About your soul."

"I don't have a soul. I'm an animal." Gideon rose to leave, but Luke's firm hand pressured his chest hard enough to settle him back in the chair.

"I won't preach to you. I merely want us to talk."

"Jabber all you want." This time, Gideon rose quicker than Luke could stop him and made for the door. "I've got work tomorrow. I'm heading home. Don't bother looking for me tomorrow because you won't find me in Shakespeare's Row. I'm off to the Sturgis home after work."

Luke gripped his arm. "Sturgis? The lawyer Edward Sturgis?"

"He's allowed me to court his daughter. She asked me to call on her. My beer drinking you so rudely interrupted was my celebration of that, former friend."

"You can't court her. Don't you realize what sort of woman she is?"

"She's not a woman. She's a lady. A very nice and handsome lady. Never let me hear you call her a woman again, else you'll regret it." Gideon slammed the door behind him and struck out for home. His unsteady strides carried him beneath the glow of street lamps. Elvira's image blossomed. That evening, during supper at her house, she'd doted on him. She spoke nice words, words so soothing they were a blanket over his heartache. A fine lady she was. Beneath a street lamp, he plucked his watch out of his coat pocket. Eight o'clock. Late for a weeknight. Better pick up his pace. He'd get his horse he'd stabled at his Government Street home and ride on up to his Spring Hill residence.

Two shadows darted out of a side street. One tackled him and smashed his nose on the banquette. Gideon passed out.

Minutes later he came to and rubbed his sore head. He rolled over, onto his buttocks, and fumbled for his wallet. Gone. The poker winnings from the previous night. He'd better report this to the police. What description would he give them? It happened so fast, he didn't get a good look at them, not in this darkness. Nor did he have the chance to pull his derringer on them. His palm shifted to his nose. What was it now? A pincushion? "Ouch!" Was his nose broken?

"Is that you, thou mighty man of valor?"

The kind voice to his left. Familiar Bible words, "mighty man of valor," which he was not. He recognized the speaker. "Er. Reverend Eagleton. It's my nose."

"Let me inspect it." The minister stooped down and examined Gideon's nose. "One of your nostrils appears to be bleeding." He helped Gideon stand. "What happened?"

Gideon waited for his former pastor to smell his beer-breath and lecture him about the evils of liquor. "Two men waylaid me when I was on my way home. Stole my wallet."

"Did you get a description? We'd better tell the police."

"Unfortunately, sir, I did not. Too dark." Gideon reached up and with his finger, touched a drop of blood.

"Let's at least go alert them regarding the incident."

"A good idea."

The minister steered him toward his buggy. "It was a stroke of Providence I passed by you. I was on my way to visit a parishioner. We'll report this incident to the police, then I'll take you to a doctor."

"My doctor's probably still over at his Point Clear residence."

"All right. I'll take you to mine. He lives up the Shell Road. He'll examine you tonight."

Gideon touched his sore head. "Thank you, Reverend. You're also a good man."

Gideon breathed a sigh of relief. Reverend Jonas Eagleton made no mention of his beer-breath, nor did he preach at him on their way to police headquarters and the doctor's home. Had it not been for his damaged nose, the little trip would've been most pleasant.

13

While his bruised nose throbbed, Gideon tethered his horse to the Sturgises' hitching post. His doctor recommended rest, as did Reverend Eagleton's doctor. Both assured him it'd aid his healing process. However, why should he not take advantage of the day off Mister Cadwallader allowed him? To call on Miss Elvira? His heart somersaulted. There she sat, in a wicker chair on her gallery, an opened book in her lap. His Helen of Troy, reading.

"Goodness. You're hurt." Elvira dropped her book on a stubby wicker table and, her arms outstretched, dashed to him. Her mother hastened out the door.

Silently, Gideon thanked the men who'd ambushed him, for last night's little incident did him a kindness. It gained this pretty belle's sympathy. "Please forgive my unexpected arrival."

"Aw, you poor darling." Elvira touched his face. "Your nose. It's swollen. It's red." She lowered her hand.

"Nothing serious." Soon as he spoke, another pain stabbed his face. "A mere bruise."

"My mercy. Let me get some liniment." Elvira whirled toward her door. "I know it hurts."

"No, no. It's fine." He'd never admit to pain, not to any female.

"What in the world happened?" Mrs. Sturgis, squinting, leaned in for a closer look.

"A couple of thugs ambushed me last night. I reported the incident to the police but couldn't be much help. Too dark, and it happened too fast. They knocked me out and stole my poker winnings. My employer allowed me a day off on account of it."

Elvira clasped her hands and beamed. "How grand of him."

Gideon glanced at her mother quizzically. "May your daughter and I?"

"Don't wander off far," Mrs. Sturgis said.

"We won't, ma'am. Gentleman's guarantee." Gideon accepted Elvira's offered arm. "Where is your pleasure, Miss Elvira?"

"Let me show you our garden. You failed to see it on your previous visit."

"A capital idea. Where to?"

"Behind the house."

He escorted her to the backyard. Though she kept a discreet distance, her mother stayed with them.

Ahead rose a magnificent stone arch smothered in honeysuckle. Beneath the arch stretched a flagstone path. Similar paths crisscrossed each other at right angles between neatly-trimmed boxwoods, arranged around dogwoods, with large open squares. In its center, the garden widened, making a flagstone circle around a majestic live oak flanked by a stone bench on each side.

Beyond the garden stood a simple whitewashed building—four walls, a panel door and a gently sloping roof. A flagstone pathway led to it. He wondered what it was. Not large enough for a carriage house, yet it could hold garden equipment such as rakes and shovels and such things. Leather buckets were stacked beside it, not far from a well. He switched his attention back to the garden.

"Beautiful." Gideon released Elvira's arm.

"I know," Elvira said, giggling.

Gideon moved his hand to clasp Elvira's but pulled back. Both were beautiful, Elvira and the garden, but holding her hand without her permission … He couldn't do that. He was a gentleman.

They strolled beneath the arch toward the live oak.

"Would you by chance be familiar with David Friedrich Strauss?" Elvira asked.

"I can't say I've ever heard of him."

"He's German. A famous philosopher. Are you familiar with a book titled *Life of Jesus, Critically Examined?*"

"Can't say I've ever heard of that either."

"No matter. That's what I was reading when you arrived."

"I must warn you, Miss Elvira, I am not a religious man."

"Mercy. Do I look like a nun?"

They sat on a bench.

"Do you know?" Elvira tapped Gideon's knee. "Strauss holds the opinion that Jesus' miracles never happened. He says the Bible is full of myths. He's pretty smart."

Gideon reached for her hand again, again withdrew. "I'm inclined to agree with him."

"Well, I once read all those gospels in the New Testament. Out of curiosity, mind you. Did you know they all contradict each other? My late cousin Upton Sturgis, he was a famous naturalist, highly intelligent, and he agreed."

Gideon remembered thinking this a few years ago when he posed a question to Luke about the contradictions. "Luke Henshaw once told me everything that appears to be a contradiction is easily reconciled and proves that the gospel writers didn't consult each other before they wrote. They all believed in Jesus' resurrection. He said it strengthened his faith in the gospels being true. The writers wrote from their own points of view with different emphases and audiences in mind."

"That's preposterous. Will you read Strauss's book after I'm finished?"

"If you want me to." Gideon eyed Elvira's mother, seated in a chair near the arch sipping the coffee Elkins brought her. The butler was going back to the house. "Let's get better acquainted. As I recall from our previous dinner conversation, you enjoy dancing."

Elvira perked up, clasped her hands around the cameo pinned at her neck. "I *love* all sorts of fun."

Because his parents didn't dance, Gideon never learned how. Would he admit that to her? *No!*

"What about reading?" Elvira asked. "Do you enjoy good literature?"

"Newspapers, mainly, and business publications, *Hunt's Merchants Magazine* and similar things. I've read a few novels. *The Count of Monte Cristo*."

"Why, mercy. You must be powerful smart." Her ticklish fingers marched up and down his cheek.

Exhilaration rippled clear down to his toes.

"I like intelligent men."

Intelligent? Gideon chuckled. He wouldn't argue the point. Let her think he was the best thing since vanilla ice cream.

Their conversation and companionship continued throughout the morning. They ambled the garden's paths, discussed all manner of subjects—flowers, art, cotton prices, different religions. An unusual lady, Elvira, more interested in intellectual matters than feminine pursuits. But the way she conducted herself, yes, she was most definitely a lady. A very handsome and very smart lady.

They ate a light lunch then visited the gurgling spring behind their house, one of Spring Hill's numerous springs that gave the region its name. Gideon reached down for a small stone and skipped it across the spring's small pond in four splashes.

Elvira picked a tin cup off the ground and held it beneath the water flowing from between two rocks. She offered it to Gideon.

Gideon drank it. "Ahh." *Nice and cool.* He licked his lips. This time, he stooped beside the spring with the cup.

Elvira accepted it from him and sipped daintily. "Love this water." She finished it and set the cup back in its place.

"We're fortunate to have so many springs around here." He fell silent. The spring ... so clear, so peaceful, gurgling and splashing. A leaf floated lazily across it. Two more leaves drifted close behind. A bright cardinal lighted on a fig tree.

He considered taking Elvira to his house, except this wasn't the appropriate occasion. It would be more gentlemanly to invite her whole family first. Katie was a capital cook. Elvira's presence uplifted his sprits, vanquished his turmoil and filled that great big hole in his heart.

"My father's jockey club will host its annual ball this November to kick off its season." Elvira tugged his coat sleeve. "I do hope you'll receive an invitation."

"I'm not a turfman." Gideon hoped to avoid the invitation since he couldn't dance. He didn't want to look silly in front of her. He reached down for another stone to skip.

"What does it matter? Father's the club president. He'll persuade its board for an invitation. We don't hold this ball in a home like most folks. We used to, but not anymore. We hold it at the track." She turned for her house. "I do so hope you will accept the invitation when it's sent."

Gideon dared not look her in the eye lest she detect his lie. "I hope he sends me one." They strolled back through the garden.

MOBILE, ALABAMA
SEPTEMBER 9, 1852

Gideon visited Parker's Dance Academy during his lunch break. A lady who stood an inch taller greeted him, her emerald orbs assessed him. "Hullo, my good sir. Are you interested in dance lessons perchance?" Her bearing was dignified. Her English accent, crisp.

A Suffolk accent? Or perhaps Lancashire? Gideon couldn't be sure. He was fourteen years old the year his parents traveled to England. Because that was where their Methodist faith began, they wanted to visit some sites associated with its founders, the brothers John and Charles Wesley.

And yes, he was interested in dance lessons, except, would he learn how to dance in time for the Spring Hill Jockey Club's ball and dance well enough so as not to embarrass himself? "I was wondering, ma'am, about the cost of your lessons."

"In English pounds or American dollars?" Her pleasant smile revealed a perfect set of white teeth.

"American dollars." He didn't feel like laughing at her joke.

"Twenty dollars per week. We hold classes every night except Saturday and Sunday. On Saturdays my husband and I hold classes in the mornings and afternoons. To whom do I have the privilege of speaking?"

"Gideon Deshler."

"I am Mrs. Parker. My husband and I are the proprietors of this academy. He is away to the post office at this particular moment."

"I'm sort of in a hurry. How do I sign up for lessons? I'm due back at work in a few minutes."

"Come with me, my good sir. We'll take care of business quicker than a polka hop."

On the way to her office, Gideon wondered what a polka hop was. Also, he wondered whether he'd learn enough dances for the coming ball. He wouldn't dare embarrass himself in front of other dancers. It'd be humiliating.

14

Elvira wandered into her pet snake's shed behind her family's garden. Ever since she was little, these reptiles fascinated her. Her Cousin Upton had studied them and written about them for scientific publications. He encouraged her interest and her atheism. She specially admired the venomous ones. They knew how to defend themselves. She did too.

Many of her beaus had ended their courtship the first time they saw her snakes, whereas others threatened to kill them. Because of her interest in rattlesnakes, most of her courtships were short-lived. Mister Culpepper, though, had shared her interest in them, unless he feigned it so he could steal her dowry. Lorelei told her Mister Deshler respected snakes. Could she spark in him a more serious interest in them? Had Lorelei told him about her snake?

One thing about rattlesnakes, though. She couldn't cuddle them. Unfortunately, when Robert nearly died from a snakebite after she made him stick his hand in the snake's terrarium, her father forbade her from using them as a disciplinary measure. He paid lots of money for their slaves, he'd told her, so he couldn't afford to let any of them die from preventable things such as a snakebite.

A buzzing rattle sounded a greeting. Coiled, her diamondback's baleful stare locked on her.

"What do you think, snake?" Elvira stroked the terrarium's glass side.

The diamondback reared back its head as though ready to strike.

"Will Mister Deshler like you when he sees you, or maybe I should wait a little longer before I introduce him." She lowered her hand.

She inched around her snake while its head twisted and followed her. It hissed.

"Let me control him so he'll give me whatever I want." She picked up a snake hook and twirled it like a baton before she set it back in its corner beside a spade. "If he takes a liking to you, why, I do think I can love his money." She brushed her hands along the snake's terrarium once more before she left.

15

Dundee Horse Farm and Plantation

Tensaw River, Alabama

September 11, 1852

"Where's Marcus?" Joe asked Rattigan upon his arrival at Dundee. Rattigan thumbed the horse barn. "Talking to JB. Trying to persuade him to wear his halter, Marcus is."

"This should be interesting to watch." Swinging his arms fast, Joe headed for the barn. Rattigan tried, but failed, to keep up with him.

Right inside the building's opened double-doors, Joe halted, put his hands on his hips and watched.

"JB, I'm 'bout losing patience with you." Marcus spoke in a low voice. Snorting, the horse looked away from him.

"*Brostaigh ort.*" Rattigan spoke his Gaelic as he drew up alongside Joe. "Hurry up, Marcus. Get JB to the paddock."

"It might be easier trying it in his stall first, Mistah Rattigan," Marcus said.

"Do what you're told, Marcus," Joe snapped, though he agreed with Marcus's idea. If he took Marcus's side on this issue, however, it might diminish Rattigan's authority in Marcus's opinion. It might also embarrass the Irishman. No man liked being corrected in public.

Marcus lowered the halter, talked to Johnny Boy, scratched the animal's chest, then attempted to slip in on him, twice, before the horse allowed it.

After he picked up his saddle and bridle from the tack room Marcus led the animal to the paddock.

Joe and his horsemen knew a man couldn't rush a horse's training, but Marcus had to bond closer with JB. Marcus had devoted many patient hours working with Johnny, even slept with him in his stall, is what Rattigan had said. Joe gave Marcus credit. The jockey was trying mighty hard to train JB.

Although the Thoroughbred disliked the saddle as much as he did the bit and bridle, once Marcus had him tacked up Johnny Boy had come to understand he had no choice but to accept his situation.

At the paddock, Joe and Rattigan met Pete, who held the saddle pad and surcingle. Inside the paddock, Marcus tied him to the top fence rail. Rattigan closed the gate. Dickson, a groom of about thirteen years, sprinted to them from the farrier's shed and nodded.

"I got them things," Dickson said.

Johnny Boy slipped his neck between two of the paddock's rails to sniff Dickson's pocket. Brow furrowed, Dickson retreated to a hay wagon.

Pete and Marcus wasted little time tacking up Johnny Boy. Pad, surcingle, saddle, bit and bridle. Johnny Boy snorted and fought the bit, which Marcus finally managed to work into his mouth. On tiptoes, Marcus whispered in the horse's twitching ear.

"Now let's see if he'll let you ride him this time," Rattigan said as he came through the gate.

In his saddle, Marcus loosed a deep sigh, for Johnny Boy still didn't move, except for his curious eyes roaming to Dickson. Suddenly, Johnny shifted his hoofs and rolled left.

"Argh!" Marcus sprang from the saddle.

Johnny landed on the grass, rolled over and kicked air.

Enraged Gaelic spewed from Rattigan's tongue.

Back on his hoofs, Johnny Boy charged the Irishman.

Rattigan bolted out of the paddock, the Thoroughbred on his heels. Johnny Boy snapped at the Irishman; his teeth barely missed him as Rattigan leapt onto the hay wagon. The horse galloped around it twice, paused to rear up on his hind legs, lay back his ears and scream angry neighs.

Next, Johnny Boy swerved toward Dickson.

Joe hurried to the horse. "No, JB." He forced a soft tone and reached for the animal's bridle.

Johnny snapped at him. Joe sprang back, grinned hugely. "What a horse!"

Dickson quivered as Johnny Boy sniffed his trousers.

"Don't give it to him." Marcus sprinted out the paddock gate.

Too late. Dickson reached into his pocket and grabbed a carrot, which he dropped at his feet.

His head lowered, Johnny Boy sniffed the carrot again.

"Dickson, I told you not to give him them carrots yet." Marcus worked off Johnny Boy's bridle so he could eat the treat.

"But, but—"

"Me an' Pete was gonna get him off you before he could hurt you."

"And you was gonna be fine," Pete said.

"I-I'm sorry," Dickson stammered.

"Go wash the horses," Joe snapped.

"Yas sah, Massa." Dickson hurried on his way.

Rattigan sprang off the hay wagon.

"JB," Marcus tipped back his cap and scratched his head, "me an' you gotta have us another li'l talk. Another long talk, me an' you. And that means working hard on correcting your behavior."

"You can do it, Marcus," Joe said.

"Sah, I can't 'xactly promise he'll be ready by November."

Promises. Joe understood. He hated giving promises because if he broke them … Such things never set easy on his conscience. "I know you're trying hard. Keep working." Joe pivoted and went to where grooms hotwalked other horses.

16

Mobile, Alabama

September 12, 1852

Elvira looped her arm in Gideon's as she and her mother swished into their dressmaker's shop. A drop of vanilla perfume behind each ear … What man could resist a lady of her beauty wearing such an alluring fragrance? Now, she needed to execute the scheme she and her mother had devised. "There it is!" She spoke in a lively manner. "Oh, Gid. See that red fabric? Isn't it pretty?" She dragged him down a wide aisle and stopped at a rack holding bolts of silk cloth. She tested the red silk's quality between her thumb and forefinger. *Nice.* She jerked Gideon closer.

"Ugh." Gideon freed himself from her grasp.

"We're sorry, Mister Deshler," Mrs. Sturgis said. "My daughter didn't mean to jerk you so hard. She gets a little excited about clothes."

"So it appears." Gideon massaged his arm.

"Sit, Gid, my dear." Elvira pointed at a cushioned chair in a corner of the store. "Mother and I must speak with my dressmaker. We'll only take a minute."

Gideon obeyed.

They continued toward a counter at the rear of the store. Elvira glanced back at him. *He's fidgeting.* She made a soft giggle. "Obedient as a well-trained dog, Mother."

"If he keeps lapping up your flatteries you can get your way with him in everything," Mrs. Sturgis said in a low voice. "I doubt this one will steal your dowry like Mister Culpepper did, if you two get married."

"No man will ever use me again."

Mrs. Sturgis placed her palm on Elvira's cheek. "That's my sweet daughter."

A stout woman came out of the back room.

"Elvira, Mrs. Sturgis. How may I help my favorite ladies today?"

"I need a new dress, Mrs. Simpson." Elvira indicated the bolt of red silk fabric.

"Are you certain that's the material you want, Elvira dear?" Mrs. Sturgis asked.

"Yes ma'am."

Mrs. Simpson led them into a side room. Though Elvira suspected her twenty-seven-inch waist hadn't expanded by much, because it never had, it was always worth the time to let the dressmaker take her measurements. She and Mrs. Simpson would discuss fashion details. Mister Deshler would pay for it once the dress was made.

A half-hour later Elvira ate at a restaurant with her mother and Gideon, who paid the bill. Next, Mrs. Sturgis's carriage carried them to a road not far from Mobile Bay. Today, with Mister Deshler's assistance, she'd get even with those foolish Henshaws. "You know, Gid. It's not fair."

"What's not fair?" Gideon's brows lifted.

Elvira tapped her reticule. "The Henshaws. The way they treat my family and me. You know they charged me the full price for my brooch? They often give other customers a price break. It's just not fair."

"I don't care for them at all." Mrs. Sturgis crossed her arms. "They're ill-mannered and greedy."

Gideon recalled the day Luke had helped him cut down a tree. "They're not really bad people."

"You liked what Luke Henshaw did to you, the way he hauled you out of your celebration when my husband gave you permission to court our daughter?" Mrs. Sturgis arched her brows.

Gideon wagged his head. "That's not—"

"So, tell us, young man. What is it you mean?"

"I meant that sometimes they—"

"That family disapproves of us courting." Elvira huffed. "That's what you told me, Gid." She gently elbowed her mother. They couldn't make him defensive and angry. That risked alienating him. "I'm sorry, Gid. We shouldn't be challenging you like this."

"Who cares what they think about our courtship?" Gideon flicked dust off his coat sleeve. "They're not family. I'm not exactly their friend anymore, anyway."

"If he hadn't dragged you away from Shakespeare's Row that night when you were celebrating me," Elvira said, "you might not have been robbed." She studied Gideon. Did he buy in to her words?

Gideon's face lit up. "Well now, I never considered that."

Elvira and her mother swapped smiles.

"What is it, ladies?" Gideon asked.

"We want you to help us," Elvira said. "He didn't treat me fair. He interfered with your celebration of courting me. Will you avenge a lady's honor?"

"Miss Elvira," Gideon said, "it would give me great pleasure to defend your honor. Unfortunately, however, Luke won't fight me. He doesn't own a gun. He doesn't believe in them."

Elvira twirled a ruby ring around her gloved finger. "Not a pistol duel, dear. Another way." She grabbed his hands, pulled him close and inserted the perfect note of desperation in her tone, a ploy she'd often practiced like an actress rehearsing a role. "Ohh! Will you … will you defend my honor? Your honor? No one will get hurt if you do it the way mother and I discussed. I promise. Please!"

A moment's hesitation, Gideon sighed. "What is it you want me to do?"

When they finished discussing it, Gideon requested their carriage be halted. He stepped down and out, dropped his watch face-up on the road's oyster-shell paving and stomped on it.

Elvira and her mother applauded.

Gideon ducked into Luke's workroom while Elvira and her mother strolled the emporium fingering earrings and necklaces. "Luke."

Smiling, Luke arose from a bracelet he was making.

Gideon slapped his battered watch on Luke's palm. "Dropped the thing on a road a short time ago. Broke the crystal. Can you fix it?"

"I'll have to make you a new one," Luke said, giving the shattered timepiece a glance. "Let's go look at the styles we carry." On the sales floor, he peered past Gideon. "You came with those two?"

"Elvira and Mrs. Sturgis? I did." Three customers at a ring case kept Mister Rhodes busy. No Hannah, no Mister Henshaw. Hopefully, they were out of the store. In order for the ladies to execute their deed, Gideon knew it had to be done fast.

Luke grunted, stepped to the watch case.

Gideon made a pretense of examining the timepieces. In truth, he didn't need a new watch, for he'd left his best watch at home. Out the corner of his eye, he saw a policeman enter. Gideon pointed. "That silver watch."

Luke went around the counter. Gideon sidestepped in front of him, which blocked Luke's view of Elvira and her mother. He flipped the watch back and forth, stuck it in his vest pocket. "I like it." He handed it back to Luke and pointed at a bronze one that had a deer, a buck, engraved on its lid.

Luke removed it from the case.

"You engraved that deer?" Gideon admired the watch's artwork. He glanced over at Elvira. She and her mother were engaged in conversation with the policeman.

"I just make the watch. Our engravers do the artwork."

Gideon handed the watch back.

Thirty-minutes ticked by before he spied Mister Henshaw crossing the street, but the policeman had left. Gideon gulped.

"We're ready to leave whenever you are, Mister Deshler," Elvira said. "Would you take mother and me home?"

Gideon handed Luke another watch he'd pretended to consider. "I'll come back later, Luke. Need to get these ladies home."

Near sunset, Gideon returned to his Spring Hill cottage. Their mischief at the emporium had been easy and a bit exciting. In a matter of seconds, Elvira had swapped her old cameo for a new one before the policeman came in. The old one she hung on the display rack so the one she'd stolen wouldn't be missed. Or if the new one was discovered missing long after they'd left, the Henshaws wouldn't know who to blame. They'd avoided arrest.

He guided his horse around a bend. A stolen cameo. Such a small act of vengeance. What was wrong with stealing it? It was like fighting a duel with Luke, wasn't it? After all, he did offend Elvira. He headed up the path to his house. In a way, what they'd done had been fun.

17

Mosquitoes darted around Joe's ears when he reined his buggy's team to a stop beneath some longleaf pines. He climbed off it and, arms folded, studied the putrid swamp's cypress brake. The day's pounding heat poured sweat down his face, stung his eyes, saturated his clothes. It tasted sour, rolling down his lips. An alligator swam nearby. If Johnny Boy failed him … "Well, gator, I'll offer you my corpse for dinner."

Joe's gaze lifted beyond the gator to the distant timber. A good spot, this place. No one would see him wade into this desolate destination. No one would hear the gunshot when he squeezed the trigger. He wouldn't feel the bullet entering his head, would he? Joe shrugged. It didn't matter.

He picked up the daguerreotype of his father from off his buggy seat. A proud, dignified man, his father Frank was, with his square chin, his heavy eyebrows and somber visage. A pity Brother Sam didn't share their passion for horses, except for wagering on races. Outside of this, Sam only cared about cotton and cards. Their father didn't hold Sam's lack of interest against him. "Like colts, not all sons can be like their sires," he'd always said. "Every man must find his own path in life's journey."

His father's shiny race trophies brightened Joe's imagination. They sat in a tall glass case in Dundee's cottage, most of them won by Green Legs. One year after Green Legs's death his father died of yellow fever. A month later, the fever slew his mother.

On the day of his father's death—in Dundee's cottage—his father asked of him a promise. In his weak, husky voice, once so loud and vigorous, he beckoned Joe to his bedside. "G-Get my horse farm's reputation back, s-son."

Joe squeezed his father's hands. With all the confidence he could muster, he'd said, "Yes sir. I swear it."

Minutes later, his father breathed his last breath. Joe set the daguerreotype back on the buggy seat and drove back to Dundee. "Father, if JB doesn't win this season, if he doesn't retore your honor and the honor of your farm, I'll join you in death."

RIVER ROSE HORSE FARM AND PLANTATION
THREE MILE CREEK, ALABAMA
SEPTEMBER 12, 1852

When Gideon arrived at Owen's estate to tell him the good news—his courtship of Elvira—Owen's exercise boys, leads in hand, were walking Thoroughbreds around a clay track. Colorful blankets draped the animals' backs. The chestnut, gray and roan horses flicked and twitched their tails at mosquitoes and flies. Comet was not among them.

Although Selah Plantation required Gideon's present attention, his dance lessons prevented his trip there. He enjoyed steamboats, in particular those that allowed gambling. Sometimes when he traveled the river, he encountered that gamester he'd seen in Shakespeare's Row, that dandified scoundrel Austin Vanderporte, who on several occasions tried getting him into a game. Vanderporte probably figured he was a sucker. Gideon, however, knew better than to trust him, the reason why he always declined Vanderporte's offer.

Since he couldn't go upriver for now, he'd telegraph instructions to his overseer, John Spears.

"I'm heading to you, Hoke." Tyce jogged past him, toward the stables where the groom called his name.

Owen and Lorelei cantered up from a nearby cotton field.

Lorelei wore a deep blue riding habit and top hat. As gracefully as a queen, she dismounted her gelding.

When Owen dismounted, he examined Gideon's bruised face. "Did you get hit by a brick?"

"Got waylaid a few days ago." Gideon pumped his fists in the air triumphantly. "I've done it, Owen."

Owen's narrow forehead creased. "Done what?"

"Started courting Elvira."

"Wonderful news." Lorelei clapped.

"She's a smart girl," Owen said.

Lorelei thumped dust off Gideon's coat sleeve then looked him up and down as though inspecting him.

Barracuda. Gideon swallowed his rebuke. "I sure like what I've seen in her so far. I signed up for dance lessons a couple days ago."

Owen punched Gideon's shoulder playfully. "I reckon you expect an invitation to our jockey club's ball this November, eh?"

"More'n likely," Gideon said.

Lorelei mounted her horse. "I'll ride to the house and get us a bottle of claret. Y'all sit in our gazebo yonder. We'll enjoy our conversation there." She galloped down the road to their house.

"Bossy woman," Owen snapped.

"Why'd you marry her?" Gideon asked.

"She was an enjoyable person for the first few years of our marriage. Then something happened."

"What?"

"Never mind the 'what.' We started arguing over things I wanted her to do, even when I gave her sound advice. I grew weary of it, so I decided to let her have her own way. Do what she says and if bad consequences result, I always blame it on her. Not only that, I always withhold my sympathy. One day, I hope she'll learn to listen to me more."

Tyce burst out of a stall.

Owen thrust his horse's reins into a groom's hands. "What is it, Tyce?"

"Comet might have lung fever. Hoke jus' put him back in his stall after his walk so he could drink and noticed he was breathing pretty hard."

Gideon hurried with his friend to Comet's stall.

The horse held his mouth over his water bucket, coughed and wheezed and made sounds that resembled snorts. His neck turned. His big agonized eyes looked at his side. His chest moved in rhythm with his quick breaths.

Breathing, definitely difficult for the poor beast, Gideon told himself. He also noticed Comet's flared nostrils.

"It come on him all of a sudden," Hoke said from behind them.

"Easy now, my champion." Tenderness flowed from Owen's mouth. "I don't mean to hurt you, but I have to do this. It's the only way I can find out for certain." He touched Comet's barrel, where his lungs were located.

The horse squealed.

Owen jerked his hand away. "Sorry, good boy. Hoke's right. It is lung fever." Owen barked commands. "Tyce, fetch the Liquid Blister and tell Leander we need a bucket of water. Hoke, some blankets. Nitre and lavender too."

The horsemen sprinted off.

Now oblivious to Gideon's presence, Owen stroked Comet's forehead.

Gideon took a step back. Lung fever. Pneumonia.

"Owen, I need to talk. I have more questions about Elvira." Gideon waited for his friend's response. "Owen? When you're finished with Comet?" He waited longer. He couldn't stand his dreary home without someone to talk to other than his servants.

"Go home, Mister Deshler," Lorelei said, accompanying their butler who carried their drinks on a tray. "You've overstayed your welcome here."

Gideon's hackles rose. "I have not."

"Yes, you have."

Owen grunted a "thank you for coming."

Well, he guessed this wasn't the time to keep pursuing the matter, not with Comet's suffering. "Would you like me to fetch a veterinary surgeon?"

"Nuh uh," Owen said. "I'll send George for him."

"I'll be going now. Keep me informed on how the boy's feeling."
Owen's taut eyes never left his horse.

"Well, so long." Gideon departed past Lorelei' s stern face.

MOBILE, ALABAMA

SEPTEMBER 12, 1852

After he stabled his horse at the nearest livery, Sam walked to the
Henshaws' emporium. He'd told Gloria about meeting Hannah there
and how he'd teased her. What an earful Gloria gave him for doing
that! Miss Henshaw had already inquired of her about him two days
after they'd met. Miss Henshaw was a nice girl, Miss Henshaw was a
friend, Miss Henshaw was in her sewing circle … Miss Henshaw this,
Miss Henshaw that. Gloria's verbal barrage battered his conscience and
dredged up his guilt. He had no idea of these ladies' connections. He
seldom asked Gloria about her social life. As he pondered everything
she'd said, he realized Gloria was correct. His teasing Miss Henshaw
and winking at her had been wrong. Since she was a friend of Gloria
and Joe … well … he'd befriend her too.

Earl greeted Sam from behind a counter. "The part for your watch
has not as of yet arrived, Mister Quarles."

"I'm as worried about that as I am about burnt water." Sam
surveyed the store. A lady was speaking with a salesman whom she
kept calling "Mister Rhodes."

"Actually, I'm looking for Miss Henshaw," Sam said.

"Luke's taken her to lunch," Earl said. "She'll be back soon."

Minutes later Hannah and Luke returned. Luke held a book
at his side, Longfellow's epic poem, *Evangeline*, Sam judged by its
cover. He figured men like Luke only read the Bible. Maybe Luke
was different.

Soon as Hannah saw him, she rushed to her father's side. "I know
who you are now, Mister Quarles." Her air, though polite, stayed
defensive. "Gloria told me."

Sam didn't blame her for her attitude because of how he'd acted. "Good day to you, Miss Henshaw. My sister-in-law mentioned to me that you two were friends."

Luke posted himself beside his sister. "It's only been a few days since you were here last. I said repairing your watch would take a few weeks."

"I didn't come for my watch." Sam drew a deep breath as he studied Hannah's wooden face. "Miss Henshaw, I've come to ask your forgiveness." Sam shifted. "Forgiveness for bragging and teasing you. I feel sort of silly." He looked straight at Hannah, sincerity filling his heart. "Will you forgive me, Miss Henshaw? It was wrong. I'll not do it again." He crossed his heart. "On my word of honor."

"Over and done with, Mister Samuel K. Quarles," Hannah said, her facial muscles relaxing.

"Well now," Sam said. "I reckon we're off to a fresh start." Sam shook Luke's and Earl's hands while his attention wandered back to Hannah. Though he was tempted to wink at her again, he refrained.

"Always nice to have a new friend," Earl said.

"I quite agree," Sam said.

18

Spring Hill, Alabama

September 14, 1852

Bone-weary and aching muscles complaining at the end of his long day and second day's dance lessons, Gideon returned to Spring Hill before the evening erupted into tears. Blinding rain pelted his cottage windows, gale winds rattled shutters and thunder roared like the broadsides of a thousand ships. An oak tree's huge limb smashed earth.

Thaddeus, Katie and Isaac scurried around the dismal dwelling lighting candles and candelabra. Dark spaces lightened like dawn.

"Don't forget the oil lamps in the parlor." Gideon removed his India rubber raincoat and set his soaked top hat on a mahogany foyer table.

Thaddeus lit a five-branched candelabrum in the hallway. "How did your lessons go?"

Gideon snatched up a thin packet of mail. In the hallway, beneath a brighter chandelier, he thumbed through it.

"I pretty near forgot." Thaddeus's long fingers reached inside his frock coat's pocket and handed Gideon a folded page. "Mister Washburn's jockey, George, brought this message today."

Gideon read it: *Our dear Comet has recovered and outruns every horse in my stable. Come see.* Recovered? From so serious an illness as lung fever? "Good news, Thaddeus. My friend's horse is no longer sick."

"Comet, sir? The horse you were telling me about?"

"One and the same."

"We were all praying for him."

"That a fact? Reckon the ceiling heard you this time."

"But Mister Gideon."

"Stop it." Gideon spun on him and aimed his finger at a chandelier. "That thing may fall on us if you keep telling me how much you and Katie pray."

"As you say, sir." Thaddeus's shoulders slumped.

"My wine. Bring it to my study. I'm writing Mister Sturgis an invitation to dinner Friday. Be sure it gets delivered."

Thaddeus headed for the pantry.

Gideon carried the candelabrum into his small study and penned an invitation to the Sturgises. He'd forsake his usual poker game for this because he knew Mister Sturgis almost always went to the Eastern Shore on Saturdays to check on his Thoroughbreds.

His invitation finished, he set aside his pen and rested his head on his desk. Was Comet's recovery a coincidence, or was it an answer to prayers? A coincidence. He massaged his arms—too much twirling and arm-lifting at the dance academy today.

Thaddeus set his uncorked wine bottle beside him, but he paid no heed. No need to apologize to him for snapping at him. It was the only way he could stop him from blabbering about prayer. He'd snapped at him before, just as he'd snapped at Katie and Isaac. Verbal whipping. Yes, that's what he'd done.

His thoughts drifted to Selah and his overseer, John Spears. If he allowed Spears to use a whip more often, as a first disciplinary measure instead of a last resort, maybe his slaves would behave better. Maybe that troublemaker Uriah would quit giving Spears a hard time.

Gideon grabbed his wine bottle, tilted back his head, took a long sip. Verbal whipping to physical whipping. Whipping Selah's field hands more often. He'd take that under consideration.

19

The Steamboat *Alabama Queen*

September 16, 1852

The *Alabama Queen's* calliope blared a lively tune as passengers boarded her. While stevedores and roustabouts loaded freight onto her and wagons clattered through crowds, Gideon tipped his hat at Mrs. Sturgis and Elvira. "My regrets about my dinner tomorrow. We'll have it when I return. I promise."

Elvira patted Gideon's black bowtie. "We understand. I hope it's not your slaves causing you trouble."

"So do I." Gideon eyed Elvira. Always good to show manners. Should he ask her mother for permission first? Or Elvira? "May I, Mrs. Sturgis?"

"Why ask me?" Mrs. Sturgis's eyes twinkled. "You want to kiss me too?"

"Oh, Gid!" Elvira moved in closer, her skirt touching his legs and her countenance aglow as she lifted her face for Gideon's quick kiss, which he planted on her forehead.

How he wished they could've locked lips. But that wouldn't be proper, not in front of Elvira's mother. He swore under his breath. Too many social rules to abide by, with mothers or chaperones always hovering, protecting daughters.

"I will return soon, my dear, sooner than later, I hope." He lifted his valise and hustled with other passengers up one of two gangplanks onto the steamboat's bow. Urgent business, his overseer John Spears had telegraphed him: *You are needed at Selah as soon as practicable.*

It'd better be urgent since it made him cancel his dance lessons and tomorrow's supper with the Sturgises. The trip took about two days, but depending on the business that needed taken care of he might have to stay away from darling Elvira longer.

The *Queen* was a large side-wheeler, bigger than most steamboats plying the state's rivers yet smaller than the Mississippi River's boats. She made regular trips between Mobile and Montgomery. White and three-tiered, her gallery surrounded her middle boiler deck. Freight in barrels and crates crowded her lower main deck near the waterline where horses and cows jostled each other. On her hurricane deck, two black iron stacks towered above the crew's quarters and pilot house.

For a steamboat's cabin, Gideon's accommodation was tolerably spacious. Opposite its bunk bed, a small pine counter held a porcelain washbasin, a bar of soap and a white hand towel. Added to these amenities, a salt shaker. He'd mix salt with the soap when he brushed his teeth. Angled near the door that opened onto the vessel's gallery were two cushioned chairs and a small table. Sunlight spilled through the gallery door's window pane.

The door behind him, connected to the boat's saloon, opened. "Excuse me."

Gideon twisted toward the voice. "Vanderporte? You're assigned to my cabin?"

"First time for everything, Deshler." The gambler dropped his valise and sailed his straw hat onto the top bunk. "You take the bottom bunk."

Gideon cleared his throat. "Don't ask me to play poker tonight. Find yourself another sucker."

"I won't be playing tonight, nor will you. The captain and me've known each other for a long time. We're on friendly terms, but he's forbidden it."

The boat's engine sounded. Its whistle blasted.

Gideon stepped out onto the gallery. Elvira and her mother waved. Elvira threw him a kiss.

"Bye, my darling." Gideon waved back and returned her kiss.

High-pressure steam exploded from the *Alabama Queen's* boilers as her paddles churned her clear of the wharf. Gideon hoped for a brief stay at Selah Plantation, for he needed Elvira, to be in her presence, because being in her presence always made him happy.

Supper over, Gideon purchased white wine at the steamboat's bar before he strolled her gallery. The evening's riverbank seemed to crawl past. The sternwheeler's paddles slapped the water with an almost hypnotic rhythm.

A small orchestra's soothing strains floated from its saloon, where couples danced. Should he go back inside and watch them? Maybe learn a few things? Sure, he'd enjoyed learning the Virginia Reel, but the main dance he wanted to learn was the waltz … to have his arm around Elvira's smooth shoulders, to whisper endearments in her ears, to thrill to her lavender fragrance, to ….

"Not a dancer either, I see." Vanderporte was sitting in a chair, a short table before him, playing solitaire by the light shining through their cabin door's window.

"Not much of one yet," Gideon said on his approach.

"Yet? You're taking lessons?"

"Could be."

Vanderporte flicked a two of hearts over an ace of hearts.

"Those cards are marked," Gideon said.

Vanderporte gathered up his deck and handed it to him. "Check 'em out."

Gideon tossed the remnants of his beer over the side. He inspected the backs of the cards. "Are you strictly a poker man, or do you also play other games of chance?"

"Ever been to the races?"

"No."

"Play the horses too. Metairie Race Course in New Orleans, the Spring Hill Race Track, the Bas—."

"You're older than me. Were you at that race on the day Green Legs got poisoned?" Gideon sat in a chair beside him.

"Ruined my wagering when he died."

"Do you believe Frank Washburn did it?" Gideon handed him back his cards.

"I got other suspects in mind, Deshler." Vanderporte returned them to his coat pocket.

"Who?"

"You nabobs usually avoid us professional gamblers. Blacklegs, you call us behind our backs. Don't much care what any of you call me. I saw something before that race, a—" Vanderporte cut off his words.

"A what?"

"A nothing. No more talk about Green Legs."

"But—"

"Shut up."

Gideon's questions stopped. Maybe, by "playing his cards" right, he'd discover who or what Vanderporte's "nothing" was. "I'll bet you have some marked cards in that coat pocket."

"Making a wager?"

"A guess."

Vanderporte stood and removed his coat. "Check it and see."

Gideon checked. He found the one honest deck the gambler had put there. That was all. Perhaps he'd misjudged him. "I'm thirsty. I'm going back to the bar for some wine." Gideon strode off.

20

MOBILE, ALABAMA

SEPTEMBER 19, 1852

"Hurry, hurry, else we'll be late." Hands on her hips, Hannah stood on the porch watching Luke and her father drag two Saratoga trunks toward their wagon.

Earl set down his trunk for a breather. "Be patient, Hannah dear. The orphanage will still be there when you arrive. Gloria's on her way here too, don't forget."

Luke hefted his trunk onto the wagon bed, followed by their father's. "We'll make it on time."

"We're here."

Gloria Quarles's cheery voice caught their glances. Hannah waved as Mister Samuel K. Quarles drove her up in their wagon.

"Ready to go to the orphanage?" Sam asked.

"Reckon so," Luke said.

Earl assisted Hannah up onto the wagon bench.

The wagon team's reins in hand, Luke sat beside her. "Let's get these horses moving, folks."

Sam and Gloria followed.

Orphans of all ages ran from a playground beside a three-story brick structure. Laughter, joking and loud talking bubbled, a joyful ruckus thronging Luke's and Gloria's parked wagons.

Sam enjoyed the merriment. He'd always considered himself a fun-loving fellow who didn't take life too seriously, except in regard to cards and betting on horse races and when he almost died from Deshler's pistol ball. Eternity had flashed before him then, sent icy shivers through his body. What would happen to him if Deshler had killed him? He'd never admit such a fear to anyone, not even to Joe.

Unlike his brother and late father, he wasn't a turfman. A gambler's blood coursed his veins. If he could maintain his respectability and become a professional gambler like Austin Vanderporte and other blacklegs, he would've done it. However, his father would've disowned him, he'd have become the family's pariah, so like most planters, he wagered as a pastime, an acceptable activity in polite society.

He pulled himself from his thoughts. Hannah struggled to lift a trunk off her wagon. He assisted Gloria down then set down Hannah's and Gloria's trunks then helped distribute gifts to the eager children.

A redheaded boy punched Luke's leg after he tickled the boy's shoulder. A blond girl put on her new bonnet and, giggling, did a slow spin, clearly pleased with the gift. Excitement rippled through the young crowd, grasping at the clothes and shoes being distributed.

A small man with a coffee-colored beard went straight to Sam. "Hello to you, sir. I'm Reverend Richard Davies."

"Samuel K. Quarles. A pleasure."

"Reverend Davies is the orphanage's director." Hannah grasped a tiny girl's hand.

Sam patted the child's head when she looked up at him.

"Are we ready, children?" Luke held up his Bible

Their excited voices responded with various affirmatives.

Luke waved them forward. "Well, come on, y'all. Today we'll learn about a big fish that swallowed a man, and if you're all good, we'll play some horseshoe pitching."

"And Puss in the Corner?" an older girl asked, her serious face studying Hannah.

"Yes, Jane." Hannah clasped the girl's hand. "We'll play that game too."

The children traipsed behind Luke, Hannah, Gloria and Reverend Davies toward the orphanage's building. Sam kept behind them at a slower gait.

With the tiny girl on one side of her and Jane on the other, Hannah marched with them, teased and encouraged them. Sam heard Hannah call the darker-skinned girl Marie. Since Marie was a French name, the little girl was probably Creole.

Sam's pace slowed. A man swallowed by a fish? It sure wasn't a speckled trout that swallowed ole Jonah, nor a Spanish mackerel. He'd heard this story many a time, thanks to his mother who'd taught it to him and Joe. She'd also been religious and attended church whenever they visited Mobile. His father attended with her but not for the reason she did. He attended because it helped a man's career, made him respectable in the opinion of polite society. Real men didn't need religion, he'd said, whereas religion fit the female species just fine.

Inside a large room on the orphanage's first floor, the children sat on the floor. Luke sat in front of them. Hannah led the congregation in a couple of songs. Her lilting soprano voice comforted Sam, like a wool coat on a winter night. Her songs finished, she stood along the wall beside Reverend Davies and Sam.

Luke opened his Bible and told the old story. The way he spoke, with various expressions blended with mild humor, captured the children's attention. When the great fish swallowed Jonah, Luke's cheeks puffed out like a balloon, followed by an exaggerated, "Gulp!"

Gales of laughter rang out.

After Jonah called out to God, Luke made a loud spitting sound, burped and twisted his face comically. "Yuk! Jonah sure tasted bad."

More laughter, louder than before.

Luke turned serious. He described how Jonah wandered the streets of Nineveh, a huge ancient city, preaching for it to either repent or expect God's judgment. Elbows propped on his knees, Luke leaned forward. "God did spare Nineveh because the city repented."

A girl with auburn hair raised her hand.

"Yes, Rebecca?"

"Mister Henshaw," Rebecca said, "what does repentance mean?"

Luke scratched his chin thoughtfully. "Well, it means turning away from doing bad things, from doing sinful things, things God doesn't like and giving our hearts to our loving Savior who died for us. Do you want to do that, Rebecca?"

The little girl nodded.

Luke scanned the attentive children. "Every child who would like to turn away from doing bad things and put their trust in the good Lord Jesus and do good things, like Rebecca here wants to do, bow your heads and pray with me."

Before Luke finished, Sam stepped outside into the breeze, his conscience pricked. He couldn't quite touch it, all the joy he'd witnessed, not only among the children but also Reverend Davies and Miss Henshaw and Luke. Although Gloria possessed a religious nature, even she seemed to lack whatever those three had. For her, good Christian deeds such as this was her duty to society, something she'd mentioned in past discussions. For Luke and Hannah, though, their joy seemed genuine, as though it gave them pleasure, as though it wasn't an obligation.

He gaped at the clouds scudding across a clear azure sky. He was happy, wasn't he? Well, why'd he feel miserable?

MOBILE, ALABAMA

SEPTEMBER 20, 1852

Sam sipped beer, shoved the glass aside and screwed up his face. "What'd they put in this garbage? Vinegar?"

"Be careful, Sam. I thought I saw them pour turpentine in it," one of the players at his poker table said.

That comment gave the other players a chuckle. Not Sam, though. Bad beer, bad lighting. Sam gathered up his cards. And another bad poker hand Cole dealt him. He was bored.

Cole studied him beneath hooded eyelids. "Your turn." His olive-skinned hands folded his fanned cards into a neat stack.

"My turn." Sam tugged his chin.

The other players laid their cards face down.

Suddenly, Sam stood.

"Hey." Cole's voice rose. "Where you off to?"

"Joe's house." Sam slid his chair back beneath the table. Its legs scraped the oak floor.

"Why?" Cole's voice rose louder as though demanding an answer.

Sam ignored him. Back on the street, he noticed the emporium's shades were down, so he retrieved his horse from a nearby livery. His bad poker hand didn't make him quit. He'd held worse hands, but for the first time in his life the game didn't interest him.

Yesterday, everyone enjoyed playing with the orphans, as did he. Except, he didn't play with them a lot. No laughter at the poker tables, save for the turpentine joke. The Tivingtons and everyone else were so dang serious about winning money. Life was too short to be serious all the time. In fact, yesterday was more fun than today.

He clucked at his horse and guided him down a street. Why was gambling losing its allure? He must solve this riddle, get the fun back in his life. Too much boredom could drive a man crazy, as it almost did tonight.

21

MOBILE, ALABAMA

SEPTEMBER 24, 1852

Valise in hand, Gideon hastened down the *Alabama Queen's* gangplank. Since her captain didn't allow card games he talked to fellow passengers, drank wine and tried to sleep, but sleep eluded him. Elvira's hovering image, filling his mind, kept him awake. During one stop on the river, the steamboat's engineer repaired a leaky boiler. "All will be fine," the captain told them in a reassuring voice. Neither he nor anyone else worried.

Since he'd dealt with an issue regarding Uriah, his field hands' driver, Selah no longer worried him either. It'd be all right. And he'd be all right once he and Elvira reunited.

He quickened his pace past warehouses. Thoughts of Elvira sent his heart soaring higher than a balloon. Her charming manner, her alluring lips, her high-cheekbones, soft hands, lamblike touch.

A boom spun Gideon toward the sound. Splinters flew at him like buckshot. His arms shielded his face. Flames roared up from the *Queen's* lower main deck through her upper boiler deck, a horrific conflagration. Fiery tongues licked air. Her stacks and boilers launched over the river like rockets. Her shattered hurricane deck caved into her boiler deck. Fragments, large and small, spewed everywhere—into the water, onto the wharf. Screaming. Lots of it. Several passengers jumped off the boat onto the dock, others hurled themselves into the river, wailing, madly swimming to shore against a strong current.

Along with other witnesses, Gideon gasped, horrified, at the mangled bodies scattered across the dock and in the river. One poor lady's head was severed and quickly sank out of sight. He dropped his valise.

A policeman galloped his horse up the street, to the nearest fire company for help, Gideon hoped.

A youth's desperate cry yanked Gideon's attention. The boy flailed in the river. His arms splashed water as the current swept him toward the bay. No survivors in the river paid him notice.

"I can't swim," the boy yelled. "P–Please. Somebody."

Throwing off his coat, Gideon dove in after him and swam hard and fast till he reached the screaming boy.

Gideon swam around behind him. The panicked youth's arm smacked his face when Gideon tried grabbing him in a special hold. The frightened lad turned and slapped his hand atop Gideon's head and shoved him underwater.

Kicking and struggling to surface, Gideon ... His breath ...*can't hold it long.* As if by instinct, he shot up a prayer. The boy's hand relaxed. Gideon swam up and by the time he dragged the boy to the dock, fire wagons were spraying water on the *Alabama Queen* while charred bodies floated toward Mobile Bay.

An elderly man rapidly limped to Gideon and the youth. "Douglas, are you—"

"I'm fine, Grandfather." The boy, coughing, pushed a strand of soaked hair from his forehead as water poured off his clothes and puddled his feet.

The man reached for Gideon's dripping hand. "I'm obliged to you, Mister. I watched everything from shore."

"Yes sir." Gideon almost turned away. He didn't want to discuss what he'd done. All he wanted was a bath and a change out of his waterlogged clothes.

"Are mother and father okay?" the boy asked.

"We are, son." Douglas's father ran to him.

The boy's mother stooped and wrapped her arms around him.

"They barely made it off the boat in time." The grandfather tousled Douglas's wet hair. "Your father was about to jump in after you when we saw this gentleman do it."

"We're all indebted to you," Douglas's father said.

"Very much so." The mother's voice shook. "What is your name, sir, if you don't mind my asking?"

"Gideon Deshler." Gideon shook the father's hand. "It was nothing, what I did. Truly nothing."

"Of course." The father smiled at him. "Nothing."

Arm around his son's shoulders, Douglas's father led him through the onlookers to a parked hackney cab with the boy's mother and grandfather behind them. Gideon waded through a sea of congratulations. As he left the crowd, his bones trembled. He could've been one of those passengers who'd perished. He quickened his pace. He must get home. Fast.

DUNDEE HORSE FARM AND PLANTATION
TENSAW RIVER, ALABAMA
SEPTEMBER 25, 1852

Joe led Gloria and Sam past a shed where his farrier sat on a stool trimming a horse's hoofs. He waved a greeting then continued on his way.

On the shed's opposite side, slow hoofbeats. Odors of horse and hay drifted their direction. They circled around the shed, where Joe met Rattigan outside Rattigan's office. A crow landed atop it, prompting Joe's small grin. Better not tell Rattigan he saw one perched on his office. "Is JB ready for a trial race today?" Joe asked the trainer.

"Nay," Rattigan said, "but *the capall* is almost ready."

"He's learned how to stand still in a line, hasn't he?"

Rattigan hesitated. "Aye."

Joe folded his arms. "And he's finally learned to back up and walk abreast by now." He leaned into the Irishman's face. "Hasn't he?"

"Alas. That he has."

Joe indicated the track. "He's started training with other horses over yonder?"

"Aye, aye. Marcus has been teaching him a lot."

Joe, hands on his hips, surveyed the yard where jockeys and grooms went about their tasks. Frowning, he seized the trainer's shirt and jerked him off the ground. "My patience is wearing thin. I want to see him run. Where's Marcus?"

Rattigan pointed at him coming out of the feed barn.

"Marcus," Joe yelled, gesturing. "Come over here and tack up Johnny Boy. Take him to the track. He's running today."

"But—"

"Don't argue with me."

Marcus's narrow shoulders slumped as he dragged himself to the tack shed.

"Meet us there." He let go of Rattigan. "And JB better start running today."

"Aye, sir. Aye." Rattigan blinked then hurried ahead.

"Irish is a strange bird," Sam said.

"Agreed," Joe said.

"He's also superstitious." Gloria giggled. "He hates crows. The poor man thinks they're bad luck."

"Like I said." Sam winced. "He's a bird."

Joe eyed his brother with concern. "Ribs still hurting from Deshler's pistol ball?"

"I'll manage."

Gloria harumphed. "I'll never forgive Mister Deshler for almost killing you."

At the track, the trio went to the starting pole. Rattigan sent Marcus and Johnny Boy to it along with Pete astride another horse, Applecart, a gray Thoroughbred with a white blaze.

The jockeys steered their horses into position. Applecart didn't concern Joe. That horse knew what to do.

And so far, Johnny Boy behaved like a proper racehorse. He stood still beside Applecart.

Joe studied his stopwatch. "Applecart's a year younger than Johnny, but he has the advantage since he's had some racing experience. Don't worry about losing this one, Marcus. I mainly want to see how fast JB runs today." He raised his hand as a signal. "Now."

Applecart shot down the track like a cannon ball.

Johnny Boy balked.

Marcus's knees pressured him to move.

Johnny Boy stayed put, shook his mane and snorted.

Applecart closed on the track's first turn.

"The crows curse you, *capall*!" Rattigan screamed.

Sam's and Gloria's laughter roared.

Joe's pent-up rage was a keg of gunpowder with a lit fuse. Suddenly, his eyes narrowed. What was Marcus up to? The jockey leaned close to Johnny Boy's ears and whispered to him.

With that whisper, Johnny Boy launched down the track. Marcus wasn't using a quirt, yet the horse's legs pumped hard and fast, like his life depended on it.

Joe cheered the horse and dropped his stopwatch when Johnny Boy closed on Applecart on the backstretch. Applecart kept three lengths ahead. Around the second turn. Johnny stayed on Applecart's tail.

"Catch him! Catch him, JB!" Joe slapped the fence rail.

The horses ... nose to nose. Hoofs thudded and kicked up dust down the final stretch.

Johnny, his neck outstretched, pulled ahead.

"Hurrah! By a nose." Joe grabbed Gloria's hands. "JB won by a nose." He planted a big kiss on her lips.

Gloria's lashes fluttered over her soft gaze. "I think it's grand, dear."

Marcus, beaming like the sun, sprang out of his saddle. "I figure JB's ready to get hisself to racing now."

Joe pulled Marcus's jockey cap down over his forehead. "How'd you get him moving so fast?"

"A word, sir."

"A word?"

"I spoke a word, Massa. Carrot. JB thinks he's a rabbit, the way he loves carrots better'n anything else. I whispered the word *carrot* to him, an' he took off. I promised him a carrot if he won the race."

"Well, Marcus, take him to the feed barn and get him two carrots. He deserves it." Joe clapped Marcus on the back.

"Let me get him cooled down first, sah," Marcus smiled at some crows strutting in front of Rattigan's office.

"Of course." Joe chuckled. "I like what I'm seeing now."

"You like it that he balks before he runs?" Gloria said.

"Fire, my dear." Joe slipped his arm around his wife's shoulders. "Get JB running, he's got a fire and determination to win. He'll be a true champion this season. My champion, your champion, our champion."

"Our stables' champion, eh?" Rattigan scowled at some strutting crows.

"Indeed." Joe, a bounce in his stride, led Gloria and Sam back to their cottage.

22

River Rose Horse Farm and Plantation
Three Mile Creek, Alabama
September 26, 1852

Owen's strides devoured earth in Lorelei's wake as she stormed around the stables to a small barn, where grooms were washing horses. Her swaying skirt upended a bucket of soapy water, doused a groom's trousers, but nevertheless, the groom continued currying a horse.

Her twisted face flushed, Lorelei's lithe figure loomed large in the barn's entrance. "Leander. Get yourself out here. This minute."

Leander, a groom aged about ten years, dashed out of the barn. His lips quivered. "Wh-What'd? M-M-Mis-Miss—"

"Stop stuttering." Lorelei slapped his face.

Leander flinched. "Y-Y-Yes, m-m-ma'am."

Lorelei slapped him again. "Stop it."

Owen simmered. Leander didn't typically stutter, except when he was scared out of his brogans. "Lorelei, stop yelling at him."

Ignoring him, her wrath bombarded the youth. "Want me to send you to work in our cotton fields, boy? Maybe a good whipping on your little naked back?" From her skirt pocket, she produced a fistful of hay. "See this." She thrust the sample at his wide-eyed, twitching face. "Look at it. Do. You. See. It?"

Leander nodded nervously.

"I just found a whole bale of it in Comet's stall."

Tyce sprinted to them from the track where exercise boys were cooling down their horses.

Lorelei thrust the hay at Tyce. "It's wet."

Tyce took the sample, rolled it over in his hand then handed it to Owen. "I'm sorry, M-Missus Washburn."

Owen studied his fistful. "Leander, this hay's not only wet, it has mold. Let's have it. Where'd you come across it?"

"Where the … the hosses was g-grazing." Leander lowered his eyelashes.

Lorelei backhanded Leander's face.

A tear rolled down the groom's cheek.

She whirled on Tyce. "As River Rose's trainer, Tyce, you bear the ultimate responsibility for this. You know better'n to leave hay out in the dew."

"Missus Washburn—" Tyce stammered.

"Husband, send these two to the whipping post. I'll fetch Mister Zeller to give them a good taste of the cat. Lung fever almost killed my Comet. I *will not* let him almost get killed again."

Owen recoiled before his wife's fury. She was right to be angry over moldy hay. He was too, but he disliked his overseer whipping his horsemen with his cat-o'-nine-tails. They worked harder and tried harder to win races when he treated them decently. Sometimes he believed Lorelei loved the whip as much as Elvira.

"Be reasonable, dear." Owen stretched forth his arms. "We found the problem before anything happened. Why not have Leander clean out all the bad hay and replace it with fresh bales? I reckon we can whip him if he makes this same mistake again."

"We'll whip them now. We'll rip the shirts off their backs and flay the skin off 'em. Comet is *my* horse. You bought him for *me*. Or have you forgotten?"

"Let's be reasonable."

"Reasonable?" Lorelei shrieked. "Feeding a horse moldy hay is most certainly unreasonable."

Zeller trotted his horse up a wide dirt path.

"Mister Zeller," Lorelei called through cupped hands. "Over here."

Zeller cantered up.

"Tyce and Leander need a whipping. They nearly killed my Comet." Again, Lorelei's palm popped Leander's tear-soaked face. Tyce glowered at her.

Zeller grasped the whip strapped around his waist. "A good way to end my long day. Gives me some exercise."

"You will not do it." Owen spoke without thinking. "I'll handle the situation."

Zeller glanced back at Lorelei.

"You'll do what I say, Mister Zeller." Lorelei delivered Owen a threatening look and spoke in a menacing tone. "These two will be disciplined the way I want, or else I'll tell Mister Cadwallader how you falsely pack your cotton bales for a higher price."

Owen reared. "If you tell him, you'll suffer as well."

"You think so?" Lorelei huffed. "People will pity me for having such a sorry-headed dishonest husband. Father will write that horse farm in the Tennessee Valley he promised you out of his will, that lush two-thousand-acre farm you love so much."

Owen's resistance collapsed, her threat a punch in his gut. If Gideon's employer, Mister Cadwallader, discovered his misdeeds, he'd most certainly sue him. He'd done it with other planters. Sure, they might be able to reach a compromise on his dishonesty, but suppose they didn't, well, he couldn't take the risk. Because Gideon trusted him, Gideon never inspected his cotton. His reputation would be lost, and his chance at Valley Farms lost forever because his cheating disgraced Mister Glenville's daughter. She was right. Her father's horse farm would be his biggest and best one when, and if, he inherited it.

Darkness permeated Owen's farm by the time Gideon arrived.

Owen's butler allowed him inside Owen's house where two other servants moved a sofa out of the men's parlor through a rear door.

Gideon swore. He'd sure timed his arrival wrong. Lorelei's stormy voice swamped Owen's. Neither had noticed him yet.

"Not there." Lorelei jabbed her index finger at another room. "My parlor. Move it."

The servants shifted the sofa around step by slow step as they backed the piece into Lorelei's parlor, puffing from their exertions.

"You don't need to put it in there." Owen peeked inside Lorelei's parlor. "Yours already has too much furniture."

Lorelei planted her hands on her hips. "It's *my* parlor, Husband. It's where I want it." Her volume increased. "That's all that matters. More places for us ladies to sit and converse on our visits. I'll be entertaining my friends this race season. You are fully cognizant of my intentions."

"The season's still a month away."

Lorelei patted Owen's cheek as though he were a child. "I know exactly when the season starts. I am *not* some simpleminded belle, so don't talk down to me like I am. You sound like dear brother Bob."

"Calm down, my dear. I meant nothing by what I said. I'm sure Bob doesn't mean anything by what he tells you either. He's only being a big brother."

Lorelei flipped up Owen's lapel. "*You* calm down."

Gideon smiled to himself when he detected Owen's tone, when he said *my dear,* it sounded flapjack flat. More furniture in the ladies' parlor at the expense of the men. With the sofa gone, the men's parlor only had a settee, two wing chairs and one side table set against the wall. Why did Owen put up with her? Did she have some sort of secret on him? A way to control him and make him do what she wanted? When Owen noticed his arrival, Owen mouthed, *I'm miserable,* at him.

Lorelei swept back into Owen's parlor. "Mister Deshler, I did not expect your arrival." She peeked in a sterling silver salver on a narrow stand. "I see lots of visiting cards in there from today. Where's yours?"

"I ran out of them."

"We did not send you an invitation either. Rude manners are inexcusable."

Gideon feigned regret. "My mistake. However, I daresay I did not come uninvited. Your husband invited me. Business upriver prevented my coming until now."

She plucked one of his frock coat's buttons. "Every time I see you, your coat's unbuttoned. Do you always go around everywhere with it hanging on your body like a drape? You think you're a coat rack?"

"Elvira doesn't mind." Gideon almost told her to go lock herself in her room but stifled his remark on account that Elvira may not appreciate his doing that since she and Lorelei were close. Thank goodness, Elvira wasn't like her. "How is Comet?"

"One of our grooms tried feeding him moldy hay," Owen said.

"That would've killed him," Gideon said.

"It's a good thing Lorelei discovered it."

Lorelei's expression hardened. "One of our other grooms showed it to me. I saw to it Leander and Tyce got themselves a good twenty lashes. Mister Zeller knows how to lay the rawhide on their scrawny little hides."

Gideon studied Comet's portrait, set in a gilt frame above the fireplace. "Mister Troye did a capital job painting him."

Owen eased up beside him. "Lorelei and I are pleased. Would you care for some coffee?"

Gideon hadn't had coffee in a long time. He briefly considered his friend's offer. No, he'd lost his taste for it. "I'd prefer wine."

"Wine it is. White wine?"

"Suits my fancy."

Owen clapped for his butler and delivered Gideon's request.

Minutes later the butler brought them their drinks.

"I'm glad to hear Comet's recovered." Gideon savored the wine. "What time did his recovery start?"

"Start?" Lorelei squinched her face. "Quite odd. It didn't start. It just sort of happened."

Owen sniffed his wine. "One minute he seemed like he was at death's portals, the next minute he bolted out of his stall frisky as a yearling. It took us pretty near a half hour to chase him down. He's resumed his normal routine. It happened in the early afternoon." Owen rolled his eyes toward his chandelier. "Between two and three o'clock, thereabouts, I think."

Lorelei nodded her agreement.

Gideon's visit stretched to an hour. He and Owen relived their boyhood adventures and shared stories that even made Lorelei laugh. Before he left, their conversation shifted to Elvira.

"I'm having her and her family over for dinner soon," he said.

"She is a wonderful girl." An affected smile flashed from Lorelei's face. "I'm so glad you two are getting to know each other better."

"She likes snakes." Owen grinned.

Snakes? "Hey," Gideon said, "do you remember that rat snake we caught with Alex Jessup? Alex told us the Hamiltons were having trouble with rats, and he couldn't find them a cat to take care of the problem."

Owen guffawed. "Scared the wits out of Mrs. Hamilton and Mary when Alex took it over to their house."

"Nice neighbors, but the Hamilton females are terrified of snakes."

Another round of stories were told before Gideon rode home. Miss Elvira was a snake-lover, was she? What kind did she have? He'd like to see it.

23

MOBILE, ALABAMA

SEPTEMBER 27, 1852

Sam almost collided with Charles Rhodes as he rounded a street corner. "Good evening to you, Mister Rhodes," Sam said, tipping his hat. "Your store's closed, I take it?"

The salesman tipped his derby and nodded. "My apologies for being in such a rush. My little woman is expecting me early. Taking her out to dinner tonight."

"Understood." Sam raised his hand bye then resumed his walk to see if his watch had been repaired. A scream from the emporium sent him sprinting into it. From the opposite direction, Luke and and Hannah's gig hastened there, its horse drawing it at a gallop.

Sam charged a man who'd lunged at Earl with a knife.

The man spun; his blade slashed at Sam.

Sam dodged it, charged in before the man could slash again and seized his arm, pinning his knife against his leg. They scuffled for the blade. Sam finally disarmed him, then slugged the man's jaw, upending him against a square post that stood between two jewelry counters. He lay on the floor, out cold.

Luke pummeled another man beside the cameo display, parrying his fists and answering with his own. Face. Chest. Stomach. The man doubled over and groaned.

"Stop!" a policeman shouted from the entrance.

Two policemen dashed inside with Hannah.

"The man over there tried to kill my father." Luke aimed his finger at the robber Sam had knocked out, who'd come to shaking his head. Squinting, he sat up.

Sam indicated the money strewn across the counter. "Tried to rob this place too."

"We'll take care of them," one policeman said, his pistol drawn. "And we'll see Mister Henshaw gets taken to the hospital."

"I don't think he'll need a hospital, sir." Luke choked on his words. He knelt beside his father, sprawled on the floor. Blood saturated his shirt. Luke stroked his arms. "He's going home."

Hannah joined her brother at their father's side.

The policeman waved his revolver at the robbers. "Hands behind your backs, you two."

Albeit grudgingly, the robbers obeyed. The policemen cuffed their hands.

Sam watched Earl's passing, for he knew Mister Henshaw's wounds were beyond what a doctor could repair.

His speech unintelligible, Earl clasped Hannah's and Luke's hands, tilted his face heavenward, his joyful eyes froze open in death.

Joyful? Sam scratched his shoulder.

Bent over her father, Hannah sobbed.

"He's with Mother now, Sister," Luke said. "In the presence of Jesus. In Heaven."

"Yes, with Mother and our Lord." Sniffling, Hannah gripped Luke's arm. "Oh, Luke! I know he's happy, but—" Her fingers splayed over her face.

"But we'll surely miss him here on earth." He put his arm around her shoulders while they walked past Sam.

Sam's eyes followed them. They seemed so sure he was in Heaven. How? How could they be sure? *In the presence of Jesus.* Luke's words echoed in his head.

24

Ned looked at the pine floor when Sturgis hung the counterweight off the balance bar's hook. If he didn't make his master's weight this time, he'd be doing more than sitting in a pile of horse manure like he'd done the previous month. Old Man Sturgis would strip him naked, chain him to a post and whip him senseless. Sturgis wouldn't be pleased with Robert either. Robert was a good trainer, but neither of them seemed able to live up to the old man's demands.

"Look at me, boy." Sturgis spoke in a monotone.

Ned looked up and stared at his master's fierce face.

"Eighty pounds." Sturgis slapped the counterweight in Robert's palm. The trainer placed it on a shelf.

Sturgis's eyes swept the empty stalls. "Where's Mystified?"

"I got him exercising." Robert stepped back to the scales. "I sent someone to fetch him."

Sturgis strode to the barn door and gazed at the clear morning sky. "A perfect Saturday for a ride. Have Ned ride him a little. Mystified's his horse this season. The grooms better muck out these stalls."

Riding again. Ned blew out a soft breath. *At last.*

"I'll see it gets done, sah." Robert inspected a stall.

Sturgis took two steps out of the barn, then turned back. "Before I forget, Ned. I have a reward for your present accomplishment. Come by the big house after you ride Mystified. I'll give it to you."

"I thank you, sah."

Sturgis left.

Yas sah and *no sah* and *thank you sah* and *massa.* Those words sure made him want to vomit all over the old man. One day, he'd do it.

25

Outside the church, Sam blinked. Parishioners in their Sunday best filed past him, the Sabbath service over. Several folks spoke to him on their way out. Did Reverend Eagleton hear his troubled thoughts? Did the man detect his uneasiness?

The minister's oratory contained no flowery language, nor did fancy theological terms riddle his speech. Too many preachers he'd known tried to impress their congregations by the timbre of their voice and a high-blown vocabulary few people understood. Not Reverend Eagleton. His straight-forward sermon troubled Sam. He hoped he'd succeeded in concealing his discomfort. He'd squirmed throughout the preaching. The minister's words made him feel like a dang fool.

"A fine sermon, Reverend," he said, upon most everyone's departure.

"I appreciate you coming, Samuel." The minister gripped Sam's hand firmly.

Strong, confident. Sam liked that. Handshakes revealed a lot about a man. In Reverend Eagleton's case, it told Sam he was secure.

"I trust I wasn't long-winded." Reverend Eagleton peered over Sam's shoulder at his wife, who chattered with another lady while they gathered up hymnals. "My missus tells me I get long-winded at times."

"Not at all, sir."

"You will visit us again soon?"

Sam spotted Luke and Hannah aboard their buggy. "I live up the Alabama River. Own fifteen hundred acres and two hundred slaves." Sam caught himself. There he went, bragging again. Somehow, in this good man's presence, bragging didn't seem appropriate. He cleared his throat. "I'm only staying with my brother long enough for Luke to repair my watch."

"You'll be heading back home after it's repaired?"

"We'll see, Reverend." Sam jogged around the corner where Zacchaeus awaited him on his buggy's bench. He, along with other slaves, had been in the church's balcony during the service.

Sam climbed into his vehicle. "Tell me, Zacchaeus. What'd you think about the reverend's preaching?"

"I enjoyed it, Massa Sam. I like Missus Gloria's preacher too. So do Sallie and Reuben."

"They didn't want to come with us today, did they?"

"Naw sah. Say they like that 'piscopal church of hers."

Sam pointed. "Over there. The Henshaws' buggy."

Zacchaeus stopped Sam's buggy alongside the Henshaws, in front of the church where Luke and Hannah bid Reverend Eagleton and his wife farewell.

"I enjoyed the service." Sam waved at them.

Hannah waved back. "Visit us anytime."

Gideon rode past.

"Mister Deshler." Hannah called after him. He ignored her.

Another church member likewise called his name.

Gideon kept riding.

"Wonder where he's going?" Luke said.

"To Spring Hill, it appears." Sam settled back and tilted his hat lower over his forehead. Next time he came to this church, if he did attend again out of friendship with Luke and Hannah, he hoped Reverend Eagleton didn't talk so much about sin. "Drive on, Zacchaeus. Drive on."

Zacchaeus slapped the reins. The two-horse team drawing the buggy clopped down the street.

BELLE GLADE HORSE FARM AND PLANTATION
MOBILE BAY'S EASTERN SHORE
OCTOBER 3, 1852

Beneath a sprawling live oak's shade, within sight of Mobile Bay, Ned and Becky sat on the ground. Time alone with her, his reward for losing weight. Also, a new pad and pencil so he could draw birds. His dream from childhood was to become an artist. To draw and paint animals, especially birds. His mother not only taught him about birds. She also encouraged his artistic dreams. So did his father, who wished he had a similar talent and was weary of shoeing horses. But because he was a slave, would his art ever be seen by others? He'd never become famous. He wasn't that good. He set his pad in his lap.

In the distance, gulls swooped, screamed and glided through salty air. Two egrets, their large white wings spread wide, rode the wind and touched down in a marsh as graceful as ballerinas. Birds, such free and pretty creatures.

Becky laced her short fingers in his and leaned her head on his shoulder. She wore her best bonnet and dress, hand-me-downs from Old Lady Sturgis. So soft, her hand. His heart jumped. It was the old man's meanness that kept them apart for long stretches of time. Separation from the girl he loved was torture.

With his free hand, Ned sketched a blue jay from memory.

Becky stroked Ned's chest. "You sho' is good at drawing, Ned."

"Only good at drawing birds," Ned said. "Can't draw much else."

"I ain't believing that."

He finished off the bird's crest.

Becky tapped his shoulder.

He turned. Their noses touched. So did their lips. Ned withdrew after their kiss. "Becky. We gotta find us a way outta here."

Becky gasped. "You talking 'bout escaping? How?"

"Ain't sure yet. Maybe sneak on a riverboat or find a canoe and go up the river north. I'm taking you with me when I can do that."

"They got slave patrols watching the docks. How we gonna sneak past them? My momma tried it once. When she got caught, Old

Man Sturgis put such a whipping on her she never forgot it. Cried all night for her, I did."

"I remember you telling me that tale. Your pappy got killed trying to escape this place too."

Becky squeezed Ned's hand so hard he felt her fear. "Drowned in the Tensaw running from the patrols."

"We'll find us a way." Ned stared at the boats and ships in the bay. Maybe they could find a boat and row out there. Or swim. "Wish one of them ships from England would anchor close enough, we could maybe swim to it. They ain't got slaves in England. I heard a person tell the old man that once."

"That's a far place to swim."

"Shallow close to shore." Ned set aside his pad. "Don't you worry none. We'll find us a way outta of this devil's brew. Jus' you keep praying." As he reached for his pencil Elvira, alongside Mister Overton, the overseer, swooped on them.

"I see you two." Elvira yanked Becky to her feet.

Ned scrambled to face her. He ground his teeth and balled his hands.

The burly overseer wiped his almost non-existent lips with the palm of one pudgy hand. Menace twisted his obese face. The folds in his double-chin quivered. Ned thought he looked like a tortoise. "You drawing something?" Overton said. "You think you're an artist?"

Ned showed him.

"Little birdies." Overton guffawed. "Going to fly off like them one day, are you now?"

Elvira snatched Ned's pad. "A cute little cyanocitta cristata."

Ned scrunched his brow. "A—?"

"It's the scientific name for blue jay, Stupid." She ripped it off the pad, tore it three times and tossed its remnants to the breeze. She seized Becky's faded white bodice and dragged her away.

Ned burned. That devil woman, if he could get away with it, he'd kill her.

Becky glanced back at Ned, her expression that of painful ire.

Ned's heart snapped in two. Like a twig.

26

Gideon hitched his horse behind other horses and vehicles on the Henshaws' moonlit street. Mister Cadwallader gave him the day off on account of Mister Henshaw's funeral. They'd both received invitations to this woeful observance.

Gideon hesitated. Had Luke and Hannah suspected him of helping Elvira steal that cameo, provided they'd discovered the one she'd taken gone? Surely not, since they invited him to this observance. Because he'd satisfied Elvira's honor by helping her, he approached the brick home's white door with a big black bow hanging from it, and feigned innocence.

At the front steps, Gideon halted. Dare he enter? How would he be received? He hadn't attended church in a long time. Would he be able to handle another death of someone he knew well? He turned to go back home and drink his wine.

"Gideon." His next-door neighbor's voice sounded from the doorway.

Gideon halted mid-stride. "John Stephen Hamilton. Hello."

"Hello to you, neighbor. Come on inside and grace us with your presence. I was wondering when you'd show up."

"I'm going back home."

"No you are not." Stephen's long legs carried him down the steps fast as a flea's jump. He steered Gideon up into the house, its rooms and hallway dimly lit by flickering candles in wall sconces.

Familiar faces swarmed Gideon. His tension snapped. No cold shoulders. No shunning. No one behaved toward him in the way he'd expected.

Stephen nudged him into a line of people inching past Hannah and Luke at their parlor's entrance. "I'll be at the refreshment table down the hall. See me when you're done."

As Gideon shuffled in the snail-slow line toward Hannah and Luke, he looked beyond them. In the parlor, black crepe draped furniture, portraits, mirrors and the fireplace's mantel. The mantel's ormolu clock stayed mute, drawn drapes blocked the moonlight and positioned in front of the fireplace, Earl Henshaw's coffin.

Hannah's black veil fell behind her black bonnet. Only widows' mourning veils covered faces and heads. Her dress was made of dark Henrietta cloth, a woolen fabric Gideon knew from his mother and Harriet.

He'd tossed away his black-bordered funeral invitation. It reminded him of that horrific day his Harriet died. Only last February had his two years of grieving ended, the first year for his parents, the next year for Harriet and Billy. Though the rules of mourning weren't as strict for men as they were for women, he happily discarded the trappings, the black clothes and black cravats and black armbands and such, that Luke wore now.

Hannah's black-gloved hand clasped Gideon's.

"I am deeply sorry, Miss Henshaw." Gideon trembled. Images of his parents, of Harriet and baby Billy made him want to flee, but he couldn't. It'd be impolite.

She beamed through moist eyes. "Thank you, Mister Deshler. My father is in the presence of Jesus. My brother and I will be all right, though we will miss him here on earth."

He stepped over to Luke, and the former friends shook hands. Luke's grip remained firm as he said, "Father thought the world of you. Hannah and I feel the same way."

They thought the world of him? Gideon's stomach clenched. They wouldn't think so highly of him had they known he'd help Elvira steal that cameo. And Hannah and Luke were joyful too. Why? He hated that poor Mister Henshaw had died. His time on earth was done, just like his parents, Harriet and poor baby Billy. *Oblivion.* He forced this notion from his mind.

Guests continued streaming through the front door.

Gideon joined others down the hall where they sipped tea, nibbled shortbread cookies and engaged in subdued conversation.

Reverend Eagleton and his wife mouthed for him to come over and chat with them and Stephen.

The minister swallowed his cookie. "It was good of you to come, Gideon. A tragic thing, Earl's death."

Stephen toyed with his cookie, brought it to his mouth then lowered it. "How have you been faring? It's been pretty near a year since we last saw each other."

Gideon glanced around. "Where's the rest of your family?"

"Visiting my grandmother in Huntsville. I'm their representative here." Stephen finally ate his cookie.

"Still managing your father's plantation in Washington County?"

"I am." Luke went to the refreshment table.

Mrs. Eagleton tilted her head at Gideon. "Do come back to church, won't you?"

Unsettled by her soft voice, Gideon froze. "Someday, Mrs. Eagleton." *A lie.* He followed Stephen to the refreshment table.

Stephen grasped the pitcher of iced tea. "Allow me, friend."

Friend? He sounded like Luke. He'd severed his friendship with Stephen soon after Harriet died. Gideon lifted his glass of tea. On one occasion a few years ago, he'd overheard Stephen and his father, in their backyard, argue about slavery. Though Stephen never let it be known publicly out of concern for getting tarred and feathered or similar treatment, his family knew he wasn't fond of slavery. They kept it a secret lest some ill treatment befall him, and Gideon never let on that he knew Stephen's true views for the same reason as Stephen's parents.

A minute later, Gideon and Stephen sat together opposite the front parlor.

A door's creak caught Gideon's attention. Mister Cadwallader slipped through the entrance, also Joe and Gloria and Sam, the last ones to offer their condolences. Once they finished, they found chairs angled against a wall in the foyer. Hannah and Luke sat with the minister and his wife, who faced their seated guests, all of them somber.

While a pianist played "Amazing Grace," Gideon wrestled his emotions. Memories of his parents, Harriet, Billy ... He swore under his breath. *Stop it, Gideon. Elvira. Focus on Elvira.*

The music stopped. Luke stepped to a podium and opened his Bible. "I would like to read a passage from Paul's first letter to the Corinthians, chapter fifteen, verse twenty-two. It reads as follows: *In a moment, in the twinkling of an eye, at the last trump: for the trumpet...*" He glanced up for a moment, his serious eyes locked on Gideon.

Gideon averted his gaze. He disliked the way Luke looked at him. Disturbed him, it did. Was Luke judging him? Did Luke know about the stolen cameo? Luke didn't seem like he knew. He shouldn't have accepted Luke and Hannah's invitation. He'd only accepted it to appear innocent of any wrongdoing in the emporium in case they'd suspected him. Yet their joy, he didn't expect it.

Luke closed his Bible. "My dear sister Hannah and I may mourn our beloved father's sudden passing, but not as those who have no hope, for we also rejoice because we know he's reunited with our mother. And, dear friends, he's rejoicing in the presence of Jesus. We'll see them again someday. That is my confidence, my sister's confidence, our hope." He sat back down.

Reverend Eagleton stepped to the podium next. He preached a short sermon using Earl Henshaw's righteous life to illustrate his points. "Our friend Earl loved our Lord and Savior." Reverend Eagleton's sermon wound down. "He would say to everyone here today, to those who've not put their trust in our Savior, to do so. Do so today, because tomorrow may never come." He gestured at the door. "We will now allow each person who hasn't done so to view our departed brother's body and pay their final respects."

Gideon didn't do that. He had other plans.

MOBILE BAY, ALABAMA
OCTOBER 9, 1852

The bay boat's paddlewheels slapped Mobile Bay's dark waters; Gideon navigated a path through and around its partygoers toward the bar. Mister Sturgis hired this boat for this excursion. Weekend trips on these vessels, a popular pastime particularly in the summer months. Gideon had only done this once before, on a church outing in his youth.

Sturgis "held court" with his wife and other jockey club members. Cigar in hand, he gestured with exaggerated sweeps of his arms and bragged about Mystified.

Owen, sipping champagne, sidled up to Gideon. "Have you met Elvira's snake yet?"

Gideon shook his head.

Owen tilted his drink's flute at Lorelei and Elvira heading aft, out a door onto the boat's gallery. "Why not ask her?"

"Ask her about what?"

"Her snake."

"Why?"

Owen finished off his drink. "I'm getting some more champagne. Go ahead. Ask her."

"Since you're so interested in me asking, I think I will." Gideon joined the ladies.

His palm shielded his eyes from the scorching noon sun. Seagulls and ospreys soared overhead. Lighters towed by tugs plied the bay's Main Channel to and from anchored ships, picking up and delivering freight. He drew up alongside Elvira, whose delightful fragrance set his heart a-gallop. Once it slowed to an easier pace, he asked the question. "Owen tells me you like snakes. Any particular kind?"

Elvira's wooden eyes stayed fixed on the bay. "Rattlesnakes."

"Rattlesnakes and cottonmouths." Lorelei peered past her friend. Amusement played across her lips.

"Are you scared to meet my rattlesnake?" Elvira kept watching the bay's busyness.

Gideon shrugged. "I've seen plenty of rattlers and cottonmouths in my time."

"Have you ever been bitten by one?" A soft glow emerged in Elvira's violet eyes as she studied him.

Bitten by one? "Can't say I have." Gideon watched the marsh. "Why does a pretty lady such as yourself like poisonous snakes?"

Elvira tweaked Gideon's cheek. "Let's say I respect them, Love."

"Me too." *Enough to stay away from them.* When she called him "Love," his heart galloped faster.

Elvira prattled endlessly throughout their excursion, especially after Lorelei left. Not a single word about Mister Henshaw's passing, however, not after he told her he'd been killed. Nor had her parents expressed sympathy. They'd exacted their revenge by stealing the cameo. Her honor was satisfied. He'd done his duty by attending Earl Henshaw's funeral and was convinced, now, that Luke was ignorant of his and Elvira's theft.

BELLE GLADE HORSE FARM AND PLANTATION
MOBILE BAY'S EASTERN SHORE
OCTOBER 9, 1852

Elvira and her mother disappeared into their mansion to change clothes.

Sturgis led Gideon to his stables where grooms carried buckets of soapy water to three horses tied up beside the barn and another groom curried a fourth horse, his black ears twitching and tail flicking. Manure's ammonia odor assaulted them.

"Ned!" Sturgis called to him at the track.

Ned, with Mystified on a lead rope, met him at the track's gate.

"Take Mystified over to the other horses. Time for washing and grooming. Where's Robert?"

"Ain't sure—"

"Ain't sure!" Sturgis lowered his speech volume, sighed. "After you take Mystified over to the grooms, find him. Tell him I need him here."

Mystified in tow, Ned hurried off.

Mister Sturgis's outburst reminded Gideon of himself. Sometimes, when Thaddeus's whistling irritated him, he'd yell at him. It was a puzzle as to why whistling irritated him, but it did.

"Ned may not be the best jockey in our turf world, mind you," Sturgis said, "but he is the best and most competent one I own." Sturgis's monologue about Thoroughbreds continued.

Gideon had looked forward to this weekend with Elvira and her family here on the Eastern Shore. A little pride puffed his chest. He was feeling like part of their family.

Sturgis reached for a cigar in his shirt pocket. "I'm sorry, young Deshler. My last one."

"I understand."

"Massa Sturgis." Robert raced toward them. "I'm coming."

Clothed in a blue organdy dress, Elvira soon returned, reached out and touched his arm. "Gid, my love. Let's go watch the sunset. It's so peaceful when it sets over the bay."

Sturgis lifted his cigar to his mouth. "Young Deshler strikes me as a gentleman. Go ahead, my dear. Enjoy yourselves."

Gideon lifted his arm for her acceptance. "Your daughter will be safe with me. I intend her no harm."

"I trust you." Sturgis poked his cigar between his teeth.

Though sunset remained a few hours away, Gideon escorted her to the property nearest the bay.

For most of the afternoon Elvira caressed Gideon—not his body—his pride. Through flattery and endearments, her silky words fondled him much like Culpepper had fondled and flattered her. Thus far, she'd succeeded with the fool stretched out on the grass before her, his hands behind his head. His gaze, one of admiration.

As she sat beside him her dress, expanded by layers of petticoats, rustled and billowed. Her gloved fingers danced a jig up and down his chest. Now, all she needed to do was wriggle deeper inside his heart to obtain the fool's money. To accomplish that, he must do more than love her. He must adore her, worship her. It was the only way she envisioned him proposing marriage.

"Look at that. The sun!" Elvira's finger-dance stopped.

Gideon sat upright.

At long last the sun kissed the horizon. Its golden glow illuminated a pristine sky. Marsh grasses rustled. In deeper water, mullets jumped southward.

"Helios," Elvira said.

"Helios?" Gideon blinked. "I see. You're talking about the sun god."

"Looks like he's going to sleep again. Soon, Selene will arise."

"Selene the moon goddess." Gideon pulled her close. "You're no atheist. You're a pagan, my gorgeous Venus."

"Merely interested in mythology, my love."

Gideon laughed.

She felt Mister Deshler's warmth in his embrace, a desperate passion telegraphed by his lips when they pressed hers.

"Since Helios will soon be asleep," Gideon said, "we'd best get on back."

Arm in arm, they strolled back to her house. Elvira smiled to herself. Not much longer till Mister Gideon Deshler would be hers.

SPRING HILL, ALABAMA
OCTOBER 15, 1852

Gideon folded his napkin edge to edge and placed it on his dining table next to his empty ice cream dish. He patted his belly. Katie's sumptuous supper, she outdid herself tonight. Suitable for a king. *Or in Elvira's case, a queen.* Wine and champagne, turkey, potatoes, bread, rice, all topped off by his favorite dessert, vanilla ice cream. Its sugary taste lingered on his palate.

"A delectable meal." Sturgis fiddled with his unlit Havana.

Katie and Isaac gathered up their silverware.

"It was wonderful." Mrs. Sturgis pulled on her red kid gloves. "A nice cottage you have as well, Mister Deshler."

Elvira winked at him. "Katie cooks better than our cook." She buttoned on her gloves.

Emotionless, Katie nodded at Elvira before she led Isaac back down the hall.

"I am honored you all appreciated it." Gideon scooted back his chair and assisted Elvira out of hers. "Would you care to go for a little jaunt?"

"Why not?" Sturgis assisted his wife out of her chair.

In the foyer, Gideon removed his top hat from his hat rack.

Sturgis took his flattened hat, a gibus, off the same rack. "I must say, young Deshler, your turkey was especially delightful." Gently, he stretched his hat out to its full size so that it resembled Gideon's hat.

"Baked turkey's her specialty." Gideon gathered his black leather gloves from off a marble-top table and handed Sturgis his brown ones.

Elvira slipped into her scarlet burnouse and pulled its hood over her head. "It's regrettable she's not a slave."

"How true." Mrs. Sturgis viewed herself in a tall gold-framed mirror in the hallway. She secured her bonnet on her head, its bow snug beneath her chin. "You'd pay top dollar for her, would you not, Edward, if she were a slave?"

"Without question, Margaret. Top dollar. Top dollar."

Gideon stepped aside for Elvira and her mother to exit the front door. "Supposing she was a slave and you offered me the highest price in the world for her, well, sir, I would politely decline the offer."

"And I wouldn't blame you," Sturgis said, fiddling with his cigar.

Gideon wondered why Mister Sturgis didn't make his usual offer of a smoke.

"Perhaps you can have her help cook for our jockey club's dinner coming up in a few weeks. We already have cooks, of course, but we can always use one with Katie's unique talent." Sturgis stepped out onto Gideon's gallery where Elvira and Mrs. Sturgis awaited them. "Pheasant will be on the menu this year, as it is every year. Do you savor pheasant?"

"It'll suit my palate." Gideon had never eaten pheasant, though he was eager to try it. He shivered, not from the evening's chill, but from Elvira's lamblike touch when she clasped his elbow. Over his shoulder, Gideon shouted, "Thaddeus. Come here. Thad-dee-uus!"

With a giggle, Elvira squeezed his arm. "You sounded like a child calling his dog."

"Guess I did, didn't I?" Gideon chuckled.

Thaddeus, his expression quizzical, hastened to them from out the door.

"You and Isaac go hitch up my landau. We're going for a ride."

With a quick nod, Thaddeus pivoted and left.

Sturgis slipped his cigar back into his coat pocket. "I assume you don't smoke. I saw no cigar lighter in your house."

"I hope that's not a problem, Mister Sturgis."

"Not at all. You have your vices, I have mine. Enjoy life. Eat, drink and be merry, as the old saying goes. We only live once."

Eat, drink and be merry. Gideon couldn't recall which book of the Bible contained those words, but they were in it somewhere, and Mister Sturgis likely didn't know it came from that book. He'd heard his parents quote it a few times. "About your horsemen, sir. How many do you own?"

"Twenty."

"Thoroughbreds?"

"Thirty. Most are retired from racing. Only three participate these days. My Mystified will make my fourth challenger next month."

"I plan on attending the races this season and learning more about the sport."

"Good. Very good. We'd be glad to have you join us."

A yellow landau clattered to a stop, its hoods folded down, with Thaddeus atop its driver's box. "All aboard."

"This isn't a train," Mrs. Sturgis snapped.

"I'm only trying a bit of humor, ma'am," Thaddeus said.

"Well, stop it." Mrs. Sturgis lifted her chin haughtily. "We don't need a clown driving us. And quit staring at me. It's not proper, boy."

Unaffected by her rudeness, Thaddeus looked straight ahead.

Once everyone "climbed aboard," the two-horse team drawing them clopped down the road. Thaddeus whistled a hymn.

Gideon gritted his teeth.

Seated beside him, Elvira tapped his knee. "Please tell that boy to stop."

Gideon rose halfway. "Stop your dang whistling, Thaddeus. It's bothering these nice ladies and me."

"Wouldn't wanna to do that." Thaddeus tilted his top hat forward.

For the next couple of minutes, Gideon and the Sturgises engaged in lively conversation.

Elvira's hands fluttered. "Gid, my love, you simply must see my snake. Will you do that on your next visit?"

"I promise I will." *A rattlesnake. Hurrah.*

Thaddeus began singing in his baritone voice. "A mighty for-or-tress is our God, a bulwark never fa-a-ailing. Our Helper ...."

Mrs. Sturgis clapped her hands over her ears.

"Stop singing, Thaddeus." A storm blew through Gideon like a Mobile Bay squall. Sometimes it seemed Thaddeus whistled and sang for no other reason than to get on his nerves. "No singing, no whistling, no tapping of the hands and feet. Just drive the carriage."

"We are approaching a fork in the road." Thaddeus glanced back at him. "Shall I go left, or right?"

Gideon thumbed "take a left."

So, Thaddeus steered the carriage down the left road while he hummed a hymn.

"No humming either, boy." Gideon's order launched off his tongue.

The humming stopped, prompting a grin from Elvira and her mother.

"That's telling the boy, young Deshler," Sturgis said. "Keep 'em all in line."

Gideon folded his arms. Keep them all in line. Whatever it took to win Elvira's heart, he'd do it.

27

S am sat in Earl Henshaw's former pew spot, Luke sandwiched between him and Hannah. When his late father attended church with his late mother, he must've felt the way Sam did now, a respectable and responsible citizen from the state of Alabama. He cleared his throat and hoped Reverend Eagleton preached a sermon that helped him keep all the warm feelings that he presently felt.

Sam put ten dollars in the offering plate during some organ music. He'd never given a lot of money to the church, much less any charity. He was growing into a great big ball of fur these days, too big a fur ball for a cat to spit out. His father had spurts of generosity too. Well, seems he was becoming more and more like his father, with the exception of raising and breeding racehorses. Was attending church every Sunday the thing that made Luke and Hannah joyful? He'd have to ask them more about this church-business.

When Reverend Eagleton stood at the pulpit, he opened his Bible. "My sermon this morning, my brothers and sisters, is taken from Matthew chapter nineteen, verses nineteen through twenty-six."

"The rich young ruler," Luke whispered to Sam.

"Huh?"

"Shh. He's preaching about the rich young ruler."

Sam thumped his knees, looked left and right and turned his watch over and over.

"The story ends with this poor rich man leaving Jesus." Reverend Eagleton gripped his pulpit. His penetrating gaze surveyed the congregation. "Yea, rich in this world, yet poverty-stricken in soul."

Sam wanted to leave. He was a rich man. He came to church today, didn't he? He was no sinner, yet some invisible power pinned him in his seat.

The minister's voice rose. "This poor man had great possessions, great wealth. These things prevented him from following our Lord. 'Then Jesus said unto his disciples, Verily I say unto you, That a rich man shall hardly enter into the kingdom of heaven'...."

Hardly? A rich man like me, doomed to Hell? Sam shot up from his pew. He didn't want to hear it. Those near him stirred. Luke jerked him back and touched his lips for quiet.

"... Oh, be not dismayed, all who are rich in this life." Reverend Eagleton's deep voice resonated throughout the sanctuary. "You too can enter Heaven, though it is easier for a camel to go through the eye of a needle, as our Lord said. It is difficult because those who are rich trust in their riches, but as the Lord Jesus said: '... with God, all things are possible.' Joseph of Arimathea was a wealthy man, and ...."

Sam peeked at Hannah, her brows knitted in concentration with her attentive eyes fixed straight ahead. The longer Reverend Eagleton preached ... He squirmed. Wouldn't that preacher ever get quiet?

His sermon finally at an end, Reverend Eagleton raised his hands. "While the choir sings, if there is anyone who would like to put their trust in Christ today, I invite them to come forward. I will pray with you."

Pray? In public? Sam quit turning his watch over, clenched it so tight it dug into his palms. *Not me.*

Luke and Hannah bowed their heads.

Praying? For me? I ain't going to do it. I ain't going up front. He bolted forward like a Thoroughbred and collapsed on his knees at an altar bench.

"Welcome, friend." Luke grasped his shoulders.

"Oh, Sam." Hannah wept, for joy, Sam supposed.

When Reverend Eagleton clasped Sam's hands, a warm peace blew through him like the wind, chipping away its rough edges, knocking off every hardness his heart once possessed.

The moment his butler entered the parlor, Joe set down his newspaper.

"Mister Cole Tivington has arrived, Master Joe," his butler said.

"Send him in." Joe arose from his chair, seized his friend's hand and crunched Cole's fingers with a hearty handshake. "What brings you here?"

"Went to Owen's stables and saw him run." Cole massaged his fingers. "Comet. Twice Friday, twice Saturday. Thought you'd be interested."

"Did you now? What was his time?"

"For a mile heat, his average time is," Cole twirled his watch between his nimble fingers, like a magician doing sleight of hand, "one minute fifty-eight seconds."

"JB's beaten that time when he's of a mind to run fast," Joe said. "The fact of the matter is, he has to be in a fast-galloping mood. You saw Comet run four miles?"

Cole shook his head. "Not yet."

The front door slammed.

Almost at the same time Joe, Cole and Gloria converged on Sam in the hallway.

His countenance aglow, Sam provoked Joe's curiosity.

"Hello, Joe." Sam seized his hand and nodded at Gloria and Cole.

"Uh, hello." Joe bumped Cole's arm, Cole bumped him back, which told Joe they had the same question. What was wrong with Sam?

Cole sniffed Sam's coat, Sam's face. "What kind of liquor you been drinking?"

Sam touched his throat. "I'm as dry as a desert. I attended church this morning, spent the entire day with the Henshaws. I've become a Christian."

Joe and Cole swapped skeptical glances.

"Now you look here." Joe tugged his brother's coat sleeve. "Let me tell you this, Sam. You and me, we're both Christians. We were baptized in the Episcopal church and let me tell you this," he poked Sam's chest, "Gloria and I attended church this morning, same as you."

Sam smiled.

Gloria clapped softly. "I'm happy for you, Sam."

"Appears me and Father lost us a good poker player." Cole snatched his hat from Joe's butler before he turned on Sam. "Till your foolish fanaticism wears off. My goodness, wait'll I tell Father about you. He won't believe it." Cole guffawed himself out the door.

Joe marveled at Sam. His brother couldn't stop smiling.

28

Gideon grabbed the wire cage off his buggy seat. A mouse, its whiskers quivering, scurried back and forth inside it. "Searching for a way out, you little rodent? You're as good as dead, mouse meat. Might as well forget it."

On her gallery, Elvira set aside her book and arose from a chair.

"A little gift for you, my dear." He stretched the cage toward her.

Elvira's eyes sparkled as her fingertips formed an arch. "My mercy, Gid. You didn't."

"I most certainly did." Gideon lifted the cage higher. "For your pet. I set a few traps and caught this little feller sometime last night."

Elvira's bright eyes shifted back and forth, keeping them on the scurrying mouse. Briefly, it stopped, stared at her, twitched its whiskers then scurried off another direction. "Why, Gideon will love it."

"Gideon?" He pointed at himself.

Elvira tweaked his cheek. "I hope you don't mind me naming my pet after you."

"That's, er, fine." He wasn't sure whether he should be flattered or insulted by her snake's name. However, he had to admit, it was sort of amusing.

Elvira patted the cage with the edge of her book. "Wait till you see Gideon's excitement when it sees the mouse."

The snake's rattle greeted their entrance into its shed. Coiled inside its terrarium, the serpent lifted its triangular head and flicked its tongue.

Gideon noted, in a corner of the shed, a snake hook, spade, hoe, rake and other garden tools. He set the mouse's cage on a table.

"Will you feed it for me?" Elvira kissed his earlobe.

"Why not?" He dropped the mouse inside the terrarium and let its pocked lid drop.

Elvira squealed. "Look at that mouse run."

Gideon pointed. "Look at it swallowing him."

Hands clasped, their fingers laced, they swung their arms back and forth in wide arcs.

Happiness bubbled inside Gideon. He released her hands. Her dress wasn't filled out like it usually was, which meant she only wore one petticoat. He recalled she'd said she didn't wear so many when she was home, so he enveloped her in his arms. So close did he hold her, he felt his heart pounding a rhythm with hers and breathed in her vanilla scent. He could stand it no longer. He broke away and gazed into her clear violet orbs. "Miss Elvira, would you permit me the honor of becoming my wife?"

"Oh! Mercy! My handsome Gid. I accept. I do! I do!" She parted from him, fluttered her lashes, locked her fingers in his then added, "But there's one thing you must do before you ask my father for permission."

Gideon kissed her soft cheek. "Whatever you wish, my dear."

"Take my parents and me to your home on Government Street. I haven't seen it yet. Is that where you keep your family's Bible?"

"It's where I keep it. If you and your parents can visit me next Thursday evening, I'll make a point to be there."

"Good!" Elvira clasped Gideon's face between her palms and smothered it with more kisses.

"Forever together, my dear." Gideon smiled, relishing her fragrance.

"Forever." Elvira stroked his hair. Once again, their lips met. And they kissed, for a time that seemed to Gideon, a blissful eternity.

On the way out the shed door Elvira smiled over her shoulder, at her snake.

Mobile, Alabama
October 21, 1852

Adrenaline coursed through Elvira, riding with her parents in their coach. Within minutes, Mister Deshler would encounter her ultimate test, the one that would determine her marriage to him. The fool had enough money to please her, but if he failed it she'd kill their relationship and seek out another wealthy, vulnerable gentleman. She'd rather die than become a spinster. She'd rather die than waste her life on the fringes of society. She'd rather die than be used by a man again.

"Do you think he'll do it, Father?" Elvira fiddled with the curtain hanging over her seat's window as their vehicle rocked along Government Street.

"Only one way to find out." Sturgis plopped his gibus on his head.

Sturgis's coachman brought the vehicle to a stop. He opened the door for the ladies. Sturgis followed them into the chilly night.

Lights glowed in Mister Deshler's home. Elvira had always admired its architecture. Tall and white, with thick Doric columns and a spacious gallery, with four dormers that projected their panes toward the dusty street.

She imagined herself with Becky in its attic, the crack of her whip on Becky's face and back, Becky's screams and wails. Mister Deshler hadn't seen her whip slaves yet. She'd not done it in front of him because she wasn't sure he'd approve. Suppose he didn't approve yet passed tonight's test, well, she'd persuade him into whipping them after he married her. Lorelei controlled Owen. She could control Mister Deshler just as easily, provided he proved his love for her tonight.

Thaddeus received their cloaks and bonnets and Sturgis's hat. "Allow me to inform Mister Deshler of your arrival. We have a nice warm fire going in the parlor." His shoes clicked down the long hall.

From near the fireplace's blazing logs, Elvira surveyed the furniture. "Where is it?"

"I don't see it either," her mother said.

"Perhaps it's in one of his drawers," her father said.

Before she could check Gideon made his appearance, accompanied by Katie and Isaac.

162   JOHN M. CUNNINGHAM, JR.

"Tea, coffee, port, beer or champagne?" Gideon asked.

"Port for me," Elvira said.

"Margaret and I will have champagne," Sturgis said.

"You heard them, Katie. Port for me too." Gideon shooed her away.

And Elvira ambled about the parlor. A portrait had been turned around to face the wall. What sort of painting was it? Why did it face the wall? No matter. She'd get an answer later. Her gloved hand touched furniture, window sills, an oil lamp. Every piece looked expensive, even the huge rug and the small mahogany table with the cabriole legs. The table's blue porcelain vase with its artificial roses grabbed her interest. She'd make him throw those ugly things away if they married.

"My late wife's." Gideon lifted a rose from the vase. "She put those flowers in there before she died."

She received the rose and moved to a tall bookcase to skim its titles. "I love your house." She turned to him. "Where is your father's Bible?"

"Upstairs. Why?"

"Well, Father knows how much we want to get married. Isn't that true, Father?"

Sturgis nodded. "She told me, and I've agreed to permit it on one condition."

"My condition." Elvira stepped past Gideon. "Would you be so kind as to get Mister Deshler's Bible for us, dear Katie?"

Katie's brows knit. An angry glance at Gideon, another angry glance at Elvira … She set down the drink tray.

"You heard the lady," Gideon said. "It's in Father's trunk. Get it."

Katie passed out the liquors then scurried up the stairs.

"Dear Gid." Elvira's voice resembled a purr. "When we are united in glorious matrimony, we must be careful not to allow religious fables in our home when we have children. We don't want them to believe lies, do we?"

"Definitely not," Gideon said.

"Will you toss your father's Bible into the fire for me? Please. I don't want them influenced by fairy tales."

The book in hand, Katie returned, her typically soft face now stone.

Gideon snatched it and sailed it into the flames. He grinned at Elvira.

Elvira and her parents grinned back.

Sturgis laid both hands on Gideon's shoulders. "Welcome to our family, son."

"Welcome, my beloved son-in-law." Mrs. Sturgis lifted Gideon's hand and kissed it.

PART THREE

NOVEMBER

1852

29

DUNDEE HORSE FARM AND PLANTATION
TENSAW RIVER, ALABAMA
NOVEMBER 5, 1852

Moonlight streamed through a window in Johnny Boy's stall as Joe leaned over it. There the Thoroughbred stood, one foreleg resting in a small hole on a bed of straw, his lips aquiver, his big brown eyes sad, his leg swathed in an India-rubber bandage over splints set on its sides and front. Joe's eyes misted. His Johnny Boy, so fiery and spirited. His heart cracked like a crystal goblet.

Marcus stroked Johnny Boy's neck and back to keep him as still as possible. Doctor Harold Harrison, veterinary surgeon, entered the stall. Johnny Boy injured his leg when Marcus did a turn on the track, Rattigan had said.

Rattigan eased up alongside Joe to watch the surgeon work.

Since he didn't see it happen, Joe withheld judgment. Marcus was his best jockey, and he loved Johnny Boy. Perhaps Marcus had been at fault. If he was, it wasn't intentional. Joe never reprimanded Marcus for it, though Rattigan most likely did. Joe never reprimanded any of his slaves until he had all the facts and found out who to blame. On some occasions, he'd reprimanded his overseers and even Rattigan. Like his father, fairness coursed his blood.

Doctor Harrison knelt at Johnny Boy's forelegs. With great care, he unwrapped the Thoroughbred's bandage and removed the splints.

Joe breathed easier. Johnny Boy's lower leg, coated in tar, no longer resembled the big log it was a few days ago. "Some swelling appears to have gone down."

Doctor Harrison reached inside his medical case for fresh bandages. "His injury hasn't subsided enough. Let me put a fresh bandage on him, then I'll bleed him again and physic him to get its inflammation down. I may try a boot on him later. Boots are good on the condition they're padded well. He can't move much yet, Marcus, not until all the inflammation subsides completely."

"I'll see he don't move much, Doctah." Marcus stroked Johnny Boy's neck. "Me an' him getting along jus' fine now."

The surgeon rummaged through his medical case. "What are you feeding him?"

"Mashes. Bran an' oats. Three, four times a day."

"Are you physicking him every day?"

"Yas sah. Jus' like you say."

Doctor Harrison gave Joe a side-glance. "You have a good jockey there."

"Marcus was, at one time, also an outstanding groom." Joe quieted. Doctor Harrison needed to concentrate on his work.

Once the veterinary surgeon finished his examination and put fresh bandages on Johnny Boy, Joe drew him aside. "When will he be ready to race, you think?"

"Fortunately for Johnny, his tendon wasn't sprung like we first feared. I'm sure his short pasterns helped in that regard."

"In what way?"

"Most of the horses I've doctored over the years, those who've injured their tendons, have long pasterns. Not true in all cases, but in more cases than those with short pasterns. I expect Johnny Boy will be ready to run in six or seven weeks, maybe, on the condition all goes well. I'll bring a boot for him Monday evening. Meanwhile, keep giving him his medicine. He should be able to start walking again in ten days thereabouts, but take it easy on him when you first start doing that."

"Thank you, Doctor."

The surgeon mounted his horse. "I will return some time Monday." He rode off.

Ten days, seven weeks. Joe's spirits plummeted. "No racing in Mobile this season for Johnny Boy, Mister Rattigan. We'll cancel his entry for next weekend. What other horse do you recommend?"

"Major Minor," Rattigan said.

"I agree. Fortunately, I have Pete entered to ride Applecart Monday. Tell Jakes to be ready to ride Major Minor next Saturday. I'll see he's entered in time for that race."

"Aye, sir. It's a pitiful way to begin the season." Rattigan hurried off.

Blame the crows. The sarcastic words struck Joe. "No, you superstitious Irishman. The crows have nothing to do with poor Johnny's problems." In April of next year, though, Johnny Boy would shine in New Orleans.

MOBILE, ALABAMA
NOVEMBER 5, 1852

Hannah closed her Bible. Outside her window, clattering vehicles, clamoring children and chattering adults passed her house. From the Mobile River, a steamboat's whistle blared. Yellow fever season had passed. Mobile, once again alive. Their street pulsed life.

Wealthy citizens back from their havens over Mobile Bay or up Spring Hill, planters from the state's fertile Black Belt region returned to conduct business and participate in the city's winter entertainments. Cotton bales by the thousands choked the city's wharves, destined for shipment across the Atlantic or up the eastern seaboard for Northern ports. Patrons packed restaurants, theaters and cafes. An overnight transformation, or so it seemed to Hannah, a sleepy city roused from its slumber.

Because of her mourning, she couldn't participate in parties. She hadn't worked in the emporium all month. It didn't seem right, working during her time of mourning. Luke had no choice. He had to work, to support her and himself. When the front door clicked behind Luke, she met him in their hall.

"What do you think, Sister?" Luke hung his sack coat across the back of an armchair. "Should we close for the day next week?"

"Father's 'Welcome Home' gathering? How can we have it so soon after Father's death? What would our friends think? Or say?"

"What would Father and Mother think if we didn't? You know how much they enjoyed hosting these parties for our returning friends."

"Banners and festivities?" Hannah shook her head. "No, Luke. It is not proper at this time."

"No festivities, no banners." He looked her in the eye. "A small gathering. Coffee, tea, perhaps cookies or other treats. Don't you think our parents would want us to continue their tradition, since they were the ones who started it?"

Hannah pondered her brother's words. Some folks would gossip about Luke's gathering being in poor taste. However, having a few friends over, their comfort and encouragement, well, she'd appreciate their company. "I guess it's a way we can honor Father's memory."

"Sure it is." Luke headed for the pantry. "Our parents loved people. Father wouldn't want us to stop having it. I'll allow it is a wonderful family tradition."

Hannah followed her brother. "All right, but let's keep it somber. I'll only invite a handful of friends to this one."

"Invite Sam too. Is supper on?"

"I have some chicken in the oven." She grabbed some thick rags off a pantry counter. Let folks gossip about them. Who cared? They were honoring their parents.

30

SPRING HILL, ALABAMA

NOVEMBER 6, 1852

The orchestra struck up a waltz. Gideon led Elvira onto the ballroom floor, her arm looped in his. The Spring Hill Jockey Club spared no expense with this building's construction, reserved for its meetings and special events. Built of red brick—long and spacious with a vaulted ceiling— its twelve ornate chandeliers arranged in two rows of six illuminated it. Colorfully-gowned ladies wore white evening gloves. Bedecked with diamonds and pearls and corals, rubies and emeralds, they glided up and down the ballroom floor in the arms of gentlemen wearing white gloves and black swallow-tailed suits.

Though people usually held balls in homes, this was a special event for a special club, one he hoped to join upon his marriage to Elvira.

Tonight, though, satisfied his eagerness, a chance to practice what he'd learned at Parker's Dance Academy. A chance to waltz. Elvira, nature's perfection, his fiancée, his princess wearing her pearl tiara, waltzing.

His heart drummed while they whirled and turned with the music of Strauss. Her skin so delicate, her perfume so fragrant, her smile so gentle, her laughter so delightful, whirling and gliding, whirling and gliding. He lifted his arm. Her hand in his, Elvira twirled beneath it. Her gold lioness brooch pinned at her gown's neck, her emerald earrings and her snake pendant outshone other ladies' jewelry. He laid his palm across her shoulder blade and around they turned, smiling at each other, his eyes transfixed by hers. Passion consumed her countenance as he led her around the room with other couples.

The music ceased. She curtsied. He bowed.

"Shall I escort you to your seat?" Gideon asked. "Or would you prefer to promenade?"

"Please escort me to my seat." She clasped his elbow .

He led her back to her chair between Lorelei and Mrs. Sturgis. "May I be of further service, my dear?"

"Not for now." Elvira rested her hands in her lap. "Thank you."

"And I thank you for the pleasure, truly." Gideon stepped up to Lorelei. "Mrs. Washburn, will you honor me with your hand for the next dance?"

Lorelei consulted her dance card and its list of dances. She smiled up at him, a sugary, dimpled smile. "I see you are next after the waltz. The dance is a polka."

Gideon's jaw went slack. "Why'd I sign on for that dance? I didn't notice it on your card."

"Did not notice?" Crimson flooded Lorelei's pale complexion. "You do not polka?"

"I fear I do not."

She thumped her dance card. "All right. Why did you sign your name beside that dance?"

"I-I don't know." Gideon applauded silently. Thanks to the Parkers' instruction, he understood ballroom etiquette, yet why should he dance with this barracuda? He'd only signed her card out of obligation to Owen because Owen was his friend and Elvira was her friend. The only way to get out of it, he figured, was to sign his name beside a dance he could not dance. He didn't care to have Lorelei in his arms. Couples were expected to smile while they danced—one of the rules of ballroom etiquette, so the Parkers had said. He was sick of Lorelei's silly simpering.

"All right. Answer me this. Why did you not look at the dance on my card before you signed it, for by the rules of etiquette I can't refuse it, but because of your inability to polka, I must breach that rule for tonight. You have, I believe, given me a good excuse to refuse."

Me too. "I ask your forgiveness, Mrs. Washburn."

"He's still learning, Lorelei," Elvira said apologetically.

"Of course."

Gideon bowed stiffly. "Again, please forgive my carelessness."

Lorelei huffed again. "I always have a good time. It's loads of fun sitting here ornamenting the ballroom floor."

Two gentlemen whom Gideon didn't know offered their arms to Elvira and her mother and led them onto the dance floor. The orchestra struck up a polka. Lorelei turned her attention to them. Gideon watched from behind her.

When the dance ended, the gentlemen escorted Elvira and Mrs. Sturgis back to their chairs. A bustle of activity and voices rumbled from the orchestra's stage.

"The musicians are taking a break," Mrs. Sturgis said. "We're having an intermission."

Gideon lifted his arms. "Mrs. Sturgis, would you and Miss Elvira care to join me in the supper-room?"

Mrs. Sturgis got to her feet. "Delighted."

Arm in arm, he led them into an adjacent room where earlier, a hearty supper had been served. Now desserts and liquor and tea and punch filled three long tables that five servants worked.

A servant cut Elvira and her mother a piece of chocolate cake. Gideon helped himself to an apple tart. At the sound of Owen's voice, Gideon excused himself to join his friend, engaged in conversation with Joe. "There's a rumor running round you can't get your alleged champion to run," Owen said.

"Johnny Boy's been giving me quite a lot of trouble of late." Joe peered past Owen. "I may need to race other horses this season. Pete's a good jockey. He handles Applecart quite well."

"My Comet can and will beat any of your horses, Quarles." Owen straightened. "He's well-trained and has lots of experience from the past season. I'd pit George against any of your jockeys any day. A pity your alleged champion can't compete."

"He will, in good time." Joe shoved Owen aside and strode off.

Gideon assumed Owen was taunting Joe in an effort to make him disclose information regarding Johnny Boy. However, Joe's blank expression might mean he was hiding something. Which horse should he wager on if they ever did race each other?

"Congratulations on your pending nuptials, Mister Deshler." Gloria Quarles spoke over his shoulder.

Gideon turned on his heel to face her. Accompanied by her father, a wealthy businessman, she was also in company with a lady Gideon didn't know.

Not much jewelry adorned Gloria— two small pearl earrings and a simple silver linked bracelet was all. A wreath of flowers crowned her head. Her modesty in such things as jewelry didn't surprise him. Much like Joe, she never flaunted her family's wealth.

"Thank you." He turned to move on.

"When will the wedding be?" her father asked.

Gideon halted and spoke over his shoulder. "We've not set a firm date yet, nor have I bought her a ring. I'll buy it come Tuesday."

"She'll want the most expensive ring in the store." Sarcasm soured Gloria's tone. "I declare, all that jewelry she's wearing tonight? It is most unbecoming for an unmarried lady. That should tell you what kind of girl she is."

"Still haven't forgiven me for what I did to Sam?" Gideon said.

Gloria looped her arm in her father's. "Sam's a changed man."

"Changed? How? Has he turned into a dog?"

"You'll observe it next time you see him. Know what I think, though? I think you and Elvira will make the perfect pair. I hear you both like snakes." Gloria and her father left, her lady friend with them.

For once, Gideon agreed with her. He and Elvira, they were, indeed, the perfect pair.

31

River Rose Horse Farm and Plantation
Three Mile Creek, Alabama
November 6, 1852

"You won't get away with it. Not this year." Owen's indignation propelled him on the hem of Lorelei's skirt and Zeller's heels. "You'll not do it, Lorelei. I said stop it."

Her party ended for her jockey club friends and all of them gone home, Lorelei was about to do something he expected ... and detested. Every year, she did the same cockeyed stupidity. Always after supper or after her party and always close to time when his horsemen were resting up for race season. The only consolation—no outsiders witnessed it, which fact relieved him of some embarrassment.

Upon her arrival at the stables, Lorelei cupped her hands round her mouth and shouted up at the horsemen's quarters on the stables' second level. "All of you. Get your bodies down here."

Jockeys, grooms and Tyce poked their heads out of their small windows.

"Coming," George said.

"Me too," another jockey said.

"Hurry up." Lorelei called to them again through cupped hands. "I'm tuckered out. I need to go to bed."

"Lorelei." Owen stood at her side. "Let them rest. They've all worked hard today."

"They'll rest when I'm finished." Lorelei counted each man who descended the creaking pine steps.

Owen raised his fist to smack her. "The way you're behaving is childish." He lowered his hand. He couldn't bring himself to do that, not to a lady, provided Lorelei could be called a lady. He could never hit a female, no matter who she was.

"A little thing I know might interest Mister Cadwallader." Lorelei withheld a glance.

Cowed by her threat, he fell silent. To this day, he regretted it when Lorelei caught him packing his cotton bales with hay.

Minutes later, George and the other horsemen assembled before them, shoulder to shoulder like a squad of soldiers. No fear did they evince, no emotion at all. They'd grown accustomed to his wife's strange drill. Tyce stepped forward.

Zeller, swinging his cat-o-nine-tails, swaggered behind Lorelei who halted at each jockey to comment. "Tuck your shirt in, Leander."

Leander did so.

"Where's your cap, Sandifer?"

The jockey looked straight ahead. "My room, Missus Washburn."

"Wear it next time I call you."

"Yas'm."

She simpered. "Where in tarnation are your shoes, George? Did a horse eat them?"

"Forgot 'em 'cause I rushed to get on down here," George said.

"Don't forget next time."

Five minutes later, after she'd inspected the horsemen, she and Zeller stepped back.

Seated on a stump, Owen fretted.

Lorelei's hands clapped her hips. She scanned their stoic faces. "I expect every one of you who will race this season, to race hard and win."

Zeller slapped his cat-o'-nine tails in his palm.

"Let any of you come in last or next to last," she indicated the overseer, "I'll have Mister Zeller whip the flesh off you when we get home. I prefer that every one of you win. Seeing how it's impossible to win all the time, let's say I'm being reasonable." She wagged her finger at them. "No last places or next to last places. Next time I call you all out, you all better be properly attired. Go to sleep."

She and Zeller left. Owen brought up the rear.

"Calling them out," Owen said, "and lecturing them and threatening them like you did. It's disgraceful. They're not in the Army."

"What's done is done." At a fork in the road, Lorelei wiggled her fingers goodbye to Zeller. "Work the hands like dogs tomorrow, will you?"

"Yes ma'am." Zeller continued on to his house.

Hot blood rushed to Owen's head. What a fool he'd been, marrying her. Gideon was right. She is a barracuda. Or maybe worse. A shark.

SPRING HILL RACE TRACK—1ST DAY OF RACING
SPRING HILL, ALABAMA
NOVEMBER 8, 1852

Gideon, buttoning his topcoat, hastened after Elvira and her mother. The ladies' bell-shaped poplin skirts rustled and swayed and parted a path through the Spring Hill Track's rambunctious crowd.

At numerous booths, proprietors hawked snacks and sandwiches, candies and cookies. Shouts and low conversation surrounded them, men making wagers and people of all social classes and colors in attendance. Horse racing broke down the city's social divide, if only for a few hours.

"Wait for me, my dear." Gideon caught a whiff of a passing man's beer. "I need a drink."

Elvira tweaked Gideon's cheek. "Oh, my sweet Gid. Let's not go to where all that riffraff is."

"Indeed not." Mrs. Sturgis turned her nose up at the crowds. "There's a saloon behind the Ladies' Stand for us respectable citizens."

Gideon smacked his forehead. "Right. I forgot."

"We'll go to the backside first." Elvira resumed walking. "I want to see the horses."

They proceeded along the perimeter of the oval track, past poles of various colors that stood at set distances along its inside rail. Gideon wondered what the poles were about, but he didn't care to ask Elvira or her mother even though they'd know the answer, but he would ask Elvira's father privately when he had a chance because as a matter of principle, he only consulted females on domestic concerns.

On their approach to the backside's walking ring where boys led their equine charges, sweet hay's aroma mingling with faint manure lingered. The clopping horses followed each other single file, heads bobbing and tails switching, their pace slow and easy.

"Horses are always exercised in the morning," Elvira said. "Races are in the afternoon."

"Wonderful animals." Gideon wedged between two other men to get closer. "Shiny coats."

Elvira, hiking her skirt and petticoats barely above her ankles, maneuvered between a cluster of men. "Yes, my love. Every horse out there in that ring. Lovely."

Men wielding pencils and pads studied the animals and jotted notes. Gamblers, Gideon figured, since he spotted Vanderporte chewing on his pencil while studying them.

Mystified walked in the vanguard. Gideon suspected Ned would be riding him.

A boy of about ten or eleven years led a gray horse with a white blaze on his face. Gideon pointed. "Who owns him?"

"Mister Quarles." Elvira clasped the ring fence's top rail. "His name's Applecart. He's pretty fast."

Gideon withdrew from the fence. "Are you two ladies ready to go? I've got a thirst hankering for a beer."

Elvira tweaked Gideon's cheek. "Let us be off."

Near the Ladies' Stand, Mrs. Sturgis called Gideon's attention to Joe on the track's far side engaged in conversation with another race official. Small red ribbons on their topcoats' lapels identified them as race stewards.

Inside the saloon, Elvira adjusted his bowtie, then patted his chest. "You go on now and have a good time. Mother and I need to refresh ourselves."

Gideon gave her a peck on her forehead. "I'll wait for you outside your refreshing room."

"I assure you, Mister Deshler, no harm will befall us." Mrs. Sturgis punctuated her words with a smile.

Therefore, Gideon purchased a beer. From a window, he viewed the track. The sun pounding its glass warmed him a little.

Two men beside him conversed. One was tall, broad-shouldered, with a Roman nose set between droopy gray eyes that reminded Gideon of a basset hound. Tawny muttonchops sloped down his cheeks and spread above his thin lips. His hair fell down behind his neck from beneath a stovepipe hat.

The other man, his light blond hair yielding to a receding hairline and about Gideon's five-foot six height, wore no hat.

"I'm wagering two hundred on Applecart," the blond man said.

"Oh, I suppose that may be a wise choice and all," the tall man said. "However, let me warn you of this particular, my dear Henley. My Lightning Bolt possesses the speed and endurance to defeat Applecart. If you'd welcome my friendly suggestion, I recommend you place your money down on him."

"Two hundred dollars, Mister Frederickson." Henley pulled his wallet from his inside coat pocket. "Care to match my wager?"

Frederickson reached for his wallet. "Of course. I did not bring my swift steed way down here from Virginia to lose."

Gideon eased up to them. "Excuse me. I couldn't help overhearing you."

The men stared at him.

Gideon continued. "I've just been informed by someone that Applecart is a plenty fast horse."

Henley looked Gideon up and down.

"The name's Gideon Deshler." He sipped his beer. A glance out the window. Jockeys were leaving the backside with their horses, heading for the weighing room.

"Are you making a wager?" Henley asked

The scent of vanilla perfume announced Elvira's return. Vanilla, his favorite flavor ice cream, her favorite perfume. Gideon took her hand. "Maybe some other time."

"Lightning's the bay horse," Frederickson called behind them. "My jockey's wearing the red and purple liveries."

Within minutes, Gideon sat in the Citizens' Stand apart from the ladies.

Club stewards kept busy. On the track's far side, Joe devoted his attention to its second turn. Three other stewards manned key points around the track. Owen rode his horse past and shooed two men up into the stands with a warning to stay clear. He shouted a greeting to Gideon before he rode on.

"Deshler."

The familiar voice called from two rows up. Gideon stood. "What is it, Vanderporte?"

"Next race, we'll make a wager." Vanderporte waved his wallet at him.

"Some other time, Blacklegs."

Ten minutes later, five jockeys dressed in various colored liveries rode their horses to the starting poles. Gideon recognized Frederickson's bay horse and Applecart. The competitors assumed their positions, the starter lowered the flag and the horses shot ahead. Applecart hung back. Lightning galloped toward the front of the pack. Animated spectators shouted and urged on their favorites.

Gideon dodged a flailing arm.

Around the second turn, Applecart and his jockey made their move. Though Lightning galloped ahead of the others, Applecart closed fast.

"Hurrah for Alabama," spectators roared when Applecart finished ahead of Lightning Bolt by a length.

Men paid up and collected their bets. According to the race schedule, the next heat took place in twenty minutes, a break for the horses to have their rub downs, so Owen had told him. He snatched Vanderporte's coat sleeve as he passed.

"Tell you what, Blacklegs." Gideon thumped his race schedule. "My friend's horse races with the three-year-olds. I'll lay five hundred down on him."

Vanderporte grinned. "To win?"

"To win."

"Five hundred it is." Vanderporte consulted his race schedule. "What's the horse's name?"

"Comet."

The gambler folded his schedule. "Washburn's horse, is it? I'll match your five hundred on Sturgis's Mystified, to win."

"If neither of our horses win, we'll pay up on whichever horse beats the other one."

Vanderporte shook Gideon's hand. "Suits me fine. Want a drink?"

"Later. Already had one beer today."

"I'll see you in twenty. Save me a seat." Vanderporte continued down the grandstand to the track.

Poker was one thing, horse racing another. Gideon saw no risk when it came to betting on horses for unlike cards, they couldn't be "marked."

Cole, coughing and clearing his throat, leaned back in his chair. Isham, seated opposite him, puffed his pipe. Smoke from his father's pipe and from other smokers in the track's saloon provoked his spasms of coughs. Tobacco smoke irritated him, the reason he never took up the habit. Only because Isham was his father did he tolerate it. He was grateful for all his father taught him about poker and horses.

"Lost two hundred on the first heat," Isham said.

"My research said Applecart was fast, but my oh my, I didn't think he'd beat Lightning Bolt." Cole coughed on his fist. "Lightning Bolt has a good reputation in Virginia and the Carolinas."

Isham lowered his pipe. "You wagered on Lightning Bolt too?"

Cole shrugged. "Today's purse?"

"Eight hundred dollars."

Cole whistled. "Look who's heading our direction."

Before he noticed Gideon's and Elvira's approach, Isham puffed his pipe twice.

Cole and his father stood, not for Gideon but for Elvira.

"Pshaw." Elvira laughed. "You gentlemen and your manners. Do sit down. Please."

Gideon pulled out a chair for her before the Tivingtons sat.

"Hey, Deshler," Cole said. "How much money you lost so far?"

"None." Gideon sat opposite him. "Haven't wagered yet. I plan on doing it when the three-year-olds run."

"On which horse?" Cole coughed between words.

"Comet. Vanderporte and I have a wager."

"Vanderporte?" Isham drew back, aghast. "You're crazy wagering with that scoundrel."

"He can't cheat playing the horses," Gideon said, "not like he does cards."

"I see your point." Amused by Gideon's ignorance, Cole shot his father a sidelong glance.

"Excuse us." Gideon scooted back his chair. "I see Lightning's owner is talking with one of my neighbors." He assisted Elvira out of her seat.

Once Gideon was gone, Cole whispered in his father's ear, "Deshler doesn't know much about this Thoroughbred business. Men can't cheat at playing the ponies. Ain't that a joke."

Isham lowered his pipe. "The less he knows, the better for us. We'll wait till Johnny Boy's ready to race Comet before we make our move."

Cole tossed his race schedule on the table. "With Johnny Boy's injured leg, we'll probably have to wait till April when they race in New Orleans."

"Be virtuous, son Cole." Isham aimed his pipe at him. "Patience is a virtue. Remember what I taught you."

Cole coughed, smiled. "You taught me well."

"How are you, Mister Jessup?" Gideon raised his hand in greeting. "How'd your horse do?"

Jackson Jessup set his beer on the bar counter. "Hasn't raced yet."

"I wish you success."

"Much appreciated, neighbor." Mister Jessup quaffed the rest of his drink. "Have you met Rufus Frederickson from Virginia?"

"Briefly."

"I'll leave you two to get more acquainted. I must attend to a few matters before my horse runs his heats." Mister Jessup headed out of the saloon.

"Now where'd your lovely wife wander off to?" Rufus peered past Gideon.

Gideon searched those milling about drinking and conversing. "Likely gone to refresh herself. She's not my wife yet. We're getting married in a few weeks."

"Then that deserves my hearty congratulations, my friend." Rufus clapped his shoulder. "She is quite the belle. What with those violet eyes of hers, why, if I weren't married, I might would have a chance at winning her gracious hand, but I do so love my wife."

Gideon was glad of that. The last thing he needed was competition for Elvira. "I'm sorry about your horse's loss."

"Banish those tears, my friend. Metaphorically speaking, naturally. There are yet other heats."

"Other heats?"

"Why, yes. Best three in five."

"Oh." Gideon wasn't sure he wanted to admit his ignorance of the sport. "This is the first time I've attended a race."

Rufus, at an easy gait, steered Gideon to a table. "Ah. My dear sir, it appears to me you lack sufficient knowledge regarding the sport. Would it be permissible for me to offer you a friendly suggestion?"

"Go right ahead."

"Don't make any wagers yet, not until you understand Thoroughbred racing and the qualities necessary for a good racehorse. My horse has four more heats to run. He may still be declared the winner, depending on how he does in the next heats."

Gideon liked this amiable fellow. "I'd be interested to learn more about this. How long you figure on staying?"

"In Mobile? Till its race season is over. I'll be participating in other races around the state, finish up in Florida then take a packet back to Virginia. My plan is to race my horses in New Orleans next year."

"Maybe we can talk more." Gideon glimpsed the clock on the wall. "Almost time for the next race. Good day to you, sir."

"And good day to you as well, friend Deshler."

Gideon found Elvira and Lorelei cornered against the wall at an exit, with Gloria wagging her finger in their fiery faces. As he shoved aside her finger, Gideon wedged between them. "What's all this fussing about?"

"Mister Deshler, my love." Elvira's soft words floated past him. "Mrs. Quarles insulted me,"

"I did not." Gloria scrunched her brows.

"You calling my friend a liar, Gloria?" Lorelei snapped.

"Calm down, calm down." Gideon retreated two steps. "Now then, y'all tell me what's happened. Mrs. Quarles, you first."

Gloria flipped up Lorelei's necklace.

Lorelei slapped her hand.

Gloria flipped up her necklace a second time.."See this. Mrs. Washburn is wearing emeralds today. I do declare, look how big her necklace is. I merely warned her about wearing it to these races. Some ruffian might abduct her and steal it."

"True, Mrs. Washburn?" Not that he cared about Lorelei. He was simply trying to smooth ruffled feathers and get Elvira out of this hen fight. Lorelei huffed. "It's a free country. I can wear whatever I like." She gripped Elvira's arm. "My closest friend, dear Miss Sturgis, gave it to me."

"More than I'd ever give you, Mrs. Quarles," Elvira said.

Gideon offered his arms to Elvira and Lorelei, which they both accepted.. Next time, Mrs. Quarles, I suggest you mind your own affairs."

"That's right," Elvira said. Hers and Lorelei's laughter exploded on their way back to their seats.

Gideon bit back his anger. He came here to watch the races, not settle a female fight.

Late afternoon, the races over, Ned and other jockeys bustled about the weighing room changing out of their liveries into their regular clothes. Outside its door, a race steward awaited them to take them to the vans where grooms were loading the horses.

Ned breathed easier than he had before his heats. He and Mystified finished a respectable second. George, astride Comet, finished first in all of their heats. Good thing Old Man Sturgis and Washburn were friends, else he'd suffer devil woman Elvira's whip tonight.

Already dressed, George approached. "A good race today, Ned."

Ned reached for his shirt. "Glad it was you who beat me. Means I ain't gonna get a whipping." He looked over at Pete, seated on a bench pulling on his shoes. "Good racing for you too, Pete. Sorry you only won the first heat."

"I'll win more tomorrow." Pete tied his shoes.

"Do you figure Mistah Joe's going to be angry with you?" Ned slid his arm through his shirt's left sleeve.

"Angry, disappointed." Pete snatched his cap off a peg. "But he ain't whipping me. Missus Gloria don't much cotton to that whip either. He'll just tell me to try harder tomorrow. Ain't no telling what Mistah Rattigan'll do. Know what I'll tell him?" Chuckling, he gestured at the ceiling. "Mistah Rattigan, sah, I jus' plain dunno what happened." He shook his head in an exaggerated manner. "I saw this crow when I was racing today." He shrugged. "Applecart just couldn't get the legs on him. It was that crow's fault."

Ned and George guffawed.

"Hoo-whee!" A cold hand touched Ned's spine.

Ned turned to a jockey whom he hadn't yet met. The man had a narrow face and a mustache straight as a ruled line above his upper lip.

"Looks like you got yourself a mess of welts and bruises." The jockey shook his head. "They must love whipping you." He extended his hand. "Call me Hezekiah. Hanks is my last name. I ride Lightning Bolt."

"Ned Jenkins." Ned shook Hezekiah's hand. "You the man from Virginia?"

"I ride for Mistah Rufus Frederickson. Pete and Applecart beat us. We came in third in the last heat."

"I'm sorry." Ned slid his arm into his shirt's right sleeve.

"For what? It's only a race." Hezekiah, yawning, stretched his arms high.

"You mean," Ned buttoned his shirt, "your massa don't get angry?"

"Mistah Frederickson?" Hezekiah tipped his cap back of his head. "Aw, no. Firstly, he ain't my massa. He freed me and all of his slaves years back. He pays me to ride. Secondly, he don't like slavery. And thirdly ...." He glanced around them. The other jockeys were heading out. He lowered his voice to a whisper. "... in the third place, I'll swear you all to secrecy so Mistah Frederickson don't get in trouble down here. He's a abolitionist."

Ned's heart practically leapt out of his chest. "A—"

"Shhh." Hezekiah's palm flew to Ned's mouth. "Don't tell nobody."

"We won't," George said.

An idea popped into Ned's head. An abolitionist? Could it be, possibly, a chance for him and Becky to finally escape the Sturgises? He'd ask Hezekiah for a chance to meet him, but he'd ask him in private. The fewer folks aware of his plan, the better. Also, the less chance it'd have of the wrong folks finding out. Freedom. He could smell it.

32

NOVEMBER 9, 1852

Fifteen minutes before the Henshaw Emporium's closing time, Gideon steered Elvira into it while her parents awaited them in their carriage. Mister Sturgis didn't have a horse entered for this second day's racing, but he had attended a few events there earlier.

Gideon gripped the derringer he carried in his trousers waistband. If Luke refused to sell him an engagement ring, he had something else in mind. He and Elvira headed for the watch display where Luke counted the day's earnings.

"Farewell till tomorrow, Mister Rhodes," Luke said, not looking up from his counting.

Mister Rhodes waved bye as Gideon and Elvira passed him.

"I'm cutting out of here too." This from an employee Gideon hadn't seen before, a young man who looked close to Luke's age.

"Visiting your brother tonight, Daniel?" Luke asked him.

"Where else?" Daniel said.

"Our lady customers seem to like you." Luke put the cash in the cash drawer and locked it.

Daniel, his arms spread wide, kept a straight face. "Ladies always cling to me." He departed, plopping his tweed cap on his narrow head.

"Luke, my good man." Gideon slapped his hand on the counter. "This pretty little lady and I are engaged."

Elvira dragged Gideon to the ring case. "I want the most expensive engagement ring you have, Luke Henshaw. A 15-karat gold snake ring with garnets."

Luke's eyes shot daggers at them.

"Aren't you going to congratulate us?" Gideon lifted his chin.

"No," Luke said. "And I'm not making you a ring, nor will I have someone else make it, nor will I sell you a display. We're closed. Do not come back tomorrow."

Elvira's dark demeanor sparked menace. She fingered a row of necklaces hanging on a table rack. "You'd best sell me a ring, Luke Henshaw, else—"

"To sell you a ring means I condone my friend Gideon's marriage." Luke thrust back his shoulders. "I do not condone your marriage. You are an evil woman, Elvira Sturgis."

Gideon reached for his derringer.

Her visage glacial, Elvira wound one of the rack's pearl necklaces around her forefinger. "A child of the devil?"

"Yes."

"Retract that insult, Luke." Gideon's veins pulsed.

"Why?" Luke said. "She is a child of the devil. I spoke the truth."

Gideon aimed his derringer at Luke's stomach. "Either sell me a ring, or die."

Luke folded his arms.

Gideon cocked his derringer, squeezed its trigger.

Gideon and Elvira strolled the banquette, on their way to a theater playing *Macbeth*. Her parents brought up the rear.

Although he'd read *MacBeth* in school, he'd never seen it performed, but Elvira had. It wasn't because his parents disapproved of theater-going. They didn't, depending on the play. They just didn't much care for Shakespeare.

His Harriet enjoyed concerts more than theaters, played the flute and sang in their church choir. Memories of her standing in the parlor, a sheet of music on her wooden stand, her flute touching her lips, music spreading warmth and beauty throughout their house. He squashed this memory.

His thoughts shifted to Luke. "Henshaw's got his head screwed on backwards. My derringer didn't even scare him. Do you suppose he'll report me for carrying a concealed weapon?"

"If the ninny does, my father will defend you in court," Elvira said. "He's a great lawyer."

"That I know, dear Elvira. Before we met, I read many articles about him and his cases in the newspapers."

Elvira slipped her arm from around his. "From now on, let's not shop at Henshaw's. I like the store where we purchased my ring far better."

"Let's hope it's made in a timely manner. I've washed my hands from those Henshaws."

"Not my kind of people," Elvira said.

"Agreed."

They turned a corner. Gideon opened the theater door for her. He breathed a sigh of relief. Thanks to Luke's refusal to sell him a ring, he had the perfect excuse to quit visiting him. Killing him would've meant getting hung for the crime. It wasn't worth it. His derringer wasn't loaded, nor did Luke flinch when he squeezed the trigger. Strange. *Uh-oh.* One problem— that fanatic Stephen Hamilton, his next door neighbor. He'd avoid him like yellow fever.

Soon after Gideon and Elvira took their seats the curtain opened for Act One. "Here we go, Lady Macbeth," Gideon said in a low voice.

Elvira wriggled, giggled.

Small gaslights ringing the stage floor flickered on. The dark blue curtains drew open. A sound of thunder echoed from somewhere behind the stage. The story's three witches made an entrance. The play began.

MOBILE, ALABAMA
NOVEMBER 12, 1852

Gideon twisted in his office chair, tapped his foot, drummed his fingers on his lap. His glances constantly ricocheted from Mister Cadwallader to a window.

His crimson cheeks quivering, his scowl lines fierce enough to intimidate a lion, Mister Cadwallader paced with strides so long they seemed to devour the floor.

Gideon fidgeted, thumped specks of dust off his coat sleeve. *Wow!* He'd never seen his employer this angry, not since last cotton season. Quitting time fast approached. He'd promised Elvira he'd pick her up and take her to dinner. Because of his work, he'd been unable to attend more races with her. Why wouldn't Mister Cadwallader close this dang business like so many other places did during race season? It only lasted one week. Thanks to him, he couldn't attend it with Elvira and her mother. Why did he have to sit here and suffer his employer's wrath? He might be watching the Thoroughbreds run. With a goddess on his arm.

"Gentlemen." Mister Cadwallader sailed a folded letter across the middle of the long table. "Do y'all know who sent me this?"

Everyone, including Gideon, shook their heads nervously.

"An important client over in Scotland. Or might I suggest, a former important client. A major firm over there. I received this letter an hour ago at the post office. That client's been a reliable customer ever since my father was alive. Do y'all know what it has done? It has severed our business relationship. That's what it's done."

Gideon and the other factors stirred.

His pacing stopped at an open window. A steamboat whistle rent the air. Odors from the fish market on the river wafted around them.

"They found lots of bad cotton on our last shipment," Mister Cadwallader continued. "Inferior grade cotton packed inside a layer of higher-grade cotton. Other bales, packed with hay." He whirled on them. "I am an honest businessman, gentlemen. I do not, will not, tolerate dishonesty."

"I won't tolerate it either," the Yankee John Eason said.

Mister Cadwallader pounded his desk twice. "If we get a reputation for turning a blind eye to such fraud, not only will Cadwallader and Company go out of business, you gentlemen will likewise lose your employment. All of you, from this minute forward, you must and will do a more thorough inspection of our clients' cotton before shipment. If you discover any fraudulent bales, you will inform me, and the offender will be facing a very serious lawsuit."

"Yes sir," everyone except Gideon said.

Mister Cadwallader lifted his gray brows at Gideon.

Gideon nodded quickly. "Yessir. I'll be more thorough in my inspections." Soon as he spoke, he knew he'd lied. He'd never inspected Owen's cotton. He'd always taken his word that he was honest because they were friends.

"Whoever among you was negligent," Mister Cadwallader scanned their faces, "it will be my sad duty to discharge you. Go home. Sleep well tonight, for I will not, not with this blemish on our firm's record and on my conscience."

On his way to pick up Elvira at her father's law office, Gideon pondered his employer's words. The bad shipment, surely, must be Owen's. Should he confront him about it at the risk of losing their friendship? Maybe, even, at the risk of losing Elvira since she and Lorelei were friends? *Nah.* He'd gotten away with helping Elvira and her mother steal that cameo from the emporium. He'd get away with this lie even easier.

Moonlight, and streetlamps aglow, illuminated the dark evening enveloping the Mobile River's idle wharfs. Dodging stacks of lumber and crates and barrels, Sam quickened his steps past brick warehouses and cotton presses. His nose battled the stench. Three rats skittered ahead, chased by a mangy gray cat.

His steamboat had encountered several shoals on the way down from his plantation, the reason for his tardy arrival. Too late for the

Henshaws' get together. His invitation stated it was supposed to have been tonight. He hoped they'd understand.

A pinprick of pain stabbed his chest, courtesy of Gideon's souvenir from their duel months back. He welcomed it, a reminder to never engage in such folly again.

A rangy figure swaggered out of the shadows into his path.

"Watch where you're going." The gruff voice wielded a sharp edge.

Sam opened his mouth to spout back. He didn't. For some reason, sarcasm didn't set right with him anymore. "I'm sorry."

"Saying 'sorry' to a black man?" The man spread his legs wide and planted his fists on his hips.

"I'm sorry about lots of things." Sam stepped past him.

"If you're as sorry as you say, you'll buy me a beer from that saloon up that away."

Sam studied the small saloon a block up a street. Liquor was illegal for people such as this man yet here he was, trying to make him break the law. Even if it was legal, he'd lost his taste for it and wouldn't buy this man one.

The man raised his fist. "You buying it for me?"

"No."

"You ain't doing what Cougar Jed says?"

"That's right. I ain't."

Cougar Jed's fists flew, knocked Sam to the ground. Sam's jaw and chest felt like he'd been slammed by a two by four. Sam scrambled to his feet and kicked his hat aside. He'd teach Jed a lesson.

Jed's fists lifted to strike him again.

His hands balled, Sam hesitated. "I won't fight you." He opened his fists at his sides. "I won't buy you any liquor either."

"Scared?"

"Of you? A few weeks ago, I might've knocked you unconscious. Tonight, however, I choose not to inflict bodily harm on your person."

Jed threw a punch.

Sam dodged it and stepped back. "I don't want to hurt you."

"I think you got lots of yellow down your back."

"Go ahead. Hit me. I'll not hit back." Sam kept his hands at his sides and hoped he didn't get hit in the chest again.

Fortunately, Jed stormed off.

Stupid . . . Sam caught himself. Name-calling and insults, he needed to quit saying and thinking such things about people.

"Hurrah!" Luke drove his clattering wagon toward him from a nearby street. "That took some courage, Sam."

Sam snatched his hat off the ground. "The old Sam could've handled him easy as pie."

"I've seen Jed before. He's free and has a vicious reputation, so I've heard."

"Is it permissible for me to visit Hannah at this late hour?"

"She'll be delighted. She was worried about you when you failed to show up for our little 'welcome home' gathering. As was I, which is why I came here after our friends left to see whether your boat had arrived."

Sam stepped to the other side of Luke's wagon. One of the horses in its two-horse team snorted. "My boat encountered some difficulties on the way down."

Luke patted the wagon bench. "Hop aboard. I'll drive you back to our house."

Sam climbed up beside Luke.

33

On the Spring Hill Race Track's backside, at the far end of the stables where grooms loaded horses into vans for the ride home, Ned breathed a word of thanks. The race season was over. He'd not done badly. The worst he'd finished was third but not on Mystified. On another horse. Old Man ought to be pleased.

"I enjoyed meeting you." Swinging his arms lazily, Hezekiah sauntered to him from the paddock. "Maybe we'll race again soon."

"I'm sho'nuff glad we met." Ned glanced every direction, lowered his voice. "My girl, Becky, also belongs to Old Man Sturgis."

"He's having a chat with your massa." Hezekiah indicated the dirt lane separating the row of stables.

Having himself a chat? It seemed to Ned that Mister Rufus Frederickson was doing most of the talking and gesturing while Old Man Sturgis simply stared at him.

"I'll make mention of her when me and Mistah Rufus are alone."

"Thank you, Hezekiah. You a good friend."

Sturgis weaved around busy grooms on his way to them. Slow and easy, Rufus followed.

"Mister Frederickson enjoyed your riding," Sturgis said. "He wants to purchase you."

"He's a good jockey, Edward." With a quirt, Rufus lifted Ned's chin. "Yessir, I'd say the boy's a mighty good jockey."

For a moment, Mister Frederickson's condescending tone rankled Ned, till Hezekiah's nudge calmed him. Maybe he was putting on an act for the old man's benefit since the old man didn't know his abolitionist views.

"You still won't sell him, Edward?" Rufus held his quirt at his side.

"No, but I do have some horses I'm willing to consider selling. Call on me at my stables on the Eastern Shore sometime and look them over. Perhaps you'll find one or two you'd care to purchase." Sturgis handed him his card. "My address is on it. You have my official invite."

"A mighty good plan that sets well with me. I've entered Lightning Bolt in a race up near Tuscaloosa for next weekend. Once he's finished there, I go to Florida. Perhaps, with your permission naturally, I can return when I'm done racing in these parts." Rufus turned on his heel. "Come along, Hezekiah. Time's a-wasting. Let's get our limbs to moving."

On their way back down the path, Hezekiah glanced over his shoulder. Mister Frederickson did the same thing. They winked at Ned before they rounded a corner for their van.

Robert hastened to them. "All the horses done loaded up and ready, Massa. And the missuses already on their way home."

"Let's get out of here," Sturgis said.

RIVER ROSE HORSE FARM AND PLANTATION
THREE MILE CREEK, ALABAMA
NOVEMBER 14, 1852

Tyce bolted through Owen's door and startled him out of his reading. "Sah, sah, she's doing it, sah."

Owen rocketed to his feet. "The barracuda?"

"Her and Zeller."

Owen dropped his newspaper. "Let's go."

They sprang into their saddles and galloped off, to the field hands' cabins.

Owen seethed so hot, had he been a steamer's boiler he would've exploded. It was high time Lorelei ended her foolishness. Her domineering ways had exhausted him to a frazzle. To get his sanity back, he needed peace and quiet in his life.

Reluctantly, he'd decided only one thing would regain his sane existence. Not a pleasant way, and he may suffer for it, but after agonizing over his decision in recent days, he knew the time had come. Time to escape this miserable marriage, the biggest mistake of his life. If she was doing what he suspected, it'd end tonight.

He and Tyce drew rein, dismounted. Every slave, including his servants and horsemen, were assembled around a whipping post. Didn't that woman know the jockeys performed better on the track when they weren't whipped?

"Make way!" Owen waded through the crowd.

George and Sandifer, stripped to their waists, had their hands screwed in stocks and their ankles bound by strong cords. Blood crisscrossed their backs and streaked their trousers—gashes, gaping wounds, flayed flesh. The previous day, they'd finished last in their heats, but neither rode Comet. On the way home after the last race, he'd told Lorelei not to whip them because they'd done nothing wrong, that winning and losing were all part of the sport. She'd sworn to him she wouldn't do it. She'd lied.

Beneath two brilliant torchlights illuminating her heartless visage, Lorelei stood while her steady hand covered her yawns.

Zeller whirled his cat-o-nine-tails high then slashed skin off the jockeys' backs.

George screamed. Sandifer wailed.

"Stop." Owen boomed like a cannon shot.

Zeller lowered his whip. Lorelei yawned louder.

"Lorelei, this whipping of my horsemen ends tonight." Owen stomped to Zeller. "Zeller, put your whip away. Don't whip any slaves unless you have good reason. I don't care what Lorelei says."

"Continue." Lorelei flicked her hand at Zeller. "Fifteen more lashes. Fillet 'em like fish."

"No!" Owen screamed. "You, Wife, will go back home, go to your bedroom, close its door and change into your nightgown. Tomorrow, you will return either to your parents or your so-kind brother Bob. I never want to see your face again."

"Are you confident that's wise?" Lorelei kept her tone cool.

"I'm telling Mister Cadwallader that I've falsely packed my cotton bales. A lawsuit, my dear, may harm me. I've finally reconciled myself to that fact. I'm seriously considering a divorce."

Lorelei huffed. "On what grounds?"

"Insanity." Owen aimed his finger at her. "Yours."

"How dare you talk to me that way. Daddy'll disinherit you. You'll never get his horse farm up in the Valley if you kick me out of the house. You don't care about that?"

"I care about peace of mind. I no longer care about you."

Lorelei flushed, mounted her horse and galloped home.

The divorce would, hopefully, come later, Owen told himself. For now, he just wanted her out of his life. He turned to his trainer. "Tyce, untie their ankles and unscrew their stocks."

Tyce proceeded to do so.

"Also, be sure to rub some tallow on their wounds."

"I'll do that, Massa Owen." Tyce unscrewed the stocks and lifted them off George's and Sandifer's hands. The bloodied jockeys collapsed to the ground.

Zeller blinked, his neck muscles twitched, a clear indication to Owen that the overseer feared Owen's wrath would thunderclap him next.

"From now on, Zeller, you will obey my orders." Owen pointed at himself. "My crazy wife will be moved out by tomorrow afternoon."

Zeller nodded.

"Tyce, help George and Sandifer back to their rooms after you apply the tallow. Zeller, you lend a hand as well."

"Whatever you say, sir."

"As it should be." On the way back to his house, Owen harbored dread and triumph. Dread, at what might happen when he confessed his crimes to Mister Cadwallader and triumph for finally discarding Lorelei.

Owen halted inside his house. Still clothed in her evening attire, Lorelei sat on a piano bench facing him from her parlor, her lower lip thrust out like a pout.

"I told you to put on your nightgown and go to bed." Arctic coldness laced his words.

"Not until you promise me you'll not get a divorce," Lorelei said. Owen's fury mounted.

"I told you Daddy will write you out of his will and leave Valley Stables to Bob. Two thousand acres you'll forfeit."

"Bob'll inherit all of your family's horse farms then, won't he? Eh? The one he'll get after your father dies, the one your father left me, plus the one he at this moment owns. He'll become a big Alabama turfman, won't he?"

Lorelei tapped two low notes on the piano. "I think you understand."

Owen spat. "He can have those farms. Let your dull brother Bob challenge River Rose's rising dominance in this state. I throw down my gauntlet to him as a challenge."

"Mister Cadwallader may sue you."

"I'll throw myself on his mercy. Go to bed."

Lorelei fell on him, clutched his arms, boohooed on his shoulder.

Owen peeled her fingers off him. "I'm no longer deceived by your little games."

Lorelei straightened and hissed. "Go ahead. You're supposed to be Mister Deshler's best man next week and I, Elvira's matron of honor. Look sort of strange, wouldn't you think, us being separated and also in their wedding."

"I can handle that. Can you?"

"Can you handle what will happen when you confess your crime to Mister Cadwallader tomorrow? Can you risk getting sued and causing your best friend to possibly lose his job? Will you enjoy not inheriting one of the finest horse farms in the state? Will River Rose go downhill after I get Comet back?"

Owen stirred. Gideon might indeed get discharged if Cadwallader discovered he'd never inspected his cotton, a matter he hadn't considered. She could forget about getting Comet in any divorce settlement, though. Although he'd bought that fine horse for her, he intended on keeping the animal. It was his money that purchased him, after all. Not hers.

Triumph shone in Lorelei's face.

The barracuda. "Go to sleep, woman. It's late."

As he retired to his own bedroom, he pondered what might happen to Gideon. But living with Lorelei … How much more of her misery could he tolerate? Give up inheriting some of the best horse land in the Tennessee Valley? Was separation, or possibly divorce, worth losing it? Although he'd eagerly anticipated inheriting it, and he was ambitious, he hadn't been eager for Mister Glenville to die. He wasn't that cold-hearted.

He clicked shut his bedroom door, lit an oil lamp and sat at his desk. He must reach a decision before sunup. A wonderful horse farm in the Tennessee Valley or divorce from a crazy woman? The horse farm would be a tremendous addition to his holdings and the equine empire he'd envisioned. He rested his head in his upraised hands. A headache came on fast.

River Rose Horse Farm and Plantation
Three Mile Creek, Alabama
November 15, 1852

Owen pulled on his sack coat and left his bedroom. In the dining room below, his servants set out a breakfast of scrambled eggs, ham and cathead biscuits.

"Where will you be off to today, my love?" Lorelei cradled her coffee beside a wine cart.

Owen pulled out a chair for himself. "I have to discuss a business matter with Zeller."

Lorelei's doe-eyes pleaded. "You won't pull my chair out for me?"

Owen sat and worked on his breakfast fast. One item at a time he ate, his usual habit, unlike many folks who ate a bite of this and a bite of that, mixing up their meal. The eggs he gobbled down first, followed by his ham and finally his biscuit, which he chased with coffee.

Lorelei set her coffee mug beside her food. "I'm sorry for my recent behavior and the difficult times I've given you." Her lower lip protruded. "Please forgive me. It will never happen again."

"I'll take it under consideration." Owen grabbed his hat and left. He had no more conscience regarding her. She could jump into Mobile Bay and drown, for all he cared. Maybe crabs would eat her for lunch. No. She'd likely give them indigestion.

Nor did he visit his cotton fields or Zeller. Because she'd lied to him about not whipping his jockeys, he lied to her today. He went to Mobile. Either he'd suffer her combativeness for the rest of his days, or he'd betray his best friend Gideon. At this point, Gideon's fate was of no concern. His own happiness took precedence over his friend's, over everyone's.

Gideon was nowhere in sight in Mister Cadwallader's office. Several factors, though, seemed hard at work, bent over their desks engaged in correspondence while another one discussed a matter with a man Owen assumed was a client. Conversation from another room drew him into it, where Mister Cadwallader and a man he didn't recognize were examining a large cotton sample spread out on a table.

Mister Cadwallader looked up from the sample. "Hello to you, Owen. Mister Deshler's not in right now. Gone to our warehouses. May I be of service?"

Owen took several short breaths and tugged at his gloves. "I've a personal matter to discuss with you, sir." Now that he'd leapt into his confession, he breathed easier.

"We'll resume our business in a few minutes, Mister Pine."

The man Owen didn't recognize, Mister Pine, departed.

"Jim Pine's a cotton broker." Mister Cadwallader indicated an armchair. "Have a seat. What's on your mind?"

Though Owen backed toward it, he didn't sit. He wrung his hands, which sweated inside his gloves. "I don't exactly know how to tell you this." He drew a deep breath. "Dang it all. I've been packing my cotton bales with hay and inferior grade cotton."

Mister Cadwallader recoiled. "Sooo, you're the one, are you? The reason I lost my client in Scotland? The one giving my firm a bad name?"

Owen dropped into the chair and hung his head. "Go ahead. Sue me. Anything's better than living with Lorelei."

"Is Mister Deshler aware of your dishonesty?"

"No sir. I reckon he trusted I was honest since we're friends."

Mister Cadwallader softened. "You came clean, Owen. Because you came clean on your own and confessed your wrongdoing, I won't sue you. Promise me you won't falsely pack your bales anymore."

"I give you my word."

The old cotton factor rested a reassuring hand on his shoulder. "I believe you."

Like a freshening breeze, freedom blew through Owen when he left. Confessing his wrongdoing unlocked Lorelei's shackles. "I don't care where you go, Lorelei, so long as you're out of my life. I recommend a deserted island somewhere. Try living with cannibals."

Back on the street, he hastened to the livery for his horse. He couldn't wait to evict Lorelei. What about her brother, Bob Glenville? He'd better find a way to deal with him provided he came down to "defend her honor." Should he shoot him? In a duel? Not a duel of smoking muzzles. Fisticuffs, unless he could determine a way to avoid him while not appearing a coward. Her father's horse farm? A major loss, but she and her barracuda ways left him without a choice.

When Gideon returned to his firm's office, his employer's steely gaze followed him to his desk.

"Mister Deshler."

Gideon's head snapped Mister Cadwallader's direction.

His employer arose from his squeaky swivel chair at the far end of the room. "Let's go. The hall."

The other factors cast curious glances at them.

Gideon's knees knocked. What had he done wrong? Whenever one of them committed an error, Mister Cadwallader almost always called him into the hallway for a private reprimand.

With his back against the hallway's wall, his employer's eyes bore into him like a carpenter's drill. "Do you inspect all of your clients' bales like I told you?"

"Yes sir." Gideon steadied his voice.

"And Mister Washburn's?"

"Owen Washburn? Yes sir. Of course."

"You will collect all of your personal items and leave. I no longer require, or desire, your services."

"But—but—"

"Your friend Owen came here a few hours ago and confessed his wrongdoing. I gave you a chance to do the same. You didn't confess to anything. Because he confessed voluntarily, I'm not suing him." Mister Cadwallader jerked Gideon into his angry face. "However, young man, you lied to me. I now know, full well, you were negligent regarding your responsibilities. You have not followed a road that would please your father. You have also disappointed me. You no longer work for me, or this firm."

Gideon stammered.

"I'll file the necessary papers for your discharge and have them delivered to you."

Gideon darted into the office, gathered his hat and topcoat, his pen and some paper. On the street, he dodged pedestrians and buggies and wagons and stray animals. *Owen, you traitor. Thanks to you, my reputation's ruined.*

34

NOVEMBER 15, 1852

Elvira, puffed up with self-admiration, did a slow spin in front of her bedroom's full-length standing mirror. Why, mercy! Didn't she look enchanting! Mrs. Simpson did a marvelous job, making her this white cashmere wedding gown. It fit perfectly, tight at her waist, flaring over her six petticoats. A cameo was centered at her bodice's neckline, a white satin ribbon circled her white gloves on each wrist.

She imagined herself entering the parlor bedecked with glittering jewelry, Gid standing at the mahogany breakfront anticipating her entrance, exuding adoration.

"Beautiful, Elvira. Simply beautiful." Her mother stroked one of Elvira's sleeves. "Mister Deshler will be absolutely beside himself when he sees you in this."

Elvira clasped her cameo. "You really think so, Mother?"

"Indeed. You'll be his princess."

I'll be his goddess. Elvira did another slow spin in the mirror. She looked so pure in this dress. *Why, mercy! I am a goddess!*

She'd only mailed a few invitations—to two aunts and two uncles, three favorite cousins who lived in Mississippi and four friends from the jockey club with Lorelei her matron of honor. The special event would be held here this Saturday, performed by a judge. At last, she'd snared her wealthy man. She couldn't wait to get ahold of his money. He'd grant her every wish. Mister Gideon Deshler, a foolish man she could manipulate till her heart's content. "I love it."

"And I'm very happy for you." Her mother put on her spectacles. "I'm in the garden crocheting. Change out of your dress and join me. I'll have Elkins bring us some coffee."

"I prefer just plain water from our spring. I'm not in the mood for coffee today. Send Becky to help me out of these clothes."

"I'll see to it, dear."

MOBILE, ALABAMA

NOVEMBER 15, 1852

Thaddeus ducked the baseball sailing past his shoulder. "Doggone you, Isaac. Quit showing off."

Isaac chuckled. "You're s'pposed to catch the ball, Thaddeus. Not dodge it."

"Not when you throw it so fast. We all know how fast you can throw a ball. No need to keep proving it." Thaddeus picked it up. "If we could ever get up a game, I'd want you on my team."

"A sure thing we'd win with my pitching arm."

Thaddeus tossed the ball back to him with a gentle throw. Isaac tossed it back.

"No more baseball." Gideon plodded through his gate. "Why aren't y'all working?"

"We're on our lunch break." Thaddeus handed Isaac the ball. Mister Gideon knew he and Isaac always pitched baseball on their lunch breaks. Something must be troubling him.

Gideon grumbled words so low Thaddeus didn't understand them. "Where's my wine?" Gideon barked as he stepped through his doorway. "I need my wine. Give it to me."

Thaddeus and Isaac hastened behind him.

"I'll get it." Katie spoke from the hallway.

"Everyone, get in this room, *after* I drink my wine." Gideon slouched in a parlor chair.

Within minutes, Gideon gathered his servants around him. "Mister Cadwallader just discharged me." His fists hammered his knees.

Thaddeus gasped. "He what? For what reason?"

"Look for a job somewhere else. I can no longer afford to pay you."

"Mister Deshler," Isaac said. "We'll work for less money. None of us mind doing it."

Gideon tossed his empty wine bottle onto the carpet and stormed out, slamming the door behind him so hard, windows rattled.

"Oh, what will we do, Thad?" Katie said.

"We'll quit working for him?" Isaac scooped up the wine bottle.

"No." Thaddeus spoke decisively. "He's not in the poor house. He still has money from Selah. He's so upset right now he's forgotten it."

RIVER ROSE HORSE FARM AND PLANTATION
THREE MILE CREEK, ALABAMA
NOVEMBER 15, 1852

Gideon galloped his lathered horse up the road to Owen's house. Owen would answer for it, he would, breaking their trusted friendship by confessing to Mister Cadwallader how he'd falsely packed his cotton bales. Because of that, he'd lost his employment. Birds scattered from the swift horse. Gideon reined him in at the foot of Owen's outside staircase, swung down from his saddle. Through cupped hands, he bellowed. "Washburn! Get your sorry hide down here."

Owen emerged from a room on his home's upper floor. He lifted his hands, palms out. "I'm sorry, Gideon. It was either confessing the truth to your employer or living with Barracuda Lady till my dying day. I paid a price too. Lost a great horse farm I was supposed to inherit." Owen sauntered down the gallery's staircase.

"You betrayed my trust. I've lost my job, my reputation." Gideon punched air.

"Lorelei's gone." Owen lowered Gideon's fist.

"Gone? You mean … for good?"

"Two hours ago. She'd discovered my packing the bales and kept holding it over my head, so I finally confessed it to Mister Cadwallader. He might have sued me, but I was so desperate to get out from under her thumb I took the chance. It was either peace of mind and losing her father's two thousand acres in the Tennessee Valley or winding up in an asylum."

"Well done. Where'd the barracuda swim off to?"

"Don't know, don't care. Come on and get your body inside. We can enjoy a decent conversation without her interference. Do you still want me to be your best man?"

"Naturally, but what about Lorelei being Elvira's matron of honor?"

"Elvira's problem. Reckon you'll be moving to Selah after your wedding."

"Reckon I will." Eager to learn more about Owen and Lorelei's separation, Gideon joined his friend in the house. About time Owen stood up to her.

Spring Hill, Alabama
November 15, 1852

"Give it here, you little thief." Elvira swooped on Becky, seated at her dressing table wearing her wedding veil.

Calmly, Becky tilted her head left and right and admired herself in its small mirror.

The little imbecile wore the red lipstick she'd made for her special wedding day. Elvira snatched the veil off Becky's head.

"I was thinking 'bout what a wedding would be like," Becky said. "Me and Ned getting married one day."

"Sure you are. Let's go. To the attic."

Becky shot to her feet, whirled on her. "I ain't going to it this time, *Devil Woman*."

Elvira shrieked so loud everyone in the house could've heard it, clear down to the wine cellar, except her parents were visiting a friend up the road for the evening. And no servant, except stupid Becky, dared enter her bedroom without her permission.

Elvira modulated her voice—calm, fatal. "Remember what I told you a few months ago? That the next time you called me Devil Woman, you remember what I said? That I'd kill you?"

Becky retreated to a flickering candelabrum. "Dying's better'n living with the likes of you."

Elvira snatched her whip from out of the crimson sash circling her waist and cracked it over Becky's head. Becky fled downstairs. Free of her layers of petticoats save one, Elvira gave pursuit. Her father's revolvers. They were in his office. She lit an oil lamp and pulled one of them out of its desk drawer, fumbled bullets out of the same drawer. One bullet. That's all she needed.

"Elvira. Elvira."

Lorelei's cry yanked her to a window. She threw it open when Lorelei met her there.

"Owen," Lorelei said. "He kicked me out of our house. We must talk."

"Meet me in the garden. Join you in a minute." Elvira shut the window, secured its latch, loaded the revolver, loosed another blood-curdling curse. What else could go wrong? Becky stealing her veil, and now her matron of honor kicked out by Mister Deshler's best man.

She moved swiftly. Past candlelit sconces, she practically flew. Elkins and other servants gaped at her fury. "Elkins, search the pantry and dining room. If you find Becky and don't send her to me, you're dead too."

Elkins hurried off.

"The rest of you, spread out and search for her."

The other servants scattered.

Elvira rushed through the parlor and music room. Her skirt swept a table as she searched behind the settee and swore. Where was that imbecile? She stood at the fireplace. Logs popped. Flames danced. The servants' quarters? Of course. That's where the pest went.

On her hurry to the hall, her elbow knocked over a candelabrum. She sniffed. *Smoke?* She glanced down. "The candelabrum! I'm on fire!" She hit the floor to snuff out the flames, knocked over the fireplace's screen. Flares shot out, singed her bare shoulders. She screamed, rolled to smother them, which ignited the carpet as her legs upended a small table. Another lit candelabrum fell on her, sizzling her back like a branding iron, like a fiend torturing her. "Help! Help!"

She rolled, extinguished it, gained her feet, slapped at sparks. The odor of smoke, the stench of burnt flash, her skin scalded and her clothes devoured. Screaming curses, she raced toward the foyer. Her arm knocked over an oil lamp that set wallpaper ablaze. Sparks spewed every direction. Her arm raised to shield her face, she moved through the rapidly-spreading inferno. Overcome by the dense smoke, she coughed and retreated. Flames compassed her. "Mother! Daddy! Becky!"

Blazes roared. Blazes expanded. Blazes scorched. She collapsed on her face and clawed the floor. Wails and curses screeched from her throat above the crash of walls and timbers. "P-Please! I don't wanna die!" She howled. The fire snuffed out her life.

Gideon galloped his horse toward Elvira's home. Had Lorelei visited her? If she had, what would Elvira do, since Owen still planned on being his best man? Even though Owen had kicked the barracuda out of his house, would Lorelei still be in his and Elvira's wedding?

From the Sturgis home's direction, a strong wind carried smoke above and beyond the trees. Its acrid smell assaulted him. Was someone burning trash?

Yet the mountain of ash and rubble, where the Sturgises' house once stood, stupefied him when he arrived. He drew rein. Crackles, sparks, clouds of swirling smoke. He stayed in his saddle. He cursed. His heart tossed and tumbled, a hurricane devastating his mind and heart.

Upon dismounting, he hitched his horse and sprinted to the garden where the Sturgises and Lorelei sat on stone benches.

Absently, her eyes downcast, Lorelei turned her gold bracelet round and round her wrist. The Sturgises stared at him with ashen faces.

"She's dead." Sturgis's voice cracked.

The news slammed Gideon. "How?"

"We don't know," Mrs. Sturgis said weakly. "We weren't here when it happened."

"I was here. I … I tried putting it out," Lorelei said, sniffling. "N-No one helped me. The servants. T-They didn't move fast with the … with the water b-buckets."

"A tall candlestick. Looked like someone knocked it over." Sturgis pointed in the general direction without looking. "An accident, or else Becky did it."

Gideon watched the servants wander around the rubble. "Where is Becky?"

"We'll find her." Sturgis's fists opened and closed.

Gideon's chest tightened. "The snake?"

"In the shed."

Gideon sprinted to the shed, rage shredding his heart into a million pieces. He wanted to, needed to kill something, somebody. He lit a lantern that shined in the gloomy space. Then he inched toward the serpent coiled tight in its terrarium. Lanternlight flickered off its menacing pupils, locked on him.

"Gideon, my namesake, life did me dirty again. So, you know what I'm going to do?" Gideon eyed a back corner of the shed. "I'm going to kill you, Gideon."

His namesake vibrated its tail, reared its head, swayed. Its jaws opened wide; it displayed its fangs.

Gideon spotted a spade leaning in the back corner against a rake. He set down the lantern. His perspiring hands seized the blade's long handle, cold in his firm but nervous grip.

Poised to strike, the serpent hissed, buzzed its rattle.

With the spade behind his shoulder, Gideon crept around the terrarium. The serpent's venomous stare followed him.

"Die. Oblivion." In one swift, smooth stroke, the spade shattered the terrarium's glass. In his blind fury and grief, he missed the serpent.

Fangs out, the serpent attacked.

35

The serpent's fangs latched onto Gideon's wool topcoat.

Gideon hurried his arm out of his coat's right sleeve then reached behind him and jerked off his left sleeve then flung the garment against the far wall. He seized up the spade. "Die, snake. Die."

The serpent slithered behind the rake, coiled and rattled angrily while glaring at him.

Gideon's heart drummed an alarm and his mouth was desert dry. Carefully, he set the spade against a wall. Slowly, he gripped the derringer in his trousers waistband and cocked it. He had but one shot. Right in the head. He'd been so angry he'd forgotten he had his pistol with him. His palms, clammy.

Coiled tighter, the snake reared to strike.

Gideon fired.

The snake collapsed, dead, shot in the head.

His furor expended, Gideon unbuttoned his shirt and rolled up his sleeve to check for a possible snakebite. He sighed, relieved. He'd not been bitten, probably due to his heavy coat. He buttoned his shirt back and reached down for his coat. He vowed to tell this tale to the next person who criticized him for always wearing it unbuttoned. This unfashionable habit probably saved his life.

By the time he rejoined the Sturgises and Lorelei, Becky stood before them, her defiant demeanor the picture of hate.

"Found her in the woods." Sturgis told Gideon.

"I ain't killed her." Becky's icy eyes challenged Sturgis's.

"The laws in our state say Imbecile's allowed a fair trial." Sturgis's lips curled up in a sneer. "However, in view of the fact that I lack clear evidence and reliable witnesses, it's a trial I may not win. As a lawyer, I hate losing cases." Sturgis smiled at Becky, that thin smile Gideon knew often belied the man's rage. "I will make your life miserable forever, Imbecile." Sturgis chuckled. "Between your missus and me, you'll wish you were as dead as our dear, sweet daughter."

Gideon plopped down on the garden's stone pathway. Elvira, gone. His happiness, gone. Life had no meaning anymore. *Why? Why? Why?*

36

Mobile, Alabama

November 16, 1852

Gideon trudged through the city's darkness. He bit back tears. Mister Sturgis's servants buried Elvira's charred body in a plot beneath some trees. The peace she'd once given him had now abandoned him. Was life even worth living? He shook his head, blotted his moist eyes with his damp handkerchief.

Inside Shakespeare's Row, he darted in and out of game rooms in search of a familiar face with whom he could talk and play cards, to divert his mind from the tragedy. He punched a wall, shot back out to the street. No one. Not even Vanderporte.

Shades were down in the Henshaws' store windows. *Bah.* Who needed them? He didn't need anybody. Another drink. That's what he needed. Whiskey. Yes, whiskey to fill that big canyon inside him. He worked his way to the saloons near the riverfront. Dawn broke the horizon.

In the Taffrail Saloon, Gideon finished off another bottle of whiskey. A hefty woman approached from behind it, her plump cheeks as red as her hair. She handed his bottle to a totally bald man who'd joined her.

"I'm cooking ye some eggs fer breakfast, sir." The woman disappeared into another room, probably a kitchen.

"Don't need eggs," Gideon snapped

With his arms folded on the counter, the man leaned in close. "It'll cost ye nothing."

By the couple's accents, Gideon figured them to be Irish. "Ugh." Gideon took off his hat and gripped his head. "An ache."

"Headache, is it?" The man set down Gideon's empty bottle.

Gideon nodded.

"No wonder, what with all that drinking ye've done an' it ain't even noon yet."

His vision blurred, Gideon squinted. The man's kindly gray eyes were set deep within his wide, bronzed face.

Eggs sizzled from the kitchen. Their aroma wafted out the kitchen door. He looked about the room. He was the saloon's only customer. He squeezed his eyes. His heart grasped at Elvira's image. She vanished. Like a ghost. He swore.

"O'Reilly's my name." The man straightened to his full height, a head taller than Gideon, and wider. "Kevin O'Reilly. The pretty lady cooking fer ye is me wife, Doreen. We own this establishment."

"Hurrah for you." Gideon slumped.

O'Reilly leaned further forward and studied Gideon closer. "Fergive me fer saying so, sir, but ye look in a bad way, an' most folks don't come in here till later. An' whiskey so early in the morning, right at dawn ye came in."

"Bad way, Mister O'Reilly? Bad way?" Gideon shoved aside Doreen's plate of scrambled eggs and bacon. *Bad way.* He swore. Then, in a sudden outburst, he spilled to them the whole tragic tale—Harriet's and Billy's deaths, how he'd fallen in love with Elvira, how she'd died days before their wedding, how he'd lost his job and thus, his reputation. He talked on and on for what seemed like hours while he ate breakfast between pauses.

Rarely, did Mister O'Reilly or his wife speak.

When he finished, Gideon reached in his pocket for his wallet. "My bill—"

"No charge fer this one, sir," O'Reilly said. "Go home. Get ye some rest. It'll do ye a world of good, it will."

"I don't take charity." Gideon slammed a wad of bills on the counter and departed, nursing happy, torturous memories.

37

The Steamboat *Princess Belle*

Lorelei fussed, Lorelei fumed, Lorelei tossed a pillow on the upright piano in the corner of the ladies' cabin. Other ladies gaped at her. "What's wrong, child?" A matronly woman came through the folding doors that connected to the steamboat's dining area. Silverware clattered and voices rumbled while folks dined. "Everyone outside heard you talking to yourself."

"None of your business, Mrs. Manchester. None of their business."

"Come, come, child. I don't mean to be nosey. I want to help." Mrs. Manchester reached for Lorelei's hands.

Lorelei clutched her skirt. The old biddy and her crotchety husband, Owen's friends, lived near River Rose. "You can help me by shutting your big fat mouth." Lorelei simpered at her traveling companions, most of them strangers, their mouths agape. "And I better not hear any of you girls gossiping about me."

One younger lady straightened on a small sofa. "You're traveling alone, Mrs. Washburn?"

"Now why would I be doing that?" Lorelei hiked her skirts and disappeared into the dining area. She'd spoken the lie. Tossed out by her idiot husband, no gentleman to escort her. Worst of all, Owen was determined to keep Comet. Well, she'd fight tooth and nail to get Comet back. Comet was *her* horse, *her* champion.

What would her parents think about what happened? Her father would be furious, disinherit Owen and give Bob his Valley Horse Farm. Sweet revenge, since Owen had been so eager to acquire it one day. Now, that day would never come. Her gallant brother Bob. He should've been born in the days of King Arthur, the way he behaved. Sir Bob, King Arthur's bravest knight. A huge joke, that.

But she'd also suffer some consequences—her parents' severe reprimand— because she traveled unescorted. Before her first meal, she must find a gentleman who'd be her escort, at least until she reached Montgomery. From there, she'd take the train to Opelika and hire a hack to carry her to her family's acreage. They'd not take kindly to Owen tossing her out on the street. Stupid men always got their way. Somehow, some way, she'd get her Comet back.

"Mrs. Washburn."

The friendly voice spun her toward a man with an olive complexion and of average height and build. "Why, Mister Tivington. What on earth are you doing aboard this boat?"

"On a business trip for my father." Cole petted his thin mustache. "Designing a building in Montgomery."

Lorelei toyed with his coat buttons.

"Heard about Elvira. A tragedy." Cole lowered her hand.

"I saw it happen." Her voice wobbled. "I try not to think about it. Owen and I are separated."

"An interesting, and sad, development." Cole escorted her to a table and pulled out a chair for her. "May I be permitted to ask what your maiden name is?"

"Glenville. I'm on my way to visit family in Opelika." Elbows on the table and fists beneath her chin, she batted her lashes. "Let's forget these silly formalities, Mister Tivington. We've known each other for a few years. Please, do call me Lorelei."

"Done. And you may call me Cole."

"Done." Lorelei picked up a menu. "Let's eat. I'm starved."

Cole signaled a waiter.

Lorelei took heart. Although Cole was neither a rich planter nor a turfman, he might as well be. Everyone who was anyone in Mobile knew he and his father practically rolled in money. Their prominence as architects and builders were well known and in much demand throughout the South.

38

BELLE GLADE'S HORSE FARM AND PLANTATION
MOBILE BAY'S EASTERN SHORE
NOVEMBER 26, 1852

Rufus Frederickson and Hezekiah Hanks rode a dirt lane on Mobile Bay's Eastern Shore, their horses' lather thick on this unseasonably warm day. Behind them Rufus's groom, Jacob Styler, drove a horse van.

Today, Rufus intended to keep his promise to Ned, the one he'd made during the Spring Hill Jockey Club's race season. Rufus's white trainer, Pomeroy Wilkins, had traveled ahead and crossed Mobile Bay with Rufus's horse, Lightning Bolt, to purchase passage on a packet. Hopefully, they'd be sailing back to Virginia with Ned and Becky tomorrow and those two would soon be "aboard" the Underground Railroad bound for Canada, out of the reach of the grubby hands of slave hunters. In Canada, fugitive slaves were automatically free.

Taking them to Mexico, or perhaps to the Seminoles in Florida or the Bahamas were other options, of course. Such destinations were closer. However, he'd promised his family he'd be home by the first week in December to help prepare for Christmas. December wasn't many days away.

A gig approached.

Rufus rose in his saddle. A young man of sober countenance drove it. Beside him sat an attractive blonde, also in mourning, her veil behind her head and an opened black parasol shielding her pale face from the unforgiving sun. He drew rein and, palm out, requested them to stop. He tipped his stovepipe hat. "My apologies, but am I correct in my assumption that this is the right direction to the Sturgis estate?"

The young man lowered his horse's reins. "My sister and I've just come from there. We got turned away."

"He's hurting," the girl said.

"He's injured?" Rufus asked. "Or heaven forbid, sick?"

"The poor man is injured in his soul." The girl's suspicious blue eyes shifted between Rufus and Hezekiah, as though debating whether she could trust them. "His daughter perished in a horrible fire several days ago. We read about it in the newspaper."

"We wanted to deliver to them a card of condolence," the young man said.

The girl puffed a wayward tendril out of her face.

"Ah. Would either of you perchance know how many slaves he owns?"

"Slaves?" The young man frowned. "To be honest, I have no idea. Whether one owns slaves or doesn't is their business."

"Do you own slaves, my good sir?"

The young man lifted his reins to move on. "It's my business, sir."

"If you must know," the girl said, "we don't."

"Ah. Neither do I." Rufus pointed at Hezekiah and Jacob. "All of my horsemen are free, as are those who work my plantation in Virginia." He noted a gleam in the siblings' eyes. Could it be they opposed slavery? It wasn't wise for them to admit it straight out, especially to a stranger such as himself. Time for the test—*code words.* "I'm an agent looking for a conductor."

"Huh?" The young man glanced at his sister, who stared at him with a blank expression.

Then Rufus remembered what a friend told him before he came down to race—Alabama didn't have an organized Underground Railroad. Perhaps they didn't know what the code words meant. He'd try something else before he requested their help.

"Now, sir, please excuse us. My sister and I must move on." The young man slapped the reins. The gig started to move.

But Rufus reached toward the young man. "Please. One more minute of your time." He nodded at Hezekiah.

The jockey dismounted. "My name's Hezekiah Hanks. I ride for Mistah Frederickson." He glanced up at Rufus. "He pays me to ride for him. Mistah Frederickson bought me from another turfman when I was eight. Then he freed me." From his trouser pocket Hezekiah produced a folded paper that confirmed his freedom, which he showed to the young man. Then he inclined his head at Jacob. "My friend Mistah Styler's free too."

"Miss," Rufus said, "if you'll kindly turn your head so as to avoid seeing such an indecency, Hezekiah will take off his shirt and show your brother. Not one slash or bruise on him anywhere. As you heard from my friend Hezekiah, I do not own slaves. I pay my horsemen and my farm's field hands for their labors."

"No need for that," the young man said with a sigh. "My sister and I believe you now."

"Have you ever owned slaves?" Hannah's question came slowly, carefully.

"No, miss."

Hannah tilted her parasol farther back, behind her shoulder. "So why did you ask about Mister Sturgis's slaves?"

Should he tell them what he was up to? Rufus cleared his throat.

The young man lowered his voice just above a whisper. "Might it be, sir, that your interest in Mister Sturgis's slaves ... is it that you intend to help them escape? That you work with the Railroad?"

Rufus took off his hat, scratched his head. Time to admit his intentions. "Yes, I am an abolitionist. And yes, I do work with the Railroad."

Coruscating smiles suffused Luke's and Hannah's faces. .

"My first name is Rufus, from the great commonwealth of Virginia."

Jacob made a small grin. "Them funny words Mistah Frederickson was using, 'agent' and 'conductor,' them was code words the Railroad uses. He was testing you."

"Then I suddenly recollected that your state doesn't have a Railroad." Rufus dismounted.

"What do those code words mean?" Hannah asked.

"An agent is a person who sympathizes with slaves. A conductor is a person who guides a slave to freedom." Rufus shook Luke's hand.

Hannah twirled her parasol. "How interesting."

"Well, it's a high honor to meet a fellow Southerner of a like-mind. I'm Luke Henshaw." Luke gestured at the girl. "And my sister, Hannah Louise."

"A pleasure, sir." Hannah dipped her head.

With a deep bow, Rufus swept his hat beneath him in a grand gesture. "It is indeed an honor. I sailed down to these parts to race one of my horses. Presently I'm on my way to purchase a slave named Ned. It is my intention to help him reach freedom."

Luke and Hannah swapped glances.

"Would you perchance know Ned or a slave by the name of Becky?"

Hannah's brow crinkled. "I'm afraid we don't know any of their slaves. The Sturgises are customers at our jewelry store in Mobile. That's about all the contact we have with them."

Rufus returned his hat to his head. "Well now, I promised Ned I'd help his girl Becky escape too. They want to get married. I pride myself on being a man of my word. Therefore, I'm eager to help."

"If we can be of service—"

"Miss Henshaw, your offer is most definitely appreciated. We'll need someone to quarter them until we can sail out of this area. Would it be permissible for us to discuss that possibility?"

Luke climbed down from the gig. "We'd do anything we can to help those poor people."

"Our late father owned some houses he rents out. Luke owns them now." Hannah arched her brows at Luke. "Don't we have one vacancy this side of the bay?"

"That we do," Luke said. "Tell us what you want us to do, Mister Frederickson."

"And we'll do it," Hannah said.

"Capital. I say, let's discuss it." Rufus gathered everyone near his van and hashed out his plan's particulars.

Hezekiah aimed his jockey cap at the house. "Looks to me like Belle Glade's up that a-way."

Rufus squinted at the white three-story mansion about a half-mile distant. Four dormers projected from its steep roof. A low parapet followed along its edge. A wide gallery with Corinthian columns wrapped around its first and second floors. They halted at an iron gate, where a wooden sign nailed onto a tall wooden pole confirmed Hezekiah's observation. Etched on it, in bold black letters, the words: "BELLE GLADE."

Rufus turned in his saddle. "Hurry up, Jacob. Time's a-wasting."

Jacob clucked, urged on the team drawing the van.

Dismounted, Rufus jiggled the gate's padlock. "It's open. I'm counting on it being permissible for us to enter. Sturgis probably expects me to purchase one of his horses." He pulled back the squeaky gate for Hezekiah and Jacob then mounted his horse.

Up ahead, a lady in mourning clothes shoved a copper-skinned girl across the road. Leather straps bound the girl's wrists.

"You two stay here. I'll check on her." Rufus trotted his horse to them and doffed his hat.

The lady jerked the girl to a stop.

"My apologies, dear lady," Rufus said. "I am Rufus Frederickson of Virginia. It is not my intention to trespass on this wonderful property. However, I am seeking a gentleman whose name is Edward Sturgis."

"I'm his wife." Mrs. Sturgis held her whip behind her shoulder.

"Ah." Rufus put on a pleasant smile. "Your husband and I chanced to meet each other at the races. He suggested I might return after my racing was done and purchase a horse. Is he available to discuss a possible transaction?"

Mrs. Sturgis pointed in the general direction. "He's over at the track."

"Much appreciated, dear lady." He walked his horse around them. Hostility flamed from the girl's scarred face. "Please forgive my curiosity. What foul deed did this girl commit?"

"Becky's done lots of things. She's an evil one. Evil clean through. Taking her for another whipping."

"Ah. Thank you for informing me of your husband's location." Rufus steered his horse past them. "Let's get a move on, Hezekiah, Jacob. Time's a-wasting."

No sooner did he arrive at Sturgis's stables than Rufus spotted him standing beneath a pine tree at the walking ring, puffing hard on a cigar.

Straightening, Sturgis likewise spotted him. Dark circles rimmed the man's vacant eyes. He flicked his cigar on the grass. "Do I know you?"

In no great hurry, Rufus eased down from his saddle. "We discussed a little business transaction awhile back. At the Spring Hill track. Do you not recollect it, Edward? I am Rufus Frederickson. From Virginia. You permitted me to pay you a visit and inspect your horses."

Sturgis crushed his cigar beneath his boot and thumbed at the track. "You see 'em."

"I don't see Mystified."

"He's with the farrier getting some new shoes put on him. He'll get his exercise later."

"Ah. An excellent horse, that one."

"She's dead." Sturgis's frail voice broke. "On her wedding week, she d-died. In a fire."

"Who?" Even though Rufus knew the answer, he wanted Sturgis to talk because talking was a good way to handle grief.

"Elvira. My daughter."

"I'm sorry."

Sturgis blew his nose in his handkerchief. "One of our servants, Becky, killed her. I can't prove it, but my wife and I know she did it."

Rufus perked up. That explained why Mrs. Sturgis was whipping Becky. Based on what Hezekiah had learned from Ned, Becky was likely innocent. If anyone in this household epitomized the devil, it was the Sturgises. "My dear sir, if you'd care to sell Becky to me, I'll take her out of your life for good."

"Sell her?" Sturgis laughed bitterly. "When my wife and I enjoy dealing out justice on her? When we enjoy executing her sentence? Deprive us of our final pleasure?"

Frederickson flashed a huge smile. "Ah. I do most certainly understand your position. Is Mystified, by chance, for sale?"

"I may can be persuaded."

"May I have your permission to examine him?"

"I'll see that he's brought to the paddock after he's reshod."

An hour later Ned, his demeanor impassive, led the Thoroughbred to the paddock rails alongside a groom.

Rufus opened the horse's mouth to count his teeth, the only way a horse's age could be determined. "His teeth appear to be in fine shape." He let go Mystified's mouth. "He's not yet four years old. A few years remain for his racing endeavors."

"You already knew that." Sturgis shot him an irritable glance. "You saw him perform at the track."

Rufus sauntered to the paddock gate and studied Mystified's powerful hindquarters. "A fine animal, Mystified is. I do believe he'd be a wonderful addition to my stables. How much will you take for him?"

"Two thousand."

"And the boy?" Rufus jabbed his finger at Ned.

"Ned's not for sale."

"Ned's a good jockey, Mistah Rufus." Hezekiah spoke from beside the van parked outside the paddock. "I enjoyed racing against him."

"Silence, boy." Rufus hated himself when he snapped at his horsemen and called them boy, even though Hezekiah and the others were in on the show, them pretending to be his obedient bondsmen and he the cruel master. A great ruse whenever they were trying to liberate a slave. He reached for the paddock gate. "May I?"

Sturgis opened the gate for him.

Rufus went through it and patted Mystified's shoulder. What could he say to persuade Sturgis to sell Ned? Ned was counting on him. Becky too. And Luke and Hannah awaited him at the bay boat landing to take them to a home they rented out. He must buy himself time to think.

"Does Ned cause you any trouble?" Rufus's forefinger touched Ned's stubbly chin. "Does he know how to obey?"

Sturgis smirked. "His girl Becky gives us lots of trouble. Those two think they're in love."

An idea. Rufus raised his forefinger. "Why not separate them?"

Ned flinched.

Elbows propped on the top rail, Sturgis leaned back against the paddock. "Separate them?"

Rufus lowered his hand. "Please hear me out. My offer. Let's say I pay you two thousand for Mystified and another two thousand for Ned. That way, Becky will never see Ned again because he'll be way up in Virginia. More punishment for Becky, would you not concur?"

Sturgis's doleful face brightened. "Now, that's a thought I never considered. Let's go to my house and get this sale done."

After feeling around in his pockets, a pretense of searching for his wallet, Rufus sighed as though disappointed. "Might it be permissible for us to do it tonight? It appears I've left my wallet in my hotel room."

"That'll work fine."

"Capital!" Rufus swung back into his saddle. Ned's furrowed brow told him the slave thought he'd forgotten Becky. One way or other, he'd rescue her too.

At the bay boat landing, Rufus delivered his report to the Henshaws. "I couldn't get Becky, but that nincompoop Sturgis has agreed to sell Ned and Mystified. Will you be able to return here tonight? Do you think you can recross Mobile Bay with a wagon?"

"I'll allow that I can, provided the bay boat's captain has room for one." Luke hopped on his gig's seat beside Hannah.

"What time do we need to return?" Hannah asked.

"Six o'clock will be acceptable?"

Luke lifted his reins. "Six o'clock it is. We'll pray there'll be room on the boat for my wagon. If not, perhaps I can hire one on this side of the bay just as I hired this gig."

"Jacob," Rufus pointed at him, "I need you to accompany the Henshaws after we discuss my plan. Now, my friends, gather round." They plotted their next moves.

In the afternoon's waning light, while dockworkers off-loaded barrels and crates onto ox-drawn wagons and herded several mooing cows into a nearby pen, Rufus and his horsemen hustled off the bay boat onto Mobile Bay's Eastern Shore. A seagull lighted on one of the boat's paddle boxes before winging toward the sunset. The boat's passengers scurried along a wide pier and hastened every direction. One man, his horse on a lead, lagged behind everyone else. Rufus patted his chest, inhaled deeply. *Salt air.* It rushed up his nose and cleansed his sinuses.

He scanned the busy scene. What in tarnation could've happened to the Henshaws? They ought to have been back by now. He nudged his stable supervisor. "Pomeroy, why don't you and Hezekiah go pick up our horses and van at the livery."

"Will do." Pomeroy, who'd fought in the recent war against Mexico, did what soldiers called an "about face" and hastened off. Hezekiah struggled to keep up with him, for fast was Pomeroy's usual speed even when he had no cause to hurry.

Ten minutes later, Luke and Hannah clattered up the road in their wagon, Jacob sandwiched between them.

"Are you all set?" Rufus asked them.

Luke lifted a trunk off the wagon bed. "Ready as we'll ever be."

Hannah brightened. "Let's get going."

"We'll meet you at the third crossroads." Rufus set Luke's trunk inside the van.

By the time Rufus and his men reached Sturgis's mansion, lights flickered from its galleries and windows on its first floor. Darkness, though, shrouded its second floor. An owl hooted. A possum scurried past.

"Jacob, I'll need you to go inside with me," Rufus said. "Everyone else, wait outdoors. First let me ascertain Becky's whereabouts. I'll dispatch Jacob to tell you. Y'all know the song and dance. Well time's a wasting."

They trotted their horses up Sturgis's carriageway. Rufus accompanied Sturgis into his parlor and studied a portrait above the fireplace's black marble mantel, a young lady clad in a scarlet evening gown and gloves, her hands clasped in her lap. Pearl earrings dangled from her small ears. A tiara adorned her bountiful black hair. An unusual figure in the portrait aroused his curiosity. A snake, coiled beside her at the hem of her gown. *Strange.* "Is she your daughter?"

"A wonderful girl." Sturgis spoke from the parlor entrance.

"She's a beautiful lady." Rufus faced him. "My groom's out on the gallery. Is it permissible for him to enter?""

Elkins let Jacob inside.

"Forgive my neglect." Sturgis turned toward the hall. "May I offer you a drink?"

Well, the wicked old goat has some manners. "Brandy would be acceptable."

Sturgis clapped. "Elkins, brandy for our friend."

"Jacob, go help him." Rufus's order signaled the groom to inquire where the domestic slaves lived. "Where's Mrs. Sturgis?"

"Upstairs asleep. Every night, at sunset, she does it. It's how she deals with her grief. Also whipping Becky. I handle it through drink and work and devoting as much time as possible to my horses."

"That's how I'd handle it." A small stone sculpture atop a table, a horse reared up on his hind legs, prompted Rufus's interest. "That is a majestic piece."

"A friend gave it to me for my birthday five years ago."

Once Elkins brought them their brandy, Jacob posted himself behind Rufus and poked the small of his back. *The signal.* "Jacob, I need you to go outside. Mister Sturgis and I have important business to discuss."

Jacob darted out the door.

A chuckle hung in Rufus's throat. Thus far, events flowed along smooth as melted butter.

Hands in his pockets, Hezekiah sauntered down the oyster-shell road behind Sturgis's mansion. Jacob had said the servants lived a half-mile beyond it. When he closed on the square brick cabins, two servants made their appearance out their doors. *Slaves, not servants,* Hezekiah thought, disgusted. Owners called their house workers *servants* to soothe their guilty consciences. A man with a heavy gray-flecked beard stopped him at the path's tall lamp. "Who are you?"

Hezekiah rocked back on his heels. "A friend. My massa's in the big house buying himself a horse and a slave."

"Which one of us he buying?" A heavyset lady spoke from a porch.

"A jockey. Name of Ned."

More slaves poured out of their quarters.

"Ned?" another girl cried.

The bearded-man snatched Hezekiah by his shirt sleeve. "It ain't right for Old Man Sturgis to go selling Ned. He's Becky's man."

From the farthest end of a short path, a tiny lady sprinted to them. She dropped to her knees, trembled violently and clutched Hezekiah's hand with such force he feared the little lady would break his fingers. "T-Tell me it's not true."

Hezekiah helped her stand. "I saw you earlier today, remember? Your massa gave me permission to let you bid him a final farewell."

"He did? *My* massa?" Becky wiped her tears.

"Lead me to him, miss. I'll be pleased to escort you."

"Oh, my. Oh, my." Sobs erupted.

However, before they reached the stables, her sorrow turned to joy. For Hezekiah explained Rufus's plan, which she rewarded by planting a kiss on his cheek.

"You'll be meeting some nice folks on the way to the bay boat," Hezekiah continued before he finished explaining the plan.

Two hours had passed, more than enough time for Hezekiah to carry out his part, Rufus observed as he closed his bronze watch's cover. "Edward, I regret the hour has grown late. I must get hold of my new property and get a move on. Most surely, you must be tired."

"I doubt the bay boat will be running at this late hour." Sturgis grabbed his topcoat off a rack. "Why not spend the night? I have a spare bedroom."

Rufus flashed a toothy grin. "That's mighty decent of you. Fortunately, I took that into account when I went back for my wallet. I've found accommodations at Point Clear's hotel." In truth, the Henshaws had secured rooms at Point Clear's hotel for him and his horsemen.

"All right. I'll go with you to my stables."

"Naturally." Rufus slipped on his leather gloves and pulled on his heavy wool coat.

Outside, Rufus introduced Pomeroy Wilkins, whereas Hezekiah merely looked at him. Jacob, on the van's seat, fiddled with the team's reins.

Sturgis's brief absence to get his horse gave Hezekiah the opportunity to nod "Becky's safe" at Rufus.

Rufus nodded back. Tempted to peek inside the van to speak to her, he squashed the notion, for as sure as he did, Sturgis would catch them.

Sturgis went up the steps to Ned's room and pounded on the jockey's door. "Come out, boy. You've been sold."

Once outside, Ned's hangdog demeanor pricked Rufus. Poor Ned probably didn't think he'd gotten Becky.

Next up, Robert's quarters. Sturgis pounded on his door. "Get Mystified. I sold him."

Robert and a groom hurried down the steps into the horse barn.

Rufus scowled at Ned. "Don't just stand around, boy. You belong to me now. You get the horse."

Ned darted into the barn.

Shattered, Ned blinked uncontrollably as he shambled to Mystified's stall. "Dawdle around some, Willie. I ain't in no hurry."

"Why?" The groom tossed a blanket over Mystified's back. "You don't wanna get out of this devil's brew?"

Ned grunted. He wanted to leave this stinking hole, a fact, but not without Becky.

"How long you figure on this trip taking?" Robert handed Willie Mystified's halter.

Lips pursed, Ned averted Robert's gaze. *Quit tryin' to small talk me.* Fire seemed to rush through his veins. On his way to Virginia without Becky. Hezekiah lied to him. He's gonna pay for it, he is.

"Hurry up, boys," Rufus shouted from the barn's entrance.

Ned's fist smacked the stall door so hard pain shot through his knuckles, but when he led Mystified past Rufus he detected a glint in Rufus's eyes.

With the van door opened, Jacob pulled down a short ramp for the horse.

"Ned?"

The familiar whisper sounded from a dark corner.

Becky? Ned squinted harder as he led Mystified into the van. Next, he saw … not her face. She wore a widow's veil.

"It's me 'scaping with you. We're going be free. We're going to be married. Mister Rufus's idea."

Ned blew her a kiss before he exited the van.

"You're mine now, boy," Rufus said. "You ride with Jacob."

On the way out of Belle Glade, Ned's heart wouldn't stop leaping. Freedom! Him and his girl, gonna be married soon. Suddenly, his heart sank. Poor Robert and all of his enslaved friends. What would happen to them when Old Man Sturgis discovered Becky gone?

Sturgis stalked past his servants, who stood outside their cabins for his bedtime head count. He ground his teeth, his lips curled, he halted and pivoted on them. "Where is she?"

"Becky?" Elkins spoke apathetically.

"Yes, Elkins. Becky. She's not here."

No one answered.

Sturgis seized Ekins's coat collar, twisted it in his fist and breathed in the butler's stoic face. "She's gone, isn't she?"

"Reckon so." Elkins remained stolid.

Rage boiled Sturgis's blood. He'd teach these slaves a lesson in cooperation. Never in his life had he let them take advantage of him. He wasn't about to do it now. They were long overdue for a good taste of the rawhide.

His strides long, he resumed pacing.

Suddenly, as though he'd been smacked in the chest, the name hit him. *Frederickson.* The man had sent out his groom after he and Elkins brought them their brandy. He seized the butler's shirt. "Elkins, you told Frederickson's groom Becky's whereabouts, didn't you?"

With his shoulders squared, Elkins snickered. "Whip me all you want, 'cause I'm mighty proud I helped her get away from this devil's place."

Sturgis mounted his horse and galloped after Rufus. "You're dead, Frederickson. Dead."

At the appointed crossroads, Hannah assisted Becky out of the horse van, into Luke's wagon.

Warned by Ned that Sturgis's nightly head count would reveal Becky's absence, Rufus directed his men to stay vigilant till Ned and Becky were safely on their way. None of them had a gun.

Becky climbed up on the wagon bench. "Miss—"

"Now you don't need to call me 'miss', Becky." Hannah climbed up beside her. "My name is Hannah Louise, and my brother's name is Luke. Call us by our first names. We're all created in God's image."

Becky peeled back part of her veil. "Thank you, ma'am."

"A mere 'thank you' suffices. We're friends."

Luke's thud on the wagon bed behind them alerted them he was aboard. "Let's go. I'll keep an eye out for Sturgis."

A shot rang out.

Rufus slapped the wagon. "Get moving, Luke. It's the nincompoop. I'll hold him off."

"How?" Luke leapt to the ground.

"Move, move."

Hannah slapped the reins. The wagon's team lit out down the road.

Another shot. Then another one. Hannah drew the team to a halt.

"What's happening?" Becky clutched Hannah's arm.

Sturgis had drawn his horse up to Rufus, whose horsemen stood side by side, alongside Luke and Ned, blocking the man's approach.

Becky gasped.

Sturgis aimed his revolver at Rufus.

Heart in her throat, Hannah gaped.

"Hey, Frederickson. You stole Becky from me." Sturgis cocked his revolver. "I don't take kindly to thieves."

"Is that a fact?" Rufus pointed at Sturgis's gun. "Well, now, let's say I don't take kindly to slaveowners. I'm unarmed. You plan on shooting an unarmed man?"

"Go ahead," Luke said calmly. "Shoot me too."

Hannah stifled a squeal.

Ned charged Sturgis, seized his leg and tried yanking him off his saddle, but Sturgis kicked him to the ground. "You die first, boy." Sturgis cocked his pistol.

Squealing, Becky leapt from the wagon and darted forward.

A rattlesnake slithered out of some bushes.

Sturgis's horse reared, his shot missed Ned. The steed tossed Sturgis high, he landed head first and his horse galloped back toward Belle Glade. The rattler continued slithering across the road.

"I'll go see." Hannah got down off the wagon.

"The fool's dead." Hands on his knees, Rufus pushed himself up from squatting beside Sturgis. "His neck's broken. Luke, you all go on ahead. We'll follow to find out where Becky's temporary quarters will be." He turned to Becky. "Our packet weighs anchor tomorrow. I need you to wear those mourning clothes, including the gloves, until we can board it so no one will know you've escaped. If anyone on board gets suspicious, let me to do the talking. This isn't my first dance, helping you and your people escape." He inclined his head at the trunk on the wagon bed. "Mrs. Henshaw has some other clothes for you in that."

"I'll let you try them on tonight. If they don't fit," Hannah lifted a small fabric basket that was at her feet, "I brought my sewing kit with me."

Rufus went to his horse. "Once we reach my home in Virginia, Becky, my wife and three daughters will make you some new dresses to wear for when you and Ned go up the Railroad."

"Oh, thank you, sah." Becky burst into joyful sobs.

"Yas sah." Ned beamed. "I thank you a whole mighty lot."

Rufus swung into his saddle. "Well, time's a-wasting."

Morning's rays pounded Mrs. Edward Sturgis's bedroom panes. Outside her window, in her garden below, her husband's saddled horse rambled the grounds. Edward was dead. A neighbor discovered him on the road at dawn and brought her his corpse. That horse probably threw him. She turned from her window. "I hate you, horse."

Someone must bury Edward, his body laid out on a mattress in the parlor. Her hands covered her face, her shoulders quivered.

Then she opened her armoire and thumbed through her gowns. The dark blue silk one. Edward and Elvira had always admired her in that dress. She donned her slippers and her whalebone corset, an older fashion that laced in the front instead of the back. She jerked its strings tight. Her insides scrunched till they ached. Every petticoat she possessed, she clothed herself in. The gown and matching evening gloves came next.

At her dressing table, she arranged her coiffure. Silver ringlets framed her ashen face. Her tremulous fingers fumbled while she made the best chignon she could and inserted a tortoiseshell comb to keep it together. She put on her eyeglasses, adjusted them on her nose.

Her pearl earrings and necklace, blood red lipstick and ghostly white face powder followed. She anointed herself with her favorite perfume. All of it, she poured over her head. It drenched her face and chest. Such a nice scent. She smelled prettier than a rose. She put down its depleted bottle.

Her breaths difficult on account of her tight-lacing, she descended the stairs and entered her late husband's office. A few minutes fumbling in his desk drawer, another minute found her in the parlor where her Edward was laid. His glazed eyes stared at the chandelier.

Elkins and two servants peeked in from the hall.

"Get some help burying Mister Sturgis." Her voice was flat.

Elkins and the servants departed.

Riveted by the coiled snake at the hem of Elvira's dress, she closed on her late daughter's portrait, one of her husband's revolvers in her hand.

The revolver, gotten from his office, was heavy, but not as burdensome as her heart. She lifted its blue-steel muzzle to her temple. It was loaded. She hesitated. Death? Was God really a myth? Would she be scared? *Time to find out.* She cocked the hammer, squeezed the trigger. A roaring conflagration blazed. She screamed. She did not hear the blast.

PART FOUR

DECEMBER 1852–APRIL 1853

39

Inside a barn, on a frigid Christmas morning, one hundred slaves and their children sat on the ground, huddled close, while Thaddeus's eyes swept his attentive congregation. John Spears, the overseer, watched from the barn's entrance. He was a big-boned man with a stubbly chin. He spat out a stream of tobacco.

Though most of the congregants listened to Thaddeus's scripture reading, those few who didn't concerned him. Nothing was more important than God's holy word. He only wished he could preach. Since no religious society had licensed him nor were five slaveholders present, he couldn't. If he preached without meeting these requirements, he'd be breaking the state's laws. He wasn't even sure the law allowed him to read the Bible to this gathering, even though Mister Gideon's parents had always encouraged it.

He closed his worn leather Bible, his reading of the Christmas story from Matthew's gospel, done. "And so, my brothers and sisters, on this most glorious of all days, this Christmas Day, our Savior was born."

Uriah, the field hands' driver in the front row, shot to his feet. A Goliath of a man, as big and powerful as a live oak, he was Selah's tallest and brawniest slave. Except for Misters Spears and Deshler, he intimidated everyone.

Thaddeus, also, withstood Uriah's intimidations. Didn't David fell Goliath with one stone from a sling? Big men like Uriah, braggarts and bullies … Thaddeus wasn't impressed.

The driver folded his arms over his massive chest. "Our Savior?" Uriah spat in the dirt. "How come we all's still slaves an' ain't free like you all, Mistah Butlah Man?"

On her feet too, Uriah's girl, Liza, raised her shrill voice. Despite her small stature, she could be a fierce wildcat. "Dat's right, Mistah High and Mighty Butlah Man." She scowled at Katie and Isaac, standing beside Thaddeus. "You all *is* free, an' we all ain't. You all workin' in de big house. We ain't. It ain't right. An' he ain't brung us no presents this Christmas like he an' his mammy and pappy used to do."

"He don't believe in Christmas no more, what I heered," another slave said, scoffing. "I surprised we even gettin' de week off dis year."

To defuse the rising resentment, Thaddeus kept his response soft. "Your freedom is coming. I see it over the horizon."

"Stupid Massa ain't freein' us," Uriah snapped.

"Alabama law won't let him free anymore slaves," Isaac said.

Thaddeus nodded. "Sadly, emancipations are now illegal in this state." Uriah spat at Thaddeus's feet. "You a lawyer man?"

"I read the papers." Thaddeus kept his composure. "I follow events, and I read about the law."

"Dat's why de Butlah Man an' his friends can talk so purty." Liza tossed back her head. "They all can read themselves a book."

"Even iffen it was lawful, he ain't doin' it." Uriah spat at Thaddeus's feet again.

Thaddeus figured it was meant to be an insult or a challenge.

"He ain't done nothin' 'cept go off on his drinkin' bouts ever' Friday night. Pinin' hisself away, what I heered." Uriah's lips curled up in a sneer.

Liza snickered. "I heered he plays cards too. Solitaire. De perfect game for de lonesome white man. An' he talks to hisself. A wonder he don't answer his own questions."

Thaddeus understood their bitterness. He, too, had once worn their shoes. His great-grandfather had been from Sierra Leone and Katie's from West Africa. Sold into slavery by a warring tribe, they were brought to Charleston by a slave ship. He and Katie had heard their parents' terrifying tales during the time they lived there, before Mister Gideon's father, Mister Peter, brought them to Mobile. Chained together in the slaver's bowels, scraps of food tossed to them from the slaver's deck above as though they were animals. Many of their grandparents' friends perished on their voyage across the Atlantic, and others killed themselves by jumping overboard rather than be sold into bondage. Isaac's grandparents had a similar story. Yet, Thaddeus could never bring himself to hate Mister Gideon. Truth be told, the way Mister Gideon spiraled downhill after Miss Sturgis's death, he pitied him.

"Pray for him." Thaddeus finally spoke once his thoughts passed. "He's suffered a great tragedy. He's a slave too. The devil's slave. The devil's got ahold of him really bad."

"Let's get goin', Liza. We ain't prayin' for no white devil." Uriah and Liza stalked out of the barn, along with several others.

After a short prayer, which included a request for freedom for everyone enslaved, Thaddeus led Katie and Isaac past Spears. Was Mister Gideon awake yet? The day neared noon. He had to lay out his clothes. Katie and Isaac had to set the table for the meal she'd cooked.

"Thaddeus." Spears called his name.

Turning back, Thaddeus faced him. "What is it, sir?"

"Send Mister Deshler to me soon as he's sober."

"I shall do so, sir." Thaddeus tipped his hat. "And Merry Christmas to you and your family."

Spears grunted.

Thaddeus prayed. *Father God, please. Help us all. Deliver Mister Gideon from the devil's claws. And raise up a Moses, Lord, please Sir. Please deliver all of my people from their sinful bondage.*

Flat on his back, on his four-poster bed, Gideon cracked open his eyes. *Ceiling. Chandelier. Where am I? Home?*

He rolled over onto his side, groaned and stared at the ormolu clock ticking on his bedside table. "Eleven thirty. Must've fallen asleep." His knuckles rubbed his eyes. *Drank too much last night.* He touched his temples. *Ugh.* His head felt like a bunch of knives were sticking in it.

He curled into a tight fetal position. Sleep— the only way he could kill his troubles. Oftentimes, though, sleep deserted him.

His door creaked. He stretched his legs back out but kept his eyes closed though his body faced the door.

"Mister Deshler?"

Gideon swore. *Thaddeus.* "Huh?"

"Are you all right?"

"Fine. Get out of here."

"Katie's fixing you a wonderful lunch. It'd be a mistake to miss it."

Gideon dug his head into a pillow. "Go away."

"Please, sir. Mister Spears says he needs you."

Gideon pulled another pillow over his face. *Stupid Spears.* "What's he want?"

"Don't know, sir. I was preaching to Uriah and others in the barn, sharing with them about Christ's birth, when he told me to tell you. Please, sir. Please get up. I'll help you get dressed if you want me to."

When he heard his closet door opening, Gideon removed the pillow from his face and watched. Thaddeus, getting out his finest clothes. With great effort, he swung his feet over the edge of his bed. He scratched his head. "What'd you think you're doing?"

"It's Christmas, sir." Thaddeus spread out his trousers on a table. "Don't you want to look your best on Christmas?"

Gideon moaned. "Out."

"Please stand up." Thaddeus spoke gently. "I shall help you dress. And then you can go downstairs and enjoy that delightful lunch my wife is fixing you. Roast beef, plum pudding."

Gideon flopped back down on his mattress. "Get my laudanum. I have a headache. Then leave me be."

"We have no more laudanum." Thaddeus pulled him to his feet.

Gideon shrugged him off. "Get me a beer."

"On a Saturday, sir? You only drink your liquor on Fridays."

"Today is Saturday?" Gideon sat on his bed and pulled off his slippers.

Thaddeus unfolded Gideon's linen shirt and handed it to him. "Yes sir."

"Get out of here. I'll dress myself."

Thaddeus did as he was told.

Gideon got dressed and fussed at himself and at his overseer for interrupting his rest.

Gideon entered his dining room where Katie and Isaac were setting out a big plate of roast beef, side dishes of lima beans and acorn squash and plum pudding for dessert.

He struggled to remember. This day. It was? Was drinking affecting his memory? "What'd you call this day, Thaddeus?"

"Why, it's Christmas, sir. The day of our Lord's birth."

Isaac smacked his lips. "Yum, yum. I'll be making you some vanilla ice cream. Both our favorites."

"Merry Christmas, Mister Deshler." Katie handed Thaddeus the carving knife.

Gideon crossed the hall. A fir tree decked out with long strands of popcorn touched the ceiling. He hated it. "Why's that thing there? I didn't cut it down."

"Mister Spears's doings," Isaac said alongside him. "He and Thaddeus put it up while you were sleeping. Katie and I decorated it."

While his eyes swept the room, a painful memory stabbed Gideon. "Billy's presents. Where are Billy's presents? And Harriet's? And Elvira's?"

"They won't be coming." Thaddeus barely spoke above a whisper.

"Not coming?" He backhanded a candlestick off a table. Last year, it was the holiday without Harriet and Billy. This year, without Elvira. Well, her family didn't celebrate Christmas. He shouldn't either. Wasn't he still an atheist? Uttering a curse, his fist slammed the wall. "Ouch!" He gripped his scarred knuckles. "Thaddeus, you said Mister Spears, uh?"

"He needs you." Thaddeus said. "I don't know what it's about."

"Sick and tired of being needed. Always some blame somebody needing me for some blame something." Gideon snatched his hat and topcoat off a coat tree and stomped out.

Merriment rang from Mister Spears's small brick house, the voices of his wife Julia and young son John Jr. Gideon halted. A Christmas tree filled their window. "Mister Spears. I heard you need me!"

The overseer threw open his window. "Heading out." Within seconds, he joined him. "Uriah's been upsetting things again."

Gideon tapped his foot. "Didn't we settle that matter when I came up here this past fall?"

"Ain't just him now. Liza's joined him in the troublemaking. Uriah's authority's gone plumb to his noggin. Ever since you made him a driver, he figures he's a big man now. An' he beat a few hands before I could stop 'im an' kicked ole Amos pretty near to death."

"Kicked him? Why?"

"Amos was making repairs on Uriah's cabin. His hammer slipped outta his hand some kinda way an' landed on Uriah's foot." Spears bit off a piece of tobacco and chewed and rolled it from cheek to cheek. "Amos apologized. It didn't do no good. Uriah dragged him into a stall an' went to kicking. Amos is getting too old an' frail to be doing that kinda work. Took me an' two others to wrestle him off the ole boy."

"Assign Amos a task more suitable for his age." Gideon pondered Uriah living in one of the dogtrot cabins fifty yards distant. He deserved some serious discipline. "Your whip. Get it."

"You gonna—?"

"You heard what I said."

Spears got the whip and handed it to Gideon.

"After I'm done with him, demote him." Gideon swaggered to the slave quarters.

Spears kept on his heels. "Or else sell his big stupid carcass."

"If you have to." Kicking an old man. Stirring up trouble. That ogre would pay for it, he would. Use the whip on him. The only way he'd learn.

Music quickened Gideon's steps. A fiddle, a drum, a bugle and slaves clapping and singing and enjoying the holiday around a bonfire. But Uriah, nowhere among them. Nor Uriah's girl, Liza. She was probably with him in his cabin.

"Come out, Uriah," Gideon roared.

Uriah emerged from his quarters. Liza, her eyes amused, leaned against the door jamb and watched. Once he stepped down onto the path, he snickered.

"I heard you like to do lots of kicking." Gideon cracked the whip. "You figure on makin' me stop?"

Everyone gathered close. Amos peered past another slave.

Common sense told Gideon he didn't stand a chance against this brute, but he couldn't back down. To do that would destroy his respect among the others, which would hinder his plantation's productivity. Before he could say or do anything else, Uriah charged.

Gideon flew backward. Uriah clutched his throat. Gideon coughed, gagged as Uriah's weight pinned him, his fingers digging into his Adam's apple.

40

Beneath Uriah's weight pressuring his chest and lungs, Gideon's life flashed before him.

"Get off him, Uriah, else I'll kill you." Spears's stern command. Uriah's grip relaxed.

When Gideon turned his head, he spotted Spears's revolver.

On his feet, gagging and gasping and heaving, Gideon massaged his aching throat. "Listen to me, you big ogre. You're no longer a driver."

Spears offered his revolver to Gideon. "I'll get the shackles. We'll turn 'im over to the sheriff."

Gideon pushed Spears's gun aside. "No sheriff or judge this time. I am judge and jury. I will make him pay the penalty. Move it, Uriah. To the whipping post. One hundred lashes."

The giant cursed Spears's pistol before he lumbered ahead. Other slaves swarmed them.

While Spears's revolver kept Uriah at bay, Gideon made him strip to his waist.

Uriah, spewing insults, flung his shirt aside.

"Hands. On the crossbeam." Gideon gestured with the whip.

Uriah clapped his hands on the crossbeam then spread his legs wide.

Gideon steeled himself against the man's hate. Uriah had kicked a frail old man, so he was getting his just desserts. Gideon secured the driver's hands to the beam with strong leather straps.

Next, he bound Uriah's ankles, which he secured to the post. He reared back with the whip then cracked it on Uriah's back. Blood spurted. Uriah quivered from the rawhide's impact.

Again, the whip cut deeper. More blood. His broad shoulders shook. A sharp cry flew off his tongue.

Time and again, Gideon's whip slashed Uriah as he counted aloud. " …Twenty-two. Twenty-three. Twenty-four, twenty—"

Uriah pleaded for mercy.

Gideon kept whipping till Uriah slumped against the post and wailed uncontrollably, his face soaked in tears and his back a bloody mass. The stench of flesh and sweat engulfed them. Uriah's nose pressured one of his massive biceps.

Shouting, and despite his aching whipping arm, Gideon raised his whip to strike again. "Uriah, you almost killed me. I'll whip you till you die." *Die? Murder?* He let the whip fall to his side. Had he really said that? That he wanted to kill someone? What was happening to him?

"Shackle him," Gideon told Spears.

"Who'll be our new driver?" Spears took Gideon's whip.

"No one. Lock him in the cage for a week. One meal a day, supper only, till his sentence ends. And sell Liza."

Spears jogged to a shed where he kept those restraints.

Gideon glared at Uriah. "I'll put an ad in the Montgomery paper tomorrow to also sell you … you …you piece of trash."

Uriah, his eyes brimming with hate and murder, spat

After Spears executed Gideon's instructions Gideon, massaging his exhausted arm, trudged home. He trembled. The hate he himself felt brought no pleasure. Had he resolved the matter by simply moving Amos into his domestic household, Uriah wouldn't have attacked him. Seldom had he locked a slave in the large cage near Spears's home. It was only for drastic measures such as this one. He should've followed Mister Spears's advice and had Uriah arrested. Hopefully, his stiff sentence would keep that giant in line. If not, arrest by a lawful authority would indeed be his final option.

His steps slowed. He clutched his head. What was he becoming? A monster of some sort? All this hate and whipping? *Dear Lord.* Lord? There he went, talking to God like he'd done that day he'd feared he was drowning. Tomorrow, he'd make Amos part of his domestic staff where he'd receive kinder treatment.

41

MOBILE, ALABAMA

JANUARY 10, 1853

When Lorelei's hack brought her and her brother Bob to Mobile's Camellia Boardinghouse, Lorelei wasn't impressed. A four-story stone masonry structure with two chimneys on its hipped roof, it dwarfed nearby stores. A pillared gallery offered access to a paneled door made of oak. Its narrow windows faced the street. Lorelei sighed as Bob assisted her out of the vehicle. At least it was a place to live till she could get her way.

Despite the fact that her parents disapproved of how Owen had treated her, her father had insisted she return to Mobile and make amends. "It's not fitting for a well-bred Southern lady to be separated from her husband," he'd told her. If Owen refused to forgive her and they did divorce, however, her father promised her he'd disinherit him.

At this point, she cared less about a divorce or whether Owen would lose that horse farm in her father's will. All she wanted now was Comet. Although she'd told her father she'd go back to her husband to apologize, she had other plans. She and Mister Cole Tivington had discussed vengeance on the steamboat during her trip home this past November. Mister Tivington's vengeance. Not hers. She'd get hers, though. That was a certainty. She scowled at her brother. To her disgust, he'd accompanied her at their father's insistence.

Bob, a cotton planter and turfman who lived not many miles from their parents, was of average height but above-average build. Had it not been for his thick red beard smothering his broad chest and his heavy mustache, his face would resemble a bulldog. His physique, however, reminded her of an ox. A skilled fighter, he imagined himself as every lady's knight in shining armor. A matter of pride for him, but at this particular moment Lorelei preferred not to have her brotherly knight defending her honor. He might interfere with her plans.

Once he paid the hack's driver, Bob carried her Saratoga trunk and his own trunk into the establishment's lobby and let her carry her rosewood case containing combs, brushes and other feminine toiletries. Black-and-white checkered tile spanned its floor. Ebony armchairs and tables stood against pale blue walls decorated with large paintings in gilt frames. Several depicted horses and racing, others showed boats sailing on Mobile Bay. Eight gaslit chandeliers accented nature's light streaming through windows. Up ahead, a white marble counter.

Bob set down the trunks. "I have kind of a strange feeling about this place, Lorelei. We're going back home."

"You go home, Bob. I am staying here." Lorelei approached the desk but halted when her brother grabbed her sleeve.

"I told our parents I'd stay with you," Bob said. "And besides, a boardinghouse is no place for a lady of your breeding."

Lorelei harumphed. "It's a nice establishment, Mister Tivington said. I am not helpless. I can take care of myself.."

" All right. What is it? It's improper for me to travel alone since I am such a genteel Southern lady?" She touched the tip of his wide nose.

"Yes, it is. I am renting a room here, next to yours if possible. Father may think otherwise, but I doubt Owen will take you back."

What a complication, this brother of hers was. How would she and the Tivingtons concoct their scheme with him around?

A wiry man behind the desk sorted mail at a pigeon-holed shelf. Lorelei cleared her throat.

The man turned. A red patch covered his left eye. "Welcome to the Camellia. May I be of service?"

"Miss Lorelei. I see you've at last arrived." Cole strode through the front door.

"A few minutes ago." Lorelei faced him.

Beneath hooded eyelids, Cole studied Bob head to toe.

"He's my brother," Lorelei said. " Bob Glenville. Bob, this is Mister Cole Tivington. He and his father are architects and builders, quite well known in the state."

"I've heard of you," Bob said. "You built this place?"

"Designed it too. My father's firm owns it." Cole slapped the desk "Chadwick, Miss Lorelei is my guest. She'll reside here free of charge."

"Yes sir."

"Would there be, perhaps, a room for me as well?" Bob hefted Lorelei's trunk and set it atop his own, then hefted them waist-high.

Cole received her toiletry case. "Why not? Would you be a poker player?"

"I've been known to play a few hands."

"Maybe you'll join me and my father at Shakespeare's Row during your stay. We can get up a game. Let me take you to meet our boardinghouse manager before you settle into your rooms." He tapped Chadwick's desk. "See that Mister Glenville gets a room as close to his sister as possible. His is rent-free as well."

Chadwick nodded.

Trunks and toiletry case in hands, Cole and Bob led the way.

Lorelei took heart. Mister Tivington didn't seem concerned about Bob's presence. It could be he knew how they'd get some privacy *and* get rid of her brother.

Inside the office, a matronly woman closed a desk drawer. Her lips were full, her brown eyes stern, her bronzed complexion pocked and her girth wide. Her silver hair fell straight behind her large head, not exactly the coiffure preferred by high-class ladies. Nor did she wear gloves like all proper ladies wore, except when they were eating or bathing,, of course. Not only that, they also wore their hair in the current styles.

Cole's palm touched the woman's desk. "Mrs. Underwood, let me introduce you to our new boarders. Miss Lorelei we've saved a room for. Mister Chadwick is locating a room for her brother Mister Bob Glenville. They're friends of mine, staying rent-free. My father's firm'll handle their lodging expenses."

"As you say, Mister Tivington." Mrs. Underwood's eyes shot daggers at Lorelei.

Lorelei scoffed to herself. That tough old biddy didn't scare her. Like Elvira, she didn't scare easily, except when that horrible fire killed her dearest friend.

Minutes later, Chadwick led them to their rooms on the third floor, assigning Bob a place two doors down.

Good. She and Mister Tivington might have some privacy. Lorelei proceeded to unpack her clothes.

Cole brought Lorelei her toiletry case. "Don't worry about your brother. Me and Father expected you'd have someone bring you back here. We'll handle him so we can discuss our plans."

"Bob and my father expect me to visit Owen and ask him to take me back." Lorelei opened her toiletry case and pulled out a hairbrush.

Cole shrugged. "Who's worried about him?" He reached for her hands. But she reached for her bonnet and pulled it off her head. He was coming on to her too fast. "Later. My brother's here."

"Of course." He left, his heels clicking on the wood floor.

She finished unpacking, slapping garment after garment onto her bed before she put them into the armoire. *Men. They all think they own us.*

Stars stole behind forbidding clouds. Evening's frostiness permeated Mobile. Time and again, Joe slapped his rolled-up sports magazine in his palm. Comet won again. Reading about his rival's victories rankled him. One long-winded article dubbed him "The Pride of Alabama."

Pride? He'd show them what pride was about. Without doubt, Comet had been "tearing up" the tracks all over the South, but they hadn't seen Johnny Boy race yet.

Joe settled into an armchair beside his parlor's fireplace. Another visit to Dundee this weekend to check on Johnny's progress. He couldn't wait to start JB racing. That ornery Thoroughbred would prove himself by becoming the real Pride of Alabama. If not, he'd have broken his promise to his father … Joe's finger touched his temple like a pistol. "Bang."

42

Dundee Horse Farm and Plantation

Tensaw River, Alabama

January 14, 1852

Dundee's jockeys, in heavy wool clothes, were engaged in their daily ten-mile walk by the time Joe arrived. Grooms led horses into a paddock. Because Marcus was the only horseman Johnny Boy trusted, Johnny Boy stayed in his stall.

Joe met Rattigan at the horse barn's entrance.

"How's our champion?" Joe asked. "Is he ready?"

"Methinks JB's leg is fit to race now," the Irishman said.

"Soon as Marcus finishes his walk, have him saddle JB."

"Which horse should he race against?"

"Applecart. Pete rides him."

"Aye. I will see it done." Rattigan headed for the jockeys.

Inside the barn, Joe relished fresh hay's sweet scent. Sunbeams slanted through windows over the horses' stalls.

His bright intelligent eyes alert, Johnny Boy hung his broad head over his stall door, twitched his ears, softly nickered "hello."

"Well, now. We sure are turning into a beautiful horse, aren't we?" Joe lifted his hand to pet Johnny Boy's nose, hesitated, then yanked it to his side. Johnny was pretty finicky about who he let touch him, sort of like a cat.

Johnny Boy nodded, snorted and shook his mane.

"And we're going to show everyone who the real Pride of Alabama is, aren't we?"

Johnny bobbed his head.

"Good boy. G-o-o-d boy. My champion."

"I'm here, sah." Marcus arrived some fifteen minutes later with Dickson, who held an armful of jockey saddles, bridles and halters.

Joe snapped his fingers. "Marcus, let's do it. Give JB his exercise walk, then tack him up. Tell Pete to do the same with Applecart. I'll be at the track."

"Yas sah."

When the two horses finally took their posts, ears perked forward and tails flicking, Pete turned in his saddle. "See you at the finish line, Marcus. Don't take all day getting there."

Marcus grinned. "JB's making Applecart eat dust."

Joe appreciated those jockeys' friendship. Marcus and Pete were practically brothers. Unlike Pete, Marcus didn't have a quirt. Now this was bound to be an interesting experiment. Marcus had told him he had a trick in mind. Maybe it would work. "Boys, just one lap around the track." Joe raised his stopwatch.

"We're ready." Pete, leaning forward in his saddle, fixed his determined eyes dead ahead.

"Yas sah. Ready," Marcus said.

"Go," Rattigan said.

Applecart thundered down the track's clay, his gallops powerful and swift, Pete urging him on with his quirt. Johnny Boy snorted and watched, disinterested.

Marcus looked at Joe.

Joe waved his hat—the signal.

"Carrot," Marcus shouted.

At that "magic" word, Johnny Boy galloped down the track. Dust swirled around his muscle-packed legs, his nostrils flared, his breaths rapid and hard. Sweat coated his outstretched neck. His stride devoured the distance between him and Applecart.

On the backstretch, Johnny's stride settled in. His neck stretched forward. His hindquarters propelled him with the speed of a swift locomotive. He soon closed on Applecart's tail. Yet Applecart's legs scissored along the clay, kept him several lengths ahead.

Marcus steered Johnny Boy around the second turn, which forced Johnny to cover more distance. Then Johnny caught Applecart again. They galloped nose-to-nose. Marcus moved closer to Pete. Pete lugged closer to the inside rail.

Joe groaned. Marcus made a mistake, doing that.

"Carrot. Carrot." Marcus's shouts rang out clear as the blue sky.

"Shout that word again," Joe yelled.

Johnny responded, for a new burst of speed sent him practically flying. Marcus pulled the horse to the outside of Applecart and surged forward by a head, a half-length … Within seconds, Johnny finished a length ahead.

Joe and Rattigan laughed, backslapped and cheered.

With their horses lathered and winded, Marcus and Pete walked them to Joe.

"Well done, Marcus Adams. That idea of yours worked just fine."

Marcus swiped his forehead with his shirt sleeve. "Yas sah. That magic word sho''nuff did."

"JB's time?" Rattigan asked.

Joe slipped his stopwatch back into its pocket. "One minute and fifty seconds. JB's going to be famous!"

"What next?"

"What next, Rattigan?" Joe shoved Marcus's shoulder playfully after the jockey jumped off Johnny's saddle.

"First, I'll enter Johnny Boy in a few races to give him some experience. Once he has that under his hoofs, I'll challenge Washburn to a match race." Again, he shoved Marcus playfully. "Marcus, you'll help me prove to everyone in this state that Johnny's the superior horse. I want the whole state to know he's the real Pride of Alabama. Every turfman in the South will send their broodmares to breed with him."

Marcus wrapped the reins around his fist. "We'll prove it, Massa."

"Go cool them down." Rattigan spoke to Marcus as well as to Pete.

"And give our champion his carrot reward after that," Joe said. "JB's earned it."

"He sho''nuff did." Marcus led Johnny Boy to the ring for his cool down, Pete alongside him.

River Rose Horse Farm And Plantation
Three Mile Creek, Alabama
January 14, 1853

Owen rode to his stables from the pasture where Sir Walter grazed with mares. He knit his brows. Up ahead, Bob was helping Lorelei out of Cole's dark blue carriage. He cantered his horse to them. Erect in his saddle, he swept his arm toward the lane leading out. "Leave." He barked the order.

"But Owen." Lorelei's voice quivered.

"You're trespassing." He'd grown wise to her trembling act. He shook his finger at the lane. "All of you. Off. Get off my land."

Bob strode to him. "Don't talk to my sister that way."

Owen didn't dare dismount. The last thing he needed was for him and Bob to engage in fisticuffs. Bob could lay him out in one punch. "That sister of yours tricked me into marrying her."

"Well, honey, at least we tried." With a thin-lipped sneer, Cole spun toward the carriage. "Let's go."

"Farewell and good riddance." Owen waved an angry goodbye.

"You're wrong," Bob shouted. "She didn't trick you. Get down from that animal and fight like a man."

Owen shook his head. "Don't reckon I will. And y'all have two minutes to get off my land, else I'll have every one of you arrested."

"By whom?" Cole wheeled on him.

Hot blood coursed Owen's veins. "You heard me. Get off my land." He'd make them leave, even at the point of a gun.

"One day, Washburn, you'll regret this." Bob shot Owen a last, steely glance.

The carriage clattered out of sight. Owen cantered home.

While Cole's carriage jounced to Mobile, Lorelei glowered at her brother seated opposite her. "I will not go back to Opelika," she said.

Bob twiddled his thumbs. "We'll collect your necessities at the boardinghouse and leave tomorrow. I'll buy us passage upriver."

"Buy yourself passage." Lorelei twirled her gold bracelet around her wrist. "I am staying here."

"Not by yourself, you're not."

"That's what you think, Sir Lancelot." She cut a hard glance at Cole, seated beside her brother.

Eyes shut, Cole leaned his head back against his leather seat. "A lovely damsel needs a male protector."

Huh? Lorelei bit back her retort. "I have you, do I not, Mister Tivington?"

"Of course you do, honey." Cole 's eyelids lifted halfway.

"I forbid it." Bob gripped Lorelei's arm, his tone demanding.

Hand to her chest, Lorelei scoffed. "Me, live like a spinster? I think not."

"Mister Glenville, I assure you, you can trust me with your sister." Cole's eyelids lifted halfway. "She and I are the best of friends. Not lovers, sir, but very good friends."

"Nothing doing." Bob wagged his head vigorously. "I'm taking her back to her parents. As her brother, it's my duty."

Cole's eyes now fully opened, he reached inside his coat pocket and produced a deck of cards. "You told me you play poker?"

Bob grunted.

"How about vingt et un?"

"Vingt et un?" Puzzled, Lorelei screwed up her face.

Cole shuffled the cards on his knees. "French for twenty-one, Miss Lorelei. The simple little game started in France. The player plays against the dealer. If his hand is higher than the dealer's, he wins. But, if the player draws a hand higher than twenty-one, he loses. An ace counts for either a one or an eleven."

"Sounds easy."

"It is."

Bob received Cole's cards, shuffled them. "I've played the game many times." He handed Cole back his cards.

"You are a man of your word, Mister Glenville?" Cole ruffled the deck on his knees.

"I am."

"Meet me and my father at Shakespeare's Row this evening. Does six o'clock sound suitable?"

"It does." Bob studied Cole's fingers ruffling the cards.

Lorelei's tension broke. Maybe Cole would use that game, a wager, as a way to send him home.

43

Raucous singing startled Thaddeus out of reading.

Katie, rubbing her sleepy eyes, came down their small cabin's short hall. "Poor Mister Gideon. Another of his Friday night drinking bouts and drunk out of his poor mind." She lifted the corner of a curtain and peeked out.

Thaddeus, too, peeked out a window. Beneath a pale moonlight, near the big house, Gideon staggered in circles like a fish trapped in a bowl. He doddered around a column on his gallery, circled a lamppost in his yard and resumed a tighter, doddering circle. His nonsensical singing and slurring intensified.

Katie shook her head. "Do you think he'll ever come back to his senses?"

"I don't know." Thaddeus sidestepped to Katie's window. Mister Gideon had experienced so many brushes with death—robbed on the street, barely escaped a steamboat explosion, almost drowned in the Mobile River. Wicked Elvira almost snared him, and he'd lost his employment. The Lord was dealing with him. Why couldn't Mister Gideon see that? The only good thing he'd done since he'd returned to Selah? He got Amos away from Uriah. Amos helped Katie with small jobs around the big house and now lived next door with Isaac.

Katie gasped. "Thad. Look."

An ugly, contorted face lowered and glared at him through his window. Thaddeus gulped. *Uriah.* "A big mistake, Katie, Mister Gideon turning him loose."

The giant's thick forefinger curled twice for Thaddeus to come outside.

Katie squeezed Thaddeus's arm. "Don't go. Please don't."

Thaddeus patted her hand. "Maybe I can reconcile with him." He peeled off her grip and entered the chilly night. Out the corner of his eye, he noticed Isaac on his porch. Likely, Amos watched this from one of Isaac's windows. "What is it you want to talk about?" He glimpsed Gideon making another drunken circle, then drop onto his gallery.

"Talk?" Uriah burst into a huge guffaw. "You gonna preach at me again like you did on Christmas, Mistah Butlah Man? All dat fancy readin' and writin' you can do. Dat makes you smart?"

Thaddeus, whispering a prayer, stepped up to him. "I'm done preaching to you, Uriah. Maybe we can become friends."

"Friends? You are some stupid. I'se sick of lookin' at you and hearin' your fool talk and knowin' how smart you is." Uriah stepped closer. "I don't care for your God, neither. I'm gonna kill you first, then I'm gonna kill drunk Li'l Massa." He indicated Gideon.

"You won't kill him," Thaddeus said, swallowing hard.

"You think you gonna stop me?"

"I am."

"He's got a knife!" Katie squealed from the doorway.

Uriah's blade flashed at Thaddeus. Thaddeus dodged it, seized Uriah's wrist, struggled to wrest it from him. The giant broke loose. His blade sliced Thaddeus's stomach.

Thaddeus clutched it, collapsed, saw Isaac hurl a big rock, nailed Uriah's forehead. Footsteps. Katie sobbing beside him. He reached for her hand. His lips moved to speak. Words failed him. His eyes shut. They opened again. Voices. Praising God. The most glorious singing ever in a brilliant, joyful, glorious light.

Gideon squinted at the brilliant sunrise, sat up, looked down. The gallery? He'd fallen asleep on his gallery? How? Why? Sniffling? Sobs? He twisted in the direction of the sound.

Katie, Isaac and Amos were kneeling beside Thaddeus's body. Nearby, Uriah's corpse was sprawled on the ground, a crimson gash in his forehead.

Thaddeus? Dead? Despite his throbbing head, Gideon managed to stand. "Wh-what happened?"

Isaac's voice cracked. "Uriah was going to kill you last night. Thaddeus tried stopping him, and I … I killed Uriah with that rock yonder."

Gideon crumpled to earth. He'd been so inebriated last night he couldn't remember a thing. Had he not been drunk, Thaddeus might still be alive. Thaddeus had died … *defending rotten me?* Tears battered his resistance. Who cared if crying wasn't manly. Grief swelled up, overwhelmed his soul, breached his masculinity, exploded with piercing wails.

Gideon staggered to Thaddeus's body. Accusations pummeled his mind: *YOU KILLED HIM. DRUNKEN FOOL. IDIOT. KILLER! MURDERER!* "Shut up!" Gideon's hands flew to his ears, as though that would silence the words. "I'm so, so s-sorry, Katie. Isaac." Gideon coughed through his tears.

Katie's mournful countenance touched his.

What did she think about him now? That he'd become mean? Cruel? He was a rotten man, letting this happen. He hadn't been nice to Thaddeus in a long time, yet Thaddeus had always been respectful and died to protect … *me?* "It's my fault this happened." Gideon choked on another sob. " I shouldn't have let Uriah out of his shackles. I shouldn't have gotten drunk last night. I'm a killer. I let him die."

Katie's tears puddled her nightgown.

"We forgive you, Mister Gideon." Isaac placed a hand on Gideon's shoulder.

"We do." Katie blinked back tears. "And so does the good Lord Jesus." *NO HOPE.*

"Quiet!" Gideon screamed, his hands cupping his ears tighter.

Katie, Isaac and Amos stared at him curiously.

A verse his parents once taught him, long-forgotten, flashed in his heart: *My peace I leave with you, my peace I give to you, not as the world giveth* ... Jesus' words? Didn't He say that?

Gideon crumpled, banged the earth. "Lord, if You are real, if-if those words are true, show me now. Give me peace! I don't want this to happen again to anyone, not on account of my foolishness."

Amos, along with Isaac and Katie, circled him. Isaac prayed.

Shattered, Gideon asked God's forgiveness for all he'd done wrong, for wandering so far from Him. A warm gentleness calmed his torment. *Peace. God. You are real. Oh, thank you!*

When Gideon rapped on his overseer's door a freckled woman cracked it open. She took a sniff of snuff before allowing his entrance.

After he whacked dust off the toes of his boots, Gideon stepped inside. The Spears's young son, whom everyone called Little John because he was a Junior, rolled a toy wagon back and forth along a battered yellow rug.

Mrs. Spears, her snuffbox lowered, blushed. Clearly, she was embarrassed. Her tangled, yellowish hair hung down to her calves. "I weren't expecting no comp'ny, so I didn't fix myself up this morning."

How females handled such masses of hair, Gideon never understood. "Is your husband in, or is he at the fields?"

"Over at the fields. I'll put on some coffee if'n you care to sit and do some waiting. He said he was coming back for a quick minute after he got them hands working." She sniffed more snuff then turned away.

"Coffee will do me good."

She disappeared down her hall.

"Whatcha playing, pardner?" Gideon sat on the floor beside Little John.

"Wagon train." The child stopped rolling his wagon.

Gideon picked up a toy horse and placed it in the wagon. "Going out West, are we?"

"I'm going to Texas." Little John rolled the wagon back and forth. "I'm gonna be a cowboy."

"A cowboy?" Gideon widened his eyes as though impressed. "Well, now. I don't think I've ever met a real cowboy before."

Little John stopped rolling his toy. "You have now."

"Well, I reckon I have." Gideon chuckled.

Mrs. Spears brought in the coffee.

"Mamma," Little John said, "I need me another wagon. I can't go to Texas without supplies."

She patted his head. "We can ask yore daddy if'n we can buy you another one next time we're in town." She peered past a faded orange curtain. "He's heading this a-way. Let's scoot, Little John. Yore daddy's got to have hisself a sit-down with Mister Deshler."

Little John gathered up his toys and followed his mother down the hall.

Pondering what just happened, Gideon watched them leave. He'd talked with a child not much older than his Billy would've been. All the hurt he'd felt, gone. Was he finally delivered from his grief and pain?

"Uriah's hightailed it out of here," the overseer said when he joined Gideon.

Gideon got up. "He's dead."

"That so?" Spears smacked his palms together. "Reckon we don't need to worry no more about that ugly brute. How'd it happen?"

"Last night. I was drunker'n a skunk. He tried killing me, but Thaddeus and Isaac stopped him. He killed Thaddeus, but Isaac pulled a David on him."

"A David?"

"David in the Bible. He killed Goliath. Isaac got Uriah right here with a rock." Gideon touched his forehead.

"I see." Spears laughed. "*That* David."

"Isaac hurled it at him and caught him square, just like David did Goliath. Isaac's always been a good baseball pitcher. He's usually pretty accurate."

"Glad we sold Liza last week. She'd be powerful upset."

Selling people, somehow, didn't set right with him anymore. He'd study the Bible on slavery and form his own conclusions. "Amos and Isaac'll build a coffin for Thaddeus."

"What about the brute?'

"I've forgiven Uriah." Gideon's gaze wandered back to his house. "But we'll bury him in a coffin without a formal funeral on account of the way he acted. Especially bullying Amos. We'll bury him quietly in the slave cemetery. However, we'll give Thaddeus a formal Christian burial first. It's the least I can do for his years of faithful service and saving my life in more ways than one. Where's your whip?"

Spears thumbed at his hallway. "My office."

"Get it." Seconds later, Gideon shook the whip in Spears's face. "I hate this thing. I never want to use it again." He flung it on the floor. "I'd burn it, but it's not mine to burn." He gathered it up and handed it back to Spears. "Take it. I never want to see a whip again. I'll send for you later to get a few hands to help bury Thaddeus. First, Amos and Isaac need to build his coffin. I'll get a minister up in Montgomery to do the service."

Gideon paused at the doorway on his way out. "My parents were right."

Spears held the door open, his wife and Little John at his side. "About what?"

"About God. About faith. I tried finding peace after my Harriet died. Looked all over for it. I felt a little peace around Elvira before she died, but that peace never stayed. And when she died, it pretty near killed me. And Uriah pretty near killed me. And I'm responsible for Thaddeus's death. No sir, Mister Spears. The only one we can ever rely on is the good Lord, even when things happen that we don't understand." He tipped his hat at them. "Well, my sermon for today is finished. God bless you."

Their mouths agape, the Spears family watched him leave.

44

From deep within his belly, Gideon's volcanic laughter erupted. Wine bottle in hand, he hurled it at a square pine board target Amos had nailed on a tree. The bottle smashed it, shattered and splattered red wine everywhere. He shivered beneath his heavy wool coat. Cold weather. *Bah*. He pinched his nose. No longer did he love wine's smell.

Once he'd smashed all of his bottles, he'd pour buckets of water on his grass to dilute it and hope it seeped quickly into the sod. No more drinking binges to manage his problems. For most of his steamboat trip downriver, he kept to himself in his cabin, only venturing out to dine with two other teetotaling passengers, one of them a minister. He was done with liquor. "Come on, Isaac. Let's see the baseball pitcher hit it."

Isaac reared his arm way back then hurled a bottle. Smack in the center. Wine splattered and glass shattered. Isaac did a deep bow. "Take that. I imagined that target being Uriah."

"Amos?" Gideon offered the elderly man a bottle.

Amos, who sat on the back steps, shook his head. "Naw sah. I'se just enjoying watching you all doing it."

"Doing what?" Mary Hamilton, Stephen's fourteen-year-old sister, spoke from the Hamilton's side of the iron grille fence. "Mother and I are trying to read, but every one of you are horse-laughing so hard out in all this cold. It's quite annoying."

"Come on, Mary." Gideon waved a bottle at her. "Where's your sense of fun? Go get Stephen and you two join us."

She flounced back to her house.

"Mister Gideon?" Katie came down the steps holding a black leather-bound book.

"Hurrah! You found it." Gideon dropped his bottle and snatched it. His parents' Bible. He pressed it against his heart. His thumb stroked its smooth, worn leather. "This is one thing we got over on Elvira."

Katie thumped dust off it. "That evening when you yelled at me, telling me it was in the trunk when that woman kept telling you to throw it in the fireplace, I knew you didn't want to burn it 'cause I knew you'd put it in your daddy's armoire."

Gideon held out the book. "I couldn't bear parting with this even though I didn't believe it at the time. My father wrote in it. His memory."

"Hey, you. Gideon."

Katie smiled at Stephen's merry voice as he and his sister entered the backyard. "Mister Stephen. Miss Mary."

"Good day to you, Katie, Isaac," Stephen said. Tugging at his leather gloves, he smiled a greeting at Amos, who smiled back.

Mary, too, smiled and spoke a greeting.

"When did you get back, Gideon?" Stephen asked.

"A couple hours ago." Gideon handed his friend a wine bottle. "Care to join us? I've given up drinking. Isaac's helping me smash my temptations on that target Amos made." He indicated Amos behind them.

Stephen grabbed the bottle, hurled it, missed the target.

"Watch me." Mary threw off her mantle's hood. For half a minute, she aimed the bottle at the target. Then she hurled it dead-on, the bottle crashing and shattering on the lawn. She pulled her hood back over her head. "That's how a girl does it, brother dear."

Stephen gave her a friendly pat on her shoulder.

"The beer bottles are next." Another of Gideon's wine bottles caught the target's edge when he threw it.

An hour later, with all the liquor bottles destroyed, Gideon invited his neighbors into his house. He hung his topcoat on a rack. Isaac made a fire in the fireplace. Katie brought them cups of steaming coffee. Seated in his parlor, Gideon recounted his recent experiences at Selah. He told Stephen and Mary about Thaddeus and Uriah, his own descent into heavier drinking after Elvira's death, and how, through Thaddeus's heroism and death, he'd come to realize his foolishness.

"From this day forward, I'm living clean," Gideon said. "I've returned to my Savior."

Grins suffused Stephen's and Mary's faces.

Gideon set his coffee aside. "I'm going to tell Luke and Hannah. Will you two come with me?"

"We'd be delighted," Stephen said.

Gideon slapped his knees. "Let me fetch my topcoat."

"Pardon me, Mister Rhodes." Gideon passed the emporium's watch case where the salesman assisted a young boy and his mother.

"Mister Deshler?" Mister Rhodes slipped a watch back into the case and pulled out another one. "May I be of service?" He handed the boy the watch.

"I'm looking for Luke."

"He's wearing out his office chair with his nose in a book." A clean-shaven man with a head full of light brown hair wedged into view between a bevy of females. He held high a fistful of earrings. "Daniel Lyman, a new employee."

"Good meeting you." Amused, Gideon watched the ladies vainly grasping for the jewelry.

Daniel held the earrings higher. "Now let's not be too eager beavers, your ladyships." He merged back into the feminine flock. "You may each try them on, one pretty lady at a time."

The ladies giggled.

Two steps toward Luke's office, Gideon bumped a man bent down bent down behind a display. "Pardon me. Uh... Sam?"

Sam straightened. "Howdy. I was picking up a card I dropped." He acknowledged Stephen and Mary before he gave Gideon the card. "Thought I was hiding from you like a mouse hiding from a cat?"

Gideon's eyes switched from the card to Sam. "I thought you meant you'd dropped your visiting card."

Sam pointed at it. "John 3:16. I was memorizing it."

"The first verse my parents taught me."

Sam took back the card. "I'm not the same man. Gloria told me what you said at the jockey club's ball, when you asked her whether I'd turned into a dog when she said I'd changed. Gave me a great big ole laugh."

"I'm glad you found my sarcasm amusing."

"May we have a truce in our dispute?"

"Indeed not. I think a treaty's better. I'm not the same man either."

Sam gripped Gideon's hand warmly. "A treaty it is."

"What's this business about a treaty?" Luke spoke from his office doorway.

Gideon spread his arms wide. "I'm home, Luke. I've come home."

"Home?" Luke knit his brows.

"I'm right with the good Lord now."

"About time." Luke laughed.

"Uh, Luke …" Gideon stammered. "A while back, a cameo—"

"You distracted me so Elvira could steal it."

"You knew that?"

"Not for sure, but we suspected it when we saw an old one hanging in a new one's place a few minutes after y'all left. Not to fret, my friend. Forgiven and forgotten." Luke raised his voice a notch. "Mister Rhodes, Daniel, y'all mind business here. Hannah must know this good news immediately."

"We'll be fine, Mister Henshaw," Daniel spoke above his female customers' conversations.

"Lead the way." Gideon followed his friends out the door.

45

A bitter taste cleaved to Gideon's palate. The brass plate attached to his former employer's business—"Cadwallader & Company"—brought him to an abrupt halt. Would Mister Cadwallader believe he'd changed? Would he let him return to his employ?

With his elbow, he wiped a smudge off the plate. Next, he pressed his ear to the door. Mumbles. *Praying?* He adjusted his tie, tugged at his coat sleeves. Mister Cadwallader's loud "amen" prompted his entry.

Every eye riveted on him, the silence so thick he could hear a feather drop. Maybe he'd made a mistake coming here.

Mister Cadwallader, seated in his swivel chair, clutched his chair's arms so tightly his knuckles went white.

What went on through Mister Cadwallader's mind at this moment? Gideon grasped at fleeting words. Maybe he should forget it. Maybe he should leave. "Mister Cadwallader, sir." He searched the curious faces of everyone watching. Words stammered forth. "God has shown me my foolishness."

Those men who held a strong faith clapped.

Mister Cadwallader's tense face blossomed into a broad smile. "Say no more, Gideon Deshler. As the Good Book says, 'there is joy

275

in the presence of the angels of God over one sinner that repenteth.' You may return to work tomorrow."

Gideon slumped against the wall. At long last, things were truly looking up.

46

Lorelei set *The Sportsman's Magazine* on the restaurant's table after she perused its race report. A waiter bearing a tray of coffee mugs passed her, coffee's aroma wafting over her table. "Johnny Boy's won several races and finished second a few times. Why haven't I seen Comet listed?"

"He's resting till New Orleans's season." Cole cut up his juicy steak.

"Since Johnny Boy is becoming well-known, and popular I might add, I do believe the time has come for us to persuade Joe to challenge Owen to a match race," Isham said, reaching inside his coat for his wallet.

"You arrange it, I'll do it." Lorelei fingered a bottle of morphine she pulled from her reticule.

"As you wish, dear lady," Isham said. "Joe'll be back by the end of next week. His office told me he was done racing till spring."

"I'll pay him a visit and persuade him," Cole said.

"Finish your food. This bill is mine today." Isham waved his wallet at them, scooted back in his chair. "Excuse me. I'll go pay it now."

Cole poked another morsel of steak into his mouth.

Lorelei slipped her morphine back into her reticule and drew its drawstrings tight. The Tivingtons assumed she'd mix it in Comet's feed trough on the morning of the match race as revenge against Owen. *Stupid men.* Comet belonged to her. She wanted Comet back, even if she had to poison Johnny Boy first.

Her eyes shifted to a familiar figure sitting in the restaurant's farthest corner. She smiled to herself. *Brother Bob has returned.* So, losing that card game at Shakespeare's Row didn't keep him away. The Tivingtons told her they'd made a wager with him at the twenty-one table, that if he lost the game's first round he'd go home. It didn't surprise her he'd come back, shaving his beard and wearing that ugly straw hat and carrying a cane. What a silly disguise. He could spy on her all he wanted. She'd deal with him at the appropriate time.

47

MOBILE, ALABAMA

FEBRUARY 18, 1853

Just as darkness settled in, Joe greeted Cole outside his house.

"See. What'd I tell you? Johnny Boy's been leaving 'em all behind." Joe thrust *The Sportsman's Magazine* at him.

Cole whipped his horse's reins around a rail. "Me and Father've followed JB's progress. Impressive times."

"Let's get out of this blame cold." A bounce in his stride, Joe ducked back inside his house.

Gloria peeked out of her sewing room. "Welcome, Mister Tivington. Might I offer you a drink?"

"Not tonight." Cole removed his hat and gloves but held them, an indication he didn't intend on a long stay.

Gloria returned to her sewing.

Joe sailed the magazine onto a parlor table.

"Did you follow Comet's times?" Cole warmed his hands at Joe's fireplace. "Only came in third once, lost to two Louisiana horses. Most of his races, he finished first."

"Except for that race over in Mississippi. He finished second in that one. A pretty close race, what I heard." Joe next extended his cold, numb palms toward the flames. "'The Pride of Alabama' they all call Comet. Have you read what they call my Johnny?"

"JB, usually."

"Just plain ole, ordinary JB." Joe snatched the magazine off the table and thumped it. "Let me tell you this. I don't give a dog's bark what they call him so long as he wins. And based on their times, he and Comet are pretty near equally matched."

"Winning is the important thing." Cole took Joe's magazine from him and flipped a few pages. "An idea has occurred to me."

Again, Joe stretched his palms toward the fire. "I'm listening."

"Let's say JB defeats Comet, say, in a match race. Just him against Comet. He might—"

"Appears we have the same idea."

"Suppose JB were to win? Farewell, 'Pride of Alabama,' for Washburn's horse." Cole turned sideways to the fire. "That'd become JB's moniker."

Joe withdrew his thawed-out hands from the flames. "Yessir. Let me tell you, Cole. Johnny Boy's day of destiny and fame is upon us. I'll meet with our jockey club's board and perhaps we can arrange it. Mister Crews has replaced Sturgis as president. I believe he can be persuaded."

"You do that." Cole put his hat back on his head and pulled on his gloves. "Best be going. Business appointment in town with father."

Lorelei flung Cole's calling card across the floor and, after brushing her hair, descended the Camellia Boardinghouse's stairs. She wasn't dressed to go out, if that's what he intended. The only use she had for Mister Tivington was to stop him from giving Comet morphine.

In the lobby, she found him seated in an armchair. Upon the sight of her, he stood.

Hands propped on her hips, Lorelei closed in. "Well?"

Cole broke into one of his rare, thin-lipped smiles. "Joe wants his horse to race Comet in a match race."

"When?"

"Jockey club's board has to approve it first. It will. Board members'll hash out the particulars. My guess is it'll be sometime this spring." He offered her his arm. "May I escort you to a fine restaurant?"

"Your parents took me to supper."

Cole tipped his hat at her. "Keep your morphine handy."

"Don't you worry about that."

Cole's yearning eyes searched her.

She considered saying something to get rid of him but if she did that, it might jeopardize her chance of saving Comet, so she excused herself to return to her room to make herself more presentable. When she came back down, she permitted him take her on a promenade. They discussed Green Legs.

Cole told her that he and his father were confident they could count on her since she'd grown to hate Washburn. "We'll make it up to Joe this year for what we did to Green Legs back in '49. We'll have our revenge for Washburn's father's lawsuit. Kill Comet, Johnny will be the winner and Dundee's reputation recovered."

"I know all the details, Mister Tivington. A broken business contract, wasn't it?"

"That is a fact, my dear. But don't believe what Owen told you. It was his father who broke that contract, not me and my father. The stupid judge had a different opinion on the matter."

"Y'all were supposed to design some new buildings for his stables as well as an addition to his house?"

Cole nodded. "That, too, is a fact. In Frank Washburn's opinion, we didn't move fast enough in our work, the reason he hired someone else to do it. The man was impatient, and the suit affected my father's reputation."

"How sad." Lorelei, however, knew differently. It was the Tivingtons who'd broken the contract, which explained why Owen's father hired someone else then brought the suit against them. She'd heard the story from more than one person.

"We lost lots of money because of that lawsuit."

"A shame, that is, Mister Tivington. A shame, too, that you and your father couldn't recover the money you'd lost in that lawsuit when Green Legs died."

"If I hadn't given him so much morphine, Legs wouldn't have died and we'd have probably won our wager on him and recovered some, if not all, of it back. I wasn't sure how much to give him at the time, so I gave him too much."

"So you told me before."

While he prattled on, Lorelei mostly listened. A half hour later, she asked him to take her home because she was tired. He did.

48

On the way to Owen's stables, Gideon clutched his reins tightly. How would his friend react when he told him what happened? He so wanted him to share his newfound joy.

The clang of a farrier's hammer striking an anvil echoed from a shed, riders trotted Comet and other horses on an exercise track and a lumber wagon clattered past. Tyce's voice rose and fell while he swung a surcingle back and forth in a fidgety groom's face. "Next time, buckle this strap around the horse's girth correctly. Must I show you again?"

The groom wagged his head.

Other grooms scurried about their tasks. Jockeys exercised. Gideon fell in behind the lumber wagon, toward the clangor of hammers and saws. There Owen supervised his carpenters repairing a paddock fence. When Owen caught sight of him, he brightened.

Gideon dismounted.

"Well, I reckon it's about time you came back." Owen strode to him.

"I'll be in Mobile for a spell now." Gideon wrapped the reins around his fist to steady his nerves. "Mister Cadwallader's rehired me."

"Great news. You have your job back, and I'm getting my herd ready for New Orleans come April. I'm counting on Comet to beat Mister Duncan Kenner's horses. And Joe's provided he enters any of his."

"I hope Comet wins too."

"You'll be attending those races, won't you?" Owen watched the carpenters pulling a paddock rail out of the lumber wagon. "Quarles and I—"

"Wait. I've something to tell you." Gideon hesitated. How should he phrase it? He didn't want their friendship to end. He must word it carefully. "I'm sorry, but I'm no longer interested in racing."

Owen's pleasantness vanished. "Why not?"

"Because I'm no longer interested in gambling."

"Not even poker?"

"Not even poker." Gideon bucked up his courage. "I've rededicated myself to the Lord. I did it in church two Sundays ago."

"Really, now." Owen's brows lowered. He folded his arms and rocked back on his heels. "I thought we'd put that dog to rest months ago."

Gideon stammered.

"Get on that sway-backed mare of yours and leave. Our friendship's over." Owen closed on the paddock where two carpenters were setting a rail.

Gideon's quarter horse was no sway-back, but he knew Owen meant it as an insult. He kicked a clod of dirt. "All right. I'll go. I haven't ended our friendship. If you ever need me, I'm always available for you."

"Leave." Owen's attention on his carpenters didn't waver.

On his way back to Mobile, Gideon ached, not from Owen's rejection but heartache for Owen's soul.

Mobile, Alabama
February 26, 1853

Gideon met Sam at a restaurant for supper. While he ate spicy seafood gumbo, Sam worked on baked speckled trout sprinkled with lemon juice. Waiters moved every which way. A pianist played a relaxing melody from a small stage.

Seafood. Gideon licked his lips. What man living on the Gulf Coast didn't like seafood? Gumbo, his favorite soup, full of shrimp and crab meat. He licked his lips again.

"Chopin." Sam aimed his fork at the pianist.

"What's his first name?" Gideon's spoon brought up some shrimp.

"Frederic."

"Fredric Chopin? He plays pretty good. Maybe we should give him a tip."

"The pianist's name isn't Chopin. He's playing a tune Chopin wrote."

"Whatever you say." Gideon's spoon stirred his gumbo. "I finally got the gumption to tell him."

"What'd Owen say?" Sam sipped his water.

"What I half-expected. 'Get out. We're not friends anymore.' It happened once before, back during college."

"You are aware of what's being planned for next month?"

"The match race? I read about it in the papers. Your brother placed a big advertisement in several papers challenging Owen to it. Owen accepted the challenge."

"Johnny Boy versus Comet, the state's top Thoroughbreds. The papers are promoting it as the state's biggest race. The Pride of Alabama Stakes, they call it."

Gideon grabbed his napkin. "They're all saying whichever horse wins the meet will become the true champion of our state, the real Pride of Alabama. It could mean thousands of dollars for whoever wins. Many, many thousands."

Sam cut his trout into manageable pieces. "My brother says JB has to win. If he doesn't, I fear Joe will inflict serious harm on his person."

"Harm?"

"He may kill himself."

"Seriously?"

Sam nodded. "Ever since our father died, I've been gravely concerned about him. He feels obligated and honor-bound to live up to our father's expectations and keep a promise he made to him before he died. Joe has a death wish. He lives and breathes racing, just like our father did."

Gideon's mind raced. "You remember what happened to Green Legs a few years ago?"

"I don't have any clue who poisoned him," Sam said, "but the circumstances were similar. Green Legs and Sir Walter were supposed to race each other in a special match race. Joe fears failure will dishonor our father's memory."

"Suppose Johnny Boy gets drugged this time. Or Comet." Hands on the table, Gideon leaned forward. "I suggest we find out who killed Green Legs."

"Agreed. But how?"

Gideon pushed aside his gumbo. "For starters, we'll question certain folks. I have to work Monday. Maybe you could ask around. I'll meet you at the emporium after work. Say, six o'clock?"

"Done. I'll take care of the bill tonight. See you in church tomorrow."

"Next time, I'll pay."

On his way home, Gideon pondered his questioning. Sam knew most everyone familiar with Green Legs's tragedy, whereas he was acquainted with a mere few. He consulted his watch. Close to seven. He'd promised Katie, Isaac and Amos he'd have a Bible study with them tonight. He hoped Luke and Stephen attended. They knew the Bible much better than he did and were far better teachers. So were Thaddeus, Katie and Isaac. Frankly, he felt inadequate.

A bang on her room's door alerted her. Nevertheless, Lorelei continued taking off her jewelry. *Bob.* She dropped her earring into her toiletry case. *It's Bob.*

"Open up, Lorelei," Bob roared. "I know you're in there."

Lorelei took off her other earring. "Why, Brother Bob, what a ferocious temper you have."

He kicked the door. "Open it, I said."

She flung it wide and blocked his entrance with her hands on her hips. "Well, well. Look at you. My knight in shining armor has come to my rescue, the defender of damsels and the helpless." She pointed at his vest. "Button that awful looking thing. Getting your shave and wearing a silly disguise. Cole and I were on to you the entire time you spied on us." She simpered.

Between her expansive skirt and the doorframe, Bob managed to work his way into her room. "Noticed me, did you? Why didn't you say something?"

Lorelei flounced to the bureau mirror and snatched up a hairbrush. "You couldn't hear our discussion." She jabbed her brush at him. "You never saw him stay with me overnight, did you?"

"Can't say I did."

"You followed me to Mister Isham Tivington's house and saw his wife, didn't you?"

"True."

"There now. Like I told you. The Tivingtons are perfect gentlemen."

Bob made a beeline to the bureau, snatched up her reticule, rummaged inside it, tossed it aside. "Where is it?"

"Where's what?" Lorelei brushed her hair with jerky strokes.

"Your morphine."

"Why in the world would I have morphine?" She looked back at the mirror and fluffed her hair. "Mercy. You did see me with it. I had it because I was suffering a pain in my neck." She aimed the brush at Bob again. "Namely, you."

Bob's blood heated. "Where is it? What'd you plan on doing with it?"

"Me? Have a plan?" Lorelei feigned innocence.

"I know you. You're up to some mischief." Bob searched the bureau's drawers. At the armoire, he rummaged through her clothes. Beneath her folded chemise on its top shelf, he found the bottle. "Morphine." He held it up. "The bottle's full, which means you lied. You weren't using it for any stupid headache."

"Dear brother, it's like I told you. *You* are the headache."

"I'm about to be worse than that." He growled. "Why'd you buy this? I want the truth. And why did the Tivingtons make me place a wager at the twenty-one table? Said if I lost the first round, I had to go home. Well, I lost, but they were crazy to think I'd leave and not come back. I'll not let you stay here all by yourself."

Lorelei's jaw dropped as she stared at the bottle, her eyes suddenly moist. She couldn't lose Comet. She just couldn't!

Gently, Bob tilted up her chin. "Lorelei. You're my sister. I truly care about you. What's happening? Please tell me about it. Why are you upset?"

Lorelei licked her salty lips. "Do you promise me you'll help? If I tell you?"

Bob assisted her to a chair. "You have my word of honor, as a gentleman and as your brother."

Lorelei sat. "It's a-about Comet and Mister Cole Tivington."

For a quarter of an hour, Bob listened while she told her story, including Cole's admission to her that he'd been the one who'd killed Green Legs. She said she'd involved herself to protect Comet because the Tivingtons intended to kill him with morphine, an overdose. In that way, they believed they'd correct their mistake when they accidentally gave Green Legs too much of it in '49. They believed this would help Joe's horse become the state champion

Bob frowned. "I've seen morphine used a few times on the track. Good for relieving a horse's pain, given in the proper dosage. It also helps a horse run harder."

"If Comet gets the right dose, he'll run faster?"

"He might, because he wouldn't feel any pain while he ran." Bob kissed her moist cheek. "Comet is rightfully yours. I'll go offer Washburn more money for him than he can refuse. We'll put Comet in my stables. We'll split the winnings when he races."

Lorelei shook her head. "I like putting him in your stables and splitting the winnings, but I have a different plan on how to get him. May we discuss my plan, first, Brother?"

Bob smiled at her, a gentle and understanding smile. "Let's hear it."

49

February 28, 1853

Shortly before the emporium's closing time, Gideon accompanied Sam into it and gave Mister Rhodes and Daniel Lyman a quick greeting. He peeked inside Luke's office where Luke sorted mail. Luke glanced up. "Come on in."

"Hello there, Mister Deshler," Hannah said.

Gideon peered around the door. She was seated in a chair.

"I heard you on the sales floor speaking to Mister Rhodes." She clasped her black-gloved hands in her lap.

"Miss Henshaw." Sam, behind Gideon, doffed his hat.

"Hello to you also, Mister Quarles."

Luke gestured at some chairs. "Please sit. What brings y'all here today?"

"We came to explain something," Sam said. "You may see me going into Shakespeare's Row occasionally, but don't misunderstand. I'm not going inside to gamble."

Luke sat on his desk. "That's good to know. So tell us. Why are you going back inside if not to gamble?"

"Hopefully, to prevent my brother's suicide."

"Suicide?" Hannah gasped. "I've never seen your brother act suicidal."

"Well, he may do it if his horse doesn't win his match race against Comet next month." Sam wagged his head sadly. "JB's his greatest hope for regaining our father's reputation. Several years ago, someone drugged our father's champion, Green Legs. After Green Legs died his horse farm never had another Thoroughbred of his quality. Green Legs never had a chance to become a sire. He feels honor-bound to keep that promise."

"We have reason to believe the guilty party's still alive," Gideon said. "Sam and I are determined to find him before what happened to Green Legs happens in this race."

"You're going inside to question folks." Luke got down off his desk.

"To question one person in particular," Sam said, "who may have some information, provided I can locate him."

"You're going inside with him, Gideon?"

"Not me." Gideon shook his head. "I'm not sure I can handle being around liquor yet."

Luke relaxed. "Hannah and I feared you were losing yourself in a bottle. Perhaps that wasn't the case."

Gideon smiled at Hannah.

Hannah returned the smile. "I hope you find him. For the Quarles family's sakes."

"As do we." Gideon turned toward the door.

"We know you're busy trying to close the store." Sam put his hat back on his head. "So we'll leave you to your work."

Searching Shakespeare's Row took mere minutes. While Gideon waited in a nearby shop, he hoped Sam found Vanderporte there. However, when Sam rejoined him, he told Gideon he'd learned Vanderporte had left town on a packet to New Orleans three weeks ago.

"Where to now?" Sam asked, back on the street. "New Orleans?"

"I wouldn't know where to begin looking in that big city," Gideon said. "What else did you learn today?"

Sam tipped his hat at a young couple in a passing buggy. "I did speak with Doctor Harrison. He's the track's veterinary surgeon. He knew nothing more than we do. Morphine was discovered in Green Legs's feed was about all."

"Did he see anyone loitering around the backside the day of the race?"

"Rattigan did."

"Who's Rattigan?"

"Joe's trainer. I asked him. He said Cole and his father visited it before the race, but they're hardly suspicious. They'd come there to tell Joe's father about a problem. He and Owen's father had to leave the backside to handle it."

"What sort of problem?"

"Vanderporte and several other gamblers were arguing about a wager. A real brawl. Fisticuffs. Frank Washburn and William Quarles stopped it before it got more out of hand."

"The race stewards couldn't handle it?"

"They did, but the Tivingtons insisted Frank and William were also needed. The stewards decided Vanderporte and a friend of his were the innocent parties, so they were allowed to stay. The fight's instigators were kicked off the track permanent."

"Did Rattigan see them do anything out of the ordinary on the backside?"

"Rattigan and the other horsemen were too preoccupied preparing for the race to pay them much notice." Sam paused. "Rattigan said Isham kept distracting him and Tyce from their work by asking all sorts of questions. Said he was a real pest, called him a mosquito, the way he hovered around them all the time."

"A distraction. Probably for Cole?"

"A possibility. With everyone else being so busy, Cole might've had the opportunity to put the morphine in Green Legs's feed. Rattigan said the horses hadn't eaten yet when the gamblers' ruckus broke out, and the grooms had left the animals' stalls for a few minutes after they put feed in the troughs."

"Why did the grooms leave?"

"To get the animals' tack out of the vans."

"Thanks to Mister Tivington's distractions, I'd say Cole had opportunity." Gideon briefly considered Sam's report. "However, my question is, why did they do it? That is, if they did it."

"What about Vanderporte?" Sam proceeded down the street. "He may have been in on it with them. He and his friend might have staged the fight. But to repeat your question—Why?"

Gideon walked alongside him. "I suggest we keep an eye on the Tivingtons, and on Vanderporte provided he shows up at the race."

Gideon poked Sam's arm. "Down yonder. You see what I see? That dressmaker's shop?"

Sam squinted. "Lorelei. Isn't that Bob with her?"

"Let's go." Gideon jogged past Sam. Maybe Lorelei or Bob knew someone or had an idea that would help them.

They entered the shop.

Lorelei, examining bolts of fabric, strolled its aisles.

Bob sat in a cushioned chair yawning, obviously bored. But when he spotted them, he grinned. "Are you two ladies looking to buy some new dresses?"

Gideon glowered at him. He'd challenge him to a duel for that insult. No, no more duels. "Sam and I saw you from down the street. We have a few questions."

Bob's brows lowered into a jagged line. He snarled. "About what?"

"Green Legs," Sam said. "What do you know about his being drugged?"

Palms upward, Bob stretched his arms toward them. "No more than anyone else. I always assumed Frank Washburn was innocent."

"But you can't be sure?"

"No."

Her cheeks red, Lorelei swooped on them from a nearby aisle. "Don't say anymore, Bob." She slapped at Gideon's unbuttoned sack coat. "You two need to leave."

Sam propped his big hands on his hips. "Do you know anything about it?"

Lorelei harumphed. "What I do know or don't know, Mister Quarles, is none of your concern."

"I think it is."

"Keep my sister out of this." On his feet, Bob's chest butted Sam's.

Sam stared indifferently at Bob's white-knuckled fists. "I'm aware of your reputation with fisticuffs. A boxing match between us would be close, for I'm equally skilled. However, I won't fight you, but not because I'm scared of you. I'm not."

"Fighting serves no good purpose." Gideon turned on his heel. "Let's go."

Gideon led Sam out the door amid Lorelei's and Bob's scathing laughter.

50

Dundee Horse Farm and Plantation

Tensaw River, Alabama

March 25, 1853

The moment he spotted Marcus, Joe withdrew from his front door's sidelight. "Here he comes. Let him in."

His butler opened the door.

"You sent for me, Massa Joe?" Marcus stepped onto the brick gallery.

"Get your body inside, Marcus."

Marcus, hands in his pockets, hesitated.

Joe yanked him into the house. "Settle down. You're not in any trouble. I want to discuss tomorrow's race with you. Private-like."

Marcus's tense face melted into a smile.

In the parlor, Joe pointed at a portrait of Green Legs then peered down at the jockey, who stared up at him with crinkled brow.

Since Marcus likely wondered what he was about to say, Joe held his tongue a minute or two as a tease. At last, he spoke. "Green Legs was a great horse, wasn't he?" His finger traced the edge of the gilt frame that displayed Green Legs's portrait. The power in that bay Thoroughbred's legs, his bulging muscles and the competitive fire shining in his eyes the artist defined well. Marcus, clad in his jockey silks in the painting, stood alongside him holding his reins.

"I always liked that painting of him," Marcus said. "But don't think I got bragging rights about me up there. The artist got my riding boots a li'l short. Mistah Troye, if he done that painting, wouldn't have made that mistake."

Joe analyzed it closer. "You're right. They are a little short. I never noticed it till now." He went to his fireplace. "Green Legs's portrait is a bittersweet reminder of bygone days."

Marcus nodded. "Them was great racing days."

Joe pivoted from the fireplace. "We can have those same days again. In fact, tomorrow will probably be the most important race of your lifetime. My lifetime as well. You must win it. It'll be best three in five four-mile heats."

"Don't you worry none, sir. I'll win it."

"I'm counting on you." Joe looked Marcus straight in the eye. "Marcus Adams, if you win tomorrow, I'll make you Mister Rattigan's assistant trainer. If Alabama's law allowed me, I'd even free you, but sadly, those days are long gone now."

Marcus beamed. "You talking 'bout a promotion?"

"Sure as the sun rises."

"I'll try harder'n I've ever tried before." Marcus glanced back at Green Legs's portrait. "JB'll become greater than Legs."

"Let me tell you, Marcus, you've done an outstanding job training JB. I also enjoyed watching your carrot training."

"Assistant trainer? You really mean it?"

"That is what I said."

The gleam on Marcus's face, the quiver in his throat ... He released the loudest whoop Joe had ever heard. Joe's whoop joined his. Their yells echoed off walls.

Gloria rushed into the parlor. "What on earth?"

Joe clasped Gloria's hand. "I just told Marcus about tomorrow if he wins."

"You'll win." Gloria winked at Marcus. "We all have confidence in you."

"Thank you, Missus Gloria."

"Go get some rest," Joe told him. "Tomorrow's our big day."

Marcus bolted out the door and sprinted back to his quarters.

51

Thirty minutes after dawn, Gideon paid the gate fee and stepped onto the track's grounds. Sam, well-known in the Spring Hill Jockey Club as Joe's brother, sauntered in for free. A smattering of folks awaited the race in the grandstands. Several others purchased refreshments at booths.

Mentally, Gideon ticked off their suspects: Cole Tivington, Cole's father Isham and Austin Vanderporte topped his list.

Sam scratched his cheek. "Any suggestions about where we should begin?"

"Let's split up," Gideon said. "Pretty near everyone associated with this track knows you. Why don't you take the backside?"

"Joe'll appreciate my charming presence there." Chuckling, Sam patted his barrel chest. "But Owen'll complain."

Gideon shrugged. "Let him. I'll stay around here and wait for the Tivingtons and Vanderporte."

"Well, I'm on my way faster'n a jackrabbit."

Meanwhile, Gideon sat in the Citizens' Stand's second row. He slipped his small binoculars out of his sack coat's pocket, unwound its leather strap and hung it over his neck. Any time now, the main suspects should arrive.

When Sam showed up at the backside's ring Marcus was leading Johnny Boy around it while Owen's groom led Comet.

Numerous folks had congregated there to watch, a few of them professional gamblers jotting notes. No sign of Vanderporte, however. Still in New Orleans or on a Mississippi riverboat? Sam shrugged. Only Vanderporte knew.

"Come to watch the race, Mistah Sam?" Marcus asked, walking past.

"Indeed," Sam said. "How's Johnny today?"

Marcus raised the halter's reins. "He's gonna win."

"No doubt." Sam wandered to the stalls searching for anything that didn't belong, places where a drug might be concealed, or a person who had no business back here.

Unlike a regular race season, when the backside bustled, a handful of horsemen worked it today. Four grooms, Joe and Owen and their trainers, Rattigan and Tyce. Also, Marcus Adams and Owen's jockey, George Moore.

Sam sauntered to the row of apartments where out-of-town horsemen lived during race season, peeked through the small windows, jerked doorknobs. Everything seemed in order.

His next destination was the club's meetinghouse where it held its annual balls. All seemed in order there. His inspection finished, he joined Joe and Rattigan, engaged in conversation about race strategy at Johnny Boy's van.

"Tell Marcus I need him," Joe said. "We'll let him know our plan."

Rattigan doffed his cap at Sam before walking off.

"I'm glad your new religion hasn't prevented you from attending the races," Joe said to him.

Sam's fist covered a cough. "Ever since your club planned this race, you and I've discussed what happened to Green Legs. We both fear the same thing might happen to Johnny Boy today since the circumstances are similar."

"If Washburn tries—"

"We don't think Owen's going to do it."

"We?"

"Gideon and me."

"Deshler?" Joe closed the gate to Comet's van and hooked on a padlock.

"He's in the grandstand keeping an eye on things there." Sam shut the padlock for his brother. "We have certain suspects in mind."

"Who?" Owen approached.

Sam hesitated. Should he tell Owen the names of every suspect and why they're on the "wanted" list? Joe wasn't involved. But could Owen be? "Vanderporte, for one."

Owen's knuckles wiped his nose. "I wouldn't put it past that blackleg. The others?"

Lorelei's soft voice silenced them as she "baby-talked" Comet at the walking ring, Bob at her elbow.

Owen jogged to them.

Sam sighed, relieved that his conversation with Owen had ended. He didn't want to disclose other suspects' names.

Standing in the grandstand's highest section, Gideon's eyes roamed the throngs pouring through the track's entrance gate. In his search for Vanderporte and the Tivingtons, he focused his binoculars and bounced its lenses from person to person. No sign of them yet. He returned to his seat but before he sat, he spotted them. Cole, Isham and Isham's wife were hurrying toward the Ladies' Stand.

Likely, they were on their way to the saloon. Should he follow? Could he handle being so close to the liquor? He had no choice. He might learn whether they planned any mischief. Though he kept his distance, he trailed them.

From a window that overlooked the track, he noticed Isham and Cole seated at a table while Mrs. Tivington disappeared into the ladies' room. He whiffed a man's beer. He hadn't had a drink in weeks. Yet, to his surprise, he discovered he'd lost his desire for liquor. With his back facing them lest they recognize him, he sidled within earshot of the Tivingtons' table.

"Do you still trust her?" Cole asked his father. "Will she give him the morphine?"

"Shhh. Speak softly," Isham said. "Don't lose confidence. She'll do it. We'll all get our revenge."

"When will it happen? The last heat?"

"It depends on how the horses run. And keep quiet. Your mother's coming back."

Revenge? She? Gideon waited till the Tivingtons were gone before he headed out. Who was *she*? Not Vanderporte, obviously. A lady was involved. He must get word to Sam. *Lorelei?* It couldn't be her. Could it? She'd never drug a horse. *Hmm.* Or would she?

He picked up his pace. Owen did buy Comet for her as a gift, he recalled, but Comet was too much a champion for Owen to let her or Bob acquire him.

Quickening his steps further, to locate either Joe or Owen, Gideon sidestepped a race steward riding a horse through the crowd. Likewise, other spectators parted a path for him. The steward's speaking trumpet touched his lips. "The Pride of Alabama Stakes is about to begin. Everyone, please take your seats."

Ladies hastened one direction and men the other, up into their respective stands. Gideon broke stride near the Officials' Stand. "Where are Misters Quarles and Washburn?" he shouted. "I have urgent news."

"They'll be along," an official said. "Return to your seat."

"My news is urgent."

The official jumped to his feet. "I said, sir, return to your seat."

With a sigh and a groan, Gideon left. How to warn his friends? He couldn't go to the backside now, not without permission from the track authorities, who likely wouldn't give it. He spotted the jockeys walking their horses to the weighing room. A lanky race steward, with black-rimmed sunken eyes and a beetle brow, stood guard. Jim Jarvis, one of Mister Cadwallader's clients.

Once the jockeys dismounted, Jarvis took their horses' reins and let them inside.

Gideon hurried to him and reported what he'd heard the Tivingtons discuss.

"A lady, is it?" Jarvis peered down his hawkish nose.

"As I said, Jim. If she isn't stopped, we may have another Green Legs incident."

"Any particular lady, Mister Deshler?"

"I figure it's Lorelei Washburn. She and her brother went to the backside earlier today and haven't returned."

"You suspect she'll drug her own horse, do you?"

"That's my fear. She might even kill him in the way Green Legs was killed. With morphine."

Jarvis gazed past him. "I realize she and Owen are not on the best of terms, but I know her well enough to know she'd never do such a thing. Perhaps you misunderstood the Tivingtons' conversation. Nevertheless, we'll keep a watch on those men."

Gideon flushed. "Mister Jarvis, forgive me, but it's not the Tivingtons you need to worry about. It's Lorelei. May I go inside the weighing room and tell George and the other jockey?"

"You may not."

"To the backside, then, to warn Sam?"

"It's too late for that now. Let any of us catch you back there, we'll toss you off this track. It doesn't matter that I'm one of your firm's clients. I show no partiality. Rules are rules."

Frustrated, Gideon pivoted. "Will you at least tell Joe and Owen what I said?"

"My duty post is here today, but I'll try to get word to them."

Gideon walked off. Hopefully, Jarvis would do it.

Cheers shattered air when the two jockeys, dressed in their liveries, rode Comet and Johnny Boy to their starting poles.

Back in his seat, Gideon dangled his clasped hands between his legs. He hoped Sam had better success than he did.

Sam opened a brick stall's lower door for a groom. Because she was the only female back here, Lorelei's rustling skirts betrayed her approach. Weary of hers and Bob's presence, he spoke to her over his shoulder.

"I have a dandy idea, Miss Lorelei. Why don't you and your brother go on out there and watch Comet run?"

"Bob and I will not leave here until I get him back," Lorelei snapped. "He's *my* horse."

Bob's big hand jerked him clear of the stall door. "Owen refused to sell us Comet right before this heat."

Shoved against the stall, Sam whiffed Bob's breath. Obviously, the man had eaten a buttered biscuit for breakfast.

Bob poked Sam's shoulder. "Believe you me, Owen will be eating his teeth before he refuses again. Comet belongs to my sister, and *he* belongs in my stables."

"Why don't *you* go watch the races, Mister Quarles?" Lorelei said.

"Because," Sam nudged Bob clear, "I'm making sure nothing happens to Johnny Boy, as in, say, getting poisoned or drugged."

"Johnny Boy's on the track right now, in case you haven't noticed." Lorelei's eyes shifted to the sound of distant roaring from the grandstands.

The first heat had started.

Lorelei's dark pink reticule, dangling from her wrist, roused Sam's interest. She could easily hide a bottle in it. Morphine? Fortunately, she couldn't mix it in Johnny Boy's feed since he and Comet ate before her arrival. That is, if she carried morphine in it. Yet how would she use it without someone spotting her? "Comet is yours and Owen's business, but what happens to Johnny Boy is Joe's business. And mine." Sam sat on his barrel-bench near JB's stall.

At last, he told himself, everything's fitting right nicely. Lorelei, defensive at the dress shop when he and Gideon questioned her. Now, with Bob's support, she refused to leave the backside. She and her brother had to be involved in this plot. Against Johnny Boy? Should he grab her reticule and check it for morphine? Bob would try to stop him. *Try it, Bob. Just try it. I dare you.*

Sam rose to check it but sat back down. Suppose he was mistaken. Suppose all he found in Lorelei's reticule were feminine toiletries? *No. Too embarrassing.*

Several minutes later, the spectators' roars faded to silence.

George and Marcus returned astride their mounts, their winded horses blowing hard and smelling of dust and sweat.

"Who won?" Bob asked them.

Marcus, slumped in his saddle, thumbed at George.

"By three lengths." George hopped down.

"Thirty-minute break," Tyce said.

George and Marcus led the horses to the walking ring for their cool downs.

"Gideon!"

Gideon swallowed his chocolate cookie's crumbs when Owen called his name.

Joe, who stood beside stood Owen, signaled Gideon to join them. Gideon hastened to them.

"What's this Jarvis told us about a threat to Comet?" Owen asked.

Gideon licked sweet chocolate remnants off his front teeth and surveyed the grandstand. Cole and Isham, still seated, didn't look in their direction. "I can't say for certain it's going to be Lorelei, but I overheard the Tivingtons in the saloon talking about a lady drugging him."

Joe looked toward the backside.

"She's been aiming to get Comet back." Owen eyed Joe.

Joe nodded. "Sam's watching out for JB."

"If Sam sees her trying to drug Comet, he'll stop her?" Owen glowered at the Tivingtons.

"Let me tell you this, Owen. My brother'll do everything he can to ensure no harm befalls either of our horses. He's fair-minded, same as me. Same as our father was."

Owen shook Joe's hand. "I'm sincere when I say this, Joe, that I regret our years of feuding when we might've been close friends. I'll go let Sam know. Maybe I can make Lorelei and Bob leave." He gave Gideon's hand a firm squeeze. "I appreciate your telling us."

"Any time." Gideon exhaled. Finally. Whatever happened on the backside, both men trusted Sam to handle it. A good thing, too, that Owen and Joe had ended their feud. In the meantime, he'd not let the Tivingtons out of his sight.

Lorelei and Bob, accompanied by George and Marcus, went to the walking ring during the race's final break. Comet and Johnny Boy each had two victories under their hoofs. Except for the first race, which Comet handily won, their competition was close, or so Lorelei heard.

Lorelei also realized this was the last, best opportunity to make her move. Her eyes narrowed. There he was, Mister Samuel K. Quarles, at the ring's gate with Tyce. Why didn't that stupid man leave? Quarles made her ill. So did the Tivingtons, who expected her to kill Comet the way they'd killed Green Legs.

But she did need to drug Johnny Boy before this last race, not to kill him but to help him win, as Bob suggested. Once Johnny defeated Comet, Bob wouldn't have to purchase him because, why, darling Owen would be so disgusted he'd give her the horse. First, however, dear Brother Bob needed to dispose of Quarles. She clutched the morphine in her reticule.

"You need to watch us run this last race, ma'am." Tyce opened the gate for Marcus and a groom to walk the horses. "Johnny Boy's a strange one, he is."

"I have no desire to watch that nag run," Lorelei said.

Owen, his strides long and determined, made a beeline for her.

Bob, however, stepped in his path.

"For the last time, you two, get out of here." Owen shook his hat in their faces. "Either into the stands or leave the premises, else I'll have a track steward throw you out."

"We're taking Comet with us," Bob said. "I'll pay you a handsome price for him."

"Forget it. I am going back to the track. When I return, both of you had best be gone."

"We're taking the horse, Washburn." Bob's wide nostrils flared. "Comet rightfully belongs to my sister. You bought him for her."

"There'll be no more gifts from me for that barracuda woman." Owen stalked off.

"Owen's not the sort who gives up so easily," Lorelei told her brother, unphased by Owen's insult. She'd heard him use it before, though she had no idea who gave him the strange notion of likening her to a fish.

"That's what I'm counting on." Thumbs in his vest pockets, Bob gave a slow, self-satisfied grin.

Lorelei indicated Sam, watching Comet and Johnny Boy cool down. One heat left. Four miles. Best three out of five. "Time to do it," she whispered to her brother.

"It's time." Bob shed his coat then made his approach.

Sam turned from the horses. Casually, he locked stares with him.

Lorelei's hand slipped into her reticule, clutched the morphine then the ladle she'd brought. She awaited Bob's distraction.

Bob shoved Sam's shoulder. "I'm sick of looking at your sorry-looking face."

"I'm sorry my face offends you," Sam said.

His shoulders squared, Bob took one step closer.

"Are y'all about to do something to my brother's horse? Or Owen's?"

"You've been back here all day yourself too, Sam." Bob threw a slow fist at Sam. Sam dodged it easily. "You're the one up to no good. Drug Comet, will you?"

"I've no intention of doing that." Sam began unbuttoning his coat. "But you do."

"You liar."

"Am I?" Sam shed his coat, unbuttoned his shirt sleeves, rolled them up above his elbows. "Look, Bob. I don't want to fight you."

Bob threw a punch.

Sam's right arm deflected it. "All right, mister. You asked for it." He plowed a fist into Bob's ribs. Bob staggered briefly before he closed in and swung twice more. Sam continued dodging and parrying till Bob contacted Sam's chin and crumpled him to the ground. Sam rolled clear when Bob threw himself at him.

Back on his feet, Sam threw a jab.

Bob deflected it.

Then Sam attacked with a one-two that landed on Bob's nose and ribcage. Bob reeled, recovered, charged. Blows continued. Blood spurted from both men's noses and mouths.

"Stop them," Lorelei cried. "Someone, please stop them."

Marcus and Sandifer dropped their halters' reins. Cheering grooms and Tyce surrounded the fighters.

While the brawl occupied the horsemen's interest, Lorelei skimmed her surroundings. No one watched her. She scanned the row of stalls that faced the walking ring. No one in those either. *You'd better not die on me, Johnny. But if you do, oh well. My mistake.* She moved swiftly with the morphine and ladle.

"Here now, good boy." Her gentle talk betrayed her intent. She touched the morphine-filled ladle to Johnny Boy's mouth. "It's sugar, boy. I'm not giving you much. I just want you to win so I can get Comet back. Will you do that for me?"

Johnny Boy pulled his head back, perked his ears and worked his lips eagerly.

"Enough, *cailín.* Enough, girl."

Lorelei gasped. Rattigan, red-faced, peeked at her from over a stall's lower door.

"Comet's my horse, Mister Rattigan."

"Mister Washburn told me to help Sam Quarles keep an eye on you, woman." Rattigan stomped to her and reached for her morphine bottle. "I'll take that."

"No. And if you tell Mister Washburn …." She hesitated. Why did that ignorant Irishman suddenly smile at her?

Something whacked the ladle from her hand. Her reticule dropped. *Johnny Boy.* He reared his head, displayed his large teeth … attacked.

Lorelei jerked her hand clear. "Stupid beast!"

Sudden quiet dropped. Sam and Bob's fight ceased. Heads pivoted her direction.

Lorelei lifted her defiant chin.

"What's this?" Sam snatched up the ladle and her reticule. He found the morphine in it.

"I caught her trying to give JB that morphine," Rattigan said.

"Why, Lorelei?" Pity filled Sam's voice. "Why did you try drugging poor Johnny Boy?"

Lorelei clutched her skirt. "Comet's my horse."

"JB's Massa Joe's horse." Marcus stuck his thumbs in his white trousers' waistband. "JB don't take kindly to no one 'cept me. He 'specially don't like people such as yourself."

"And that's mighty good, that is," Rattigan said, "else you may have gotten away with it. Our Johnny's proven himself to be pretty smart."

"Smarter'n you, Missus," Marcus said.

Bob pivoted to leave but Sam grabbed him, dragged him next to his sister.

"You're not going anywhere, Glenville," Sam said. "Not until we sort things out. George, fetch us two stewards and tell Mister Crews what happened. There'll be a slight delay in the last heat."

George took off at a jog.

Impatient, Gideon tapped his foot. The final heat should've begun by now.

"Why ain't they come back?" a man behind him yelled.

"Been thirty-five minutes," a man in front of Gideon said.

"Hope nothing's wrong with one of the horses, Conway," said a pipe smoker beside Gideon.

"Let's get to racing," the pipe smoker's friend, Conway, shouted.

Up and down the grandstand rode murmurs and loud complaints.

Gideon shifted his attention to Cole and his father, their expressions stolid. Good poker players, both of them. They'd had lots of practice controlling their emotions when dealt a bad hand of cards.

A steward drew rein in front of them. "Attention, please," he announced through a speaking trumpet. "Please forgive us. There has been an urgent delay. The final heat will be underway very soon."

Was that them? Gideon brought up his binoculars to confirm it. *It is.* Lorelei's and Bob's wrists, bound with canvas straps, being marched by two race stewards toward the Officials' Stand. Sam, Owen and Joe followed.

The Tivingtons' section stirred. Cole and his father, uttering "pardon me's," maneuvered past spectators.

Leaving? Were they worried what Lorelei might tell the race officials? Gideon shot to his feet. "Jarvis! Stop 'em!"

The Tivingtons lit out for the main gate. Jarvis seized Isham's arm but Cole sprinted ahead.

Bounding out of the grandstand, Gideon chased Cole and threw himself at him with a flying tackle.

"Get off me, Deshler." Flat on his face, Cole squirmed.

Straddling him, Gideon pinned his shoulders. "I knew you and your father were up to no good. I've never trusted you Tivingtons about anything, not even at cards. Y'all caused a lot of grief between Joe and Owen."

"We didn't do nothing." With his red face turned sideways on the path, Cole writhed.

"I overheard you and your father in the saloon. You know Lorelei and her brother'll implicate you." Gideon pressured Cole's shoulders harder. "You poisoned Green Legs too, didn't you?"

Cole cursed when Joe and Owen came to them.

"You murdered my father's favorite horse, his beloved champion." Joe's callous tone chilled Gideon, though he knew Joe wasn't speaking to him.

"Lorelei confessed to everything." Owen pulled Gideon off Cole. "Because of you and your dear daddy, Tivington, Joe and I loathed each other for years without cause."

"Move it, Tivington." The race steward marched Cole to the frowning race officials awaiting him at the farthest end of the track.

No sooner did Gideon return to his seat than he felt a nudge. Vanderporte, having come down the grandstand, sidled over to him.

"I suspected it was him all along," Vanderporte said.

"When did you arrive here?" Gideon asked. "I heard you were still in Louisiana."

"Was," Vanderporte said. "I arrived in time for the third heat."

"Why did you suspect Cole?"

"On the day of the race," Vanderporte said, "I was on the backside making my final assessments on Green Legs's and Sir Walter's chances of winning. I noticed a bulge in Cole's coat. Didn't suspect anything at the time, until Green Legs's sudden death. Then I figured the bulge might have been laudanum. Only later did I learn it was morphine that killed him."

"If you suspected Cole, why didn't you share your suspicions with me on the steamboat?"

"Wasn't sure. I don't like being wrong about such things. I'd hoped to get Cole into a poker game."

"To make him one of your suckers?"

"That was the general idea. I'm glad you caught him, though. Care to make a wager on this heat? An honest race?"

"No, Austin."

"Austin?" Vanderporte drew back, surprised. "What happened to your always calling me Blacklegs or Vanderporte?"

"It's a long story. I'll share it with you when I have the chance."

Puzzled, the gambler returned to his seat.

Hurrahs split sky when George and Marcus guided their horses toward the starting poles. Gideon devoted his attention to the race.

For the final heat, Joe sat beside Owen. "Since we're both honest turfmen, my new friend Owen," Joe said, "I have a proposition for you."

"What kind of proposition?" Owen kept his eyes fixed on the track.

"No matter who wins this race, why not become business partners?"

Owen shook Joe's hand. "Deal."

"Yes, a deal." Joe gave Johnny Boy and Comet his attention.

The horses took their starting positions. With him and Owen in business together, and the fame their horses had achieved in this state, he and Owen would both become successful breeders of champions. As far as he was concerned now, he'd kept his promise to his father—Dundee and River Rose—the greatest stables in the state of Alabama.

"We'll need to write other tracks and warn them about those four," Owen said. "Lorelei and Bob should never be allowed on any track again, not after what they tried to do."

"Nor the Tivingtons."

"Agreed." Owen tilted his head at the track.

Johnny Boy and Comet stood ready.

The starter lowered the flag.

Comet shot down the track like a rocket. Johnny balked.

The roaring crowd burst into cheers and laughter, hundreds pointing at Johnny while Comet thundered toward the first turn.

Marcus, at last gaining control of Johnny Boy, steadied him on all fours. Yet still, the horse didn't budge.

"Watch Marcus." Joe stood and waved his hat at his jockey.

"There goes that carrot trick again." Owen also stood, binoculars to his eyes.

Marcus, leaning across JB's neck, spoke in the horse's ear.

All of a sudden, Johnny lit out down the track, hoofs pounding, dust and clay rising, cheers deafening.

On the second lap, Johnny gained on Comet by six lengths and maintained this distance till the fourth and final lap.

His grin stretching from one ear to the other, Joe focused his binoculars. "That a boy, JB. Run. Run."

"Looks like Marcus is shouting at him," Owen said.

"He is. That magic word, *carrot*. Marcus waited till the last lap to shout it."

Joe and Owen laughed.

Five lengths, three lengths, two lengths ahead ... Comet now, one length ahead. Johnny Boy lunged ahead of Comet then dropped behind him. Johnny's last dogged effort pulled him about even. His neck stretched forth just beyond Comet's as they crossed the finish line.

Joe sprang from his seat, flung his hat in the air. "Johnny Boy! By a nose!"

Gestures of victory and defeat animated the grandstands. Ear-shattering claps and cheers for both horses resounded from every direction, a clamor of celebration.

When Marcus and George slowed their lathered mounts to a walk, they guided them to the Officials' Stand. Sweat permeated their liveries and coated their horses. They wheeled their mounts to face the stand. Andrew Crews, the Spring Hill Jockey Club's president, stepped forward holding a shiny brass trophy. The words, *Pride of Alabama, 1853,* was etched on a brass plate attached to its base.

Joe, beaming from ear to ear, stepped down alongside him. The two men faced each other.

"On behalf of the Spring Hill Jockey Club and the state of Alabama, I congratulate you, Mister Joseph Quarles, on your horse's splendid victory." Crews handed Joe the trophy.

"Thank you, Mister Crews." Joe held it high for all to see.

Applause. From Owen too, who clapped loudest.

Swollen with admiration, Joe gazed warmly at Marcus and stretched forth the trophy. "It was my outstanding jockey, Marcus Adams, who deserves the credit." He chuckled. "And let's don't forget that ornery horse only he can ride, our Johnny Boy."

JB gave a snort, as though saying, "It was nothing."

Laughter, from everyone present.

Shoulders square, Marcus stammered out his words. "Thank you, sah." He patted Johnny Boy's neck. "And thank you, JB."

Johnny snorted again.

"Reckon he wants his carrot now," Owen said.

Once again, laughter erupted.

$\mathcal{E}$PILOGUE

In Philadelphia's Franklin Art Gallery Ned Jenkins studied himself in a mirror in a room adjacent its auditorium, squaring his bowtie. Gray streaked his hair. Shallow creases furrowed his forehead, yet he remained as energetic and youthful as he'd been during his jockey days.

His art had gained a measure of fame in Canada, where he and Becky settled after Rufus Frederickson helped them escape bondage. Along with a fellow artist who was white, Ned set up a small art store in Ontario after receiving a basic education. Becky, discovering she had a special gift for numbers and math, managed the studio's business end along with his friend's sister. Ned and his friend, meanwhile, taught art classes and sold art supplies. Once he and Becky learned how to read, they "devoured" every book they could get ahold of.

When war broke out in the States he moved to New York where he found a job with *Harper's Weekly* as a sketch artist. His drawings depicted various black regiments in combat and in camp. After the war he returned home, resumed painting wildlife and rejoined his friend in their store. Moreover, he exhibited his paintings all over Canada, quickly gaining an artistic reputation and following as "Canada's Audubon."

Today, Philadelphia was the first stop on his first American art tour. He'd not been in the States since the war. Would his art be as well-received here as in Canada? His new painting about to be unveiled ... Was it good? He dusted his coat sleeves and faced Becky as she hurried through the door. "How do I look?"

Becky stroked his chest and arms and patted his head. "A little bald at the top, but you still look plenty pretty to this girl. Now shoo. They've already introduced you. Mister Frederickson says times a-wasting."

"Good ole Rufus, helping us on our art tour. Never known a finer gentleman than him."

"Me either." Becky wiggled her fingers impatiently. "Now would you please shoo? They're growing restless out there." She gave him a firm shove through the door, into gallery's airy auditorium then sat on the front row beside Mister Frederickson's wife and turned her admiring gaze upon him.

As Ned stepped up onto the stage, Rufus arose from his chair and stood near a tall easel draped in a white sheet. His long, bushy side-whiskers had turned iron gray, his broad brow furrowed, but his easygoing demeanor and stride hadn't changed.

Thrusting back his shoulders and clearing his throat, Ned faced his audience. The silence ... *deafening*. Lots of art enthusiasts and art critics out in that audience. *Ned, don't say nothing wrong. Don't make a mistake.*

After a brief recounting of his life as a horseman, how Rufus rescued him and Becky and their flight through the Underground Railroad, Ned nodded at Rufus.

Rufus whipped off the sheet.

Oohs and aahs echoed everywhere.

On his canvas, a watercolor painting of a large woodpecker surrounded by a forest, with sunlight seeping through the timbers. The bird's wide, black feet clasped the dark brown tree. His triangular crest was red and his body black. Two stripes crossed his white face: a black one went past his eye, and a red one crossed his cheek to his bill. The bird seemed to be moving toward a pale rectangular hole in the tree. The scene was so real, it almost came alive.

Did they know what kind of woodpecker he'd painted? Ned gripped the podium. The murmuring and finger pointing continued. What did it all mean? He coughed to get everyone's attention.

Once again, silence.

Ned's voice rose. "As everyone can see, my bird is climbing a tree and eating a meal, so I've titled this work *The Beetle Hunter*, because that's one of the things woodpeckers eat. Beetles, and of course, other insects. And, as you observe, my friends, he's a rather large woodpecker. About the size of a crow."

"A pileated woodpecker." A big man leapt up from near the front and clapped. He faced the audience. "I'm an ornithologist, a bird scientist, and Mister Jenkins here painted a wonderful representation of the species. Canada's right. Mister Jenkins is Canada's John James Audubon." Suddenly red from embarrassment, he sat down and sheepishly sank in his seat.

Grateful for the compliment, Ned smiled at him. "My pileated woodpecker is a male of the species. We know this because of the red stripe crossing his cheek. Females don't have it."

Soon, Ned moved into his main lecture—his artistic technique and woodpeckers, the pileated woodpecker in particular. Constantly, he glanced at the ornithologist for confirmation of his bird facts. By nodding, the ornithologist gave his approval.

Near the end of his one-hour talk, Ned stepped to his painting. "I'm donating *The Beetle Hunter* to this gallery. Now, I will remain available for any questions you may have while you enjoy my work exhibited in the next rooms. Feel free to ask me anything. I'll be more'n happy to try answering."

Cheers reverberated throughout the auditorium. Chairs scraped floors as art enthusiasts bumped each other in their haste to view his exhibit. Two gallery guides directed them toward the display rooms.

Rushing up onstage, Becky grabbed Ned's face between her palms and planted a huge kiss on his lips.

Rufus clapped Ned's back. "Well done. Very well done."

Ned drew Becky close.

"Yessir," Ned said, satisfaction welling within him. "I do believe we're off to a good art tour in this country."

Rufus and Becky looked at each other, nodded and said, "Amen."

Author's Note

One detail some readers may have noticed is that my jockeys didn't stand in their stirrups during races like modern jockeys do. This riding position is called the "monkey crouch." British jockey Tod Sloan first rode this way in the 1890s, making it famous. Before his era, jockeys didn't ride standing.

Though I had considered including a reference to Africatown, a small settlement near Mobile, my research showed me it didn't exist during my novel's era. Africatown was settled in 1860 by slaves brought over in the slave ship *Clotilda*. According to the *Encyclopedia of Alabama*, it was the last slave ship to come to the United States.

Jockey clubs generally held their dinners and balls at the end of race season. However, for reasons of plot, I decided to put the Spring Hill Track's dinner and ball at the beginning of its season.

I'm indebted to Katherine C. Mooney's book, *Race Horse Men: How Slavery and Freedom Were Made At the Racetrack,* published by Harvard University Press, Cambridge and London, 2014. Her book inspired this story. The inspiration for Johnny Boy was a famous racehorse named Boston. Boston sired two other great racehorses of the era, Lexington and Lecomte.

ACKNOWLEDGMENTS

This book would not have been possible without the help of the following people. If I left anyone out, please forgive me. Thanks to all!

Jessie Bush
Joan Deneve
Syrone Harvey
Sandee Lee
LaDonna Michele McCann
Pat Margum
Tisha Martin
Terri Miller
David Parks
Michael Rogers
Diane Samson
Angela Shelton
Sherry Shindelar
Susan Sloan
Erma Ullrey
Pat Wagner

About The Author

John M. Cunningham Jr. grew up in Mobile, Alabama. A graduate of the University of Alabama and former history teacher, he has been writing professionally for over thirty years. His work has appeared in numerous Christian and secular publications. He is a member of American Christian Fiction Writers, Word Weavers International and teaches Sunday school. He specializes in historical fiction set primarily in the American South. He is currently working on a novel set in Alabama during the Creek War (1813-1814).

Visit his website at www.theauthorscove.com.

Other books by Mr. Cunningham:

Reflections of a Southern Boy: Devotions From the Deep South

Southern Sons-Dixie Daughters, Book 1: *Vengeance & Betrayal*

Southern Sons-Dixie Daughters, Book 2: *River Ruckus, Bloody Bay Squire, A Mascot's Tale*

www.ingramcontent.com/pod-product-compliance
Lightning Source LLC
Chambersburg PA
CBHW032144190626
46814CB00005BA/1831